Now You See Her

Cecelia Tishy

WARNER BOOKS

NEW YORK   BOSTON

Copyright © 2005 by Cecelia Tichi
Excerpt from *All in One Piece* copyright © 2005 by Cecelia Tichi.
All rights reserved. No part of this book may be reproduced in any form or by any electronic or mechanical means, including information storage and retrieval systems, without permission in writing from the publisher, except by a reviewer who may quote brief passages in a review.

Warner Books

Time Warner Book Group
1271 Avenue of the Americas, New York, NY 10020
Visit our Web site at www.twbookmark.com

Printed in the United States of America

Originally published in hardcover by The Mysterious Press

First Paperback Printing: February 2006

10 9 8 7 6 5 4 3 2 1

WHERE'S THE LETTER?

I take the envelope, unfold the single sheet, and read.
"Wrong man . . . bad evidence . . . if you are a moral de-
tective, you must care and act . . . do something." At the
bottom, in huge letters: "HELP ME."

A short letter, it's a disclaimer and a plea. It contains
no real information, not one fact. I hold it at the edges
between fingers and thumbs, reading and rereading from
top to bottom until I can recite it verbatim. "Wrong man . . .
moral detective . . . do something."

Then there's a shimmer, an optic flash. The moment
hastens but stands still. Yes, I stare at lines of ballpoint
ink, but the letter in my hand has turned as transparent as
cellophane, and on the other side something swirls. Coils
of red heat. The paper takes me there.

I am now posing with the letter, merely posing. Detec-
tive Devaney thinks I pause to grasp the words on the
page, but he is mistaken. My left side is hot. Below the rib
cage is a burning. It's painful. The hot coils sear and
flash. It takes everything I've got not to cry out . . .

For Bill, my partner in crime

Acknowledgments

A book is a team effort, and I thank Bill Tichi first and foremost for unflagging zest for plot and being first reader. Susan Robinette, mystery reader extraordinaire, helped keep an eye on the big picture, and Thad Davies cued the time travel, while the Nashville chapter of Sisters in Crime is the best mix of readers and writers. I thank my agent, Meredith Bernstein, for keen editorial advice as well as adroit agenting, and my Mysterious Press editor, Beth de Guzman, for the level of editing that's often said to be a thing of the past. Not so: Beth eyed the manuscript line by line and challenged this author to meet the higher standard. Bill Betts's copyediting of the finished manuscript has been scrupulous, and I am grateful for his eagle eye. Like every writer across the broad spectrum of mystery fiction, I thank the readers who support our death-dealing enterprise.

Now You See Her

Chapter One

They say nighttime fog is romantic, but a woman walking alone on dark city sidewalks gets a Jack the Ripper feeling to the marrow of her bones. The streetlights cast a sick haze. You can't see a damn thing in any direction. And footsteps are approaching right now—coming from behind, amplified in the fog.

I speed up, just three blocks from my destination on Marlborough. The steps get closer. A woman was murdered walking by the Charles River last month, less than a mile from here. Point of fact: the steps pound harder, faster, a man's stride. He's broken into a run, catching up.

Or closing in? Should I thrust at the groin with my umbrella? Smash his nose with the heel of my hand?

Or is it *two* people running? I hear many footsteps, so it's hard to tell. One or two? The murdered woman was struck from behind while walking, bludgeoned to death. I veer to the curb and stop, silent, invisible, I hope. The soles strike hard enough to crack cement.

Then a noise erupts in the fog just feet from where I stand—a sudden grunt, a scuffle. A cry of pain sucked in and stifled. Muffled? Gagged? A gargling sound too. It's over in a flash. A sound bite.

I don't move. It feels like forever. The steps recede, but with a new sound—a scraping. Dragging a heavy bag? A body? Every muscle in my body clenches.

What did I hear?

I force myself down Dartmouth to Marlborough, fighting fear as I hurry along a vapor trail of odors—exhaust fumes, balcony barbecues. Also garbage, pet waste, mildew.

At 9:06 p.m. this third of May, I meet Meg Givens at the Marlborough townhouse front door. Huge relief just to get here. Sensibly, she drove. We stare at this house in somber silence, and my pulse rate hikes back up. Neither of us wants to be here tonight. No one comes to greet us. There's no welcome mat beneath our feet. Not a single lamp glows from any window, upstairs or down. A small campaign sign for the Massachusetts governor's race pokes from the tiny front garden, but the whole townhouse is dead black, and I don't expect the interior to be a bit cozy and welcoming, not with the task ahead of us.

Meg's Lanvin wafts in the thick air, along with hints of something rotting. Compost? Sewage? Rain starts falling, thick drops mixed in the fog and mist. Should I tell her about the footsteps? The sickening sound, the dragging? As a Realtor, Meg found a tenant for my upstairs flat, but she's not a close friend. Why didn't I drive tonight?

"I appreciate your willingness to do this, Reggie," she says. "So let's get going." Meg keys in. We step into the pitch-black interior, and a sweet, sharp odor hits my nostrils.

Gas. "Meg, gas. Let's get out of here."

"They should've left a light on." Her nails scratch the wall like chalk on a board.

"Out. Now."

"Here, got it." *Click.*

Light flares to reveal a front room sectional sofa in hot orange and wall-mounted hunks of scrap metal. No, they're armor: a breastplate, a visor, a mailed glove. It's like a dismembered knight. Then I see the chandelier, a massive work of medieval blades, halberds, swords, knives. Some are fused, others swing free. The whole fixture hangs from slender wires. We're ankle-deep in a rug that needs mowing with a John Deere.

"My God, a hall of armor. What do I smell?"

"It's sandalwood, Reggie."

Not gas, but sandalwood. The joke's on me. I'm wound way too tight from the weather and the footsteps and noise . . . and those ghastly blades that look ready to crash. "Meg, I think somebody just got mugged."

"Muggings in the Back Bay are fairly common, Reggie. Should've warned you about the scent. I recommend citrus air fresheners, but this couple loves sandalwood. It's the night noises that wake them up. Random noises."

"That's it, Meg—some disturbing noises that I heard when I was walking over here."

"You walked? Reggie, I forget you're new to the city. I'll drive you home. I insist. And this shouldn't take us long. The owners are out for dinner. They prefer we leave by ten. Let's get to it."

I wrench my mind to the task at hand. Let go of that sidewalk incident, forget the weaponry of the Middle Ages, focus on the here and now—which feels, however, like a setup for failure. I tried to duck out of this, but Meg begged me. "You say these people hear slamming doors?"

"Hard slams, Reggie, always late at night. The noises started the week they moved in. I sent our firm's best handyman. Every door latch works perfectly. I hope you can help. Are you ready to start?"

"I'm ready, but are you certain there's no object or artifact left in the house from previous owners?" She shakes her head no. As I've told her, I work hands-on. To start off, I need something tangible to hold. Bare-handed, it probably won't work.

"Just give it a try, Reggie."

Closing my eyes, I try to clear my mind and concentrate on rhythmic breathing. And I wait. We wait together. Five minutes? Fifteen?

Meg's knuckles crack. She whispers, "How're you doing? Any vibes?"

"Nothing so far."

"Take your time. I'll lower the light." She turns the dimmer, and the room goes sepia. Minutes pass.

"Anything?" I shake my head. "Maybe if you sit down? Or walk into other rooms? Are you concentrating?"

"I'm concentrating." But I sound as tense as I feel in this nineteenth-century Boston townhouse whose owners think it's haunted. That's why I'm here this gloomy evening. I'm supposed to ID the ghost.

The fact is, I sense nothing but a mix of sandalwood and Lanvin. Maybe there is no resident ghost. Or maybe my sixth sense is blocked, since I'm both empty-handed and distracted by the sidewalk episode. In either case, no vision, no spirits.

Meg twists the dimmer down to brownout and stands close. "Let me prime the pump. I'll tell you some terrible things, Reggie. These quaint Back Bay houses the tourists love—the slate roofs, the ornamental ironwork, the old brick—the naive tourists think they're so charming. So do our clients."

Her voice drops low and gets grainy. "How wrong they are. Dark secrets haunt these houses. We Realtors know the true stories of Back Bay murders. Daggers, Reggie, and poisonings from tonics laced with mercury."

Is she making this up just to coach me?

"Imagine this, Reggie: under the Victorian facades, under the stiff collars and lace, are crazed opium addicts, jealous younger brothers cut from parents' wills. Fratricide, parricide. A cousin in formal evening attire trampled by a carriage horse. A beloved uncle strangled. On a night like this, Reggie, angry spirits can stir. They can slam doors. And psychic powers can summon them. You, Reggie, can hear them if you concentrate."

I try. I imagine a rearing carriage horse, the uncle whose eyes pop as the killer crushes his windpipe. I picture it all. So would you. Which doesn't make it psychic.

"You don't feel anything?"

"Wait—" Behind closed lids, I see pricks of light and hear a sudden whoosh. Ghost? No, the ventilation system. "Meg, my sixth sense is vacationing."

My laugh sounds brittle. Wrapped in her own troubles, Meg can't possibly know why I'm on edge. It's not only the sidewalk scare in the fog but also my entire new Boston life. Or, as my businessman ex used to say, the whole enchilada.

Stifling her disappointment, Meg runs a hand through her dark brown hair. Her face is heart-shaped, dark eyes quick. She's wearing a purple dress with a brooch shaped like a festive red hat, oddly jaunty in this somber scene. "It was worth a try. Anything to block a lawsuit."

"You really think they'd sue? For ghosts?"

"Or disturbing their peace, whatever. The wife is convinced the house is haunted. They paid top price in last year's hot market and spent big bucks renovating. A lawsuit could drag on for years and cost a fortune. As the listing agent, I could be named as a defendant. Even if they don't sue, they could smear our firm. The husband is a new player in big development deals in the city. They're political people. They host fund-raisers. You saw the yard sign outside for the primary."

We move through the dining room, and suddenly, I recognize the pattern in the wall covering: neat rows of clenched fists. "Aren't these the fists of the Black Power movement?" She nods. "They papered this room in Black Power salutes?"

"This paper was custom-milled in France."

"Are your clients black?"

"He is. They moved in two months ago, even though the kitchen's still not done. Here, sit down a minute while I write them a note."

We're now in the kitchen, a construction zone of tile and stainless steel. I verify that all kitchen door latches do work. "The new owners are the first to complain about the slamming, right?"

Her pen stops. "Why do you ask?"

"A house can have a history."

"Reggie, the whole Back Bay is historical."

"Let me ask this: I won't say 'haunted,' but is the house notorious for unexplained incidents? Do the Realtors gossip about its 'dark secrets'?"

She pauses and taps the pen. "Nothing specific, but for

some reason, this house goes on the market every few years. For Realtors, it's a merry-go-round with a brass ring. The insider joke is, who's next to grab the sales commission?"

"What do the sellers have to say?"

"When they leave? The usual, job transfer, out-of-state move."

"No compaints about night noises?"

"A seller wants a good price, Reggie. And 'ghost' isn't on the disclosure sheet." Meg meets my gaze. "Some of the Realtors are . . . shall I say, a bit superstitious? One of our younger agents did some research on the history of the house, and we teased her because she got so obsessed and moody and complained about cold and chills. Bad for business, I told her. We called her Igloo Sue."

"What did she find out?"

"We never knew. She met a pilot and moved to Dallas, one of those whirlwind romances. Personally, I think the problem is the style of the house. It's the only neo-Medieval on a block of Italian Renaissance. It doesn't get enough light on the first floor. That's my theory." Meg finishes the note and manages a grin. "Guess you're not a ghostbuster psychic, Reggie."

"Guess not." My faux buoyance hides a certain angst. Not about this Marlborough house in particular, but my health as a psychic. True, this gift has bruised and scraped me raw, scarred my arm, nearly killed me, yet it has provided a surge of energy the NFL could use in Super Bowls. The care and feeding of my sixth sense is topmost priority.

But on that sidewalk, I felt plain fear, and in this house, nothing. At the moment, I'm a psychic flatliner who can't handle the city on a foggy night.

So what? you ask. So first thing tomorrow morning,

I'm discussing a homicide case with Detective Francis Devaney. He's counting on the newfound psychic ability that recently put me in a working relationship with the Homicide Division of the Metropolitan Boston Police. No, it's not a paid position. I'm an unofficial adviser. The reward is beyond a Wall Streeter's comprehension: quite simply, it's adventure beyond my wildest dreams. Me, Reggie Cutter, ex–executive wife and twenty-five-year authority on ensembles for ladies' luncheons, volunteer committees, banquets, teas, corporate galas. I tell you, as the ultimate makeover, helping cops solve a murder beats a face-lift by a light-year.

For the past month, Devaney has waited while my wounded arm healed from my "rookie cop" adventure. Well, my arm is now hoisting ten-pound free weights, and I've counted down the hours to tomorrow's talk. Devaney'll offer me a psychic's deputy badge, so to speak, and I'll salivate like Pavlov's dog. I'm just that eager. But if I blank out, I'll be sidelined. He'll be polite and distant. "No hard feelings, Reggie." "Of course not, Frank."

Oblivious, Meg clicks her ballpoint and reaches for her briefcase with a pro's nimbleness. "My car's at the corner. Maybe lunch next week," she says. "And love that green jacket, Reggie. Bet it's terrific in decent light."

"I like your purple too, Meg, and your brooch."

"It's my Red Hat outfit. You must know the Jenny Joseph poem about wearing purple and a red hat when a woman gets older? It's about breaking free."

"Vaguely."

"It's a great women's group. You have to be over fifty."

"Not quite yet."

"We'll welcome you. You'll love us. It's a fun bunch.

I'm flying to this year's convention. I'm looking for a hard-shell hatbox for the overhead."

Outside on the stoop, I fumble with my umbrella as Meg reaches to close the front door. Neither of us can explain the next moment. Meg's arm is outstretched, fingers ready for the knob. Before she can grasp it, the door starts to move. We watch it, standing still as two statues. Neither of us touches the door, but both of us feel a sharp cold draft. All by itself, the massive front door swings shut with a hard slam.

Chapter Two

At 8:11 a.m., Devaney arrives, a burly man with a barrel chest and graying hair cut short. Blue eyes, crooked nose. "Reggie, I'm early."

"Detective Frank Devaney, come right in."

He fills the room in his tweed sport coat and a mustard tie with ovals like slide specimens. His usually ruddy cheeks are a bit colorless, like the morning.

"How about some coffee? How about a muffin?"

"Water's good," he says.

We sit in the front room among my late aunt's furnishings, the carved oak chest and hurricane lamps and shelves of books. I, in navy slacks and a cream blouse with light makeup and a natural-tone lipstick, have claimed the bentwood rocker. It was my late Aunt Jo's, as was this South End townhouse condo here on Barlow Square, which I inherited and moved into after my divorce. Devaney commands the sofa, his feet flat on my favorite of Jo's kilims. "Where's the pup?"

"Biscuit's with her co-owner. I'm now dog sharing."

"Vacation time-share pets?"

Joint custody of Biscuit the beagle is a twisted tale. "My dander allergy," I say, and let it go at that.

"How's the arm? Soreness gone?" He tells me that the scar from my first crime case will fade. Actually, my dimple-size scar feels like a badge.

"And how's the upstairs dentist?"

Is this cop-style chitchat? H. Forest Buxbaum, D.M.D., is the new tenant Meg found for the upstairs flat, which is a huge chunk of my post-divorce income, since my settlement stocks have crashed.

"The acid test, Frank, will be when I knock at Dr. Buxbaum's door with a midnight toothache."

He chuckles, asks about my kids.

"Jack's still drawing a paycheck in Silicon Valley, and Molly's probably got a sleeping bag in her sculpture studio in Providence. Both fine. And your boys, still overseas?"

"One in the desert, one at sea on a destroyer. Their mother wants them back stateside." He rubs his eyes. "I do too. They're adults, and still we worry."

I nod. "They're out on their own but still our kids."

"Maybe I will take that coffee."

It occurs to me that he's stalling. He looks tired. "Frank, was a crime reported on Dartmouth Street last night at about nine? It's on my mind. I heard footsteps and scuffling on the sidewalk in the fog."

"Walking by yourself? Reggie, you're not in a gated community anymore."

I flash to the private subdivisions and security patrols of my past. Luxury prisons. "Frank, I will not live shut in behind locked doors in Boston. Anyway, I was driven home in that fog, with visibility of about four feet." I say nothing about the slammed front door, which Meg and I murmured about in cryptic tones. "Every intersection was a war of nerves."

He can't disagree. "No, nothing reported on Dartmouth last night I know of. Nothing in the Back Bay." Momentary relief. Maybe I only imagined the worst.

"You okay, Frank?"

His thighs strain the weave of his trousers. "Let me tell you, Reggie, no police department in this country thinks there's enough personnel to do the job A to Z. The public wants blood, the media and politicians hammer you. Add a high-profile crime, like the Dempsey case, and everyone's on us like buzzards."

"Sylvia Dempsey." The woman murdered by the river. Is this the case for my psychic sense? "Do you have leads?"

He shoots me a look. "Not you too."

"A person ought to be able to walk by the Esplanade at twilight without being bludgeoned."

"Forget *ought*." He puts his mug down, takes a notebook from an inside pocket, and lays it on the coffee table between us. "Did you visit Boston in the crack years, Reggie?" This is not chitchat.

"Crack cocaine years? No."

"In those years, Reggie, you stepped on crack vials like they were seashells on the beach. People set their families on fire. Mothers threw babies off roofs. The homicide rate went sky-high. We had a hiring freeze. Openings in the division, we couldn't fill them."

This is not about Sylvia Dempsey. This is something from the past.

"It got to be a blur," he says. "Lowlifes and snitches angled for their own deals with cops and the DA. Notes got sloppy, and witnesses ran together in your mind. It's probably hard for you to imagine that."

Me? One autumn I served on three ball committees and mixed up the Baccarat and Tiffany and Waterford table favors. Tragic at the time.

"Don't get me wrong, we got some real good convictions. We put away scum. But then a few particular cases—" He twists his wedding band. "You think those cases are over and done with, past history, but then you find an old notebook in a drawer, open it up, and a detail comes back."

The notebook on the table—I know this now—is coming my way in minutes. It will be the psychic prompt. I'll be expected to hold it and to feel the extrasensory vibes, though there are no guarantees. I say, "So you have doubts about some of those cases."

"Yeah, doubts. I checked old notes and files on a case about a man named Henry Faiser. He's doing twenty to life in MCI Norfolk for shooting a man we thought was trying to buy drugs. Faiser was twenty-one years old at the time. The victim was a white college student named Peter Wald."

"Faiser's black?" He nods. "This happened close by?"

"About half a mile away on a block near the turnpike on Eldridge Street. It's a fancy condo high-rise now, but then it was three shabby houses and a body shop, which Vehicle Theft was already watching because they suspected stolen cars stripped for parts."

"A chop shop." Again, he nods. I get no points for knowing this lingo. The notebook lies untouched.

"Homicide was watching the house next to the shop. A crack house, we thought. A woman had died there, and the cause of death was heart failure, inconclusive as a criminal case. So we kept an eye on the house. The DEA was in it too."

"The Drug Enforcement Agency?"

"Feds, so there were turf issues."

"But Henry Faiser shot and killed Peter Wald. That's a fact?"

"Faiser was known to be living in the house, and also known to be at the scene of the murder. A gun was found in the weeds in a vacant lot alongside the house. Ballistics proved it was the murder weapon. We had information that Faiser shot Wald in a dispute over a drug buy."

"Faiser was a drug dealer?"

"A sometime dealer. Now and then."

"So he had prior convictions?"

"He had arrests."

"Not convictions?"

He shakes his head. "Charges were dropped."

"For lack of evidence?"

He looks me in the eye, and the moment hangs. "Reggie, how many homicides do you think I worked so far in my career, twenty years a cop? Give me a number."

"One hundred fifty."

"Nowhere close."

"Two hundred?"

"Over five."

"Five hundred murders." I am stunned.

"In the crack years, assault cases turned into homicides. I didn't even see my wife, my boys. I missed their Little League, birthdays, our anniversary. Day and night we all worked, and we still got behind."

"You think Henry Faiser did not kill Peter Wald?"

He sucks one cheek. "Does the name Jordan Wald ring a bell?"

"Wald? The candidate Wald?"

"State Senator Jordan S. Wald. He's running for lieu-tenant governor."

"Carney and Wald?" I recall the names on the yard sign at the "haunted" house. A memory kicks in. My late Aunt Jo talked about a State Senator Wald who pushed legislation for tough environmental standards. It was one of her many causes. "Is Wald the environmentalist?" He says yes. "Was Peter Wald related to the senator?"

"Peter Wald was his son. And into environmental causes too. An activist."

"What was he doing there?"

"It was a drug scene, Reggie, a dealer on every corner."

"Peter Wald was there to buy drugs?"

"We never knew for sure." Devaney's face says other-wise. He blinks and lowers his gaze. A moment passes.

"But there was pressure to find the killer," I say. "And now, years later—how many years?"

"Thirteen."

"Thirteen years later, you're not sure."

He pulls the knot of his tie, opens his collar but does not meet my eyes. "Let's say as a veteran in Homicide, I know how easy it is to convict innocent people. Plus, there's hepatitis in the prison system. Hepatitis B and C. It's almost an epidemic. Prison health care isn't exactly the Mayo Clinic."

The nub of it: Henry Faiser is in prison for a murder he maybe did not commit, and he's seriously sick. Years after the fact, Devaney is bedeviled by guilt. "So you've opened old files and"—I swallow hard, the challenge be-fore me on the table—"and an old notebook."

Here's what's next. Frank Devaney will put the note-book into my hands, ask me to hold it and to receive a psychic message. A feeling, an image, something. Will I have to tell him that my intuition is temporarily out of order?

My mouth is dry as he lifts the brown tooled-leather notebook, clasping it like a prayer book. "I'll turn to the particular pages," he says. "You can hold it. That's what your Aunt Jo did. I always had to give her something to hold."

My Aunt Jo, psychic number one, and me, the sequel, though I didn't understand in childhood that my so-called overactive imagination was really a sixth sense. All those tests they put me through from third grade on—results inconclusive. No one would listen to my aunt's explanation, which became the secret we eventually shared, aunt to niece.

"Frank, let me say something up front. I want to be honest. The fact is, I'm not sure I can help you today. In that fog last night . . . well, maybe my sixth sense fogged up."

"Reggie, when it came to psychic abilities, your aunt was also modest. She never bragged. She never promised more than she could deliver. I appreciated that."

"I'm not my aunt."

"In the police department, sniffer dogs have more credibility than a psychic. If Homicide saw this, I'd never live it down."

Perspiration dots his brow. My armpits prickle. The notebook is in my palms, clasped in my fingers. Eyes closed, I try to focus, reach deep inside, imagine that I am one with the notebook. I try not to hear Frank Devaney breathe.

What happens? I think random thoughts—my son's birthday later this month, I'm out of bananas.

Reggie, prepare to admit the truth, I tell myself. It's a

setback but not defeat. There will be other cases. Frank Devaney will come calling again . . . so I hope. For now, honesty is crucial. "Frank, it's not working. My sixth sense has come to a halt."

"You're sure?"

Eyes opened, I try to give back the notebook. He doesn't take it.

"Maybe you need time."

"Psychic messages don't work on a timer." I put the notebook next to him on the sofa.

His eyes look both hard and sorry. "You're positive?"

"Pretty much."

"Well, no hard feelings on this one, Reggie."

I force this out. "Of course not, Frank."

Slowly, he pockets the notebook and rises. I, too, rise, feeling like I'm made of wood. We move toward the door. I am rollerblading on the edge of self-pity, a crime-case Cinderella in a patch of rotting pumpkins. I say, "Maybe the moral of the story is, be careful when you clean out your desk." He frowns. "That's when the notebook surfaced, right? When you rooted through your desk?"

"No. It's when I got a letter from Henry Faiser."

"From prison? Telling you that he didn't kill Peter Wald?"

His nod is long, slow, reluctant. "He writes every once in a while. To say he's doing time for somebody else's murder, yes."

We're at the door. "Where's the letter?"

Devaney pulls a small envelope from his inside pocket. It's addressed in the block letters of children and terrorists. "See for yourself."

I take the envelope, open it, unfold the single sheet, and read, ". . . wrong man . . . bad evidence . . . if you are a moral detective you must care and act . . . do something." At the bottom, in huge letters: "HELP ME."

A short letter, it's a disclaimer and a plea. It contains no real information, not one fact. I hold it at the edges between fingers and thumbs, reading and rereading top to bottom until I can recite those words verbatim, ". . . wrong man . . . moral detective . . . do something."

Devaney waits patiently. I'm still reading. Then there's a shimmer, an optic flash. The moment hastens but stands still. Yes, I stare at lines of ballpoint ink, but *through* the paper I see a scene develop. The letter in my hand has turned as transparent as cellophane, and on the other side something swirls. Like a storm. Coils of red heat. The paper takes me there. It's an oven, an inferno.

I now pretend to read. I am posing with the letter, merely posing. Devaney thinks I pause to grasp the words on the page, but he is mistaken. My left side is hot. Below the rib cage is a burning. It's painful. The hot coils sear and flash. It takes everything I've got not to cry out, to stand as if normal. The fiery storm scene engulfs me.

"Reggie, are you okay?"

"Okay," I say, voice from an echo chamber. "Hot—"

He takes the letter from my hands. I lean against the cool door frame. The coils begin to fade as he folds the letter, tucks it back in the envelope. No flames crackle in his mind.

"Reggie, you okay? Are you sick?"

I shake my head. "Just a feeling in my side, like something hot. Terribly hot." Then I feel embarrassed. Suppose he thinks it's a hot flash?

Devaney leans close, looks hard at me. "I have something to tell you. The house, Reggie, the crack house where Henry Faiser lived—"

"Yes?"

"The day we arrested him, it went up in flames. The chop shop and all three houses on the block burned to the ground. Two bodies were found—homeless squatters. We never solved it."

"Oh."

"You felt that, Reggie. The heat. The letter did it. It means you can help, Reggie. Just like your aunt. I'll get to work on this and call you."

Relief on his face. Relief in my soul. *Bingo!* Psychic is open for business. Hoo-ray. Saved. Deputized.

Yet my rib . . . my rib is still hot. Moments pass as Frank Devaney welcomes me to the team. As I sign on gladly as his silent partner.

Even after Devaney leaves, the rib is still hot. When my whole self is willing and able and eager, why this blaze? Listen to the body, say the experts. Suppose I do? Suppose it warns me, as I plunge ahead, not to walk through fire?

Chapter Three

I'm ready to take a midday walk to Eldridge Street for a crime scene survey—just as soon as my dog comes home. The radio's on as I wash a few dishes, the violins and cellos full-throttle fortissimo. I turn it off, since Beethoven is the last thing I need at a stressful moment. The fact is, I'm jittery and my rib is pulsing. From the front window, I scan the scene on Barlow Square, where the trees are leafing out nicely in bright spring green. On the brick sidewalk, a dry cleaner makes a delivery and an older man in an argyle sweater fills his pipe. A woman carries a cardboard carton in from her car—a new toaster oven. It's a calm city scene for suburban me, the twenty-five-year denizen of enclosed malls and culs-de-sac. Sometimes distraction is the best sedative.

Seated in Jo's study, I open my laptop and start "Ticked Off," a hybrid etiquette and pet peeve column now running in seventeen suburban weeklies, three new ones signed on since last month. The weekly column was launched during my last corporate-wife posting in Oakton, Illinois—i.e., Chicagoland—where we had our biggest house. Where I had my smallest life, upscale as it was.

"Ticked Off" was the hobby that has gained a life of its own. The sight of my name in print, the check payable to me—what a thrill! Who knew that one little op-ed piece on cell phone bad behavior would turn into a bona fide column? Who knew, for that matter, that "Ticked Off" would become a flotation device when my marriage crashed—or, to be precise, when I was ejected from what Martin "Icehouse" Baynes decided was the passenger seat? Never mind that my own idea was long-term partnership, my spousal role the family copilot.

Marty, it seems, saw it differently. For him, I was to learn, a wife meant twenty-five years of cargo to be jettisoned when Ms. Trophy appeared. My era was done, finis, when Marty got Celina, one year older than our daughter, Molly, who is now twenty-three. In any case, "Ticked Off" is now modest steady income to be counted on. Serendipity, never knock it.

I'm finally past the jitters and settling into writing the column—a reader-suggested topic of women who file their nails in public—when an ungodly roar erupts outside, a sonic throbbing with firecracker accents.

My jumpiness doesn't trigger because this time I know what's up. I dash to the window and see the familiar chrome and cherry fenders, the bubble helmet and leathers, the gloved fingers on handlebar controls. I watch the motorcycle ease to the curb and back against it. This Harley is rigged with a dog seat. Sitting up in a harness thing, wrapped in a blanket, the dog has a brown-white-black furry head, floppy ears, and the blunt muzzle and nose of a beagle.

I spring out. "Biscuit. Sweetie." My voice is swallowed by the engine roar.

This black, white, and tan bundle of energy is my dog. Correction: half mine. Formerly my aunt's, she was jointly bequeathed to me and to this biker, who cuts the engine and dismounts, visor up. Standing by the chrome exhaust, I struggle with the harness straps, a Gordian knot. I am exasperated beyond words. "How can you—"

"How can I what?" He pulls off the helmet. This is R. K. Stark, who stands like a highwayman, a Colossus of Roads, in his biker leathers.

"This harness contraption, it's dangerous."

"Custom-made, a stroke of genius."

"A dog's hearing could be damaged by the noise. You didn't consult me. What about our deal?"

He deftly frees the dog, who jitterbugs into my arms and licks my fingers. As I hug her and scratch her warm belly, my dog-dander allergy acts up, the same allergy that plagued me for years while raising the children with retrievers, one Lab and one golden. I sniff but coo, "Sweetie—"

"*Sweetie*? Did I hear *sweetie*?"

Caustic as always, this man wants to turn a sweet animal companion into a *Call of the Wild*. Meaning that our philosophies on dog care are as different as day and night. Stark stows the harness contraption in the saddlebag. Biscuit darts toward a puddle in the gutter.

"Biscuit, *no*." On Stark's order, the dog halts, comes when he calls her, delights at his gruff "Good dog" and the tug at her ears. I am practically forced to invite him inside. The two of us have issues to discuss, such as fleas, ticks, and kibble.

"Coffee on?"

To a normal person, you'd say yes and issue a polite invitation. But Stark strips manners like bark from a tree. I call it the Stark effect.

"Coffee on?" he repeats.

"Pope Catholic?"

"How fresh?"

"Since last Tuesday."

At her kitchen water bowl, Biscuit laps furiously, doubtless dehydrated from the foolish motorcycle ride. I pour Stark a mugful of hot coffee, slide the sugar bowl, and wait as he spoons in his usual five. His cropped hair and trim mustache are ginger, his eyes gray as the North Atlantic. He's over thirty. His scent is unfiltered Camels. And muscles—the man might as well live at a gym.

Literally, he might. I can contact him only on his cell phone and suspect he's close to homeless. Or never sleeps. For two years, he lived rent-free in my Aunt Jo's basement, jobless, practically a derelict. He's supposedly working off his debt of gratitude to Jo by "helping" me, mostly, it seems, by showing up at odd times.

One of which saved my life. Truly. Stark is brusque and about as sensitive as a boiled owl. My neighborhood grocers call him a thug, and they may well be right. Credentials? Don't ask. I don't even know what his initials, R. K., stand for, and he keeps me off-balance by showing up and vanishing like a Cheshire tomcat.

But in my two months here on Barlow Square, Stark has shown uncanny skill where my welfare is concerned. It's as if one of my son's boyhood action figures has come to life to watch over me. What I know for sure is, the man's tongue is alkali, but his deeds are heaven-sent. Stark has been a rock. So far.

What links us is Biscuit. What divides us, among other

things, is also Biscuit. I'll never know why Aunt Jo saw fit to name both Stark and me guardians of her dear beagle. Doubtless Stark is as mystified as I am.

"I'll call her sweetie if I want to. Pets deserve pet names." I blow my nose.

Stark gulps down coffee that would scald ordinary mortals. "Today in the open field," he says, "she figured out her nose beats her eyes."

"Perfectly good eyesight. The vet checked."

"Next step, rabbits. She won't be gun-shy."

He's baiting me. I reach for the tissue box. "Biscuit," I say, "is a house dog, not a gundog."

He gulps again. "How about you, Cutter?"

"Me?"

"How'd you like to learn to hunt? Teach you how to field-dress a deer."

"To butcher dead animals in the woods? No thanks." He's goading me. I give him a stony stare.

He stares back. "Okay, then, learn to ride. Give your driver's license a big upgrade."

On this particular subject, the goading is a try at persuasion. He's brought this up before. "My license is perfectly adequate."

"Adequate for your girlie car."

My preowned VW Beetle is parked down the block. Its dashboard bud vase sports a silk rose. "The Lexus is a thing of my past, Stark. You know that."

"I'm not talking about your deluxe four-wheelers, Cutter. Your Beetle either. I thought you were hot for adventures. You disappoint me."

In truth, I *am* hot for adventure. I have pamphlets on scuba diving and white-water kayaking and hang gliding too. I have in mind a certain man—no, not this dog partner, but a man who appreciates the outdoors and whose return from an international trip I await. I won't say his name here, but cards postmarked Hong Kong, then Cairo, promised he'd call by the first of May.

Today's the fourth.

So, yes, a woman can be keen for adventure but have no pamphlets whatsoever for Harley-Davidson motorcycles.

"Boots and long sleeves, that's the gear to start off," Stark continues. "You already got the helmet."

On the top shelf of the hall coat closet sits a spare motorcycle helmet, courtesy of R. K. Stark. Stolen, for all I know.

"Coupla weekends of school, you'll get your certificate. We'll start you out in empty parking lots."

Enough of this. "On a totally different subject," I say, "do you happen to know anything about old crimes in the South End near the Mass Pike?"

"Happen to? You mean, was it me?"

"On a block on Eldridge near the turnpike?" I give him the dates, try out the names Peter Wald and Henry Faiser.

Stark shakes his head. "I was on the *Vinson*. The Indian Ocean is a few miles east of Boston."

Imagine this man in his Marine Corps uniform on an aircraft carrier. "Maybe you know somebody who remembers those names, someone here in the city. There was a crack house and a chop shop on the same block."

His shrug is nonchalant. "Maybe I could ask around." He eyes me over the rim of the coffee mug. "What's this all about, Cutter? Wait, don't tell me. You got another psychic gig with the cops, right? Am I right?"

Not that I'm hiding it. "Maybe."

"It's that buddy of yours from Homicide, isn't it?" He

puts down the emptied mug. "So which one was offed? Faiser?"

"Peter Wald. The son of Jordan Wald." Stark's face shows nothing. "The Wald who's running for lieutenant governor."

Stark shrugs. "Crooked pol."

"He's an environmentalist. He's green."

"The color of money. If it's Boston politics, it's gotta be crooked."

Pure cynic, Stark. I should have known.

He says, "And Faiser? He's doing hard time?"

"He is."

"Black guy?" I nod. "So the case is officially reopened?"

"More like informally."

"I see." He smooths his mustache. "Sounds to me like somebody's leaning hard on the cops."

"What do you mean?"

"Maybe a reporter. Maybe prison reformers are breaking new evidence that'll make the cops look racist. Maybe a DNA test is coming up. The Homicide guys want to get there first. Especially with the election."

"Stark, you have a suspicious nature."

"I'm a city guy, Cutter. I never did time in a candyass suburb."

"I happen to think ethics plays a part. I believe in conscience." Somehow my statements sound like prissy teatime chatter from my former life as Mrs. Martin Baynes.

He scoffs. "All the better reason to learn to ride. Take your mind away from all that junk."

"Stark, why would I want to ride a motorcycle?"

"Because it's the most fun a human being can have. Sex aside." He cants one hip forward. "Admit it, you like Fatso."

His Fat Boy model Harley, on which I have had two rides, one of which was to the emergency room at Boston City. In my moment of dire need, Stark roared to my side, and the Fat Boy was my ambulance.

"The thing of it is, Cutter, a passenger ought to be able to take over if anything goes wrong."

"Copilot a motorcycle?"

"In a manner of speaking."

I pause to absorb this, a statement that presumes future rides on the Fat Boy.

And also presumes that Stark stands ready to pilot while I am the copilot. Never again will I let myself be mistaken for a passenger. Never again. I say, "You owe me nothing, Stark. Jo—bless her—Jo wouldn't expect it. You're a free man."

"That I am." He reaches into a back pocket, produces a folded, crinkled sheet. "Application form," he says. "Just fill it out and send it in."

The Motorcycle Safety Foundation. Weekly courses at a local community college campus, weather permitting. Tuition about the same as scuba in a Y pool.

"Think about it. Oh, before I go—here, Biscuit. Here, girl." He digs in a pocket. "Dog treat."

The dog bites, ecstatic. "What is that thing?"

"Pig ear."

"Cute. But what is it really?" As Stark goes to the door, I look closely at the dried, wrinkled yellow-tan triangle. Good God, it is an actual pig's ear. "Disgusting."

"Better than bones. Easy on her stomach. Pure protein. Bye, Cutter." He's outdoors at the curb. The engine roars. He's gone. I'm left hoping he keeps Peter Wald and Henry Faiser on his mental "ask around" list.

*   *   *

A dog on a leash is excellent cover. By noon, I separate Biscuit from the vile chew-toy ear and head to Eldridge Place, which claims a whole city block and rises ten stories in pinkish granite that glints in early afternoon sun. Turnpike traffic murmurs in the background. Islands of evergreens soften the main entrance of glass and columns. The security cameras are concealed in stonework niches.

I walk halfway down the block and back again. Not a sign of a former crack house, a chop shop, a murder. Every trace of the violent past that Devaney described is long bulldozed. Eldridge Place now means city living for the right sort of people. Ironic that I myself might have lived here in my former life.

A familiar scenario plays out when two bulky men in crested navy blazers burst from the lobby to meet a Lexus. The taller one opens the driver's door and takes packages from a honey-haired woman in a slate linen suit. The thickset one slips behind the wheel to take the car to the underground garage.

To think that such synchronized blazers once pampered me.

I slowly stroll past. Too slowly, because here comes yet another blue blazer, a wiry redhead with eyes the color of seaweed. "May I help you?"

I assume my Regina Baynes expression. "I'm tracing an ancestor who lived on Eldridge Street long ago. I'm looking for the house where he once lived."

"Sorry, there's no houses on Eldridge. We've got both sides of the whole block."

The borrowed "we" of the staff. He looks at Biscuit as though she might squat and foul his grounds. I pick her up. Twenty feet away, a slender man in khakis prunes pine branches. "Do you know anyone who might remember the street from years ago? Perhaps a groundskeeper?"

"We sub all that out. What did you say your name is?"

"I'm Regina Cutter."

"Well, Ms. Cutter, I'm sorry we can't help." He escorts me across the cobbled drive. The pruning clippers bite, and the air smells like Christmas trees.

I'm not through. The sidewalk runs the whole block, and I put Biscuit down and stroll past the entrance, stopping to put on sunglasses against the glare. I'm three-quarters down the block when I feel it—the heat at my ribs. Warm, then hot. Bearable but insistent. So very *there*. I'm alongside the Eldridge Place pink granite wall. A small stand of bone-white birches marks the spot where the burning sensation rises. I cross slowly, pass the spot, feel my ribs cool. Back to the birches, and I feel the burning heat.

This is the spot. I know it. Literally speaking, I know in my bones that this is where Peter Wald died.

This is my own knowledge, personal carnal knowledge. My fiery ribs are the divining rod for murder thirteen years ago. The burning tells me young Peter Wald was gunned down right here. He fell, bleeding, to this very ground. And a possibly innocent man has been wrongly imprisoned all these years. If so, it's crime piled upon crime, the loss of two lives. Both the prisoner and the victim were younger than my son, Jack, is now. And these birches, merely a landscaper's accent—they're an accidental shrine. Fitting for an environmentalist.

But a secret shrine. The Eldridge Place residents don't have a clue. Who else knows this is a death site?

The killer? Accomplices?

I'm supposed to sit at home and wait for Devaney to

call. No, that's too passive. And all too familiar. The story of my life, waiting for men's cues.

I tug the leash and head down the first side street, which has no sign. So typical Boston, as if everyone's supposed to know the street names. Shingled triple-deckers with sloping porches line the block, with clustered mailboxes of apartments quarried from every floor, a sign of transience. It's trash day, with mounds of junk piled curbside, including stained rugs, mattresses, a single ski.

At midblock, a shopping cart brims with plastic bags and a filthy yellow suitcase. I veer around a figure who rises from the curbside mound. "Don't touch my cart."

She wears a black coat and striped knit scarf, which drags on the walk. She's clutching a frayed doormat. "Don't you touch it."

"I won't."

Glaring, she throws down the mat, picks a torn lampshade with chapped fingers, mumbles.

I tug Biscuit's leash as she grabs my arm. "Got a dollar?"

She looks sixty-something, and one of her blue eyes wanders. One cheek is discolored purple. "What about a dollar? I could use a dollar." Her sunken mouth is a smear of fuchsia lipstick, and the sun glares on her coat collar pin, which is a bird in flight.

In a bizarre way, this woman got herself together with a scarf, pin, and lipstick, accessories for a day of trash picking. She's about twenty years ahead of me. What happened in her life? Suppose somebody like myself ended her days collecting cans for nickels? What are the guarantees against street life with shopping cart?

Suppose that destitution is contagious?

Biscuit's tail wags, and I dig for the dollar. Not one

single in my wallet. She smells of sweat and a foul rose perfume. Biscuit is keenly interested. I hand the woman a five.

She thrusts it deep inside her coat, and the wandering eye fixes on me. Never mind thanks, I want to go.

"You look like somebody. You work at the shelter?"

"No."

"Like a volunteer? You look like her."

"Come on, Biscuit."

"Jo. Her name's Jo."

"Jo Cutter?" My Aunt Josephine?

"She got me a bed when they were full. Snow on the ground. I could've froze."

"The weather's warmer now." Dumb remark. "Biscuit—"

"Where's she been, Jo? She don't come to the shelter now." She turns sideways so the wandering eye can fix on my face. "Where's she at?"

"If it's Jo Cutter, she was my aunt. She . . . passed away last February."

She blinks. "Dead?" I nod. A car drives by. She wipes a coat sleeve across her eyes.

My eyes water too. I can easily imagine Jo finding a bed for this woman. Jo, the Jane Addams of the South End.

And me, keeping my distance.

"Good ones go first. God almighty." She sets the torn lampshade carefully on the cart and kicks at the mound. "Used to be you got something good." She taps her yellow suitcase. "Got it off a pile way back. Shuts real tight. Samsonite."

"You know these streets?"

"Lived inside all my life. Good heat all winter, me and the old man. Forster Street."

"How about Eldridge?" I catch the wandering eye, hold its gaze. "Do you remember Eldridge? An auto body shop? Houses?"

"Can't go near it now. They run you off."

"I mean years ago."

"They burned it down."

"Who's they?" Her lips move as if sampling the question. She shrugs. "I hear Eldridge Street had an auto body repair."

"They'd give you a sandwich. Tasted like paint."

"And a drug house next door. A crack house."

She spits. "Forster was my street."

"What about the crack house on Eldridge? Next to the auto shop."

"Golden rule, live and let live. They kept to themselves."

"Who lived in the house?"

"Young ones, babies. Take it from me, their trouble was music. Day and night, burst your eardrum."

"Musicians?"

"Boom box radio. Religion, they said it was. I didn't care. Summer or winter, earmuffs for the music. The big Doc in charge, he waved you off. I waved back."

"The leader was a doctor?"

"Big Doc?" She snorts. "Never saw a doctor with hair like ropes."

"Dreadlocks?"

"Ropes."

"Was he black? An African-American?"

"Never saw a doctor wear a red robe. Big like a giant. Stood on the porch to preach. Boom box music or that preaching. Morning, noon, and night. Most nights, though, I'm inside."

"Was the auto shop open at night?"

She darts me a look. "You don't listen good. Nights, you don't want to be out. Cops come out at night."

"Were the police around back then?"

"Never when you want them."

"What did Doc preach about?"

"Poison."

"Poison?"

"His people were poisoned. The car garage was poison. The air, the ground, tunnels, and pipes. Poison everywhere. Doc never gave me a sandwich. None of them in the house did. Take it from me, Doc belonged in Bible times." She draws herself up straight and flicks a hand over a shoulder as if brushing lint. "It wasn't no crack house. More like religion. Like whatsis, a cult."

Does she realize what she's saying? "A young man was killed there, shot to death."

"No flowers. The candles blew out. Rain washed the blood."

"Do you remember a young man named Henry? Henry Faiser?"

"What's he look like?"

"He's African-American. Black." I realize that's all I know. His features, his skin tone, hairstyle, I haven't a clue. "Henry Faiser," I repeat. She shakes her head. "But you remember the killing?" She half nods, half cringes. Her scarf sweeps the pavement. "Were you there?" I ask. "Did you see it happen?"

"Police cars like a funeral. Big Doc preached, then the fire. Cinders flew to Forster Street. We stamped the hot cinders. How 'bout another dollar?"

"I gave you a five. What's your name?"

"What's yours?"

"I'm Reggie. This is Biscuit."

"Me and the old man had a dog once. He ran it off." She pats her scarf in place. "I'm Mary. Suitcase Mary. They all know me. I got to get moving before the city truck beats me to it. You talk too much. Don't touch my cart."

"Okay." I watch her go down the block to poke at the next pile of refuse, reluctant to let her go, the closest thing to a witness. If necessary, can I find her again on trash pickup day, or at night in a shelter?

Whichever shelter.

I cross and head back toward the pink granite of Eldridge. There's no corner store or church in sight, meaning no neighborhood store owner or minister with a long-term memory of what happened here. The turnpike traffic is louder, and Suitcase Mary is out of sight. The redhead in the navy blazer eyes me from the Eldridge Place entrance.

I pull the leash. "Biscuit, this way, sweetie. We're going home." Past the stand of birches, my rib flares as I picture the chop shop, then the house where, unless Mary is demented, a red-robed giant with dreadlocks ranted about poison from a porch while music boomed at all hours. And the residents were crack addicts? Members of a cult? Both combined?

Was Henry Faiser one of the residents? One of the disciples?

What was Peter Wald doing here? Buying drugs?

Devaney told me none of this. Could Stark be right to think the police have their own particular reasons to re-open the Faiser-Wald case? Why didn't Devaney tell me more? Why is he the one behaving like a silent partner?

Chapter Four

TV's afternoon news reports a zoning squabble in the Back Bay, though anybody who was slugged and dragged away last night in the fog on Dartmouth is unaccounted for.

An unnamed suspect, however, is wanted for questioning in connection with the murder of Sylvia Dempsey, whose death by the Charles River last month has created a media feeding frenzy. In this TV teaser, there's no hint about the identity of the suspect, though footage of the murder scene by the Charles is replayed. Then it's on to the mayor's budget and the weather. I turn off the TV as the phone rings.

"Hi, Mom."

My daughter usually calls at nighttime. Something must be up. "Everything okay, dear?"

"Fine. I'm calling from the studio."

Doubtless up to her elbows in paint or clay, with her dark eyes intent. Her figure, like Jo's, is built for efficiency. Molly's metabolism burns up every calorie, fortunate young woman, while I fight hips and bustline to stay a size 8.

"How are you, Mom?"

"Fine, dear." She sounds preoccupied.

"Mom—your fur coat. Is your offer still good? Is it available?"

"The minks?"

"I only want one."

My heart skips a beat. I've held on to both furs in case Molly ever returns to civilization. At least the nose ring is gone. As for the tattoo, well, lasers can do wonders. "Molly, I kept both coats for you. But what about animal rights, dear?" The vivid memory surges of Molly's activist episode in front of Neiman's with the spray paint and the Russian sable. That was high school. I wrote the check, and Marty dealt with the lawyers. "What about PETA?"

"Mom, those minks of yours died a very long time ago. They're historical."

Not exactly my wording.

"Can I have one?"

"Summer's coming. Why not wait till fall?"

"Now's the time, Mom."

I get it. She plans a restyling for the next season and is reluctant to admit she wants a more youthful look. "Molly, furriers are expensive."

"Won't cost me a thing."

Meaning her artist friends will snip and slice. *Quelle horreur!* "It's not for amateurs, Mol. Remember Marge Hooper's beaver jacket resculpted on the cheap?"

"The one that looked like crop circles. The coolest."

"She never wore it again."

"Wish I had it."

"Molly dear, is it sculpting you have in mind?"

"Not exactly."

A promise is a promise. Don't ask, don't tell. "Shall I drive the coat down, or will you come up to Boston?"

She'll take the train up from Providence and have dinner. "Molly, one more thing, a hair question." My daughter, the veteran of blue dyes and spikes, should be an expert. "About dreadlocks—why do the Rastafarians grow them?"

"To symbolize roots, to symbolize resistance. Why?"

"Are their leaders called Doc?"

"Not that I know. What's up?"

"I'm doing research. They smoke marijuana for religious reasons, right? Bob Marley and all that."

"All that."

"Do they preach? Is missionary work required, like Jehovah's Witnesses? Or public preaching?"

"It's based on Bible verses about hair and herbs. And the Lion of Judah. You could ask Marfah. Remember him?"

A scowling boy who hung around our Utica house and ate everything in sight. "Where is he?"

"In law school."

"That boy got into law school?" Imagine, a lawyer with dreadlocks.

"At Northeastern. In Boston near you, in fact. You could look him up."

"Maybe I will."

"Gotta check the kiln, Mom. See you in a few days. Bye."

I go to the Web and Google Rastafarian and read, "Early Rasta mystical experience emphasized the immediate presence of JAH within the 'dread' (God-fearer) . . . Through union with JAH, the dread becomes who he truly is but never was."

Mystical paradoxes were never my strong suit. I hit another Web site, this one illustrated with lions and a map of Jamaica. "Rastafarians say scriptures prophesied the Emperor of Ethiopia as the one with feet unto burning brass . . . and hair of whose head is like wool, the symbol of the Lion of Judah." There are biblical quotations from Genesis, Exodus, and Proverbs, all about the eating of herbs, none mentioning marijuana. Their colors are green, gold, and red. The red robe—was it Big Doc's vestment?

There's nothing at all, however, about preaching or music, no Old Testament verses on poisons. I go to other Web sites, but not one lists an obligation to stand outside on a porch preaching. Rastafarians speak out, the Web sites inform me, against poverty, oppression, and inequality.

Could these be Big Doc's "poison"?

I'll ask Devaney. Sloppy case notes from the crackhead years are understandable; so are mix-ups on witnesses. But a ranting preacher with dreadlocks in a red robe in a cult house blasting music at full volume? That would make a surefire lasting impression.

Unless Suitcase Mary's brain is scrambled, that's information Devaney withheld from me.

Deliberately? For reasons of his own? What about the sideways gaze, that guilty look as he pulled his tie? Guilt at Henry Faiser's imprisonment, I thought at the time.

But maybe it's more than that. Maybe Devaney's hiding something from me. The Homicide Division is not, of course, obligated to inform psychic Reggie. I'm out of their loop.

But not necessarily out of their danger zone. Yes, I serve on a need-to-know basis, but it's my ribs on fire at a murder site. Thrilled to work with cops, I could be death's own candidate for another clump of bone-white birches. I will indeed confront the man. My ultimatum: tell me everything about the case, or else count me out.

Biscuit's water needs freshening, and I put in the call to Devaney, grab a sandwich, and get back to "Ticked Off."

The phone rings in minutes, but this voice is high and breathy. "Ms. Cutter, this is Angie from Dr. Buxbaum's office. The doctor asked me to call because the bathroom faucet in his apartment is dripping. He asks that you have it repaired. He would appreciate promptness. He wants you to know it's affecting his sleep. He trusts you will take care of it."

I stare at the phone as if it's a burst balloon. No showdown with Devaney. Instead, plumbing service for H. Forest Buxbaum, D.M.D. I picture him drilling and filling, a high-maintenance tenant. This could be the start of phone pal chats with Angie. "Dr. Buxbaum needs his lightbulb changed . . . his storm windows raised . . . lowered . . . grease trap cleared . . . shirts starched, shoes shined."

Excuse my nanosecond of self-pity, but in my previous life, plumbers were on autodial, along with the pool service guys, electricians, lawn care experts, florists, vets, hairstylists, spa technicians, tutors for the kids all through school.

But with my divorce settlement stocks collapsed, I cannot take one dollar for granted. The five I gave Suitcase Mary—an impulse I can ill afford. "Plumber" is no longer a touch-tone tap away, but a synonym for debit. I can't simply throw money at leaks. My new life isn't *calling* but *being* the plumber.

"Please tell the doctor I'll see to the faucet."

To think, at this time of year, top management and spouses always met at Amelia Island. We played doubles, and one year Martha Stewart—of course, before her trial—flew in to demonstrate bonsai. So many flights on the company Gulfstream with the onboard three-star chef.

Meanwhile, back on earth, my late Aunt Jo, a high school history teacher and community activist extraordinaire and psychic too, was probably fixing faucets for her tenant. Did she drag the toolbox from the back closet and thumb through the *Complete Do-It-Yourself Manual*? Not that she mentioned it in her holiday visits to our suburban homes.

Jo in her seventies, wielding a wrench? Knowing my aunt, I have to answer yes.

And me now in my mid–late forties, a self-pitying pampered wimp? Absolutely not. In jeans and a sweatshirt, I grab Jo's toolbox and read up on "Faucets" in the manual. Stillson wrench, spindle assembly, and knurled nut sound like Urdu. Never mind, Reggie. Get upstairs and give it your best.

Buxbaum's bathroom sink faucet is indeed dripping. Step one, turn off water below sink, then remove faucet handle and turn wrench counterclockwise. But it's stuck. I push and pull, grunt and yank. It's much worse than jar lids. Then the wrench slips. Two nails break to the cuticle, but the faucet handle gives at last.

On to the packing nut and back to the wrench, which feels as heavy as gym equipment. It's a strain. So much for the biceps of Rosie the Riveter. My cuticles sting, and this is taking a long time. What if H. Forest Buxbaum comes home to find me here? The very thought is a big incentive to get this done. Two-handed, I give the wrench a shove, and the nut loosens. Remove the cracked old washer, insert a new one. Back to the wrench, tight and tighter. The drip has stopped. It's done.

Ta-dah!

I did it. Me. Success on my maiden voyage with wrench. Break out the bubbly. Ride me aloft on a parade float. It's a one-minute high.

Then it's over. Done with. I put the toolbox back and think: what if one life leads to small deeds like the faucet washer and endless cups of tea? As the poet said, measuring life in spoonfuls. What if the alternate route means fire, danger . . . and death? Yes, maybe the ultimate big D, though it's risk with a purpose, not cheap thrills. It gives the term "to die for" real meaning. It makes Jo's bentwood rocker a launchpad, not a rest stop.

Fact: I'm damn lucky to be here.

Psychic service a la Reggie is my ace card and ticket to ride. Henry Faiser doesn't know I exist, but come hell or high water, I mean to find out what happened thirteen years ago on Eldridge Street. I know a little something of how it feels to be imprisoned. If Faiser is innocent, I'm here to prove it and help set him free.

It's almost four and overcast when I set out with Biscuit for Tsakis Brothers Grocery. On her own, the dog would sniff every hydrant and parking meter, but this isn't a leisurely stroll. Devaney hasn't called, and I need information. We walk a half mile on Tremont at a brisk pace on a chilly, overcast afternoon.

The brass bell at the store's front door tinkles. Two baritone voices call, "Beeskit!" "Mees Reggie!"

"Ari, George." The Tsakis brothers' store is an aromatic world of coffee and cheeses, parsley and strawberries and bread. Both brothers smile their warmest greeting, their black eyes twinkling beneath thick dark brows. Ari is sorting tomatoes, while George waves from behind the deli case, where he's slicing cold cuts for a buzz-cut man in a blue jacket. In white aprons against dark trousers, the Tsakis brothers could be twins, except George is clean-shaven with a thick head of hair, while Ari's scalp shines as if polished, his mustache somewhere between handlebar and walrus.

Biscuit sits, her shoulders taut. She can't wait for the trick she's about to perform. Her white front paws are out, tail whapping like a black and white windshield wiper. Ari reaches into his apron pocket and tosses a dog snack as Biscuit goes airborne to catch it. She chomps and swallows, and then they do it all over again. Paying Ari at the register, the customer scratches the dog's head as Biscuit goes to her favorite spot by the big bag of onions. She lies down. Biscuit is in heaven.

To tell the truth, my own idea of heaven is increasingly Tsakis Brothers Grocery. As Jo's niece, I am treated like family. The grocery store is my neighborhood hearth.

"So, Mees Reggie, what you need?"

"Bananas, Ari." I reach into the open produce bin, but he stops me.

"These too big. I get you some from the back."

The legendary "back" is where the best and choicest of everything are kept for special customers, although everybody who comes in seems to qualify as special. In moments, Ari returns with a ripe bunch of smaller fruit, which curls like fingers. "These taste best. Some peoples likes the big ones, these out here for them. You want some strawberries too? Here, you try." He offers a ripe berry, enjoys my enjoyment.

"Delicious."

"We say, win win."

"Win win." We smile. Ari will put the bananas and berries on my account. "Ari, George, here's a question. Do you ever make deliveries at Eldridge Place?"

George nods. "Big apartments, swanky. Customers phones us."

"Do you remember Eldridge Street before the high-rise tower was built?"

"Before was different. Peoples from before, these are not our customers. We not deliver then."

"But you remember the street, near the turnpike? A house with loud music? A big man stood outside and preached about poison. He wore a red robe. And there was an auto body shop too. Cars."

Ari bites his lip. George tightens his apron. They exchange glances but say nothing.

"I hear it all burned down. There was a big fire."

"Long time ago. Our store was new."

Both brothers seem agitated. George says, "Past, all finish."

Ari steps close. "Mees Reggie, why you ask this? Something happens with that basement guy?"

"Stark?" The Tsakis brothers take a dim view of Stark.

"Bad guy, Mees Reggie. We try to tell your aunt. Stark is one customer we never miss. Go boom someday. We say, keep away from that guy."

"This isn't about Stark. He was on a ship in the Marines when the fire happened."

"Then why you ask about fire?"

They both look worried. I have a magic word, however: it's *psukhē*, which is Greek for psychic. They knew about Jo's powers. In their eyes, she was Barlow Square's own Delphic Oracle. The Tsakises believe psychic powers run in the family. Which evidently is the case, though

I was long loath to admit it. "It's *psukhē*," I say. "I'm trying to help somebody out."

They nod. At last, George says, "We are new in America. We need a car. Somebody say go to B&B Auto on Eldridge Street. They sell cheap."

"You bought a car there?"

"We not know there is a problem."

"Stolen car?"

"We not know." They look sheepish.

"You got into trouble?"

"Police takes the car."

"Confiscated?" There must be a vehicle theft record. "What kind of car was it?"

"Ford," says Ari.

"Dodge," says George.

They confer and agree to disagree. Neither recalls the model. George says it was a four-door. "Do you remember any names at B&B Auto?"

At last, Ari says, "Carlo."

"A mechanic? A manager?" Both men shrug.

"Last name?"

"We not remember. We try to forget."

"Maybe you have old papers filed away."

"All cash."

"Maybe you'll remember later. It's important. An innocent person could be freed from prison, a person who's sick and badly needs medical care."

Ari picks up a tomato as two girls come in for chips and sodas and Newports. George says no cigarettes, the girls are too young. It's a standoff as I call Biscuit, wave bye, and head home. I'm counting on the Tsakis brothers' memories of Carlo. I'm counting on their conscience.

Chapter Five

Devaney left a phone message, but he's gone when I call the station house. I wash the strawberries and treat myself to a bowlful, one advantage of living solo—although sharing with a special someone would be nice. There's still no word from the Hong Kong/Cairo man on my voice mail. Is a promise still a promise? Suppose he doesn't call, ever?

Well, so what? There are other fish in the sea and so on. Sulking and self-pity are not an option. I used up my quota in the divorce. Life goes on.

I sleep badly, dreaming of cold riptides and swollen black sacks, grateful to awaken just before 7:00 a.m. to news about an armed robbery at a convenience store in Saugus. TV coverage of the Dempsey case continues on all stations. You couldn't avoid it if you tried. One channel even shows her college yearbook photo. The TV ads for the governor's race are starting. Michael Carney and Jordan Wald shake hands against a backdrop of flags and applauding supporters.

I move closer to the screen. Carney, the gubernatorial candidate, is pink-cheeked and jovial with squinty eyes.

Wald has a jut-jawed, chiseled look and a penetrating gaze. I search his eyes for the deep sorrow of a parent who's lost a child. Maybe the TV image quality just isn't vivid enough. Both men look like they've had their teeth whitened. I gaze in vain for a background glimpse of an interracial couple who might own the "haunted" Marlborough house. Surely, the wind caused that front door to slam. Or maybe the door hinges are off-balance. Or a pressurized closing mechanism pushed it shut. Meg and I were just too rattled to talk about it driving back in the thick fog.

I take Biscuit out, feed her, make coffee. It's cool with thin sunlight. Over cereal with a banana, I scan the *Globe* Metro section, which is also filled with feature stories on the late Sylvia Dempsey. No bodies have been reported found in the city or surrounding towns.

I move to the study and e-mail the final version of "Ticked Off," then shower and dress, rejecting a tweed wool two-piece from my Mrs. Martin Baynes days. My new closet rallying cry is "Down with heather!"

Down, in fact, with the whole palette of fade-away colors. The emerald jacket that Meg Givens admired? It hangs beside a new bolero pantsuit of indigo. I am molting, by choice, out of muted colors. It's not easy. Old habits die hard, even when you try to kill them. Today's choice is the indigo.

I'm due in Roxbury at ten. On the sidewalk approaching my Beetle, I hear—

"Good morning, neighbor."

"Trudy Pfaeltz, hi."

She crosses Barlow Square toward me in green scrubs and a trench coat, a small box under one arm. In her later thirties, Trudy has a pug nose, pale freckles, and dark blond hair pinned back. Her face has the pallor of someone who seldom sees the sun.

"Just home from work?" I ask.

"God, were we busy. Night shift is run, run, run. The hospital should issue every nurse a skateboard. The surgical floor's a zoo." Trudy shifts the small box. "I stopped at Pets Galore in Allston. This seed is supposed to promote a vocabulary in talking birds."

"Your parakeet?"

"If Kingpin doesn't get past 'pretty bird,' I'm going to wring his chartreuse-feathered neck. But you know, this box of seed is a test. If it works, I might handle a line of pet products. It's a multibillion-dollar industry."

"Along with the vending machines. Trudy, with your schedule, how do you do it? You must never sleep."

"Like Ben Franklin said, Reggie, time is money. My six vending machines are going to buy me a new minivan. Milky Ways will make my down payment. You might look into something like it. You could trade in your little car."

We both gaze at my black Beetle with its red silk rose in full flower in the dashboard bud vase. Now is not the moment to discuss automotive upsizing. I have something else in mind. "Trudy, let me ask, do you treat homeless patients?"

"When they're brought in unconscious or injured. Boston City gets most of them, but I treated a few when I worked in the ER years ago. Why?"

"Yesterday I talked to a homeless woman, probably in her late sixties. She seemed lucid but partly confused. Does street life cause hallucinations?"

"Dementia. It's a contributing factor. Street people tend to be unstable to begin with, and then a trauma pushes them over the edge. They can develop remarkable survival skills, but malnutrition takes a toll. Plus alcohol and drugs are a factor, sometimes abuse. It's hard to know, Reggie, because these people don't get regular workups. We don't have good records. But if the woman didn't make sense, it's par for the course. You're not hearing-impaired."

"Thanks, Trudy. I'd better let you get some sleep."

"Not till I turn the birdcage into a language lab. By the way, I'm going to start representing Cutco cutlery. How about a free demonstration? No obligation."

"Knives?"

"Cutco is premium cutlery for every lifestyle."

"Trudy, my lifestyle is cutting up fruit."

"Sounds like the eight-inch trimmer to me. Meanwhile, here goes the birdseed experiment. You look spiffy. Great color. Going shopping?"

"Going to work."

"Like he said, time is money. See you soon."

In moments, I'm on my way across the South End line to Warnock Street in Roxbury, a section of Boston I'd never go near in my former life. Every store has a pull-down steel grate for nighttime lockdown, and every person on the sidewalks is black.

It's jarring to be the whitefish out of water, to face a lifetime of prejudice and stereotypes. But the Roxbury streets are definitely not my comfort zone. A parking slot opens up, and I ease the Beetle in beside Bertie's Bar-B-Q. Next door is StyleSmart, the store where I work Tuesday and Thursday mornings.

"Reggie, good to see you. And that indigo looks so fine. It brings out your eyes."

My boss, Nicole Patrick, glides across the floor as if

this shop is a ballroom, as if its customer seating area is a salon, as if the racks of business-dress clothing fill a dance floor.

And why not? Our clientele comes here to learn to dance, so to speak. StyleSmart, you see, provides business-dress clothing for the low-income and no-income women trying to enter the workforce after years on welfare. The idea is to outfit them for post-welfare lives. It is a not-for-profit consignment shop of sorts, meaning its inventory is donated by women like my former self, who seasonally went through her walk-ins to thin out whatever had "expired" and replenish her wardrobe. The customers here pay little or nothing for their purchases and fashion consults. Nicole Patrick is a social-worker-turned-fashionista for the working poor. Me, I'm the chief consultant.

At least, that was the original plan. My Aunt Jo matched us up practically on her deathbed, thinking her niece and friend would cross-pollinate. It's funny how things turn out differently under the law of unforeseen outcomes.

"Reggie, step back there a minute." Nicole teeters on four-inch mules, her hair upswept today. Her skin tone is between milk and bittersweet chocolate. She raises an aerosol can and practically arabesques in her turquoise peplum jacket, its jet beads clicking as she moves. Her onyx drop earrings swing as she shakes the can.

Is she spraying bugs this early in the season? I swear, one spider sighting, and I'll quit.

"They're cookin' up spareribs at Bertie's, Reggie, and if that landlord doesn't do something about the vents, our whole inventory will smell like a smokehouse. 'All manner of baked meats,' says the scripture, but Genesis isn't Bertie's. Here goes."

A mist of orange oil rises. Suddenly, StyleSmart smells like—

"Creamsicles," I say.

"Ummm, it takes you back in time, like snow cones on a hot day. Glad you're here a few minutes early, Reggie. I sold the suit we'd put on Oprah. We got to find our girl another outfit." We stare at the nude mannequin. "Let's dress our Oprah up real fine."

"How about that burnt-brown outfit on the far rack?" It's my background that should make me valuable to Nicole. I repeat, "Definitely the burnt-brown with a nice scarf."

"Let's think on that one for a few minutes." This means no. I have struck out, backslid in just minutes to my old clothes habits. Women on the job aren't nuns, Nicole says. A little plumage keeps the season bright. She tells this to our customers, making sure I overhear.

Moreover, she coaxes me into apparel from the donation boxes. The indigo bolero I'm wearing came from one such box. But don't think for a minute I'm skimming the charity clothes. For every peacock feather, so to speak, I donate something from my closet filled with sedate heathers, bland taupes, and innocuous blues. Accessorized, they're sometimes just right for our clients.

Crazy as it sounds, the used clothes are an upgrade for me, a makeover that Nicole Patrick calls Operation Peacock, with Nicole as my consultant and personal shopper. In other words, my fashion fairy godmother.

"I got some new size tags for the racks," Nicole says. "Let's put 'em on first. You take the skirts, I'll do the tops. I'm also expecting someone I want you to meet."

The shop is ours alone for the moment, and I seize the opportunity. "Nicole, when you were a social worker, did you have Rastafarian clients?"

"My caseload had its share of families with young men in dreads."

"Were they—" I want to ask, religious fanatics? Cult members? "Were they believers?"

She shoots me a look. "Believers? They tried to find their place in the sun in a world that is mostly hostile to them. *Es*-tranged, I'd say."

"What are their beliefs?"

"The history is complicated, Reggie. Mainly, it's a mix of Marcus Garvey's back-to-Africa movement and Haile Selassie as God-on-earth in Ethiopia. It's not my religion, but one big thing: the Rastas oppose Babylon."

"You mean Babylon as a symbol of sinful luxury?"

"For them, it's more like a symbol of centuries of white power oppressing black peoples. Here in North America, the shackles of the slave days become the shackles of poverty, inequality, the trickery of whites. They eat natural foods."

"I hear they smoke a lot of marijuana."

"Tokin' offenders?" Nicole chuckles, snaps a size 16 tag, and looks my way. "Reggie, most of America is hopped up on drugs of one sort or another. Think of the pill pushers on TV. Think of all those feisty little school-children getting off the bus with their tummies full of sugary Froot Loops. They turn the kids' energy into an illness. They call it attention deficit and dose them up good, so they sit cooped up inside the whole livelong day. Who benefits? The drug makers. That's the real 'disorder' we're talking about."

I recall my son Jack's Ritalin year, practically a rite of passage for every other fourth-grade boy at Fox Country Day. Marge Hooper and Leah Stromberger had coaxed me to their pediatrician because Tucker and Brent behaved so much better. Jack did too, but we wanted our real son, not a Stepford boy. Even Marty agreed, Marty who hardly gave the family a thought.

"Okay," I say. "I take your point." We work along. The new spring hues are light and bright. "I hear the Rasta colors are red, green, and gold. Are they symbolic?"

"They're from the Garvey movement. The red stands for the Church Triumphant of the Rastas. It symbolizes the blood shed by martyrs in the history of the Rastas."

"Do their preachers wear red robes?"

"Not that I know."

"I have one preacher in mind, a red-robed preacher with dreadlocks. He was—or is—called Big Doc. What can you tell me?"

"Not very much."

Nicole can clam up when you least expect it. If knowledge is power, Nicole Patrick guards hers carefully. Years of social work made her the eyes and ears of Boston's black communities: Roxbury, Dorchester, Mattapan. She's a storehouse of information, but prying it loose is something else.

I'm not ready to be shut out. "This Doc headed a group home on Eldridge Street near the turnpike. I'm trying to find out—"

Just then an unlikely customer enters, a tall white woman in a plaid jacket and a briefcase-like handbag. She and Nicole exchange air kisses. "Reggie, would you come on over? There's someone I'd like to introduce. Regina Cutter, this is Ms. Caroline French. Ms. French represents the Newton Home and Garden Alliance."

We shake hands. Caroline French has light brown hair and ivory skin and a certain eagerness about the eyes. Her emerald-cut wedding set brushes my fingertips.

"I love this shop," she says to me, white-to-white. "The heavenly aroma—it's my favorite, *sorbet à l'orange*. And how inspiring to know so many women are rising to their full potential."

"Reggie, Ms. French and I have been talking about our StyleSmart ladies modeling their new career clothes for a luncheon benefit event. It's a fashion show that Ms. French is chairing next month in Newton."

Newton, the home of Boston College, the Chestnut Hill Mall, many large and lovely homes.

"Such a paradigm, your store," Caroline French says in well-modulated tones. "Your women bravely helping themselves to a better life . . . and the great determination of your people to get going."

Your people, so different from hers. From the shop's front window, I notice that Ms. French gets going in a Mercedes SUV.

Nicole says, "Reggie, Ms. French tells me the Alliance hopes to name StyleSmart as the beneficiary of their fund-raising this year."

It's my cue. "How wonderful! StyleSmart so very much appreciates the opportunity to work with your organization. Did Ms. Patrick tell you she envisioned this store after years as a social worker? No? Well, the store is flourishing. With the help of groups such as the Newton Home and Garden Alliance, we can continue to work with the women whose self-esteem and economic independence we strive to advance."

This goes on. We all look at our calendars and commit to a plan. Caroline French rises, and we all promise to finalize the specifics.

After she leaves, Nicole practically orders me to script and direct the Newton fashion show. "You can talk that white talk, Reggie. Those home and garden ladies can do us a world of good."

Opportunity knocks. Like Nicole, I can strike a bargain. I look her in the eye. "Before I say yes, Nicole, I want to know who lived in a group house on Eldridge Street about thirteen years ago. I want to know what happened to the red-robed preacher who was called Doc or Big Doc. The house was destroyed by a fire, and I want to know who were the people in that house and where they went."

"Well, that's a bundle."

"There's more. I need to know about a man named Henry Faiser. He's black, and he lived in that house. He's now in prison for a murder he possibly did not commit."

Silence falls like a winter night. What I hear next is a ticking sound in Nicole's throat. She lowers her voice to a throaty whisper and says, "Reggie, you got a nice new life goin' for yourself. You got a roof over your head and lights in the darkness and taps running hot and cold water. You got kids, maybe one day some grandkids. You got spirit, Reggie, just like your Aunt Jo said. But you got to be careful it doesn't turn into 'vexation and vanity of spirit' or you'll have 'no rest in your spirit.' So don't you go looking for new trouble. Take a word of good advice. Mind your business. Stay away from evil dealings."

Chapter Six

In Boston, regular coffee means with cream. I sip, wipe off donut glaze icing from my fingertips, and look at my watch. It's 3:14 p.m. Finally, Frank Devaney appears.

"Reggie, sorry. Couldn't get away. Let's sit in the back. I'll grab a coffee. You all set?"

We move to the farthest of the fast-food pink plastic molded seats, which allow you ten minutes before your spine cries out for a chiropractor. Devaney balances coffee and a cream-filled donut. With his back to the wall, he can see whoever comes in. He likes fluorescent light and quick customer turnover. They appeal to his idea of public privacy. I resist a joke about the cop-donut connection as he sits down. His eyes are bloodshot, and he could use a shave. He scans the room, flips his necktie—chrome yellow with red comets—over one shoulder, arranges a plastic fork beside a napkin, and centers his donut as if it's a first course.

"Gloomy weather." In Bostonese, it comes out "wetha."

"Bet you used to be in Florida this time of year, didn't you? Or the islands."

"Something like that."

"Must have been nice."

I will not fuel his tropical yearnings with postcards from my past. "It had its moments. It's done."

He cuts a bite of donut as if to savor a delicacy on fine china. "On the Faiser case," he says, "I want to update you."

"Good—because I want to help. I'd like to see your notes."

"From the leather notebook? Forget it. The handwriting's so bad my wife says I could've been a doctor."

"I can puzzle it out."

He puts down his fork. "Believe me, the notes don't make any sense. They're like . . . a foreign language."

"I might spot something you've missed."

He shakes his head. "Reggie, you have to understand that this is complicated. I wasn't exactly myself in the crack years."

"We were all younger thirteen years ago, Frank. And not so wise either."

"It's not that. I was more like another person, nobody you want to know—or I'd want to know, for that matter. In those years, the guy in the shaving mirror was a stranger." He fidgets with the fork. "I don't like to dwell on it. You think what's past is past, but it lies in wait like a leg trap. The notebook stirs everything up."

"I can help. Let me do my part and read the pages. We both have the same goal. We both want to find out whether an innocent man has spent nearly thirteen years in prison. We can read the notebook together."

"And have a discussion? We're not a book club, Reggie."

There's finality in his voice, and his cheeks are flushed. He snaps off the plastic fork tines. The donut lies uneaten.

Is this shame, or is he hiding something? Or is the

notebook a cop-civilian barrier? Whichever it is, I cannot simply retreat every time Frank Devaney pulls rank or becomes agitated. "Frank, do you have Henry Faiser's mug shots from when you booked him? I'd like to know what he looked like. Any distinguishing features? What can you tell me?"

"He was slender. He looked young for his age."

"That's all?"

"My recall's hazy, Reggie. I told you Homicide was a zoo back then."

"But surely, you've reviewed the files in the past couple weeks. You're working on his case, right?"

"When I can spare the time." He drinks, stares off, blinks. "There's a certain very big case right now. The whole division is pulled in. It's a media circus."

"Sylvia Dempsey?" He nods. "You're involved in that one too?"

"To lend a hand."

Meaning that he's tied up a certain number of hours that otherwise would be spent on Henry Faiser. "TV news says somebody's being sought for questioning."

"I suppose you want to know who it is?"

"In fact, I don't. I'm doing my best to avoid the whole thing, Frank, and it's not easy when one story dominates the news, day in and day out. It's like an infestation. Anyway, what good would it do to wallow in the murder of a business executive's wife who was about my age?"

"That's right, stay clear. Personal stuff is the kiss of death—that's a figure of speech. By the way, the husband is a doctor."

"Not a businessman?"

"A doctor who's in a business. A skin doctor. We're working with the Newton police."

"Newton?"

"Their place of residence. Look, Reggie, there's a reason I asked you to meet me today. I've brought a piece of evidence from the Faiser case."

"The gun?" My heart leaps.

"No, a stopwatch, like coaches use to time athletes. How about if you hold it and try to get a feeling?"

"Was it Peter Wald's? Or Henry Faiser's?"

"It came from the vacant lot where the murder weapon was found. It was lying in the weeds with empty bottles and other junk. Our blues brought it in with the gun."

"Just the watch? Why not the empties and other stuff?"

"Because the stopwatch was found a foot from the gun and looked clean, like it just came out of somebody's pocket, maybe the shooter's."

"So you think that the killer shot Peter Wald and then ran into the vacant lot and dropped the gun and also lost the watch?"

"We thought so at the time."

"The stopwatch was introduced as evidence in court?"

"No, it wasn't. The DA didn't need the watch—not when we had the gun."

I ask, "Where is the gun?"

"In storage. It's a snub-nosed .32. That probably doesn't mean anything to you."

He couldn't be more wrong. Among the furnishings in my Aunt Jo's Barlow Square townhouse condo are two handguns, one of which is a .38. Jo Cutter was not a markswoman, and I have no idea why she had these guns. It was shocking to discover them. They are scary and intriguing.

I say, "So Peter Wald was shot at close range."

He puts down the fork. "How do you know?"

"Because a snub-nosed .32 is wildly inaccurate beyond fifteen to twenty feet."

"Is someone in your family a sportsman, Reggie?"

"Sportsperson, you mean." A feminist daughter and a divorce tune up a woman's ears to gender pitch. I drink my lukewarm coffee. Clearly, Devaney knows nothing about these guns of Jo's. "Nowadays everything's on the Internet, Frank."

He looks relieved.

"So you've kept the watch all this time?"

"I got it from a warehouse."

"Why not the gun?"

"First things first." He moves the donut and broken fork to the side. "I couldn't just check out old evidence like a library book. I needed a little help from my contacts."

So the watch isn't officially in his possession. Maybe Stark is right: there's mounting pressure to reopen the case. "How about DNA evidence?"

"We didn't have test kits back then."

"Personal items? Something with skin flecks? Clothing with blood?"

"Physical evidence rots if it's not refrigerated, Reggie. Maybe you watch too much TV."

"Don't brush me off, Frank. I'm trying to help."

"It helps when you tune in your psychic station. You ready?" I feel pushed but nod yes. "It won't bother you to try it here in the donut shop?"

"Psychics can work anywhere, Frank. It's not like a seizure. I won't froth at the mouth."

"I just mean—" He looks almost embarrassed. "It seems a little cheap."

I have to laugh. "If it bothers you, we can go for

cocktails at the Ritz." He chuckles. I smile. From an inside pocket comes the watch, which he puts down on the table. It's a small black plastic digital thing with tiny buttons and a liquid crystal screen, which is blank. The battery is dead, of course, though its working order shouldn't matter. It just looks so impersonal, mass-produced.

I admit to this: a paranoid flicker of suspicion that this isn't really evidence but a deliberate feint on Frank Devaney's part. He could have taken the watch from, say, a dish of old keys and rubber bands and dried-out pens to test me, to make certain I don't fake visions in order to stay connected to police work. Or to be sure that the so-called silent partner is straight with him, even if he's not with me.

What do we know about each other, the ex–corporate wife and the homicide detective? That we come from different worlds, that our paths ordinarily would never cross. Yet both of us seek freedom from a troubled past. The Henry Faiser case offers us a fresh start.

I pick up the watch and clasp it between both hands and close my eyes. I hear voices out front—a dozen honey-glazed, three cinnamon, coffees. I hear greetings and good-byes. I press the watch between my palms as if to warm it. Still nothing happens.

I'm ready to give up and hand it back when my hearing changes. It's as though I move to a different frequency, underwater or high in the earth's upper atmosphere. Then all feeling, all sensation, throughout my body seems to drain toward my right arm, to my hand, then my thumb, my right thumb. The thumb burns, and I see something raw and red. I see red drops.

"Frank, my right thumb is burning, and I see . . . it's

like meat. It's bloody meat." My breath is heavy. "I'm not sure, but it could be human flesh." I swallow hard. My rib, my thumb—are they connected? My body is a data bank of pain, but the meaning is totally beyond me.

Don't even whisper the word "meat." Or steak, chop, or drumstick. The stopwatch vision of bloody raw flesh has driven me to a tofu and veggie diet.

And what good did my "reading" do? The burning thumb and the raw flesh seemed to baffle and disappoint Devaney. Whatever he knows about the Faiser case is not in sync with a fiery thumb. He pressed for more psychic data, and I gripped the watch till both of my thumbs turned white, but nothing else came into my sixth sense. It was exhausting. Frank doesn't seem to understand the bodily toll a psychic reading takes, how draining it is. We promised to stay in touch, but both felt down when we parted.

I'm not down for long, though. The police files are closed to a civilian, but surely, the *Globe* covered the story of the Eldridge fire and the shooting of Peter Wald. Going online in the newspaper's archive, I enter keywords to search events of thirteen years ago on March 22. Interestingly, the *Globe* covered the fire and the shooting in separate stories. The headline on page two of the first section read, "State Senator's Son Fatally Shot." Peter Wald was identified as a college student known for environmental advocacy. "Shot by an unknown assailant at approximately 1:25 p.m. on the 300 block of Eldridge Street, Boston." Taken by paramedics to Boston City Hospital, he was declared dead on arrival. Robbery is named as the suspected motive, and police were said to be searching for a black male of medium height, late teens or early twenties. Senator Jordan S. Wald, who identified his son's body at the hospital, was said to be in seclusion.

The article contained no information on why Peter Wald was on Eldridge Street, which was, according to Devaney, a known drug dealers' bazaar. Did the senator pull strings to suppress that information? As a parent, frankly, I would have.

Three additional articles report the arrest, arraignment, trial, conviction, and sentencing of Henry Faiser, all within the year, all reported in short columns on inside pages. Is it possible that Senator Wald exerted political pressure to get a swift conviction? If so, he's partly responsible for an innocent man's conviction—if Henry Faiser is innocent.

As for the fire, it received all of four inches in the Metro section, maybe 150 words altogether. A fire of suspicious origin in the 300 block of Eldridge Street destroyed three houses and an automobile body shop, B&B Auto, in the early evening hours. Firefighters arrived at 7:13 p.m. to find four structures ablaze. Though high winds hampered efforts to contain the fire, firefighters prevented its spread to adjoining streets. Residents of Eldridge Street escaped, though two unidentified bodies, thought to be homeless males, were later recovered from one unoccupied house. It is thought the fire began in that house, caused by smoldering cigarettes or drug paraphernalia.

I search for follow-up stories. There's nothing. Didn't any reporter look further into the fire? Didn't an editor assign additional coverage? Evidently not. It was on to the next day's stories and deadlines.

For the next three afternoons, I walk around the Eldridge neighborhood in search of Suitcase Mary, hoping another five dollars might pry loose additional memories of Eldridge Street life years ago. She's nowhere to be seen, even though Biscuit is in doggie Nirvana paddling in the gutter rainwater. Meg Givens has called to schedule lunch, which is nice, although she sounded tense and admitted to problems at work. She gave no specifics.

I am brushing and vacuuming dog hairs from every surface on Sunday early afternoon. Stark—without phoning ahead, as usual—roared up a couple of hours ago and took Biscuit out for training at the nearby park.

The dog finally staggers back home, laps her whole bowl of water, and promptly collapses on her bed just off the kitchen. I've turned off the vacuum. "Stark, you worked her too hard."

"Nah."

"Just look at her little chest. It's heaving."

"Look at her paws, she's dreaming about chasing rabbits. She went crazy for the puddles today, wanted to swim. You giving her too many bubble baths?"

Asleep, Biscuit growls softly, a sign of aggressiveness, which Stark loves but I find alarming in a pet. "She's about ready for field trials," he says. "I know a guy with a farm out in Acton."

"Stark, that's too far. How would you take her? Not on that motorcycle. The harness is treacherous."

"I tinkered with one strap. Bet I could get a patent."

"You're delusional."

He laughs and scans my kitchen counter. "You out of coffee?"

"I'm staging a work stoppage. This isn't Starbucks." I try to sound firm but come off petulant instead.

Stark says, "Maybe you should go for an outdoor workout too."

"I work out with free weights. I keep fit."

"Get some sunshine, vitamin D for your mood." Then he grins, the devil in his eyes. "Anyway, you oughta be nice. I happen to have the name and address of Henry Faiser's sister."

"Fantastic. I mean it, great. What's her name? Where does she live?"

"Feeling better, Cutter?" His gray eyes glint. The kitchen smells like Camels and leather. "You sent in your application yet?"

"Stark, you can't force me onto motorcycles."

"Who's forcing? It's a swap."

"It's blackmail."

"You'll love it. Forget your vacuum, you need a Harley. Besides, women love the leathers. So where's the application? I'll help you fill it out. You got boots?"

"Any woman with pantsuits in her wardrobe has boots."

"I don't mean candyass fashion boots, Cutter."

Candyass—his favorite put-down and a true measure of his vocabulary. "I'll work on it." I spend the next moments with the application. "It asks why I want to take the Motorcycle Safety Foundation course. How about 'bullied'?"

"Try 'recommended by friend.' Don't forget the check."

I write the tuition check, and he puts the envelope inside his jacket for personal courier service. "We're looking at a weekend in July. Now this." He takes out a torn paper. "The name's Kia Fayzer. She spells it different from her brother. It's *F-a-y-z-e-r.* Last known address is 3529 Roland Street, Mattapan. She's not in the phone book. I can tell you, Cutter, Mattapan's no place for a honky lady."

"I'll be fine."

"You need an armed escort." His eyes are stone-cold serious.

At this moment, I do not want to know that there's a loaded firearm concealed somewhere on Stark's body. "All right, we'll both go, if we take my Beetle."

Number 3529 Roland Street is a triple-decker off Blue Hill Avenue. I park at midblock, walk to 3529, and climb onto the porch on this Sunday afternoon. Stark keeps an eye on me from the car, but Kia Fayzer is nowhere in evidence. I knock until my knuckles hurt and then look sideways left and right. On either side are identical clapboard and shingle triple-deckers, which have seen Boston's generations come and go. Decades ago, Irish workingmen with huge families lived here, then immigrant Jews. Now it's a black neighborhood.

Each of the three floors of every house has been cut into several apartments. On this block, the porches sag and windowpanes are cracked. Plastic sheeting is taped over some of the windows. If Henry Faiser once lived here, the route that took him to Big Doc's compound on Eldridge seems, in economic terms, strictly lateral.

I start to go next door when a car pulls up to let out a woman with two children about six and eight years old and a baby in arms. "LaBron, get that bag. Anissa, come on back here. Carry that bag in. Where you think you're going, girl? Get a move on, I got to get to work. I'll be late for work." The car pulls away. Each child stares at a grocery bag set on the curb.

LaBron, the eight-year-old, pouts. The heels of his new sneakers flash bright red with every step, but he's unhappy. "They didn't give us no Devil Dogs. We didn't get no chips."

"Hush your mouth. Get that bag."

"Excuse me," I say, "I'm looking for Kia Fayzer. Does she live here?"

"No Pepsi neither."

The woman shifts the baby on her hip and looks me up and down. She looks weary but wired in grass-green capris and a cropped pink sweater. The baby sucks her tiny fist, leaving an epaulet of drool on one shoulder, an insignia I well remember. "You a caseworker?"

"I just want to talk to Kia."

The little girl stares at the bags. "They too heavy. Make my arms hurt." She wears white rubber rain boots, a long purple gown, and a macaroni necklace. Her short black braids are topped with a rhinestone tiara held fast with sparkly butterfly barrettes.

"Make like you're hugging it."

"Hug and kiss an ol' bag? Yuck. Princess don't kiss a bag. Princess Anissa kiss a frog tha's a prince."

"Frog kiss, yuck." LaBron squats, begins hopping. He leapfrogs over the grocery bags back and forth.

"Stop that, LaBron. Grab the bag. Put your arms around it and lift up."

I try to get her attention. "I just want to talk to Kia for a few min—"

The little girl's bag rips as she tugs it. Canned goods spill out: beans, spaghetti, soup.

"Look now, what you did." LaBron gloats at his sister's mishap.

Cans of food are rolling into the street. I grab one. It's sauerkraut. I catch a can of chili as a car swerves to miss it. LaBron puts a package of buns on his head. "Bet you can't do this, Nissa."

"I don't care." She stacks two cans atop one another.

"You don't got no buns. I got 'em all."

This is too much for Princess Anissa, who begins to cry. "Mama, make LaBron gimme the buns."

"No buns for crybabies, nah nah."

"LaBron, you torment your sister, you go to bed with no TV."

But he's become a bear, maybe a tiger. Paws out, buns clenched in his teeth, he's on all fours nosing the one intact grocery bag.

I help gather the cans. The mother says, "We got it ourself. LaBron, get up and behave yourself. Pick this up."

"Where's the hot dogs? They didn't give us no hot dogs, just buns. And powder milk." His face is a map of fury. "I hate it there. I wanna go to the real store."

"Quit your fussin'. Get on upstairs."

"Excuse me, about Kia Fayzer—"

"I don't know nothing 'bout where she is."

LaBron picks up the sauerkraut and makes a face. "How come we don't go to the real store? Kia took us to the real store."

"Kia lived here?"

"Hush your mouth, LaBron."

"I wanna go see Kia. She fix me a hot dog at her house."

"Boy, shut your mouth."

"Where is her street?"

"Like a farm." He moos and bellows, then makes horns and charges his sister. The mother glowers and slaps the air halfheartedly as LaBron ducks. The baby starts to cry. I hustle to the Beetle and can't wait to check the city street atlas.

Chapter Seven

There is no Farm Street in metro Boston. I pore over the atlas and stare at Mattapan. A farm street, what would it be? Old MacDonald Avenue? I've tried to find Kia Fayzer online and in the phone book, but no luck no matter how I spell the name.

LaBron was a cow . . . No, a charging bull. This feels like charades. Or is it . . . Yes, here's Angus Street, also in Mattapan.

It's almost 3:00 p.m. Monday when I drive solo to have a look. I'm deliberately drab in navy slacks and a sweater. Biscuit rides in the backseat. Stark wants to train her to hunt rabbits, but I'm on a different hunt. The dog is my magnet.

All five blocks of Angus are a mix of apartment houses, weedy vacant lots, duplexes, one corner store. A German shepherd lunges at a chain-link fence and snarls as I pass with Biscuit on her leash. Kids just out of school, however, gather to pet her, which is my plan. Setting books and backpacks down, they stroke her ears and scratch her belly as she obligingly rolls onto her back.

"She a girl dog."

"She lick me! Lick my fingers!"

"She sweet, she don't bite."

It's during this petting-zoo moment that I ask about Kia Fayzer. At the name Kia, a boy in black jeans with white piping nods and grins. Two teen girls in flowered jackets repeat the name as if Kia is a cousin. Bingo!

"Which house?" I ask. They suddenly look puzzled. "Which apartment is Kia's?" The boy starts to laugh. The girls giggle. "Where does she live? Which building is Kia's?"

Three girls in plaid uniforms start to hum a tune. "Does she live in the brick one?" Now a dozen children laugh, elbowing and egging each other on. "Kia," I say again, and they grin as if I'm a Pied Piper of the funny bone. I don't get it. They're singing about "my neck, my back." They all know the words.

And it dawns on me: there's a recording artist named Khia. She's one-name-only, like Cher and Madonna. I say, "Fayzer," and the kids all shake their heads and go blank. The girls get a jump rope and start double Dutch. The German shepherd is frantic, and Biscuit whines until I carry her in my arms three blocks up to the corner store, Fern Market.

The steel-grilled door stops me. Ads for Kools and Newports plaster the front glass so I can't see inside. "Market" sounds harmless, but what of Stark's warning about an armed escort? What if I walk in on something—a drug deal, a gun buy? No Tsakis brothers will greet me here. No Nicole Patrick will run interference. My lily-white hide is on the line all by itself.

Move it, Reggie. A man sits year after year in prison for a murder he possibly did not commit. Get going. So I step into the small market, which smells of Fritos and chicken. The sound track is hip-hop, which is hideously familiar from my Jack's teen years when our whole house was hammered by Tupac Shakur and Puff Daddy. Decent music ended with the Bee Gees, Marty insisted, one of the few points on which we agreed. Fern Market sells cigarettes, malt liquor, lottery tickets, and bobbleheads of Celtics and Patriots team members. I buy a scratch card and ask a solemn clerk in a ribbed sweater about Kia Fayzer. "I just want to talk to her for a few minutes."

He shrugs. "Can't help."

"It's about a family matter."

"Be anything else?"

Biscuit whimpers, and I hold her close and leave. In front of the store, two young men in dark suits with rumpled white shirts hang out. They eye me while pretending not to, and I eye them the same way. "I'm looking for Kia Fayzer." Their eyes go blank, and they turn away, which is my cue to exit their space. Instead, I linger. What have I got to lose? "I want to talk with her for a few minutes. LaBron says she lives here."

A minute passes. "Which LaBron that be?"

"From Roland Street. Here in Mattapan."

"You lookin' for LaBron?"

"No, for Kia Fayzer." They sway, and I realize they're either drunk or stoned. Their shirts puff out of their pants, and their pockets gape. I spell "Fayzer" and say it again.

"Sure am dry," says the taller one. "Dry as a desert."

The shorter one rubs his throat. "Colt 45 wet me down good."

I remember the malt liquor from Jack's teen drinking. The shorter one gives Biscuit a little scratch. "What you want with Kia?"

"Just to talk a few minutes. It's about family. Nothing official."

"Maybe if somebody be good to us, take care of our thirst and maybe a couple lottery tickets. Maybe we hungry."

So if I furnish the refreshments, maybe they'll tell me where she lives. If they know. If this isn't a petty con game. Am I desperate enough to buy two Colt 45s, two lottery tickets, and take-out chicken?

Yes.

After a couple of minutes, I hand out the bribes while juggling Biscuit in one arm. "But this here bottle ain't cold, lady. This here feels warm as spit." With my neck and face flushing hot, I go back inside to exchange the warm bottles for iced.

"Tha's better." The short one scrapes his scratch card with a fingernail, which a manicurist would admire. Both men clink bottles and chugalug and peer into the bag of buffalo wings. Finally, the short one points to a sky-blue duplex midway in the next block. "Try up there."

By now, it feels like a Grail quest. The woman who answers the door won't say her name. She's medium height, mid-thirties, her skin a golden bronze, hair in close-cropped black waves. She stands in ironed jeans and a ripped white T-shirt, her legs planted wide apart as if the porch is a rolling deck. Big-frame dark glasses hide her eyes.

"I'm looking for Kia Fayzer. Are you Kia?"

"You a caseworker or a cop?"

"I'm Reggie Cutter. If you're Kia, I'd like to ask about your brother Henry."

She ignores the dog. Her eyes say don't waste my time. Biscuit yips. She folds her arms across her chest.

"I'm here on my own. I'm not a law enforcement officer. Somebody thinks maybe Henry is innocent of the crime that sent him to prison. Somebody wants to look into it. I agreed to help. Are you his sister?"

"So you not a cop?"

"Citizen" sounds righteous, but "psychic" is loony. Words do fail. "If you're Kia, would you give me fifteen minutes?"

In a movement that is both sinuous and cynical, she rolls her hips and lets me into a room that's crammed with clothes and cosmetics. Her T-shirt, I see, is not simply ripped but torn cleverly. The dark glasses are unnerving.

She clears an armload of nylons and lingerie from a chair. I recognize a certain Victoria's Secret black lace bra—the Very Sexy Seamless Plunge—which also nestles among my own lingerie, with tags still on. Mine awaits debut on a romantic night, an act of faith in my future.

"What's on your mind?"

She sits on the edge of the mattress of a pullout sofa. I perch on the chair and speak to the lenses. "I understand Henry lived at a house on Eldridge Street thirteen years ago, before the mur—before a young man, Peter Wald, was killed. The house had a preacher named Big Doc. He was a Rastafarian. Was your brother a follower?"

"Was Henry a follower?" She snickers. "You could say he followed a boom box voice inside his head."

"Was it Rasta music?"

"His own kind of music."

"He was a musician or . . . did Henry hear voices?"

"He went his own way, did his own thing."

Is this possible: a loner in a group house? An individualist in a cult? "I understand he had an arrest record."

"Sure he did. Get arrested, that's how you qualify, you hear what I'm saying." The lenses flash.

Maybe I don't really hear. We could easily talk past one another for the whole fifteen minutes. "What did Henry do for a living?"

"You do what you gotta do."

"Jobs?"

"Henry was self-employed." She falls silent. I remind her I'm trying to help. I ask for specifics. "Like when he was little, he got old sandwiches from 7-Eleven and sold 'em at beauty parlors for double what they cost."

"And when he got older?"

"He sold some clothes."

"He clerked?"

"He went moppin'."

"Cleaning floors?"

She laughs loud and hard. Biscuit cocks her head and barks once. I shush her and pat her head. Her cutest expressions are going to waste. The woman is dogproof. She says, "Henry filled orders."

"You mean he made deliveries?"

The angle of her jawline says she thinks I'm hopeless. "He delivered what you want. You want Fendi? You got it. Gucci, Manolo. What you want."

"Stolen? Shoplifted?"

"Takin' care of business. Look, if you're not in school, there's the elements—the gangs and the streets. Henry didn't waste his time flippin' burgers. When it comes to something hard-boil, he had his ways."

"Was he recruited? Did Big Doc recruit him?"

"Like in the army?" She shakes her head no. "More like, when it's cold outside, where's he gonna stay?"

"With family?"

"We got split up a long while back. I don't know where all Henry stayed. But when it comes down to it, if somebody's got a house, maybe that's cool."

"Shelters?"

"Shelters," she says with a sneer. "You get robbed and hit on. Juvie, they treat you bad."

"So you think maybe he pretended to be a Rastafarian to have a place to live? He pretended to go along?"

"Did what he had to do."

"With no limits?"

"Henry didn't shoot nobody." Her voice sounds disembodied.

"How about drugs?"

"How 'bout 'em?" She tilts her face, and my own reflects double on the lenses. I try not to fidget.

"Wasn't he arrested and charged with narcotics violations?"

"They never got him on that. If they got him, that's *it*. Five years for five grams. If you black, they get you. That's a fact. You know what five grams of crack look like?"

"No."

She reaches for a suede purse, and a wave of dread rises in my stomach. She's going to show me actual crack. Am I complicit in something? Aiding and abetting? Do I glance at the crack, then shut up about it? My palms break a sweat.

"Look. Look here."

Is this entrapment?

She opens her palm to reveal two pennies. "Weight of five grams of crack. You lookin' at five years hard time. That'll get you five years stuck away. Five years for sure."

A five-year sentence for selling just five grams of crack cocaine, the approximate weight of two pennies?

"Odds of a black man spending time in prison today is one in four. One in four."

Surely an urban legend, but I won't dispute her.

"They get sick in there. They get TB, hepatitis. My brother's sick."

"I heard. Do you visit Henry?"

"Out there in Norfolk, yeah, I go out Saturday mornings when the 'F' visitors are allowed. I go when I got money for the debit card."

"What do you mean?"

"Henry likes his treats, you know, like everybody. Candy, cologne, soap."

"You can't take him a package?"

"Lady, what planet you on? They make you buy a debit card."

"Who, the guards?"

"The guards, the warden. Prices jacked way up. Toothpaste, a pair of socks, they got a gold mine goin' in there. Somebody's making big money out of prisons. No phone cards, no weekend low rates. Henry gets to feelin' bad, he call us collect, and the real crime is the phone bill. You know who ought to do hard time? The phone company."

Her lip curls. If she escalates this rant, I'll lose the moment. "Tell me, was your brother an athlete? Was he a runner?"

"No."

"A stopwatch was found near the gun that killed Peter Wald."

"Henry played ball. That white boy got shot by a white man in a running suit. Henry told me true. He wouldn't touch a gun, no, ma'am. That's how I know he didn't shoot nobody."

"What about the stopwatch?"

"Watches, now, if you wanted Rolex, he get you one. His price was right. You want Cartier, you got it. Maybe what they found is Henry's merchandise."

That cheap plastic thing? Not for a trafficker in Rolexes. No way. "Do you have a picture of Henry? I'd like to see it."

She pauses, finally shrugs, and goes to a closet door hung with a thick wedge of clothes. She feels in pockets for a key, then unlocks a bureau drawer and returns with a black-and-white school photo of a serious, thin boy in his late teens with short hair, not dreadlocks. He has soft, liquid eyes and a diamond stud in his left ear. His smile is shy and a bit sly. I wonder who's treating his hepatitis.

"May I hold the photo?"

"It's a old one."

Her sisterly undertone is wistful. Kia gently hands me the photograph, and I hold it carefully. Seconds pass without one psychic vibe. Zero. Those liquid eyes prompt a perverse thought: had Henry Faiser been imprisoned for selling two cents' weight of crack, he wouldn't have been near Peter Wald on Eldridge Street. He'd be out now, a free man.

"So who is this lookin' into Henry's case?"

I hand back the photo. "I can't say. It's someone in the justice system."

"They catch the one that did it? They got some DNA?"

"Not that I know."

"Then you playing games."

"No, I'm helping an investigation."

"With cops?"

"I can't tell you. And I can't promise Henry anything. We'll have to see." I pick up Biscuit. "Maybe it's best not to tell your brother."

" 'Cause it's lies."

"Because it's complicated."

We're at the front door. I step onto the porch and thank her. Kia's taunting voice follows me down the sidewalk past the liquor store where the two young men loiter with bottles and losing scratch cards.

"They got him in there 'cause that boy got killed was a white rich man's son. One of ours is goin' to pay for that. They're makin' money off us. They got our people locked up to make money."

"Reggie, Mattapan is off-limits. Where's your learning curve?"

Meg Givens and I are lunching in a bookstore café near Copley Square. It's nearly 1:00 p.m., and we've chatted and browsed best-sellers while waiting for the table. Meg likes my turquoise sweater set. I've admired her russet jacket. Her earrings are tiny red hats. We're both famished and irritable.

"Dangerous parts of Boston, Reggie, you have to be careful."

"Like the Back Bay?"

"Oh, you still think you heard somebody mugged in the fog?"

"And dragged off. With a horrible sound, like strangling."

"Mattapan is not for a white woman like you. Too much crime. What were you doing way out there anyway?"

"I was trying to find the sister of a man who . . . wrote a letter."

"To your aunt? I guess you've got to go through her things sooner or later."

"Actually, it was a letter from a man in prison."

Meg looks up sharply. "Your aunt was a saint, Reggie. She championed underdogs. She fought for good causes morning, noon, and night."

"It energized her."

"But she was one of a kind. Her files are probably chock-full of wacko pleas for help, and you can't be responsible. Not to smudge Josephine Cutter's memory, Reggie, but my advice is, ignore those letters. I've read that prisoners send them like dogs shed fleas. They're more or less bulk mailings, and if the prisoners don't have real paper, they use toilet tissue. Was this one?"

"Prison-issue Charmin? No, Meg, this letter was on notebook paper. The lettering was vivid and blocklike. The wording was basic."

Inside I hesitate. Did Henry Faiser send out lots of letters just like the one he mailed to Frank Devaney? What if the same plea went out to prison support groups, to ministers, to random names in the phone book? The man is a hustler. His sister admitted it. The plea for help and proclamations of innocence could be his latest scam.

The con game of a murderer?

Just then, however, as I take a bite, the air begins to feel heavy, and a certain pressure builds at my side. It takes effort to swallow. "Oh, ouch."

"What's wrong?"

An acrid odor hits my nostrils, and the air thickens. Meg's face blurs. "My side, my rib."

"Reggie, you look pale."

"It hurts—"

"Drink some water. Here."

I watch a turquoise sleeve reach for the water glass. It's my own arm. My rib is actually . . . burning. I manage an icy swallow, but in my field of vision, the light shimmers and waves, although Meg seems not to see it. I set down the ice water, but my rib is on fire. Breath held, I am seeing the letter that Devaney put into my hands. It's as if I hold it even now, as if it is part of me: "Do something. HELP ME."

"Reggie, are you okay?"

Heat warps the light like a mirage, and my rib is scorched. I smell smoke. I haven't touched anything to prompt this, but maybe the memory of Henry's letter is a trigger. Or maybe Henry beams his psychic energy at me, targets me.

Meg speaks from a distance. "Reggie, do you need help? Can I help you?"

"Just a minute. Give me a minute." But the words of clocks and timekeeping are not real. One moment melts into the next. I am suspended in smoky vapor. Meg's face is near yet far-off. I take shallow breaths and wait until the block letters begin to fade and the burning along with them. Slowly, the heat recedes, the air clears.

"Do you need a doctor?" I manage to shake my head no. "Do you feel okay?" I nod, but my rib is still pulsing. "Reggie, for a minute there, you looked like somebody in another world."

My mouth is dry, my voice thin. "Just a random twinge, Meg. I should've eaten breakfast."

"It's the stress. Listen, you're not responsible for the stuff in your aunt's files. She wouldn't want that. Barlow Square is your home now. You need to meet new people, make new friends. Like the Red Hats, wonderful women. Another year or two, you can join. You'll love us. Now you need to gear up, jump-start. That guy who promised to call you after his trip—have you heard from him?"

"One postcard from Hong Kong, one postcard from Cairo."

"That's it? Well, never mind. I say it's time for a clean slate. Toss Jo's files. You can use my office shredder. I'll get a bottle of chardonnay. We'll make it a party."

Determined to steer me out of the weird episode, Meg chats and jokes but also watches me, ready to call for help at the first sign of trouble. I reach for a pumpernickel roll to show good faith with my new friend. "Molly's coming up from Providence for dinner this weekend," I say. "And I've got to get Jack a birthday present."

"If he's like my Skip, clothes are out." I nod and ask about Meg's son. "I just sent a check for his health care and car insurance," she says. "It's a whole new world out there for young adults, isn't it?" Meg spears a blue cheese crumble. "Reggie, can I bring up something? Are you sure you feel okay?"

I butter the roll with lavish swipes. "I feel absolutely great."

"Okay, good. I hate to do this, but there's something I've got to ask you . . . another favor." Meg glances sideways at the next table to be certain no one is listening. "I have to because I'm at wit's end."

She leans close and lowers her voice. "Just for the record, Reggie, I've been in real estate here for over fourteen years. I've rented and sold places where awful things happened—heart attacks, fatal accidents, like the hair dryer that fell into the bathtub or the ladder that collapsed on a stair landing. One of my clients even fell from a rooftop. Nice woman, full of fun. The husband decided to sell the penthouse floor and buy a whole building once he got the insurance and the new live-in girlfriend. My commission paid Skip's tuition for a year." Meg looks me in the eye. "But this haunted house is something new."

"Marlborough Street?"

She nods. "The doors keep slamming. Now the crystal and china objets d'art are falling off the shelves. The lights flicker even though electricians have checked the wires. That night, are you sure you felt nothing paranormal?"

"Nothing at all. I tried my best. Maybe all that Black Power wall covering jammed the radar. Or maybe that chandelier is bad luck. Have you ever seen such a gruesome home accessory?"

"It's the husband's pride and joy."

"And those chunks of armor on the walls . . . it's as if a knight had been cut in pieces with a welder's torch."

"They're authentic, very valuable."

"So are dinosaur skulls, but who'd want them on their wall? It's not about market price, Meg. It's about taste."

"Reggie, let me tell you a little about these people. Their name is Arnot, Jeffrey and Tania. He made his money in franchises and nightclubs. I hear he also owned a women's pro wrestling team that folded. He's on a few boards around the city."

"And Tania?"

"She's an Ivana Trump type. She collects antique china and crystal but likes shopping at Target with an entourage and a camera crew taping."

"Maybe they both crave publicity. Maybe the 'ghosts' are a stunt."

"No. They want to be in the Boston social whirl, not ridiculed as nutcases. No offense, Reggie, but most people still think the paranormal is somewhere in left field."

As if I don't know. "Meg, you can probably find a

dozen New England psychics eager to take a reading on the Marlborough house."

"Too awkward, Reggie. Too tacky. The Arnots would feel insulted. They want discretion."

I nibble the roll. I know just what's coming.

"Reggie, won't you give it another try? Maybe the fog blocked the message. If you could just try one more time? Tania Arnot phones me nearly every morning in tears. Her husband is talking about filing suit. They're afraid to go to sleep. They've spent the past four nights at the Four Seasons."

The Four Seasons as homeless shelter? "You'll pardon me, Meg, if my sympathies fall a little short." Or is this personal jealousy, with my own five-star hotel days a thing of the past? Of course, the favor is for Meg, not the Arnots.

"They're hosting another fund-raiser next week, and she's terrified something will happen."

"A political fund-raiser?"

"Yes, one of several. Serious campaign money is at stake—and, of course, the Arnots' social standing."

I'm already on the edge of my chair. "Is the fund-raiser for Carney and Wald? For Jordan Wald?"

"I suppose so. Remember we saw their yard sign. Tania is begging for my help. She careens between rage and despair. These people won't go quietly, Reggie. Even if they sell the house, accusations will fly. Marlborough is one of Boston's best addresses, but a Realtor can't take things for granted. I have to consider resale values. Your Aunt Jo told me once that the first version of the Declaration of Independence said 'Life, Liberty, and the Pursuit of Property.'"

"My ex said things like that."

"I'm asking your help just one more time. Please."

Now I'm the one who leans back. "One condition, Meg. I want to be at next week's fund-raiser. Let's say it's part of my sixth-sense investigation. Let's say it's a burning issue."

Chapter Eight

Like phobic fliers, a woman of a certain age needs a martini to cross the threshold of a computer-electronics store. To my regret, I am cold sober as I search for a birthday gift for my son. The Carney-Wald fund-raiser is days away, but various tasks keep me busy. A freckled young clerk suggests inflatable stereo speakers for video games in the bathtub.

When I say no, he urges wi-fi accessories. "The D-Link System will quintuple the top speed of ordinary home wireless systems. This is based on the latest version of the wi-fi wireless standard—you know, the 802.11g. Full compatibility is guaranteed."

Compatibility? That would be me, the mom, selecting a nice necktie. Filene's Basement menswear and my budget—that's compatibility. I picture Jack taking his new girlfriend to dinner in a nice spread-collar shirt, a clothing item on which I have gigabytes of expertise. Believe me, I know my Egyptian cottons.

My son, however, lives in T-shirts and khakis. He could furnish his wardrobe from a Dumpster. I settle on a titanium stylus for his pocket PC, a sort of birthday stocking stuffer, then go home and order a big tin of his favorite special roasted peanuts from Bluff Gardens in Michigan. It's the thought that counts, though I can only guess what avalanche of dazzling gifts Marty Baynes a.k.a. Daddy Warbucks might order from a *SkyMall* catalog.

The phone rings.

"It's Frank, Reggie. Remember you asked me about a reported incident in the Back Bay on the night of the third when you heard that dragging sound?"

"I do."

"Missing Persons isn't my division. You know that."

"Yes."

"But TV local news is going to carry a story tonight. I think the media are taking a short break from the Sylvia Dempsey case."

"What is it, Frank?"

"There's a guy from Woburn reported missing."

"Woburn? Isn't that miles from the Back Bay?"

"Twenty miles, yeah, but here's the thing. He works for a Boston caterer. He went out on a job starting at five. The family expected him back in Woburn by midnight."

"The job was in the Back Bay?"

"Alan Tegier's the name. None of his family or friends have seen or heard from him since he left for work that evening. He didn't make contact with anybody known to him later that night. He left Woburn for the Back Bay and never made it back home. But, Reggie, don't let your imagination get crazy on this."

"Crazy? Did you say crazy?"

"It's probably nothing, just a lovers' quarrel or maybe a family fight or job trouble. The guy'll probably turn up in a couple weeks. That's how it usually goes in a missing person case. Nine times out of ten."

"But you're concerned enough to call me."

"Consider it a courtesy. But it's not your case, remember that. I want you to keep your head."

"Frank, after two kids and a slugfest of a divorce, believe me, what I've got going is my head. Count on it."

"I do, Reggie." His voice drops, almost shy and barely audible. "More than you might think."

Channel 4 news at 11:00 p.m. broadcasts blurry snapshots of Alan Tegier, a young white man in a white shirt and black bow tie pouring wine and serving trays of salmon roe canapés. His distraught father and sister are shown stapling xeroxed photos of Alan to telephone poles, then it's his tearful mother next, imploring anyone with information to come forward. Another clip shows the Woburn assistant chief of police and Lieutenant Tom Shabati of the Boston police say that every effort is being made.

I go to bed wondering if there'll be a follow-up. Or if, like the Eldridge fire, Tegier's disappearance will receive the gone-and-forgotten treatment from the media. It's a disquieting thought that returns to me the following morning. Despite the treacherous Harley harness, Stark has taken Biscuit for a few days, according to our custody arrangement. My nose clears, but the dog's water bowl and food dish look sad and lonely. The house feels empty. It's easy to fall into a melancholy mood about another young man who has vanished, in this case into Norfolk Prison.

Meg's idea that my aunt received prisoners' pleas for help has also stuck in my mind. It has a certain logic. Devaney could be fooled, preyed on by Henry Faiser and by his own guilt over shoddy work in Boston's crack cocaine epidemic. What if Jo's files contain letters from Faiser, especially if he copied the same message over and over and mailed them out by the dozen? My aunt was an activist on so many fronts, she might have kept a letter from Henry.

Two stout oak file cabinets flank the rolltop desk in the study, and I sit down and start in. The household accounts are neatly arranged, utilities, repairs, consumer skirmishes with appliance manufacturers. ("Surely your engineers could redesign my DeLuxe Quiet model to stop the motor sounding like a Panzer tank.") The letterhead replies reek of condescension, evasion, and corporate pieties.

I move on to the activist files, Jo's battles with the city over garbage pickup, pedestrian protection, fair housing, food donation, neighborhood crime prevention. There's a file of tribute letters too, from a church's autumn festival committee and a wetlands preservation group, among others. Also a folder of thank-you notes and cards: a woman whose son got help job-hunting, an uncle grateful for his niece's summer camp scholarship. One file folder is reserved for a single sheet: a letter of commendation from the Office of the Mayor.

So far, however, no file contains pleas for help from prisoners. I'm relieved, but only momentarily—because while replacing one file and reaching for the next, my hand smacks something hard and cold.

The guns. Just after moving in, I'd found them in Jo's kitchen, the Taurus .38 in a drawer under a stack of brown grocery bags, the Colt .44 nesting in cotton in a box high in the pantry. What woman wants stray guns in her kitchen? I'd immediately jammed them deep in the right-hand oak file drawer. Or so I thought. But no, here they are in the left one.

I close the study blinds, then those in the kitchen. I put the guns on the table and try to figure out where to store them properly.

They make me believe that Jo nurtured a secret self that she kept hidden inside her various chests and cabinets. Take the scarves as another example. In clothing preference, Jo swore by Harris tweeds and Shetland wools and dressed like a Mennonite. But she left a drawerful of neatly folded, flamboyant, store-fresh scarves in silks and velvets. Beside hers, my Hermès collection is downright sedate. Scarfwise, in fact, Isadora Duncan at warp speed in a Bugatti—rest her soul—had nothing on Jo Cutter.

Which goes to say that Jo Cutter, like most people, had her contradictions. Still, the guns are in a category all their own, a total puzzle. To my best recollection, Jo never mentioned them, never dropped the slightest hint.

Plus, other guns might be hidden elsewhere in the condo. Several of Jo's storage boxes remain untouched. Suppose she collected according to calibers, with a .22 awaiting me in an overnight case, a .357 in a canvas tote?

I run a thumbnail across a nick—or trophy notch?—in the walnut grip of the Colt .44. It looks old, like a collector's item. I pick it up. Was someone shot with this very handgun?

Or killed?

The Colt cylinder smells metallic, oily, and burned. A shiver zings down my neck. I half suspect Stark knows something about these firearms, but so far haven't confronted him. If I do, he might confiscate them.

One nasty thought lurks in the back of my mind: that the guns belong to a third party who might suddenly show up to demand them.

I put down the Colt and pick up the Taurus .38. I pull back the hammer just a little, spin the cylinder, and there's a neat click with each rotation. *Clickety-click.* Ever so lightly, I brush my finger over the trigger, frighten myself, then move my finger away with a shudder.

Did the gun that murdered Peter Wald look like these? Devaney didn't tell me. Kia swears her brother is allergic to guns. Maybe yes, maybe no. I picture the young man with liquid eyes in a cell on a thin mattress writing letters.

It starts up again, at first warm, then hot. It's the searing pulse at my rib. Leaning against the fridge, still holding the .38, I feel the burning sensation come, as if it seeks and finds me, and bears down upon me.

As if Henry Faiser's message hits me personally. It's not scattered to the winds, but beamed at me. Did his sister visit him, tell him a white woman showed up to say she's working on his case? I feel this certainty. And I asked for it, yearned for it, worried that my sixth sense might fail me and my life would shrink to mini-measures. I now wait for the heat to crest and to fade. This moment in the kitchen is a reckoning. The hot pulse signals the obligation that defines my new life. I am Henry Faiser's target.

And his lifeline.

Chapter Nine

It's a lovely spring twilight with the trees in foliage and the songbirds in lullaby chorus. It's almost seven, and the sky is mauve, the air a mix of earth and lilac. Hope is in the air. An evening like this was made for a political fund-raiser—and for knowledge that might help the Faiser case.

I park the Beetle and walk down Dartmouth. The hideous night of two weeks ago seems from another world. Kids on skateboards jump the very curb where I stood that night, cowering, hearing the gagging noise and scuffle. I pause to scan the pavement stones carefully. It's years since anybody bothered to pick up pennies. There is no mark visible on the concrete.

The Marlborough Street home of Jeffrey and Tania Arnot is bathed in pearly light, the dank Gothic mists vanished without a trace. Lamplight glows from every window of the neo-Medieval brownstone, and luminarias guide us up the stairs. The Carney-Wald yard sign of red, white, and blue looks jaunty, making the very notion of haunting silly and far-fetched.

Most guests wear business clothes, the men in suits,

"Excuse me, are you feeling all right?" It's a young woman with a tray of mushroom puffs. Her nameplate says "Brenda" just below the caterer logo, Ambrosia. "I saw you close your eyes in the front room. If you're not feeling well, can I get you something? An aspirin?"

"I'm fine, Brenda. Thanks. Just resting my eyes. Really." I smile to prove well-being. I'll tell Meg I gave it my best shot. As for the Arnots, I'll be pleasant, gracious, and firm. Tonight's close-up of Jordan Wald, however, will be my payment in full. I want to see the father of the murdered young man. I want to see the face of an influential public official whose fatherly grief and rage perhaps helped prompt the conviction of an innocent man.

The trio strikes up "Tangerine," and I head toward the front room off the entrance. The crowd is shoulder-to-shoulder, the room at maximum occupancy. A man in stunning eyewear says, "Well, of course, he's a hack. It's a time-honored political tradition."

"Cynical, Rodney. Love that about you," says a woman in knits with brass buttons. "At least Carney's a known quantity, all those years in the House. It's Wald I wonder about. What's he want?"

"What they all want, Jennifer. He's a four-term state senator from an old Boston family. What else do you need to know?"

"They say he's a loner. Steers clear of the old boys' network."

"The old boys' days are gone. Upstarts are today's fresh faces. Or haven't you heard?"

"But how'd he get in the game?"

"Real estate and heating oil. Family connections don't hurt either."

"One more bored businessman hot for a second act in politics. They say he's got Potomac fever."

"Be fair. He gets top grades from environmental groups. He's a green guy."

The woman to the left smooths her chestnut hair. "I heard something about him."

"He runs the marathon every year."

"His wife died of cancer."

"Wasn't his son killed by a crazy drug addict? It was on TV."

I lean close to hear more, but a murmur rises and shoulders tighten. Four chunky men and a woman in black with headsets wade into the room and fan out. One near me says, "A-OK for Bulldog and Boxer."

Two men in suits arrive like a magnetic force, and guests part to make way like the Red Sea. The florid face and jolly, squinty eyes of the shorter man are unmistakable—he's Michael Carney, candidate for governor. Just steps behind him marches Jordan Wald, his jutting jaw like a prow. Both men wear shadow plaid suits, though Carney is rumpled, Wald starched. Smiling, they shake hands left and right, their teeth bridal white.

"Ladies and gentlemen, your attention, please."

Applause crackles. A microphone squeals. Alison has helped a buxom woman in platforms onto a stout low bench by the front window and hands her the mike.

"My friends . . . testing, testing . . . friends of Michael Carney and Jordan Wald . . . testing, can everybody hear me?" Her voice is playful and gusting. "Can you hear?" The guests nod and murmur. She purrs, "Darlings, you've written your lovely checks for our marvelous candidates. You deserve at least to hear."

Good-humored laughter ripples. In a shantung cream

coatdress with a heavy sapphire necklace-earring set, Tania Arnot is wide-eyed and apple-cheeked, with frosted hair coiffed and sprayed to withstand gale-force winds. She cradles the mike as if the bench is a cabaret stage.

"Jeffrey and I welcome all of you tonight to our home. The beautiful spring evening promises new times . . . and a new governor and lieutenant governor. Are you ready to give a great big welcome to our guests of honor? Are you?"

Her breast heaves with the Carney-Wald button, while a badge on her shoulder proclaims "More for Massachusetts!" A few feet away, the broad-shouldered man in the midnight chalk-stripe suit grins. Just as I guessed, Jeffrey Arnot. "Are you ready to welcome the next governor of our great Commonwealth?" Yesses rise like helium.

Carney springs onto the bench, air-kisses Tania, and launches his ten-minute spiel. "Not just jobs, *good* jobs . . . a Massachusetts economy in *drive* . . . every child in the *best* of schools." He tells a story about his wheelchair-bound late mother, his voice rich as fudge as he segues to life lessons learned from his father, a metalworker of sterling character. Next he sings praises of his wife and sons, who are busy campaigning elsewhere in the state in homes as warm and welcoming as Jeffrey and Tania's.

Waiting his turn, Wald nods reverently. I search his face. No widower's flash of grief shows nor mournful gaze in memory of his own lost son. So what? Give the man the benefit of the doubt. Not every politician is required to bare his soul to a roomful of strangers.

In minutes, Jordan Wald leaps up to join Carney, grabs the mike, and quips about the two bench-pressing for Massachusetts. "We're both athletes—a wrestler to *pin* the problems and a marathon runner to *go the distance* for the people."

Time-delay laughter.

"Seriously, my friends, we're in a tough race. The future is at stake." His voice slightly reedy, Wald predicts a hard-fought campaign with victory in November. His four terms in the Massachusetts Senate, he says, are foundation stones for the future. He ticks off environmental legislation he has sponsored. The Carney-Wald administration will be pro-business and green. "Protection of our coasts, our wetlands."

Wald makes eye contact so each guest feels addressed personally. He jabs the air with a few Kennedy gestures and turns his head from the shoulders, as business executives do. Marty practiced this. It's an authority thing. Underlings twist their necks, but bosses strike the Mount Rushmore pose.

"My life is an open book. What you see is what you get. My good fortune . . . giving back in public life. My thanks to each and every one of you."

He's done. Tania invites all to stay and enjoy the party, and the candidates work the room. The black-clad headset handlers keep watch like a junior Secret Service. I turn, and a hand with a grip like wood and leather clasps mine.

"Jordan Wald."

"Oh. I'm Regina Cutter."

"Appreciate your support, Regina." He leans close, the cleft in his chin quite charming, though his handshake doesn't feel quite right. I smell wine breath, men's cologne—and underneath his starched shirtfront, something vaguely sour. "For you, Regina, for Massachusetts."

But his politician's eyes have already moved on. The

moment came and went. What did I learn—that perhaps thirteen years ago this man leaned on the DA to nail Henry Faiser whether or not the evidence was solid? No, nothing of the kind. He strikes me as a stereotype of a political candidate. The lasting impression is that Jordan Wald has an odd handshake and uses hair spray.

"Bulldog and Boxer, exit now. Repeat, exit now."

Like border collies, the headset handlers cut the candidates from the pack and escort them outside into a black Suburban with dark-tinted windows. The SUV pulls out, corners, disappears.

The party winds down fast, the house emptying quickly. The trio packs up. I linger by a foyer fireplace, its mantel lined with decorative floral Limoges plates. I note the rose pattern on the plates, fine antiques in this home dominated by armor and weaponry. Here comes Alison with a short, wiry black man. She turns to him. "Mr. Jeffrey Arnot, I'd like to introduce Reggie Cutter."

As an ex–corporate wife, I'm seasoned at hiding astonishment in social situations. So much for the midnight-blue chalk-stripe broad shoulders. Jeffrey Arnot can't be more than five-six, lean and taut, his facial muscles tense, eyes steely yet opaque. We shake hands, mine moist, his dry and hard. He wears a black double-breasted suit with a mauve shirt and violet paisley tie, the color palette perfect. His French cuffs set off heavy gold monogrammed cuff links. His skin is a dark walnut.

"I understand you are an exorcist."

"Exor—oh, nothing of the kind, Mr. Arnot, though I have experienced paranormal events. Paranormal."

"My wife has the idea you can put a stop to the disruption of this house. You cast a spell, is that it?"

"No. What I do—"

"Cast out demons?"

"Perhaps Mrs. Arnot's free to join us. I'll go see." This from a fretful Alison.

"I'm a plainspoken man, Miss Futter."

"Cutter."

"Plainspoken and business-minded. I indulge Mrs. Arnot in such things as this, but chitchat with a real estate agent is not my concern. Fair price and value are my terms. I am not a gullible man. I believe in dollars and good sense."

"Jeffrey, Jeffrey dear, and Ms. Cutter." With Alison in tow, Tania Arnot sweeps this way, her platforms marching through the shag as through a meadow. Her dress rustles. "So wonderful to meet you. We've heard marvelous things." Her low voice gusts as she touches my shoulder. "Meg speaks so highly of your special talent, your powers."

"I was just explaining, in order to correct a misunderstanding. Mr. Arnot seems to think that I'm—" I don't want to say "witch." "That I'm someone with preternatural power."

Tania nods. Jeffrey rocks back on his heels.

"But I must tell you that I've made a good-faith effort to learn whether your house is—" I resist the word "haunted." I won't give Jeffrey Arnot the satisfaction of scoffing. "To learn whether your house is susceptible to mysterious events. But I must report that I detect nothing out of the ordinary. Nothing at all."

Jeffrey Arnot's lips bend to a near sneer. Tania looks as though she might weep. Alison twists her fingers.

This much I know for certain about the moment: none of us touch the mantel. We're at least two or three feet from it, standing quietly. My eye catches the movement first. Of the four Limoges plates, two begin to tremble from side to side, as if shifted by an unsteady hand, as if inched from their grooved slots in the mantel.

We watch, all four of us, as the porcelain plates stutter and shift in a kind of dance. None of us move a muscle, not Alison, not Jeffrey or Tania. Not me. Time slows, the moment expanding as we stare, fixated. A cold current of air wafts as two plates, each delicately patterned with roses, push out, out.

The cold air strikes my neck. Tania visibly shivers. She folds her arms tight. The plates rattle. Jeffrey is stock-still. Alison's eyes are huge. The plates tremble, advance to the mantel edge, linger for an instant until another blast of icy air sends them plunging.

At the last split second, one of us might reach out, catch at least one. As spectators, however, we only watch, frozen in the moment, statues ourselves as the two plates fall to the marble hearth and smash to bits.

Chapter Ten

I saw it with my own eyes. You're thinking looks can deceive, but the plates were perfectly secure. Then they jiggled and moved as if pushed and pulled. Then they fell."

I repeat the story like the compulsive Ancient Mariner. My daughter nods across the table. We've just finished dinner, her favorite chicken with herbs. She's come for the mink coat. "Molly, those two plates moved as if an invisible hand pushed them." She smiles. "What's so funny about that?"

"Invisible hand. You know how Dad always talks about the market and the invisible hand."

"Your father is not in this, Molly."

"Sorry, Mom." She puts down her fork. "It must have been scary."

"No. It was weird. If it was an optical illusion, four people saw it. Four people picked up the shards." Which isn't exactly true. Alison got a server—Brenda—to sweep up the pieces.

"How about that cold draft? Sounds like the wind blew the plates."

"It wasn't wind. It was a cold zone, as if a freezer door opened. It felt that very same way on the night the front door closed. I was with a Realtor friend."

"I see." I'm not sure she does. "I hope you don't obsess about this, Mom. The whole thing could be a trick, hidden wires and pulleys."

"To destroy antique Limoges?"

"Maybe the plates were fake. Forgery's not that hard. If you spent time with artists, Mom, you'd think behind the scenes." Molly pokes at a stray salad leaf. Tonight her thick honey-blond hair is scissored like crow's feathers and tinted a dull brass. Stylewise, I never know what's coming next. She says, "Art's just a big bag of magicians' tricks."

"Why would anyone play such a trick on the Arnots? This wasn't the first time. Things crash and slam in that house. The Arnots are nearly berserk."

"Maybe it's his trick on her. Or hers on him."

The shocked look I'd seen on both Jeffrey's and Tania's faces tells me no way. "Maybe you had to be there."

"Maybe."

There's nothing left to say, except "No psychic message came through to me."

Molly nods. Unspoken between us is the Josephine Cutter connection, meaning that my Molly, too, has a sixth sense. On occasion, it's expressed in her art, though not recently.

"Just remember, Mom, you're not in charge of party tricks." She smiles. "Hey, did you hear? Jack's new girlfriend threw him a birthday party."

"He called. He likes the new titanium gadget. I hope this girl's nice."

"Jack's bedazzled, that's what I think."

Here's what my son said to me: "In the middle of the night, Mom, I think I love her. But by midafternoon, I think I'm just stupid." Of course, he's on my mind.

"Sometimes Jack and I worry about you, Mom."

"Me?" Talk about role reversal.

"We think since the divorce you're, like, overreaching. You need to feel personal success. Why not join a book club? People love book clubs."

They do, though the one I want to join at the moment is Frank Devaney's leather-notebook club.

"Reading is one of life's great adventures."

It's amazing how grown children can patronize a parent with a statement of fact. Behind my back, in good faith, my children want to shrink-wrap my life.

"I might take a motorcycle riding course."

"Oh, Mom, you're hilarious. Let's clear the dishes. I'd better get the mink. I have to get back to Providence. A friend's coming to the studio to help with a sound system."

"Music in your art studio?"

"I'm working on an installation featuring implants and anabolic steroids. We're putting voice boxes inside Barbies and G.I. Joes."

And she used to draw so beautifully, flowers and seascapes. "I don't understand."

"It's America, Mom. It's G.I. Joe and Barbie. I got razor wire too. It's the idea of the nation as bulked-up security state."

Don't ask, Reggie. "Let's leave the dishes, Mol, and look at the coats." I've spread out the short female mink directional and the three-quarter Blackglama. Both came from Marty, commemorating his promotions. They were, so to speak, the coonskins nailed to the wall. I was scheduled to get an ankle-length Lagerfeld when he made CEO. Dream on, Marty. You hit the glass ceiling, I hit the fur floor.

"Mom, I just want to be sure you're ready to give up a mink. Suppose you change your mind?" That hooded look I know so well on her oval face—it's guilt.

"Molly, my dear, you are the one and only reason I hauled these coats to Boston. For me, they are relics of a bygone time of life." I stop, lest my daughter think she herself is somehow from a bygone era of her mother's life. "Take your pick, but first feel each one. Notice the hair is short and velvety and has a delicate sheen. Natural mink has clarity and is understated. The longer hairs— the guard hairs—are uniform in length." I turn on an extra lamp. "Notice the depth of color. It's quality mink."

"Mom, you sound like a saleswoman."

"Molly, if you own it, you need to know."

She picks the shorter one. "This'll be great." The hooded look of guilt deepens.

"Put it on. Go ahead, Mol. Mink with jeans is stylish." She puts it on. "Very nice. Though the funnel sleeves are definitely passé."

"Today passé, tomorrow retro classic."

"Remember your cape in high school?" We giggle, recalling Molly's high school Saturdays at a warehouse where the clothes, baled like hay, were burst open so the kids scavenged and paid by the pound. "That Swiss loden cape, I rushed it to the dry cleaner. It was either that or Orkin."

"I guess I drove you nuts."

"I guess that was the point." We chuckle. "You must see about summer storage."

"I—" She looks suddenly sheepish as well as guilty.

"What is it, dear?"

"I won't lie to you, Mom. The mink is . . . I mean, when you come to my exhibit next month, how would you feel if you saw the coat in . . . in . . ."

"On display?"

"Sort of."

"Then you don't plan to wear it?"

"It's a mixed-media thing." Her gaze shifts sideways. "But it'll be fun to wear next winter."

She shakes her head and slips off the coat. "Mom, actually, what I have in mind is—" Her fingers mimic scissors.

"You're going to cut up my mink coat?"

"Just a few strips. To twine them with the razor wire."

"Oh, Molly . . ."

"Oh, Mom." She looks suddenly forlorn and nine years old. "Mom, I don't want to upset you. I think this is a bad idea. I'm sorry. You better keep the coat. I'll use something else, maybe moleskin."

It's one of those moments, swirling with mixed motives, values, costs, high stakes, low stakes, my daughter, myself, our past and future. Believe me, this isn't easy. Talk about counterintuitive. "Molly, a gift must be freely given. I'll never wear that coat. I promised it to you. It's yours. You're an artist, and if your work needs mink strips . . ." I manage a swallow, pick up the coat, and put it into her arms. "Whatever you do with it, it's yours. I can't wait to see your show."

Why did the Arnots' house turn on them? Molly sparks the question. Is it possible that a saboteur lurks on their housekeeping staff, a maid or cook working on behalf of someone trying to oust them, maybe to force a sale at a low price? Their number is unlisted, so I get it from Meg Givens, dial the Arnots, and leave a message.

I fill dead-end moments with TV news and the *Globe,* which are still full of features on Sylvia Dempsey's murder. The unnamed person who was questioned reportedly furnished no new information.

I make another phone call. "Are you still stuck on her case?" I ask Devaney. He grunts yes. "Any progress on Henry Faiser?" My heart sinks when I hear "Not really." Maybe he's telling the truth. Or it's an excuse not to tell what he knows. "How about the caterer?"

"Alan Tegier hasn't turned up yet. Missing Persons handles it."

"So when does Homicide step in?"

A noise at Devaney's end sounds like cracking peanut shells. "Tell me, Reggie," he says in his driest voice, "have you heard that Homicide requires a body? Have you heard of the centuries-old principle of habeas corpus?"

"Never took Latin, Frank. I minored in French."

He hangs up.

Next Tuesday morning at StyleSmart, I want to ask Nicole again about Big Doc. But she's eager to plan the fashion show at the Newton Home and Garden Alliance. The plan is this: we put together the ensembles here at the store, and Nicole will snap Polaroids for my reference so I can write the narration. Time is short.

We work with a few customers, then turn to the show. Nicole has six StyleSmart regulars in mind as models.

"Thing is, Reggie, this show will cost our ladies lost wages. When you're only getting six or seven dollars an hour, you can't afford a ladies' lunch even if the salad's free. My idea is, StyleSmart will pay our folks. Our budget's lean, but this is high priority."

No wonder my Aunt Jo adored this woman.

Admiration, however, can't cloud the goal, which is information on the Rastafarian preacher. As always, I first pay my dues. Nicole is at hurricane force, plucking hangers of jackets, skirts, and tops plus scarves and pins for the show. "Our ladies need to look confident, competent, pulled together. No wilting violet, no flake, no slut look. Here's a red jacket for a power look. And a pinstripe too. We got the pearls. Reggie, check our handbags, would you? How about shoes—black and brown, medium heels?"

In moments, she's snapping the photos of a dozen outfits, two for each model. "The corporate look, Reggie. Our ladies need a business image. You work up the story line and the adjectives. I'll call Caroline French and tell her we're set."

"Just one thing, Nicole."

She's caught my tone. She turns. "What?"

"Some information I need."

"What? Oh no, not that Rasta."

I describe my talk with Kia Fayzer.

"Reggie, you are courting trouble. If you think your white skin will save you—"

"Nicole, at this point in life, I have few illusions about my white skin."

She blinks. I blink back. "Truth cometh to the light, Reggie, but some things are exceeding deep. Remember the wickedness of folly."

"I just want to talk to him."

"Folly and foolishness, Reggie."

"Just a few words."

She shakes her head. "My covenant of life and peace—"

"Nicole, please."

She rolls her shoulder in a monumental shrug. "His real name is Ernest Frynard. He preaches on street corners."

"Here in Roxbury?"

"Vanity of vanities, Reggie."

"I just want to talk."

As if the words are dragged from her depths, she finally says, "Try lower Washington."

For the next two days, I walk past street vendors and panhandlers downtown on lower Washington Street but see no preacher at midmorning, early or late afternoon. I breathe subway odors from the sidewalk grates and mingle with shoppers passing Filene's windows, which feature summer beachwear. But I don't see anyone remotely fitting Big Doc's description.

Not until Friday. It's nearly three, a warm, sunny afternoon in the sixties. The weather has been spectacular. Biscuit is beside me, trotting nicely on her lead. Stark brought her back this morning, freshly shampooed and full of pep. I've walked her from the South End, crossed the Public Garden and the Common and down Park Street, where two firefighters flush a hydrant. Wouldn't you know, Biscuit leaps for the water. She half prances, half swims in the gushing stream before I step in and get her out. She shakes herself from ears to tail, droplets flying. My feet are wet. The firefighters laugh.

Tightening the dog's lead, I do not at first pay attention to the sounds coming from lower Washington. The drum rhythms and the *jing-jing* of tambourines can be heard from two blocks off. A street fair? No, these rhythms are insistent, driving, martial. I move closer to see about twenty people gathered at a corner, blacks and browns and a few whites.

Crowd control is managed by a squad of dark-faced men who seem to be in charge. They wear tight black pants and jackets with silver conchas, like a mariachi band, yet severe, military. They corral the crowd but keep the sidewalk passage clear. Two Boston cops across the street watch the scene, arms folded, eyeing the corner while talking.

I join the crowd and stand beside a woman in a head scarf. She peers intently toward a mounted poster of a winged bomb and a black steel barrel lettered "OIL" with a red slash. The drums get louder, tambourines quicken, and a portable sound system crackles with static. The crowd swells to maybe forty, young and old. Some clap with the drums and tambourines. Finally, in sync, the whole black-clad squad chants, then whoops, and a speaker mounts a plywood podium. He has a mike and a portable amp. Yes, he's a big dark-skinned man in a red robe.

His voice booms through the crackling static. "Merchants of death! Plutonium in the Canyons! Cancers from uranium 238!"

Picking up my wet dog and soaking my shirt, I crane to see.

"Cluster bombs! Civilians dead! Liquid gas in Boston Harbor!"

His dreadlocks look like roofing, and his red robe is

dark crimson. Didn't Suitcase Mary say that Big Doc preached about poisons?

"Seizures! Starvation of our people!"

Individuals in the crowd begin to call out. "Hiroshima! Vieques!" cries a man in a football jersey.

"Firestorm!" bellows Doc. "Arms race! Stockpiles of death!"

The woman beside me cries, "Chemicals!"

Doc calls back, "Mustard gas! Monsanto and MIT! Rocket gas, parts per billion! Charles River of death!" Saliva crusts at his mouth. The man is literally foaming. I hear no Rastafarian words, no Lion of Judah or JAH. An oregano odor mixes with colognes, perfumes, and truck exhaust. Marijuana? I'm not sure. "Raytheon and the devil!"

"Exxon!"

"Halliburton!"

"Bomb the rice fields! Bomb the little children of Baghdad! Ruptured lungs and blindness! Land mines!"

"Say on, Doc!" The mariachi guardians face the crowd and glower. Their silver conchas, I see, are actually bottle caps.

I am close enough to see Big Doc's face, which is broad with muscular features. His shoulders thrust forward and pull back, as if he struggles to take flight.

"Cheyenne Mountain! Nuclear winter! Niger Delta poison oil!"

"Tell it!"

"Stealth bombs! Harvard! Tunnels of waste! Subways of Boston! Sewers in the City on a Hill!"

The crowd wails in rhythm, including the woman beside me. Doc's arm now rises, palm upward, each finger circled with thick silver and copper rings. On his sleeve, on his front—grease spots. His arm is raised as if to take an oath. The preacher's robe, I see, is an academic graduation gown.

"Pox and plagues! Gas! Fuel rods!"

I see my chance. The global and the local mix in his mind, this man so far gone into apocalypse, his opaque eyes on the horizon of the mystic lunatic. My best chance is this: "Eldridge Street!" I call at the top of my lungs. "Eldridge Street!"

He doesn't lose a beat. "Fire! Fire of night! Poison flush, tanks of death in the pipes!" His arm drops, then thrusts high in a fist and glares at the sky. "Suffer the children!" he cries. He punches the sky.

"Henry Faiser!"

"In the flock of innocence."

"Peter Wald!"

"The blue-eyed boy. Suffer the children. Suffer the rock!"

What rock? What blue-eyed boy? Pipes? Tanks? Does he look my way, or do I only imagine it? Are his words focused or mere reflex? Am I shoulder-to-shoulder with gibberish? Or have I heard a real message delivered according to the Gospel of Big Doc?

Chapter Eleven

Devaney comes by to say the partially decomposed body of caterer Alan Tegier was found this same Friday afternoon in Chelsea. I'm still trying to sort out Big Doc's toxic shock terms, but Devaney barges in with his story about the body found by two workers. Off-loading forty-gallon drums of animal fat at a rendering plant, they slipped, literally lost their footing. Three plastic-lined drums of beef, pork, and lamb trimmings collected from Boston butchers tumbled off the loading dock and burst. On the concrete were slices and chunks of fat and one clothed body, identified as Alan Tegier.

"You'll see it on TV, Reggie. I wanted to tell you first." We're in my kitchen. Two untouched glasses of Diet Coke fizz on the table between us.

"So the body was . . . stuffed in a barrel? Packed in fat?"

Frank nods. "Rendered animal fat is used in making munitions. The trimmings pay by the pound."

"Then Tegier was to be . . . rendered?"

"Try not to think about the particulars, Reggie. It's about disposal of the body. Chances are, Tegier was already dead.

We're waiting for the autopsy report. I just want to ask you a couple questions for the detectives handling it." Frank opens a small spiral notebook. Dealing with this man is, as usual, a push-pull affair. He loosens his necktie, a solar system of planets and moons with a grease spot on Saturn's rings. "The night Tegier disappeared, Reggie, you were in the Back Bay and heard a scuffle?"

"In the fog. It was more like a yelp, then grunting, then gargling. Then something heavy dragged away. Heavy enough to be a person."

"This was where exactly? Commonwealth?"

"Dartmouth Street. I was on my way to a nine o'clock appointment on Marlborough. A couple of nights ago I walked down the same block and saw no signs of what I'd heard in the dark."

"What kind of signs?"

"Like on the pavement, there were no dark rubber streaks from dragged heels."

"And that's it? The whole thing?"

"I dreamt about it, about oozing black sacks."

"Like trash barrel liners?" I nod. So does he. The notion of psychic dreams is unstated. He sips his Coke, rubs a thumb over the spot on his tie. Hesitant, I offer spot remover.

He accepts, and in a wifish moment, Saturn's rings are degreased. He thanks me. "Okay, Frank, then answer this question: what color were Peter Wald's eyes?"

"Wald's eyes?"

"Jordan Wald's murdered son. Were his eyes blue? Was he a blue-eyed boy?"

He wets his lips. "Ask me the date of his death— March twenty-second. Declared dead at Boston City Hospital at 2:13 p.m."

"How about his eyes?"

"Ask me what he was wearing—a Red Sox jacket, brown corduroy pants, and basketball shoes."

"The eyes?"

"Two squad cars arrived on the scene to find Peter Wald facedown on the street bleeding to death from a gunshot wound to the upper chest."

"His eyes, Frank. Were they blue?"

"I couldn't tell you. I don't remember." He exhales slowly. "You got a psychic message on this?"

"No. A Rastafarian preacher yelled something about blue eyes. He headed a group house on Eldridge at the time Peter Wald was killed. When I called Henry Faiser's name, his comeback was something like 'a flock of innocents.'"

Devaney drinks his Coke. "What you're saying, Reggie, is you're going out on your own. Unauthorized. I thought we talked about that."

"We did. I went to a rally on lower Washington. I also took a couple of walks and struck up conversations."

He straightens the tie. "Conversations? So you just happened to walk up Angus Street and chat with Kia Fayzer?"

My neck gets hot. "What is this?"

"Because I talked to her too, just like you did. Got her address from her sister. I understand you talked to the sister too."

"No, I did not."

"Woman with two little kids, LaBron and a girl."

"She's Kia's sister?"

He winks at me. "Knocking on doors on Roland Street? Helping out with the grocery bags?"

My palms are clammy. "It was a coincidence, Frank.

That woman—I think she'd just come from a food pantry."

"Likely so. Lots of people need food help. You'd be surprised who turns up at donation centers these days."

I have a sudden realization. "So that woman is also Henry Faiser's sister." I could have asked her about him. When LaBron talked about Kia and the hot dog, I didn't think it through.

He grunts. "Tell me, what else did you learn in your mission impossible?"

Ignore the jibe, Reggie. "I learned Henry Faiser is a hustler. Kia swears he never had or used guns. I also got a lecture on drug laws and race and prisons. And profit. Is all that true?"

Devaney's eyes look suddenly weary. "True enough. Whatever she told you, the numbers aren't pretty. The race thing makes it tough. Seven years after the first drug laws, blacks made up more than eighty-eight percent of all people convicted in federal court of trafficking in crack cocaine. The odds of a black man serving prison time are one in four." So Kia had said to me. He repeats it in a flat voice. "One in four is dismal."

"Kia ranted about prison profits."

"Ranted?" He rubs his eyes. "You could rant if you saw the business side of it."

"Of drug dealing?"

"Of prison dealing. In a couple weeks, Reggie, I'll go to a convention in Orlando, take my wife."

I nod. If Frank Devaney wants to tell me his vacation plans, okay.

"It's the American Correctional Association. It's a good chance for my wife to sit by the pool. Me, I go to seminars and walk through miles of exhibits—the bullet-proof vests and prefab cells and restraint devices and firearms, what you expect."

"And don't expect?"

"Procter & Gamble's there because they sell inmates shampoo and deodorant. AT&T's there because they rake in a billion a year from prisoners' long-distance calls."

"So Kia's right?"

His laugh is bitter. "The prison industry is worth an annual thirty-eight billion. It's a corporate America wonderland, Reggie. I'm in the wrong business. I should've been a warden. Today those guys are millionaires." He stands. "Well, so what? I work my cases, keep my head up. I'm thinking about life after retirement too. Thinking about chef school. I watch *Iron Chef* on TV. I might take a night course."

"Cooking?"

"Why not? There's heat, there's action. That's the big draw of this job."

"You cook now?"

"I make a mean jelly omelet. Made one for your aunt now and then." He points. "With that pan right there."

We regard a skillet on a wall hook over the stove. I haven't used it once. "Maybe sometime you'll give me a demonstration."

"Sounds good. Meantime, Reggie, you get the notion to play cop, call me first, okay?"

"Frank, my next project is helping with a fashion show. And going out to dinner with a friend. Tame enough?"

"Call me first. I mean it."

We're at the door. "One thing, Frank. If you'd go back over the records, I'd still like to know the color of Peter Wald's eyes."

*   *   *

The answer is yes, they were blue. Devaney calls with remarks about genes and chromosomes and Sinatra and the fact of Peter Wald's blue eyes. I wish him a good weekend and grab Biscuit's leash. "Here, girl. We're going to Tsakis Brothers. We have questions to ask about Eldridge." It's almost six on this mild evening when I reach the grocery.

"Mees Reggie, welcome!" Shelving soft drinks, Ari laughs as the dog licks his fingers. From the hot food case, George puts down tongs and reaches into his apron pocket for the dog cookies. Biscuit woofs twice, leaps for the snack, repeats her trick, and heads for the onion sack.

I am not here to shop or socialize, yet must do both to set a mood. "Something smells wonderful. Roasted chicken?"

"Is *kotopoulo kyniyo yemisto.*" Ari points to the hot case, where small golden baked birds are aligned in regimental rows. "Like Christmas, the song of birds in a tree."

"Partridge?"

Ari nods. "Very old Greek custom. Sophocles say, 'Came one who bore the name of *perdiko* on the glorious hills of Athens.' This food from Artemis, sister of Apollo, goddess of hunt. Has delicious stuffing, garlic and wine, a feast. You try."

"Sounds good." So much for the tofu-veggie regimen. "Take two, invite a friend?"

"Not tonight."

"So one today, one tomorrow." George slips two birds in a foil bag. The mix of sales and hospitality are wasted on me this evening. I have Eldridge on my mind. The salad greens and pint of strawberries are a pretext to linger as customers come and go.

"Cream for berries?"

"Thanks, no."

"Oranges? End of the season, Mees Reggie, so you take oranges free today. Our gift." Ari puts several oranges in a bag. Two customers are leaving, and I pause until they've paid and scratched their lottery cards and closed the door. My order is ready. It's just me and the Tsakises.

"I want to ask you something."

Ari steps close, his scalp shining. "Mees Reggie, we not forget about the car and the B&B Auto fire. We try to ask around, peoples we know."

George shakes his head. "In America, everybody is moving all the time. Every year, like sand Arabs."

"Like nomads?" They nod. "But, Ari, George, you can help me. When you bought the car on Eldridge Street, there was a house next to the auto shop. A group lived there, some children too, and a young man."

"This house, they make loud music."

"Yes. The leader was a preacher, a black man. He wore a red robe. Do you remember him? His name is Doc. He preached on the porch. His hair—" I twist a strand of my own and say, "Dreadlocks. He preached about poisons. He still does. When you bought your car at B&B Auto, did you see him?"

George rubs his hands on his apron. "A crazy guy. He is yelling at the sky. Nobody to listen. Why you want to know about him?"

"Because of a young man named Henry Faiser. He also lived in that house. He sold things, like expensive watches. Do you remember Henry?"

Ari stands tall. "We not buying the jewelry. We go only to the B&B for a car. We not buying the leather shoes."

"So Henry tried to sell you? You went into Big Doc's house?"

"Never." George folds his arms. "We are seeing the car at B&B, and the Negro comes to sell."

"The B&B guys let him in? The guy you mentioned—Carlo?"

"This boy with shoes and jewels, he comes and goes quick, like a Gypsy."

"That house was known for drugs. Did you see drug deals? Crack cocaine, rocks? Perhaps on the porch?" Ari shakes his head. "Did you ever see a young white man around there? He had blue eyes, college age."

Both say no. "Is a long time ago," says George. "Life is different."

"Different for you and me—and Henry Faiser too. He's in prison. The blue-eyed white man was shot and killed just before the Eldridge fire, and Henry was convicted. Maybe he's innocent. The preacher might have information. What do you remember about Doc?"

The grocers glance at one another. Ari asks, "This is your *psukhē*?"

"Sort of."

George unties his apron, folds it, lays it on the counter. Biscuit naps. "The red-robe guy is wild. Crazy."

"He's religious," I say, "like a priest, maybe a prophet. Did he preach about fire? Three houses burned down, and B&B Auto too. Bodies were found. The police say the cause of the fire was never determined. Big Doc remembers 'fire of night.' Did he preach about fire?"

"We not listen. We go there for the car. Someone is crazy, stay away."

George says, "We not see him all these years, Mees Reggie. But last Thursday, maybe I hear something."

Ari frowns. "Maybe, maybe not." The brothers exchange looks. Whatever this is has been discussed.

I ask George, "What did you hear?"

"I make delivery at Eldridge Place, the back. Everything is delivered: whiskeys, laundries, furnitures. Everybody is around. Guys in blue coats."

"Navy-blue blazers? The staff?"

He nods. "And I have four orders, four different floors. Like always, I go in back elevator, for freight. We are three in elevator, two blue coats and me. I am careful of eggs and tomatoes. I not look around, but one guy in the blue coat, he is Carlo from B&B Auto."

Ari frowns. "I tell my brother, maybe just looks like Carlo. Or is a different guy. Maybe a mixing up. I say, wait till next week. Look again. Make sure."

"No." George frowns, insistent. "This is Carlo. No mixing up."

I say, "He works at Eldridge Place?" George nods. "Did he recognize you?"

"He not see my face."

"But he'd remember the whole Eldridge story."

George jabs a finger. "Maybe not. Maybe he likes to forget. In America, peoples like to forget. Maybe you should forget too, Mees Reggie. Leave Carlo with his new trouble."

"What trouble?"

"In the elevator, he is upset. A guy named Perk makes big problems. He says, 'Blame Perk. Perk kill us.' He say kill."

I ask, "Who is Perk?" They shrug. "Maybe it was slang, a way of speaking?"

Ari nods. "Like I say to my brother, maybe jokes."

"No jokes."

"You see, Mees Reggie, we discuss this."

"What does Carlo look like?"

George lifts his hand. "Six feets, big shoulders. Hair short like this."

"A flattop?"

George nods and fixes his bright onyx-eyed gaze on mine. "I not know English good, Mees Reggie. I know a joke. I know a fear. This Perk, he makes Carlo afraid. A tough guy, he is afraid."

"We afraid for you, Mees Reggie." Ari leans close. "We worry *psukhē* make you troubles. Summer comes, flowers grow. Life is good. We have melons and peaches, everything fresh. This Carlo, you stay away. Perk, he is not your business. B&B Auto is no more, gone. Big fire, finish. The red guy, maybe he is yelling far away." Ari's voice drops low. "*Psukhē* is good. You hear the spirits. But Greeks know also pride. Greeks know *hybris*."

"Hubris," I say. "Arrogance."

"*Hybris* like a sickness. If your aunt here, she tell you watch out. She tell you *hybris* makes a falling down."

"Downfall," I say. "Downfall." The word hangs. Silence builds as Biscuit rouses, shoulders tight. She plants her paws and barks hard and loud, as if warning, as if sounding an alarm.

Chapter Twelve

At 8:30 a.m. on Monday, a white limousine with black glass windows pulls up at the curb outside on Barlow Square. Nobody gets in or out. I keep an eye on it, thinking it's for my neighbor, Trudy Pfaeltz, probably a premium for selling candy bars.

Me, I'm waiting for a car to be sent by Alison on behalf of Jeffrey Arnot, who wishes to speak with me. On business, was the message.

At nine, the appointed hour, the limo is still out front, but no sign of the car arranged by Alison. It's five after. Then ten. Suddenly, a uniformed driver, a stocky white man with windburned cheeks, gets out of the limo and comes to knock on my front door. He tips his cap and says, "Mr. Arnot is here." I grab my purse and follow him to the sidewalk. Opening a door, he ushers me inside the white limousine where Jeffrey Arnot sits with legs outstretched. In a double-breasted suit with a blinding white shirt and silk tie, he's by himself, talking on the phone.

"Don't push on this, or the deal's history. You got till two. Don't screw up, surprise me for a change. Ms. Cutter, good to see you. Have a seat." The door shuts, and so does Arnot's phone. I sit opposite him on a camel suede seat amid soft pools of apricot light. A coffee, a *Wall Street Journal,* and a laptop lie on a lacquered table between us.

"Drink?"

From a hidden pullout bar? "Thanks, no."

"You won't need that seat belt."

"I always wear—"

"We're not going anywhere, Ms. Cutter. You're in my office."

"Oh." I feel the engine purr, the vented air. I'm in a light wool blue Brioni suit from the old days, deliberately muted. Jeffrey Arnot stares as if appraising merchandise.

"I want to follow up on that business with the plates."

"I'm very sorry—"

"Forget it. It's not important. Old art, you get cracks and breakage. One reason I go for armor, it doesn't bust. Michelangelo and Rembrandt need tune-ups. Mrs. Arnot sent the pieces to a restorer. The plates'll look good as new. This isn't about plates."

"I see."

"It's not about Marlborough either, not as such. The baseline is, we have a fine house, one of Boston's best. Mrs. Arnot and I agree it's a premier address in the city. No dispute."

He crosses his legs. The socks are silk. "But men and women see things differently, Ms. Cutter. For my wife, Marlborough is home. That's the woman's viewpoint. It's probably yours."

I nod for simplicity's sake.

"A business point of view, however, is different. I picked a certain wallpaper pattern for personal reasons, it's true. I'm a black man in a white city, and I fight hard for what's mine. I have a thick hide, and I'm proud. You saw our custom chandelier. It was my idea, a warrior's equipment. But to me, the house is an investment. Renovation helps the investment value. The house appreciates, and I utilize it. My wife and I entertain clients and business associates. You attended one of our candidate receptions."

"Mr. Arnot, you needn't explain—"

"But I do. The random noises are an inconvenience. We can't explain them. To a point, they disrupt our lives. Mrs. Arnot is sensitive. Again, a woman-man thing. But we now agree to cease inquiries such as yours."

"A search for spirit sources."

"Superstition, mumbo jumbo. Which can be damaging, make no mistake. Gossip and rumor take a toll. A food scare in the restaurant business can bring you down, can put the whole chain at risk. In pro sports, a sex or drug scandal, true or not, cuts your sponsors. Likewise, a house can get a reputation, even in the Back Bay. The investment could be at risk."

He steeples his fingers, his eyes never leaving my face. "Mrs. Arnot now understands the consequences of letting her nerves get out of control. She sees the smart thing to do is adjust to the situation. I protect my investment, she protects her home. It amounts to the same thing. Do you understand me?"

"Mr. Arnot, I have no intention of discussing the noises or plates with anyone."

"The plates fell. Accident. End of story."

"I only came as a favor—"

"As a misunderstanding. An intrusive mistake on a very important evening."

"Your guests had no idea why I was there. I only mingled—"

"And saw our next governor, Michael Carney, who deserves all-out support."

Whatever "all-out" means.

"You are aware, Ms. Cutter, of the slander laws."

"Slander? Mr. Arnot, I have no intention of discussing the Marlborough house noises with anyone. Are you threatening me?"

"To protect my interests, I am vigilant. I am a watchful man." He taps his fingertips on the tabletop. "But also fair. It's a give-and-take world. Arnot Enterprises might be of some service to you, Ms. Cutter. I understand you are new in the city."

"I spent childhood summers in Boston, Mr. Arnot."

"It's different now, new people, new projects on the drawing board. Politics and business dance cheek-to-cheek. You might benefit."

"I can't see how."

"For the moment, benefit yourself three ways. Zip the lip, Ms. Cutter. Stay away from my wife. Stay clear of my house. We'll all move ahead. We'll all get our piece of the Boston cream pie."

Meg Givens's grim "Good morning" over the phone is drowned by a woman in the background crying, "Tell her, go ahead, tell her." I'm just back inside my door from the encounter with Jeffrey.

"Go ahead. Tell her." The gusty cabaret voice is unmistakable over the phone, even without a mike. "A Second Empire vase. Tell her Second Empire. Tell her it jumped off the chiffonier in the master suite last night. Tell her Jeffrey saw it too. He can't deny it."

Meg asks, "Reggie, did you hear that?"

"Just like the Limoges plates, it moved and crashed. Tell her 1880-something Christofle, priceless glass with gilded silver. That cold air blew too. It was freezing. Tell her, for godsake."

"She hears you, Tania."

"Now tell her who really owns the house. Go ahead, you're the Realtor. You know the secret." Fumbling noises—a scuffle for the phone. "Who cares if it's confidential? Screw it, you tell her."

Like a hostage, Meg speaks in a voice flattened by stress. "Against my better professional judgment, Mrs. Arnot wishes you to know that the Marlborough Street house is listed in her name."

"Hear that? 'Tania Rae Arnot' is signed on the dotted line. The house is mine."

"Technically," Meg says, "for tax purposes—"

More fumbling, then the cabaret voice says to me, "Whatever Jeffrey told you, don't believe him. The goddamn house is mine, and it's haunted. He's in his limousine gallivanting all over, and I'm stuck like a prisoner in a goddamn haunted house. I'm telling Meg and you too. You hear me, Cutter?"

"I hear you, Mrs. Arnot."

"You fix it, or I'll make sure Meg Givens never sells another house in Boston. I'll contact every name in my Rolodex. I'll get you too. You do your psychic thing or—"

"But it doesn't work that way."

"Lady, you make it work, or I'll make your life hell. Sheer hell."

The phone goes dead.

Shaken, that's the feeling. The hysterical woman's threats would rattle anyone, the Arnots' domestic rage spilling to the street. Meg'll doubtless phone the second she's free.

I try to concentrate on "Ticked Off" as a sedative. But it's not easy to calm down when somebody promises "sheer hell." Did the Arnots choreograph this Monday morning drama? No, that makes no sense. It's him versus her, with bystanders caught in the cross fire. What could Tania do to me? Nothing.

Nothing at all.

I keep telling myself this, when Angie calls to say that Dr. Buxbaum needs two minor repairs upstairs. His bathtub drain is slow, and his smoke detector needs a new battery. "And, Ms. Cutter, Dr. Buxbaum wants you to know he got something special for you. It's on the upstairs landing by his door."

I trudge up. The something special is a book—*Dare to Repair: A Do-It-HERself Guide to Fixing (Almost) Anything in the Home.* The cover art is the familiar World War II classic factory queen, the manicured, pin-curled Rosie with sleeves rolled, flexing a bicep. The nerve of that dentist.

Rosie stares at me in her polka-dot head wrap, ready to open fire with her rivet gun. My own biceps, coaxed to life from dreary free-weight workouts that I maintain on schedule, were supposedly meant for sleeveless sportswear and evening dresses, for dancing in the dark on moonlit terraces. Not wrenches, not plungers.

There's a note, which says, "Hope this helps." But since when did I ask H. Forest Buxbaum, D.M.D., to be my personal trainer? Odds are, he'll deduct the price of the book from the next rent check. The nerve.

I'm on a stool replacing the nine-volt battery in Buxbaum's kitchen smoke detector when it hits me—the

"Eldridge Place, 300 Eldridge Street."

"It's the lovely pink high-rise, and I'm in the foyer." I say *fwah-yea* in a noblesse oblige voice for Pam's benefit. The young man has gone back to door duty. Still no sign of the staff men who might recognize me.

"I don't ordinarily walk in this neighborhood," I say to Pam. "I took a wrong turn and lost my way. A few blocks can make such a difference." Pam's nook, I see, has surveillance monitors showing the parking garage and the lobby elevators. The hallway of each floor appears at thirty-second intervals.

"We have underground parking for residents and staff," she says. "This is definitely not a pedestrian neighborhood."

"Well, I should know better, but the name Eldridge rings a bell. It strikes me I might know of someone who perhaps works here. He's a cousin of my mechanic. I think he might be on your staff, a man with an old-fashioned flattop haircut. His name is—" Her eyes narrow as she looks at me. I nuzzle the dog. "Biscuit, sweetie, do we remember the name of the nice man who helped fix the car? Was it . . . Marco? No, Carlo. It was Carlo."

"Carlo Feggiotti?"

"Yes, I believe so."

"He's our night manager. He's in and out during the day but on duty for the night shift. He comes on at ten."

"My goodness, a small world." Pam agrees. "Come to think, a friend of his might work here too. Perk, I believe. Perk?" Pam shakes her head. No Perk works at Eldridge. Biscuit wriggles to get down. I hug her closer. Her tail waps my rib, which has cooled but feels pressure. "I hope I'm not keeping you from your duties, though perhaps my little Biscuit's injury is serendipity."

"Oh?"

"Because this building reminds me of the peace of mind that is possible with high-level security and services. Boston's old townhouses are lovely, but with crime and uncertainty these days, sometimes I'm tempted to relocate."

Pam nods. "I know just how you feel. We have just one unit available in the building at this time, though I understand there's an offer on it. But if your needs are not immediate, plans are under way for Eldridge Place II."

"Really?"

"Across the street."

"But didn't I see houses?"

"In major disrepair. They'll come down."

"And the new building will have the same standards of quality?" I gesture around the lobby.

Pam nods. "The same company, the same architect. The same partners. In fact, one of the partners is coming in this afternoon. We're watching for him now."

"Taking a personal interest in the project is a good sign."

"Oh, this particular partner is very much involved. And we always know when he's coming. It's impossible to miss a limousine."

"Limo?"

"Yes indeed. The other partners' cars are top-of-the-line, but we can spot Mr. Arnot's white limousine a mile away."

Her pleasant smile prompts my own, a mask to conceal pure panic, as Biscuit wriggles and I fight to figure out what to do.

*   *   *

"So you took a taxi?"

"I faked a fit about Biscuit, and the concierge called me a cab."

"Good thinking. What a close call."

Meg Givens doesn't know how close. I glimpsed Arnot's Moby limo as my taxi pulled out, and hunkered down all the way to Barlow Square.

"Reggie, could you just hang in with Tania a little longer?"

"Impossible, Meg. The Marlborough house is not my psychic turf."

"Could I tell her you're trying?"

"Bad idea. Jeffrey Arnot ordered me off the property."

"Can't psychics work at a distance?"

"Not me. I first need contact with an object, something authentic from the source of the haunting. For Marlborough, something historic."

"But that's out of the question. They stripped the house." Her voice rings with despair.

"I'm sorry, Meg. No question, the woman is awful."

"Reggie, you don't know the half of it. How about this? I'll tell Tania you're researching the house. I'll tell her that you, the psychic, seek knowledge from the past. Old documents, deeds, whatever."

"Just like your coworker who moved to Dallas? The woman who felt chills, the same sort of chill we both felt when the Marlborough front door slammed on us?"

"Are you hinting the house really is haunted?"

Should I tell her about the cold blast I felt when the Limoges plates crashed? Or remind her that she brought up murders in the Back Bay—daggers, tonics spiked with poison, carriage horses run amok? No, not now. "So, Meg, you want me to be the new Igloo Sue?"

"Just get Tania off my back for the moment. Buy me time. I have two deals pending with acquaintances of the Arnots'. The spring real estate market is down, and I need these commissions. The Arnots' fireworks make me happy to be single again. Those sixties lapel buttons you see on eBay—'A Woman Needs a Man Like a Fish Needs a Bicycle'? Since my divorce, that's me."

I manage a laugh, but the words "me too" don't come out. I admit to checking the mail for more postcards from Mr. Cairo. "Meg," I say, "if it'll make your life easier, go ahead, tell Tania the psychic is burrowed in the library."

She's more grateful than she should have to be. "I owe you, Reggie. If ever—"

"Try now. There's one condo up for sale at Eldridge Place. I want to see it as soon as possible."

"You're thinking of moving from Barlow Square? From a townhouse to a high-rise? Why?"

"A modern building has advantages. I just want to see the condo at night, after ten."

"Ten p.m.? I don't know if Stu works that late. That's Stu Albritten, the listing agent."

"Tell him I'm nocturnal. Tell him your client's a vampire."

"Not funny."

"Something else, Meg. There's a new condo project, Eldridge Place II. Tell me about it."

"It's just off the drawing board. A colleague in our office will be an authorized agent. We've got the prospectus."

"I want to see it. I also want your best info on the major players. I want to know who sold and bought the land. I want to follow the money."

Meg's laugh is brittle. "So do we all, Reggie. So do we all. Stand by. I'll see about Eldridge."

Right now I'll see about Big Doc. Odds are, Nicole knows more than she told me. The upcoming fashion show has potential for a swap of services between me and my boss, so I grab a tuna sandwich and work on the Newton fashion show script, then make a beeline to Style-Smart and hang up blouses while Nicole reads my printout. " 'StyleSmart for Success!' I like it, Reggie. You got a gift with words. Oh, look at this. 'Dress today for tomorrow's career . . . compound interest in this versatile four-way suit . . . a dash of decorum makes this ensemble a big step up the job escalator!' Girl, you are good."

Great, she approves. But when I ask about Ernest Frynard a.k.a. Big Doc, she stonewalls me. "I love your write-up for the show, Reggie, but forget about Ernest."

"Big Doc."

"Don't 'Big Doc' me. Ernest Frynard's granddaddy would turn in his grave if he knew what became of that boy, the Lord rest his soul."

"Nicole, he might know whether a man serving time for murder is really guilty or innocent. I need to talk to him."

"Reggie, if you want to waste your time on a Washington Street corner when he rants and raves, that's your business. Rasta or no, you don't know whether to be scared or laugh at the man. Mostly, you want to cry and run. He's out of his mind. Don't you be going after him. He's a false prophet among the people, and his ways are pernicious. He has a vile temper."

"I only want to talk for a few minutes."

"And don't be fooled by that gang in the Zorro getups. They look like Halloween, but they're mean, they're cold as ice. Every one's an example of what can happen to our black boys and men in this day and time. Folks need to wake up. Ernest was smart in school. He got lost."

"So you won't help me find him."

"What part of 'no' don't you understand?"

Chapter Thirteen

From StyleSmart, I pick up Biscuit, head to lower Washington Street, and circle deep into rush hour. On the corner where Doc preached, a ring of young break-dancers draws a small crowd. Are they his opening act? No.

Nor are Wednesday's Peruvian reed flutes. Nor Thursday's gaunt guitarist, who is chased off by a sudden cloudburst. On a drizzly Friday at 3:30 p.m., it seems certain that Big Doc and his crew decamped long ago. I'm wasting time and gas. Beside me, Biscuit gives baleful stares. "One last loop, Biscuit, and we'll head back to Barlow Square." She woofs and thumps her tail.

As I drive off, my rearview mirror shows a huge old smoking Buick with dark-tinted windows. It swerves and stops against the curb. The doors and trunk lid pop open, and a six-man squad in black jumps out and starts to set up the oil drum, the placards, the sound system. It's them.

Four lefts get me back to Washington, where Doc's crowd has already materialized. As before, it's a motley mix of young and old, male and female, and mostly dark-skinned. It's as if they know the schedule. So far, there's no sign of Big Doc himself.

Should I keep circling the block? The drizzle gets heavier, and I turn the wipers on. Three more loops, and there's Doc himself exiting the passenger side of an SUV two cars in front. He looks the same: the dreads, the hulking shoulders and quarter-acre crimson robe. Facing the crowd, he opens his arms wide as if to embrace vast assembled multitudes. The mike is presented as if it's a scepter, and his voice booms through my window glass. "Poisons and corruption, O children of JAH."

I look for a parking spot. The SUV and Buick have driven off. It's seriously raining, and the crowd starts to thin. A few umbrellas appear, and Doc himself retreats into a Payless shoe store entryway. His squad wrestles plastic sheeting over the sidewalk setup, but the plastic billows in the wind. I'll double-park, approach him on foot, and make my pitch at the Payless doorway.

The Buick suddenly careens from behind, cuts in front of me, and rides up over the curb. Shrouded in plastic, the black squad guys shove equipment into the trunk. Car and truck horns blast behind me, though I stay put. Doc swoops into the Buick front seat. The others cram into the back. Doors slam. They're off.

At first, it's easy to follow. Downtown Boston at rush hour is a bumper-to-bumper choke hold, especially in the rain. I edge in and out to keep them in sight. We cut and dart, the Buick driver lays heavy on his horn, and I hope against hope he—they—won't notice a tailgating Beetle.

Within a mile, certain lanes open up, and I'm now in a Boston racetrack amid Jeeps, dump trucks, motorcycles. Where am I? City street names flash—Wensley, Lamar-

tine, Roanoke. Isn't the Franklin Park Zoo out this way?
The Arnold Arboretum? I have a near miss with a seafood
truck and slam into a pothole the size of a pond, then
barely glimpse the Buick's rear end disappear around a
corner. Really, it's the car's smoking exhaust I follow to
a block with houses and a storefront whose windows are
painted over in green, dull gold, and red. Rastafarian
colors.

The Buick has stopped before the storefront, and Big
Doc gets out and disappears inside. So do all the others.

I pull up to read a lettered sign over the entrance:
"House of Spirit and Health." Except that it's spelled
"Helth." Is it a clinic? No, more like a church, a house of
worship. Doc's? Is he the minister?

Do I dare go in?

"Biscuit, you stay here for a little while." I park between a pickup truck and a battered station wagon, crack
a window, lock up, and dash for the door and knock. Nobody answers, but the latch gives, and I step inside.

Odors of old wood and plaster mix with food. Ginger? Yes, and coconut too. My eyes adjust to low light,
but I see no one. Down at the front stands a grove of potted palms. They look yellowed and dry. The side walls
show pictorial murals. They aren't religious, not to my
eye. On the right rise deep green mountains capped in
chalky mists; on the left, stubby fishing boats bob on a
turquoise sea. The ceiling features whitewash clouds.
The palm grove links up with coconut. The ginger is Ja-
maican. Worshipers are supposedly transported to the
Caribbean.

How many parishioners come here? This sanctuary—
if it actually is a sanctuary—might hold two hundred, but
the seating looks haphazard, a mix of benches, folding

chairs, and one outsize oak pew that looks hacked with a saw or ax. I call out, "Hello," and walk forward. "Hello, hello," I say louder, but my voice sounds muffled. "Is anyone here?"

A man appears suddenly from behind the palm grove as if it's a curtain. He's wearing the mariachi uniform, and the squish of his shoes says he's been out in the rain, doubtless on Washington Street and in the Buick.

"I'm looking for Doc. Is he here? My name is Cutter. Your door was open. I tried to knock."

"No service today. Try tomorrow."

"I heard him preach a couple of weeks ago. It's important."

"Important to you on your personal schedule."

"I . . . it'll take just a few minutes."

"Minutes, seconds, hours—the time of life chopped into pieces. Do you see a clock in this House?" He starts toward me. "Do you see a calendar on these walls?"

"No."

He's six feet away, then five, closing in. I wish Stark were here. "Time is infinity and eternity across latitudes. Time is of the stars and oceans. Time is cosmic rhythm."

We're face-to-face. His tan skin is sallow, his jaw tight. "This is the House of Spirit and Health, not filth and sin. But welcome to all who enter. Welcome."

He motions me to a seat. Wafting from him is an herbal odor, like oregano, like marijuana. Are they all smoking in a back room? High as kites? I sit down on a folding chair. He pulls another up close, spins it like a top, and straddles it. A buck knife is sheathed at his belt. Our faces are inches apart. "Spirit and health rule here. Ours is the kingdom of spirit and health."

"Is Doc the minister?"

"From ancient times, the leader comes."

"I believe he has certain knowledge—"

"Wisdom."

"Information."

His eyes narrow, and he rubs the bone handle of the knife. "Reborn into spirit and health under the Lion of Judah. He who never was but truly is."

"Can you just ask him to see me for a few moments?"

He taps the knife handle. "The House of Spirit and Health," he says, "does not live by bread alone. Not bread alone."

Money. He wants money. I reach into my pocket. How much will it cost to get out intact?

He says, "We favor Benjamins."

Benjamin Franklin, the face on the hundred-dollar bill. "I have a twenty. And a five."

He scoffs, but his fingers wrap around my two bills. We stand. I'm getting out of here. I reach for the door latch as he says, "Minister Doc is here in the House. He will see you. He's a busy man, but he makes time for those in need."

My mind seesaws. Grab the latch and get out—to the rain, to my car, the dog, back home safe and dry. The smart thing to do. No one even knows where in the city I am, not even me. At this moment, I'm surely Henry Faiser's fool. My own fool too. Is Doc sitting behind the sickly grove of potted palms in this faux Jamaica? What price to find out? Or not to?

"Are you ready?"

My throat wants to shut. I swallow hard and hope my voice doesn't quaver or knees buckle when I nod, turn around, and say, "Yes."

We march zigzag down the aisle, behind the palms,

and then left to a badly lighted steep stairway leading down to utter darkness. To Doc's underground?

"Wait, I don't think—"

"Watch your step. I'll help you." The stairs are rickety, and there's no railing. The squad man grips my elbow—in order to prevent my fall or to secure a hostage? The pressure of his fingers hurts my elbow. Descending, I count seventeen steps. This is stupid.

Basements have windows; cellars do not. We enter a chamber turned into a cellar by blacked-out windows. Four squad men range about on sofas smoking cigarettes, one of them holding a big rusty metal lid. The air is thick with marijuana smoke. A kerosene lamp on a small table lights the leader's dreadlocks like a dingy halo. Before me, Doc sits enthoned in a recliner in his red graduation robe. He puffs on a corncob pipe.

"House of Spirit and Health greets all who enter." He nods at a squad man, who tosses a sofa cushion to the center of the cement floor. Am I to sit? To kneel?

I stand, my "escort" directly behind me, blocking the exit.

"I have a few questions."

"Spirit and Health answer all questions, sister."

"It's about Eldridge Street, years ago."

He jabs the stem of the pipe at the cushion, a signal to lower myself. I drop to one knee and repeat, "Eldridge."

"Satan, Moloch, and corporations of the Sphinx—these are false gods. Poisons and death. Health is here in the herbs of JAH and Judah. Ganja"—he holds out the cob pipe—"and maize."

"Thirteen years ago you lived on Eldridge Street."

He meets my gaze. Smoke wreathes his head. "Long season of corruption and outer darkness." He inhales. The others smoke in silence. "It was a time," he says slowly, "of great testing."

"The auto body shop, B&B Auto, it burned to the ground. Your house burned too."

"Fire of night."

"Bodies were found."

"Not of our people. Not of our knowledge."

"A man named Carlo worked there."

He blinks and pauses. "Flames of hell," he says at last, then inhales deeply.

My eyes begin to water. "A young man was shot dead on Eldridge that same day. He was about twenty years old." His response is to pass the pipe to a sofa squad man, a taut figure who looks coiled for a fight. The cob pipe in turn is passed to each of the others, who set cigarettes aside to share it, weed upon weed. My head begins to feel light. "Who was the blue-eyed boy?"

"Pale wanderer. Lost child of despair."

"Was it Peter Wald?"

"Tunnels of waste and poison. The City on a Hill, a sewer of death." He falls silent as I recall that these were his very words on the Washington Street corner. But my thoughts feel cloudy, and my head is starting to float. Doc leans down in my direction and says, "Wood and rock."

" 'Peter' means rock. And 'wald' means wood."

"The blue-eyed boy was a child of death, begotten of death."

Everything starts to sway, my vision now breaking up like time-lapse film in this smoky air. Suddenly, a scratching sound begins from the sofa. "Peter Wald," I say once again, though my tongue feels thick. "A man is in prison for his murder. He may be innocent. Henry Faiser is his name. He lived in your house."

"Warehouse of innocents. But the summons will come, and blood will cleanse the poisons."

"He's sick. He needs help. An African-American man wasting away in prison. If he's innocent—"

"Innocent, yes. Poison sewers drowned him, but this House of Spirit and Health is clean."

As I watch, Doc's damp robe brightens to a cherry red, and the fire of the cigarette tips flash like red starbursts in the night sky. The scratching sound amplifies, then changes to plinks like beautiful raindrops. I get it—the metal lid is a steel drum, and the man is polishing it. It's for reggae, Rasta music.

I am woozy. The cushion is inviting, and it takes all my strength to rise and stand up. "Thank you for your help." My mouth feels stuffed with cotton. A sofa man laughs in a guttural scoff. Two others elbow one another in the ribs, and the tense one looks ready to spring. "I must go."

But the sallow one with the knife blocks the stairway. Doc grins when I touch the wall to steady myself. Everything flashes. Strobe lights? No, it's from the marijuana smoke. Dizzy, I'm so dizzy. "No hurry," drawls Doc. "Stay. I say stay."

He sounds like a master talking to a pet. I cough, phlegm rising, eyes streaming. "No, I must leave. Someone expects me back."

The room whirls, and colors shift. "You will stay." The sofa squad stands up. Doc yanks the lever on the recliner and snaps forward to sit upright. One of the squad fingers a length of tire chain. The knife behind me—is the naked blade exposed?

"We have matters between us. We must bargain," Doc says.

Does he want more money?

"We must get personal. The House of Spirit and Health is person-to-person, heart and skin."

Meaning assault? The chain clanks, and the men stand at attention as the drummer hammers with his knuckle, bone on steel. It takes every particle of my being to look into his dilated pupils and speak. "I must go. Someone expects me."

"I expect you." The huge red-robed arms open like giant wings, the long nails like talons. "Doc is master here."

I hear a click—a gun cocked? My gorge rises, and I swallow to fight the nausea. "Whatever you say. But I feel sick. Do you have a restroom?"

"This lady wants to rest."

"For just a few minutes."

"Ganja is JAH's way."

"It makes me . . . sick. The kerosene—"

"Take her up." Doc leers, his pupils huge. "Then bring her down."

The knife man grips my elbow, and it's helpful because I'm reeling. He doesn't look so steady himself. We climb the stairs together, each keeping the other from falling. My knees are rubber, my head spinning. We stumble down a hallway, reach a door. "In there. I be out here." He snaps a light switch on and gives me a little shove inside. I latch the door from within, then noisily raise the toilet seat and cough and gag and run the taps and look around.

Thank God, a window, just big enough to crawl out of, though painted over like all the others. I steady myself against the sink, open the clamshell lock, and push up. It doesn't budge. It's the thick paint. It's painted shut.

"How you doin' in there?"

"Dizzy, sick." I stick my middle finger down my throat and gag and retch as though I'm turning inside out. Then I grab the commode handle and flush and flush again. My one hope is this window. Should I break it? Kick it out? No, he'd hear it shatter, and the jagged glass would cut me to ribbons. Dizzy, light-headed, I tell myself to focus. I open both faucets until they gush and make a big noise, then I bang both hands against the sill. Still stuck.

"You comin' out?"

"In a minute." I pull out my car key, and as I retch and heave and brace my hip against the wall, I dig the key into the hardened paint.

"Come on out of there."

"I'm throwing up. Got to puke." Which is almost true. I retch and flush again and gouge at the paint. The key slips, and I nearly fall. The door shudders. The knife man is yanking the doorknob.

"Come on, move on out of there."

"It's your fault if I puke on Doc."

This gets me maybe two minutes. The taps run, the key digs, the thick paint and rotten wood start to splinter. Then the window frame gives, rises. The window is up, and warm, wet air rushes in. Rain splashes my face. I pocket the key. It's maybe eight feet to the ground, and there's a stockade fence down below.

"Bitch, time's up." It comes out *bidge*. He's stoned. "Come on, bidge."

"I'm washing up." I'm actually standing on the toilet bowl rim, then thrusting my legs out the window and twisting around. Grabbing onto the window frame with both hands, I lower myself until I'm hanging there.

"Yo, bidge, move it."

He's thumping on the bathroom door. In minutes, the

others will join him. I let go, tuck my head, bring my knees up, feel the rain and wind—and slam on my back in mud.

"Bidge, what the f—"

I get up and limp, stumbling across a yard and under a tree. Tiny white rags cover the ground. Blossoms, they're apple blossoms. I reach the sidewalk. My car is up the block. I stagger ahead, limping and dizzy. I grasp the key, open the car, get in, and lock it. It takes two hands to crank the ignition. The engine roars to life, sweet sound. My mind's strobe light still flashes, and my brain spins. Biscuit squeals, happy. I invite her into my lap. I'm not fit to drive, can't pass a drug test. The dog licks my face and tilts her head. I put the flashers on and go slow. It takes forever. Nobody follows. It's as though I'm in a maze, a blur of mud and motion. It's pitch-dark when I finally pull into Barlow Square.

Chapter Fourteen

Stu Albritten is a dapper, compact man in a houndstooth sport coat with a foulard scarf and bridle-bit loafers. At 10:03 p.m. on Tuesday, we shake hands at the Eldridge lobby elevator. It's four days since the Big Doc episode, and I've told no one, not Nicole, not even Devaney, especially not Devaney. The whole thing hangs over me, the stupidity and close call. At home, I'm skittish, startled at the least noise. Out in public, I feel as though I'm playing a part, nervously impersonating my normal self. I've come from the visitors' parking on D level, a catacomb of gray concrete studded with surveillance cameras and blazing with fluorescents. "Meg's on her way, Ms. Cutter. She just phoned."

"Appreciate your flexibility, Stu."

"No problem, I'm a night owl. I understand you currently reside on Barlow Square, Ms. Cutter. Classic South End townhouses."

With effort, I speak brightly. "Yes, charming. But these days I'm security-minded. My alarm system doesn't seem like sufficient protection. It's a source of great concern." I turn toward Pam's concierge nook. The face of Big Doc flashes like a hologram. I blink. He disappears. Tonight the sole staffer is a sharp-faced older man with thick yellowish glasses. His thatch of iron-gray hair says he can't be Carlo. "I seek security," I say to Stu. "Peace of mind."

"Then Eldridge may be for you. Management is serious about the twenty-four-hour concierge, as you see, plus security services and private underground parking. I myself got clearance moments ago at the desk. Ah, here's Meg."

"Reggie, Stu, good to see you."

The gray-thatched man approaches to screen Meg and me, while Stu taps the elevator up button. "Have a good evening, folks." The doors open, we get in, and Stu pushes 6. The surveillance camera lens glints from a light fixture.

"Remember," Stu says with a Realtor's gravity, "availability might change any moment. Eldridge sells fast. Let me remind everyone, however, that every client has personal tastes. Sometimes clients at a showing need to see through to the future."

Meg chuckles. "Stu's warning you, Reggie, that we're about to see something extreme."

"Highly individual. Here we go." He keys in and flips the lights.

The condo is a storm of rose and pinks. The overstuffed sofa, the chaise and side chairs and carpeting— all pinks. A mounted antique carousel horse fills a corner, its wild eyes, flaring nostrils, and bared teeth not one bit softened by the pink and gold saddle and hooves. Every chair features at least two satin and grosgrain tasseled pillows in the shape of hearts, and shelves abound with china and crystal hearts, mostly Steuben. The wall art from here to the dining room—more hearts, also serigraph Cupids. A tabletop Zen sand garden is raked into the word "LOVE."

"It's a Valentine's Day museum."

"Or a cardiologist's dream." I mentally edit wet dream.

"Bet it's a divorcing couple. They OD'd on love."

"Every owner redesigns and updates. Let's see the kitchen." We note the Viking range and Sub-Zero fridge. "Caterers love an operational kitchen like this. The staff can come in and get right to work."

Meg says, "It's perfect for parties. Perhaps you plan to entertain, Reggie?"

"Perhaps."

"This way to the master."

We gather at a king-size bed whose pale pink duvet spreads like a field of eyelet lace. "Ooh," says Meg, "a mirrored ceiling over the bed."

"Indeed. And a bar and his and her walk-ins." Stu opens each closet door with a footman's flourish to reveal a terry robe and jeans jacket, a woman's driving moccasins, a man's running shoes and gray running suit. The clothes look like effigies of the owners.

"Who owns this place?"

"It's a business-owned property held in the name of a company."

"Surprising. It's so personal."

"Let's see the master bath," Meg says. "My bet's on a heart-shaped honeymoon-special tub."

We chuckle, momentary peephole conspirators. The bath is marble with gold fixtures, plump towels, and lavender sachets. I try to keep my mind clear of the bathroom at Big Doc's House of Spirit and Health, a house of pot and threats. My dreams of black sacks now mix with nightmares of the cellar and of me pounding on windows as walls close in. Did Doc say anything real?

"Plenty of closet space," says Stu. "All Eldridge residents are entitled to a storage locker in an underground level."

"And the second bedroom?" I chirp with brittle cheer.

"For guests, or a study or TV lounge." The second bedroom, however, is empty except for a NordicTrack. Its walls are gray, and the carpet shows no imprints whatsoever from removed furniture, which seems odd.

"The space would be just right for me," I say, "but security is uppermost in mind. I need to be able to come and go freely both in daytime and at night. Especially at night." We walk out into the hall, and Stu locks up. "For instance, here in the hallway to the elevator, I'd need to know the security arrangements will protect me."

"All common areas are protected. Of course, fire sprinkler systems are state-of-the-art."

"Let's speak to the night concierge for a moment." Stu and Meg are reluctant, but when the elevator opens, we cross the lobby to the thatch-haired man, who's deep into a crossword puzzle and barely looks up.

Stu says, "Our client has questions about security. Walt, is it?"

"Walt Kane, yes, sir, I keep an eye on the goings-on from ten at night to six a.m. You might say I monitor the monitors." His watery gray eyes blur behind the thick reading glasses. A *National Enquirer* and a magnifier lie at his elbow. He's nearly finished his puzzle; eraser crumbs scatter around a column of open squares.

I smile. "So, Mr. Kane, you are the night manager?"

"No, ma'am. That would be Mr. Feggiotti."

"I wonder, could we speak to him? Stop by his office for a moment? Or could you page him?" Meg looks puzzled.

"Sorry, Mr. Feggiotti doesn't stay in his office. Take it from an old navy chief, he's the officer of the deck. He doesn't stay on the bridge. He's on watch all over the vessel. You might come back in the daytime, talk to Pam Kagel. She'll fix you up."

Stu and Meg look relieved and ready to go. "Crosswords," I say. "Your hobby?"

"Mind games. Use it or lose it. Eight down. I'm stuck."

"Oh, do let us help."

Walt shrugs. "An eight-letter word for sad and regretful," he says. "The third and fourth letters are *i* and *g*."

I step closer, smile again, and whisper, "Try *p-o-i-g-n-a-n-t*."

In moments, Carlo Feggiotti is on his way.

The flattop haircut could be gauged with a Home Depot level. Carlo is six feet, broad-shouldered and taut, his arms out in a stance I recall from my Jack's season of high school wrestling. Chewing gum, he strides forward with a thrust of the hips, sidestepping the rug, his heels crashing with each step across the lobby. The Eldridge uniform of gray slacks and navy blazer is cut in fabric light-years higher in quality than the doormen's. Carlo's chukka boots are Italian leather, and his uniform is custom-tailored.

Tailored almost well enough to conceal the hip bulge of a holster. Not for nothing my time with Devaney.

"Mr. Feggiotti, I'm Reggie Cutter. So good of you to take time out." I offer my hand.

His grip is a mitt of bone and callus, his scent
Bazooka. Stu, too, shakes hands, winces, and then says
good night. Meg lingers. "I'm also a Realtor," she says.
"I'm with Gibraltar Residential." She hands him her card,
a business pitch even in a baffled moment. "We just
showed Ms. Cutter a fine unit on the sixth floor."

"Six oh three." His voice is a high tenor. His dark
eyes, which are narrow and close together, remind me of
Renaissance portraits that follow you everywhere in a
room. His jaws work the gum.

Meg says, "Ms. Cutter's main concern is security."

"Because of a robbery of my home some years ago,
Mr. Feggiotti. The ghastly memory is vivid to this day."

"Eldridge Place is all about security, Ms. Cutter."

"Perhaps I could ask a few questions."

"But before you do, Reggie, if you wouldn't mind . . ."
Meg looks at her watch. "Perhaps since we've already
seen the condo unit, I'll say good night." She disappears
into the elevator. Silently, Carlo mouths, "Level D,"
cracks his gum, turns to me, and asks, "What's on your
mind, Ms. Cutter?"

"Peace of mind, Mr. Feggiotti. The reassurance that if
I should move into Eldridge Place, my home will be safe
and secure at every hour of the day and night."

"No worries on that score here. As the poet says, 'If in
its inmost petals can reside so vast a light.' "

"I beg your pardon."

"Dante, *The Divine Comedy,* canto 30 from *Paradiso.*"
Is he joking? "Eldridge Place . . . a paradise?"

His laugh is high, a countertenor. "As much like paradise as we can make it. The residents leave security worries to us, as they should. The Eldridge staff are trained
professionals. Most have self-defense training, plus our

integrated premises control system. There's fire and HVAC, UL-listed central monitoring, motion detectors, and CCT."

"Closed-circuit television?"

"'Gazing upon every row, now upwards and now down, now circle-wise.' Canto 31. Dante knew it all. He's the genius for all time. Like he said, 'The piercing brightness of the living ray.' So to help secure the perimeter, we have V-plex polling loop technology to let us spot the exact location of any trouble spot. Our camera Internet video server has alarm capabilities. Plus the Pan Tile zoom network day and night." He pauses to shift his gum. "Of course, all outdoor mountings are weatherproof. We belong to the Electronic Life Safety, Security and Systems Professionals. The motto is, 'Our mission is to make America a safer place.'"

"That's reassuring, Mr. Feggiotti, because I've been warned about this neighborhood."

"Crime is everywhere, Ms. Cutter. We're not kidding ourselves. 'The boughs not smooth, but poisoned thorns.' *Inferno*, canto 13."

Somehow Big Doc comes to mind. At Carlo's name, his comeback was "Flames of hell." Unless I hallucinated in the haze. "Were you raised in Boston, Mr. Feggiotti?"

"Malden, close enough."

"And you have long experience working here at Eldridge Place?"

"Since they poured the first truckload of concrete. I know every rebar and I-beam in the place."

"Then maybe you can clear up some confusion. You see, I lost touch with Boston for a number of years when I lived in the Chicago area. An old friend tells me this block had a terrible fire, the whole block. Is that true?"

Carlo's eyes do not move, but the jaw stops dead. "My friend warns me against a possible move here. Maybe he's superstitious?"

He shifts his gum and pats the bulge at his hip. "Yeah, superstitious."

"Do you remember the fire?"

"Want some gum?"

"No thanks."

He pops a fresh piece. "We're high-tech watchdogs. Our mission is your security."

"I'm not a superstitious person, Mr. Feggiotti, but background of this property is a factor in my peace of mind. I want to know Eldridge Place isn't subject to fire."

"You're good to go on that score. Don't give it a thought."

"But there was a fire?"

"Years ago."

"Houses?"

"Couple old houses, yeah."

"And that's all?"

"Maybe a business."

"Offices?"

"Like a gas station."

"Underground gas tanks? So flammable." Didn't Big Doc rant about poison sewers? "And ruptured tanks would contaminate the soil."

His gaze narrows. "It's all cleaned up. It was a body shop."

"With paints and solvents, major pollutants. It all burned?"

"To the ground. 'As flames on oil will skim across the surface, so here quick fire coursed from heel to toe . . . sucked by the reddest flames.' Canto 19, *Inferno*."

"You're quite the Dante expert. Impressive."

"The man knew everything there is to know. Here's a whole verse from the *Purgatorio,* my favorite—"

But at that moment, a side door bursts open. A short, thickset balding man in black jeans and turtleneck jogs our way. He wears one thick oily work glove, carries the other. "Carlo, Carlo, we got a shipment. It's—"

"Not now, Arnie. We have a visitor."

"It's imp—"

"I said not now. Our guest comes first." His voice drops to a throaty growl. "I'll meet you after." Carlo guides me immediately, swiftly, to the elevator. "Let me take you to your car."

"It's level D. I can manage."

"I insist. Eldridge Place is all about courtesy." The flesh of his left cheek begins to twitch. "Of course we have excellent garage lighting, even 'back toward where the sun is lost.'" His knee jiggles as he hits D, and we ride down. He studies a ring of keys as if it's a poker hand. The door opens, and he walks me to the car at a fast clip.

"Thanks so much," I say. "Parking garages are claustrophobic."

"'The bottom of the universe . . . the place all rocks converge . . . that melancholy hole.' *Inferno,* canto 32. Any questions or concerns, Ms. Cutter, be in touch. We stand by to help. Good night." He shuts my door, waits until I start my engine and back out of the space, then disappears into the elevator.

It rises just one level, to C. To meet Arnie? What kind of shipment arrives at eleven at night? What unnerved Carlo? Is it connected with Perk? Who is Perk?

I debate about taking the stairwell and having a quick

look. But there's no exit window here, no mud to cushion a fall. Besides, I'm probably on camera right now—on the concierge desk monitor at a thirty-second interval. I decide to view the building from the service roadway instead. If approached, I can say I took a wrong turn.

In moments, I've spiraled out of the garage, bypassed the resident/visitor exit, and pulled onto the breakdown lane of the service entrance drive at the north side of the building. Angled on an upgrade, I'm about fifty feet from the entrance to the city street. A concrete abutment rises about ten feet high on my right. On the left, landscaped high mounds with evergreen shrubs form a scalloped pattern along the left lane of the service road. It feels as though I'm climbing out of a tunnel.

It's after 11:30 p.m. No security cameras are visible, but that means nothing, because cameras might be mounted on any metal post or a cornice of the building. If I'm under surveillance, a blue blazer should appear in minutes, or maybe a Boston cop. I open a map from the glove box so I can plead lost if confronted. The grime on my car cuts its gloss and, I hope, its visibility. Lamplight glows in a few units of the upper floors of Eldridge. Most everyone has turned in.

What am I looking for? Carlo and Arnie in a criminal act? Whatever, it's not happening on this service road. I lower the window and listen. At low volume, the Mass Pike traffic in the distance is white noise. An airliner drones, a final flight out of Logan? I move my seat back and look around at nothing. The air feels thick, the sky a molten lead. A small bird wheels aloft—or is it a bat? I shut the window fast.

Any commercial vehicle that enters or exits the complex must pass this spot. The Tsakis brothers deliver eggs

and tomatoes here, dry cleaners too and liquor stores. But
what arrives unscheduled late at night and makes Carlo
Feggiotti's cheek twitch? I could sit here all night and
never know.

I chomp a cinnamon breath mint. The map light shows
11:52. It's stuffy. I turn on the engine and crank up the
vent blower. The welcome fresh air is noisy. The blower
roars on high, fills my car with sound and air.

Then I hear a second engine noise, the grind of a
truck's low gears. It's coming from behind me, from the
service road, its lights off. Caught off guard, I twist
around to see it gaining, shifting, approaching. In a moment, it will pull alongside and pass me. I crane my neck,
ready to look up at the cab's windshield. But the driver's
face is a smudge. As the truck passes, however, I look at
the passenger side window. There's a face staring down,
dark yet visible. I recognize him. Our eyes meet for just
an instant. I'm sure he sees me. I'm sure I've been recog-
nized. It's Carlo Feggiotti.

Chapter Fifteen

Meg Givens's morning Mayday distress signal is a blessed distraction. Once again I slept badly. Eyes gritty, I'm on my third cup of coffee. "You promised to research the Marlborough house, Reggie. Can you give it an hour ASAP? Please? Tania's out of her mind. I'm losing mine."

"And Jeffrey?"

"Forget Jeffrey. Ghostwise, it's all about Tania."

On my radar screen, it's about Jeffrey warning me off. It's about tracing the Eldridge history to Henry Faiser's arrest for Peter Wald's murder and the whole street engulfed in flames. But Igloo Sue's research on the house is also on my to-do list because it can pacify Tania as well as help Meg. A calmer Tania means a less stormy Jeffrey and keeps my path clear so I can see if there's a trail from him to the lethal Eldridge fire. I need to know how a scrappy black city kid made it to the Back Bay and an office limo and partnership in a high-end real estate development.

By 11:30 a.m., I have made my way to the Boston Public Library, "the People's Palace." Founded in 1848 and the first publicly supported library in America, it's a city treasure with its Sargent murals and courtyard garden. The garden benches beckon with shade and sun, but I march straight to the catalog, enter "Boston" as keyword, and get swamped. Whole forests have been sacrificed to the city's recorded obsession with itself.

How can an amateur possibly pick and choose from these hundreds and hundreds of titles? What documents did Igloo Sue research before being swept off her feet to thaw and live happily ever after in Dallas? Everyone working in the catalog this morning seems expert and savvy. Skilled hunters, they click, they jot. I eye the pale, stern woman beside me with a Bean tote and note cards. She's researching brooms. *Straw Brooms of New England, Broom Pedlars in Vermont and New Hampshire, The Economy of the Corn Broom.* Beside her I'm a bumbling novice.

I ask myself what will satisfy Tania and let me find out more about Jeffrey. Picking titles at random is like flea market browsing, but that's what I do. My consumer picks: *Boston: A Social History, Boston Bohemia,* and *Lost Boston,* plus *Delinquents and Reformers in Boston* and a dozen others.

It's dizzying—and distracting too, because it's tight quarters, despite the fact that I've moved to the main reading room with its high-vaulted ceilings. Seated to my left at our shared oak trestle table, a gaunt, bearded man surrounded by Russian tomes mumbles in cadences memorable from *Doctor Zhivago.* To my right, a twenty-something guy with mismatched socks and black nail polish snaps the pages of *Car and Driver.* The room is crowded. I can't move because my seat number tells the staff where to bring more books from the stacks—into which, thank heaven, library patrons cannot go, or else I'd surely disappear into the labyrinth. Not to mention my claustrophobia.

I open a chapter about the prestigious Back Bay and learn something jarring: that the area was once a sewage basin, a dreadful city health hazard called "a great cesspool." Surprise, surprise, "the neighborhood smelled like the hold of a ship after a three years' voyage." By 1849, in the interests of public health, the Health Department required the area to be filled in. Amazingly, the aristocracy of Old Boston paid a premium to live atop a city sewer—a pre-EPA cleanup to turn a toxic swamp into luxury housing for city aristocrats. I reject the notion of telling Tania that the residents of neighboring Beacon Hill had "put their handkerchiefs to their noses" when visiting new Back Bay construction. She'd be revolted and furious and take it out on Meg.

Here, however, is a more Tania-friendly fact, which Jeffrey Arnot will also appreciate: 580 acres of "brand new land" were brought to Boston in railcars from "the lure of real estate profits," whereupon "Beacon Street extended westward. Two new streets were developed: Newbury and Marlborough." Bingo!

Better yet, here's a French twist: "In the 1860s, Boston suddenly surrendered to all things French . . . Second Empire style. From the very start, the Back Bay was clearly to be the most fashionable and luxurious residential section in an expanding city."

The Arnots' house, according to one of these books, was built in 1881 in the newly fashionable Medieval style, its first owner Mr. Edmund Wight. An architectural writer celebrates the house for its "forward thrust of gable" and "inward pull of the deep and spacious entrance porch."

Pure spin, this praise for a house that'd give anyone the Gothic creeps in the brightest moonlight. I'd bet nineteenth-century little children in knickerbockers and sailor straws streaked past that house in terror. My Jack and Molly would've called it a Witch House and skipped it on Halloween, assuming they trick-or-treated in the 1880s.

Yet it's bonbons for Tania if I can link the French Second Empire with the paranormal—or whatever they called it back then. Animal magnetism? Or perhaps it was mesmerism, named for Franz Anton Mesmer, who put subjects into "a sleeplike condition, a state of trance" in which "jars of ammonia passed under their noses failed to evoke even the slightest response." I say that anybody who's beyond rousing with ammonia fumes is scary.

Had Edmund Wight been a follower of mesmerism?

My book of the hour is *The Gentle Bostonians: Biography of the Back Bay Breed,* a memoir by one Frances "Fannie" Fantrell, who grew up on Clarendon Street in the last quarter of the nineteenth century. The dates fit the Arnot house, and the location is perfect for neighborhood lore on Wight. "Home for me is always the Back Bay," wrote Fannie, "where houses breathe an air of comfort and conformity." And here's Marlborough: "Henry James stood with Father at the head of Marlborough Street, looked down its long expanse, and sighed."

My pulse quickens. Surely, Edmund Wight will make an appearance in this old-fashioned book, in its own way a version of *People,* with nonstop news makers and celebs of Boston history's Who's Who. Maybe Wight went to the Pole with Captain Scott and froze and has haunted his own house ever since.

I'm midway through the book and getting hungry for lunch when Wight makes his entrance. "Father and Mr.

Wight took their customary stroll." Bingo again! Mr. Wight, according to Fannie, is "a compact man, in sober clothes, round faced, with grizzled, close-cropped mustache and eyes twinkling benignly behind steel rimmed spectacles." In springtime, "he wears a 'Boston Leghorn' hat, his walking stick swinging forward before it touches the bricks of the sidewalk."

Wight's valet, or maybe coachman, is named Boyle. "Boyle brought the coach round, and Mr. Wight took leave of us." "Boyle" is Irish, isn't it? Moments ago I read that "hauling gravel and filling in the Back Bay furnished employment for Irish laborers." If I can't find scandal or mesmerism, can I concoct a notion of a ghostly Irish servant?

I read on. Mr. Wight, it seems, courted Miss Clara Eddington of Beacon Hill, "a pretty girl with a classic nose and delicious warm voice, a flowered hat high on her wavy hair, and velvet ribbons on her bodice." She was "the fixed maypole around which Mr. W. circled as if 'twere perpetual springtime."

It seems that Miss Eddington was courted by countless suitors. Trolleys full of Harvard men made pilgrimages to her family home on Beacon Hill. To foil rivals, Wight made his big bold move, which was to build the Marlborough house. The neighborhood was reportedly atwitter when the architect, Charles Dehmer, persuaded his client to forgo the Academic French style in favor of the captivating newer fashion, Medieval.

Did Miss Clara Eddington of Beacon Hill thus live happily ever afterward on Marlborough as the wife of Edmund Wight, who was, after all, a Brahmin serving on boards of trustees and faithfully attending dinner meetings of the Monday Club, of which he was secretary?

No. Somehow his new Marlborough house affronted her. There are references to Miss E's "tragicomic dislike" of the stone of Mr. Wight's house and "intractable aversion" to the New Land. Fannie Fantrell recounts a crushing moment, a promenade when Mr. Wight proposed marriage to Miss Eddington, then "watched the tip of her parasol trace out two letters: N-O."

Why did she turn Wight down flat? Was this "compact" man more friend than lover, or his pedigree not pure enough? Was that house really the insurmountable obstacle? Maybe Clara set her sights on a big-bucks robber baron in the Gilded Age. Fannie does not venture a guess.

Within a year, the spurned Wight is said to be "storm-tossed" and "heartbroken," while Mr. and Mrs. G. A. Eddington announce the engagement of their daughter, Clara, to Mr. Charles Dehmer.

Dehmer! I can't believe it, the architect. What a twist! Dehmer hasn't figured in the picture at all except for the house. Following a spring wedding, the couple will live on Louisburg Square, Beacon Hill. Her home turf.

I smell a plot as thick as blood pudding—the architect Dehmer conniving to wreck his client's courtship. He must have known that Wight, not the Harvard boys, was his real competition. Had he drawn up blueprints calling for a house style and a location that Clara Eddington was certain to loathe? Was Dehmer a Machiavelli and Casanova combined? A snake, that's what I think. Fannie speculates on none of this, although she soon refers to "Mr. Wight, the bachelor of Marlborough Street" and regrets that "he has fallen heir to his family's fatal weakness."

What fatal weakness? "Fevered accusations" and "dreadful dislocation of nature" conceal the specifics.

But 1886 brings the "horrid" news that Mrs. Charles Dehmer, née Clara Eddington, has been widowed, the Dehmers' little boy, Charles Jr., left fatherless. The Dehmers had been in residence on Louisburg Square just two years when Mr. Dehmer died of fatal injuries in a pedestrian accident on Beacon Street. The accident involved a carriage horse driven by—"O cruelest of Fate's twists"—Mr. Wight's man, Boyle.

I see the words "crushed" and "skull," and suddenly, the "Gentle Bostonians" are as Gothic as the Marlborough house.

Here's how I read the story. First, imagine Wight brooding in his brand-new Medieval house while Clara honeymoons with Dehmer. Imagine this Boston gentleman trying his best not to conjure the newlyweds' boudoir scenes. Imagine him fighting depression and fury while Clara and Dehmer travel, for weren't wedding trips back then months long—steamship and rail journeys to distant resorts and watering holes? Imagine his reaction on learning of the birth of the Dehmers' son, Charles.

All the while, picture the bereft Wight in Boston faithfully attending board meetings and Monday Club dinners but succumbing to his family's "fatal weakness." Did Wight direct his man Boyle to kill Dehmer? Was he jealous and enraged enough to become homicidal? Not that he'd act in the open, of course. A gentleman of Wight's standing in the "Back Bay Breed" would not so crudely make his hired man a hit man.

But if hints were dropped . . . Suppose Boyle took his cue from a master whose every breath the servant could anticipate and must obey without question? After the fact, Boyle would be absolved of responsibility, "consoled" and "forgiven." Accidents *will* happen, horses startle, and pedestrians misjudge distance curb-to-curb. The less said the better.

I plod on, the task now so grim. My appetite's gone, and it's somehow par for the course to come upon an abrupt reference to "Mr. Edmund Wight's sudden and untimely death" in 1888.

"Oh—"

"You okay?" The *Car and Driver* guy is now into *Road & Track*.

"I'm fine. Something upsetting in this book." I lift it to show the front.

"The Gentle Bostonians?"

"They're not. I mean, they weren't gentle."

He half smiles and shifts his chair away.

I sink into Fannie's account of Edmund Wight's funeral at Mount Auburn Cemetery on March 20, 1888, complete with references to "the calamitous season, so vexatious in spirit to all, as if Nature herself would humble the proud at heart." What killed him? The "grippe" and "a weakening attack of bronchitis" are mentioned. I'd vote for remorse and guilt. At the funeral, "all were inconsolable," and Mrs. Dehmer, "achingly lovely in mourning silks and jet," was said to be "thrice near fainting. The servants, too, as if their own kin were struck down."

Including Boyle?

Fannie does not say. Page after page, I find no more aftershocks. There's one mention of "the star-crossed Marlborough house," but mainly, the charmed lives resume, the symphony concerts, Sunday sermons, candlelit Christmas trees, seasonal travel to lakes and shore. It's as though the passions and deaths are but ripples in time. They subside. Nothing rocks the Back Bay boat.

But why, well over a century later, does every new owner leave the Marlborough house in short order? What drives them out? Why the freezing drafts and night noises? Is it the ghost of Edmund Wight?

What to tell Tania? A tale of the loyal Irish servant, Boyle, whose spirit mourns Mr. Wight, himself a man devoted to all things French. The household noises are not to be taken as signs of anger, but as catastrophic sadness. Not rage, not conspiracy to commit murder. Sadness, in fact, could be new and novel enough to hold Tania while I try to learn whether the Marlborough house is specially "star-crossed" in this twenty-first century. Assuming "star-crossed" is the apt term for a house purchased with money traceable to the Eldridge Street fire in which the bodies of homeless squatters were found. All of which makes it a probable criminal act of arson and murder. The guilty could be at large while Henry Faiser serves hard time for a murder of which he may well be innocent.

Chapter Sixteen

The fashion show at the Newton Home and Garden Alliance looms this Friday like a huge nuisance. My library book report is written up, a piece of hackwork to appease Tania. Meanwhile, a new "Ticked Off" deadline nears, Nicole is edgy, and I'm slated to spend extra hours at StyleSmart pressing suits and stuffing tissue paper into shoulders and sleeves and zippering garment bags.

Devaney had called to report that Alan Tegier had been strangled, probably with a coated wire. On Faiser, he was silent. I need to know whether he has got hold of additional stored evidence from Peter Wald's murder, specifically the gun that killed him. These days, however, it's touchy between Devaney and me, sort of "don't ask, don't tell."

Meg and I meet late this morning, Tuesday, in a Tremont café for coffee and a swap. A silent TV on a back wall shows the city's chief of police being interviewed, the closed-captioning saying extra personnel have been assigned to the Dempsey case and that the public is invited to phone in leads on a hotline. A sure sign the case is stalled and that Devaney is more preoccupied than ever.

Meg scans my Marlborough Street "psychic" docudrama about Boyle and Edmund Wight while I finger the Eldridge Place II brochure, an ebony calfskin folio with thick cream papers, lavish margins, and engraved script seductively announcing the latest in elegant living.

"This is perfect, Reggie—the devoted Irish manservant who mourns his gentleman."

"Glad you approve." I glance out the window, where Biscuit is tied to a parking meter and licks every stranger's proffered hand. Back to Eldridge II with its Palladian design, parquetry flooring, gallery walls, clerestory fenestration, master thermal mineral spas, private elevators, valet garaging, and on and on. Worthy of Louis XIV, the cursive sweep says that Eldridge Place II is developed by the Bevington Partners Group.

"I love the walking stick and Leghorn hat," Meg declares.

"Good." But at the moment, I'm in the grip of a utopian fantasyland. "All the amenities," I say aloud. Imagine a waltz on that parquetry flooring, beautifully finished, with nary a dust fuzz rolling like a tumbleweed over the barren plain of sloping floorboards. And no tenant complaint about a dripping faucet.

Meg folds the pages of my ghostly sad melodrama and tucks them into her bag. "This will go to Tania today. And, Reggie, if you're really serious about a move to a deluxe high-rise, Eldridge II is a good bet. Trust me, by the time the foundation is dug, most units will be sold. Barlow Square is a good location, so your condo ought to fetch a nice price."

"Probably still too pricey for me." But my voice lacks conviction, and I pause a split second too long.

Meg mistakes this for encouragement. "I printed these from the Bevington Partners' Web site, the usual developer stuff about experience and innovation. They underwrite and execute development opportunities. Here you go."

She hands me the sheets. Guilt dampens my palms. Meg Givens thinks I'm really house-hunting. I try to stall her. "But they haven't even broken ground. Eighteen months for such major construction? Doubtful."

"They're fast. Bevington's subcontractors have sweet incentives and stupendous penalty clauses. Carrots and sticks, Reggie. We all marveled when Eldridge Place rose like the Empire State Building, one floor per week. Of course, the fire was a lucky break."

"The Eldridge fire?"

"Horrible to say this, but that fire saved them demolition and hauling. It probably cut red tape too. Zoning fights are a moot point when whole blocks lie in ashes."

I swirl my coffee. "Meg, let me ask you, were there rumors about that property?"

"Nothing I ever heard. But, Reggie, those were slum blocks at the time. We did no business there. Eldridge Place transformed the area."

"Slum blocks have slumlords."

Now Meg's eyes narrow, and the expression on her heart-shaped face shifts from piquant to shrewd to suspicious. She says, "You're not really considering a move, are you? You're not house-hunting."

For decency's sake, I have to say, "Not exactly."

"So that pink love nest that Stu showed so late at night—that was wasting Stu's time?" Her eyes flicker with anger and bewilderment. "And mine?"

Guilt settles in like black molasses. My gaze drops. "Meg, I owe you an apology on this. I'm acting in connection with a psychic message. No, it's not Marlborough, and I can't give you specifics, except you do know that people died in the Eldridge fire?"

"They were accident victims, Reggie, hoboes or druggies. Your aunt had her psychic projects, but she never used people."

"WWJD—What Would Jo Do?"

Meg rises with a chilly smile. "I have a showing at one. I'm disappointed, Reggie. People make Realtor jokes, but we work hard and have our pride. This is breach of faith."

Meg exits. The coffee's cold, and maybe I've wrecked a friendship in the making. One thing I know: guilt can be a useless emotion, an apology can fall on deaf ears, and my sainted aunt is an impossible act to follow.

Back at Barlow Square, Biscuit naps and I Google the Bevington Partners Group and find something Meg didn't mention. The developer is mired in lawsuits over the construction of Eldridge Place. Three of the suits claim breach of contract, the fourth negligence. Subcontractors have filed $8-, $15-, and $28-million suits alleging nonpayment for various costs, including insulation panels, pipe, ceramic coatings, labor. Bevington has countersued, alleging substandard quality of materials and construction. All the cases are pending.

As for the fourth case, negligence, the family of a fatally injured construction worker, Jahan Motiki, has filed *Motiki v. Bevington Partners Group,* which claims that no safety harness was provided for the man's high-elevation installation work. Plaintiff Sari Motiki, who is represented by the firm of Heald and Menkins, alleges that her late husband sustained fatal head and spinal injuries in a fall. Bevington contends it bears no responsibility because the worker's employer was a subcontractor and Motiki an illegal alien, which sounds like he came from a flying saucer. Suit and countersuit are pending.

My ex, Marty, said these kinds of mishaps and lawsuits are one cost of doing business. He used the old cliché "Make an omelet, break eggs." By now, perhaps his trophy and my replacement, Celina, finds the omelet and eggshells as numbing as I did. Though maybe she's better than I at faking awe at Marty's all-purpose version of Deep Thought. Anyway, try telling Mrs. Motiki that her late husband was a broken egg.

None of the suits are delaying Eldridge II, though I note a complaint which was filed last March by a group called Friends of Eldridge.

"Friends" of those dilapidated blocks in the neighborhood? Of Suitcase Mary's turf? The group claims that Bevington's environmental impact statement was flawed. It claims, too, an improper acquisition of four city blocks of single- and multifamily residential properties on Eldridge and three side streets, including Forster, which Mary said was *her* street and which the concierge, Pam, blithely dismissed as a demolition detail. The Friends' appeal to the zoning board was denied. I find no Web site for the Friends. Roll on, Eldridge II.

Biscuit stirs, drinks some water, goes back to sleep. Online, I search Suffolk County property transactions on Eldridge Street over the past two years. Seven, no, eight residential properties—houses—have been bought by one person, Steven Yung. I click around. There's a Steve Yung Web site with a grinning man in a white shirt and bow tie. "Let me put you in the car, SUV, or pickup of

your dreams at prices you won't believe!! I'm your NEW
BEST FRIEND!! Don't visit a showroom without me!!
Guaranteed Financing!! Satisfaction!! Credit Doctor at
your service!! See me, Steve, at *Brighton Auto Mart*."

It's a long shot, but at two, en route to StyleSmart, I
detour to swing by Brighton Auto Mart, which is midblock on Brighton Avenue. It's a narrow lot whose front-
row auto prices, whitewashed across the windshields, all
end in $99. The usual plastic pennants droop from a wire,
and a sign proclaims "Spring Sale." There's not another
customer or tire kicker in sight, but a slim, Asian-eyed
man dashes from a back lot crammed with fourth-
generation cars and pickups. "I'm Steve. How you doing
today?" His handshake is soft and wet. He's in Dockers
and a blue shirt and striped clip-on bow tie. He grins,
nods strenuously, keeps earnest eye contact while I introduce myself. "What can I show you, Mrs. Cutter?"

"My daughter needs a car."

"Mrs. Cutter, you've come to the right place at the
right time. We have a spring sale all this week long. Tell
me about your daughter."

The man sounds from a playbook. "She's an art student. She lives in Rhode Island."

"I've got the car for her. Follow me, please." We walk
the back rows. The vehicles are all sooty, which is
strange. The inventory looks as defeated as Steve Yung is
perky. "You live around here, Mrs. Cutter?"

"The South End."

"So you come so far out to Brighton for the spring
sale."

How can I slip the Eldridge side streets into the conversation? "I saw your Auto Mart Web site." Why aren't these
cars shined up?

"My cousin put me on the Internet. It's good idea for business. See, you come all this way from South End. Parking there, they say, is terrible."

"A challenge."

"The city, I stay away from there. Brighton is good for me. My family, we like home here in Brighton."

"Nice." I check my watch. This is dumb and I want out. Nicole is expecting me. Steve lays a hand on a metallic-raspberry car.

"Mrs. Cutter, this is your daughter's Beretta."

"Like the gun?"

He grins as though I'm Comedy Central. "It's Chevrolet, a really good deal. Less than nine thousand miles. A little sporty, great car for your daughter. It could be yours, ma'am, for a low down payment and easy finance. You can get amazing deal. How about a test drive?"

"I don't think today. I need to bring my daughter with me."

"You can surprise her. Young lady daughters enjoy a big surprise."

"Perhaps I'll come back with her."

"Let me give a price. Please come into my office, please."

It's ridiculous, yet somehow I don't want to hurt his feelings. Maybe it's the brush with Meg, or some dim notion of Asian propriety, or the rows of dingy cars, but I step into the clapboard shed with its cluttered desk and lumpy sofa and fluorescent buzz.

He grabs a clipboard and motions me to the sofa. I sit. Give this five minutes, max. "Please, how much do you want to spend?"

"Not a lot."

"You want to finance the car? I offer the whole package, easy payments. You thirsty, like a Pepsi? No? How about insurance?"

"I'm not sure." This feels like a skit.

He turns on a calculator. "The best deal, you will see."

He crunches his numbers. I sit, hands folded, looking out at the dispirited rows of sedans and coupes and aging SUVs. Inside, a dusty electric fan awaits the summer season, and a Bruins cap hangs from a nail. Framed photos of beaming children line the desk, babies in arms, tots, a pretty Asian woman in red with a golden hibiscus in her hair. The family photos are the sole bright note in the place.

My gaze is drawn to a framed black-and-white glossy that's half hidden behind the family grouping. It's some kind of official photograph, maybe an awards ceremony, a beaming Steve Yung shaking hands against a backdrop of duckpins and a banner that says "Bowl for Kids."

I shift on the sofa, my gaze steady on the glossy figures. I look away, then back again. With breath held, I focus on the man Steve shakes hands with in the photo— a wiry dark man in a double-breasted suit. I stretch, then crane, then stand up to get a better look. Partially blocked, the figure is nevertheless familiar and unmistakable. I stare until I'm positive. On the desktop is a photo of Steve Yung shaking hands with Jeffrey Arnot.

The Newton Home and Garden Alliance occupies a 1700s white colonial on a street with a tearoom, a yarn shop, a dog groomer. It's a light-year away from the Brighton Auto Mart. A historical plaque on the Alliance house says it was built over two centuries ago by Ebenezer Botts.

Four StyleSmart "models" crammed themselves into my Beetle all the way from Roxbury to this suburb, each woman proud, eager, anxious, and a bit defensive too. I pull around to the back, followed by the donated dry cleaner's van, which is our transport for the pressed ensembles on hangers. Nicole's two van passenger "models" get out fast: Rosalie, who's nearly six feet in flip-flops, and the doe-eyed Carmine, who reminds me of Kia Fayzer—and thus of the brother I'm not helping nearly enough.

"Mighty seasick in that van."

One of my backseat passengers, Beverly, cracks about the Beetle, "Itty-bitty car for circus clowns."

"Ladies, welcome!" In a powder-blue suit with box jacket, the Alliance's Caroline French opens a service entrance door.

I smile. Frankly, I have a hidden agenda. No, it's nothing to do with the photo of Steve Yung and Jeffrey Arnot, the charity event photo op signaling possible deals, maybe stolen cars, maybe real estate parcels in the Eldridge area. For the moment, my focus is on Newton. The Boston police chief's closed-captioned plea has given me an idea. Newton was Sylvia Dempsey's home turf. One way or another, I'll ask whether the murdered woman was a member of the Alliance or had friends among the members. I might get tips for Devaney, tips I can offer to exchange for information on the Faiser-Wald case. What's more, tips that Devaney can use to buy back his time to work more fully on the Faiser case. Sylvia can be leverage for Henry Faiser. If the right moment comes, I'll ask. If it doesn't, I'll create it.

"Nicole, Regina, wonderful to see you. Everybody take care to duck those puddles! It showered all morning.

We're so excited to have you here. Mickey, please give today's guests a hand."

Mickey is a bandy-legged, peppy seventy-plus in janitorial twills who jumps the puddles and grabs garment bags as our motley group hopscotches across the parking area, which is filling up with Volvos and Lexuses. A few bumper stickers say "Carney-Wald."

"Reggie, you got the makeup case in your car?"

"Makeup? Me? I thought you."

The tally of things forgotten begins. We're minus makeup, half the accessories, and one pair of size 10 snakeskin pumps for our "big gal," Rosalie.

"Then what am I s'posed to wear on my feet?" Collectively, we stare in silence at Rosalie's orange flip-flops.

Nicole rolls her eyes. "Reggie, the scripture says, 'They grope in the noonday as in the night.' But 'His hands make whole. He saveth the poor.'"

The Book of Job, if I'm not mistaken.

Nicole, however, looks nothing like the biblical master of miseries. Hers is the formal but friendly look for the ladies of Newton, a periwinkle knit suit with a deep V-neck and little regimental gold buttons down the front and cuffs, plus a gold choker and gold button earrings. Under her guidance, I represent the power palette in a fiercely feminine café au lait business suit with cream silk shirt and pearls. It's ironic—I, the former full-time homemaker, Regina Baynes, will impersonate an executive femme. The pose is perfect for a group of women who'd resent a Fortune 500 Wonder Woman casting her reproachful dragon lady's shadow over the sociable luncheon.

"Nicole and Regina, may I introduce our Alliance

treasurer, Sissie Hehrborg. Sissie also chairs the committee in charge of our clothing drive." We shake hands with a wide-eyed, auburn-haired woman in a mushroom two-piece knit who promises to bring us box lunches in the "greenroom." "Ever since the community theater group rented the building for *Candide,*" says Sissie, "we call the back parlor our greenroom."

In we go, eight of us, four African-Americans, one Latina, one white, plus Nicole and me, in a ten-by-twelve room with our thick clothes racks, folding chairs, and five windowsill pots of dying geraniums.

"Close quarters," I murmur to Nicole. Then the damnedest thing: my right thumb starts to hurt, burning as though scalded and raw. I raise my hand to see if I was stung or bitten. It looks normal but throbs. I blow on it. There's no bee or wasp in sight. No spider. But it feels like an open, angry wound.

Weak, I lean against a wall. The one time my thumb hurt this way was when Devaney showed me the stop-watch at the donut shop booth, the first and only time. It's the pain triggered by the watch the police recovered from the weedy vacant lot on Eldridge. First my rib, now this, as if my psychic wires are crossed. It's maddening, an onset that I cannot control.

"A few months ago we had a speaker," Caroline is saying, "but last month's program featured peony varieties— Regina, are you all right?"

"I'm . . . fine . . . just need a minute." I manage to smile. "I jammed my thumb last week. It's probably a sprain."

"Oh, sprains are dreadful. What can we get you? How about a pain pill?"

Pain pill? How about the identity of Peter Wald's mur-

derer, if not Henry Faiser? How about the real story of the
Eldridge fire? Those would be my real painkillers. The
fierce burning at last starts to fade, the pain to subside. It
feels like a release. "I'm fine. Really." My new smile offers proof.

Free of nursing duty, Caroline brightens. "Everybody
is thrilled to have a fashion show for a good cause. And
guess what? We have live music, a piano and choir. Oh,
here's Sissie and Jeanne with your lunches. I'll see about
your bottled water."

In moments, we arrange the chairs and unwrap sandwich halves. I am thankful for the momentary pause.

"What's this grass? What's this smeary green stuff in
my sandwich?"

"Alfalfa sprouts and avocado pear, Carmine. Pretend
it's mayonnaise." Nicole turns to the group. "Models, get
your hearts and souls ready." She looks at Rosalie and
says, "Iman!" Then she makes eye contact with each of
the other five. "Lauren Hutton! Tyra! Naomi!" It's bril-
liant strategy. Nicole has prepped the six by giving them
supermodel names. For two weeks, the StyleSmart walls
have been plastered with old *Vogue* and *Sister* covers for
rehearsals doubling as pep rallies. "Natasha! Kate! Nobody is shy when they got a super part to play."

Nicole turns my way. "Reggie, give me whatever cosmetics you got, eye shadow, liners. We'll make do while
you go find out about that music and choir. We'll wrap up
lunch and get the ladies dressing."

I hand over my makeup kit, then go down the hall into
the main parlor, where slipcovered folding chairs flank an
aisle that serves as our runway. The floral arrangements
are lovely—hanging baskets of lobelia and fuchsia, and
basket-weave planters of bright grass. The garden club

ladies are assembling at tables with their own box lunches; sauvignon blanc is poured by waiters in white jackets.

For a moment, it takes my breath away. I'm Reggie in Wonderland down the rabbit hole into my past life. At any table of six, I could claim my seat and join the conversation about opening a summer cottage in the mountains or at the shore. Yet I'm an outsider now, like a ghost staring at a scene right out of my own life.

Across the coiffed and frosted heads, I wonder who here knew Sylvia Dempsey. There are over one hundred women in this room. I can't go table-to-table to inquire. Who were her friends?

"Regina, will you need a microphone?" Sissie Hehrborg has approached to lean close and point to an oak stand. That's where I'll read my script as "Naomi" and "Tyra" and the others walk the ramp. "You're our announcer, right, Regina? Our announcer?" She slurs the word so it sounds like *announ*sher. Beneath her perfume and the wine, do I detect the odor of juniper berries? Gin? "We've set you up right here." She takes a step, steadies herself on my arm. "Scuse me."

I smile to signal no problem. "Sissie, do I understand that a choir will perform?"

"Children from the school for the blind. They're outside in their bus. PB&J sandwiches for them. They're gonna sing."

"Oh. We weren't informed."

"Three songs. Then your StyleSmart gal will say a few words."

"That's Nicole Patrick."

"And will she need a microphone?" Sissie hiccups.

"Nicole? Definitely not."

"I'll come back to the greenroom to cue you. You'll hear the choir. Wasn't my idea, by the way. Peanut butter kids' choir, cookie bones for the guide dogs. Sometimes we go along to get along, don't we?"

Indeed we do. Back in the greenroom, Nicole has the six models lined up for inspection as on a flight deck. She's worked wonders with everyone's makeup. Renee's cocoa skin is glowing, Carmine's complexion is radiant with a bronze sheen. Kayzee's shoulders are squared in her light gray jacket with a sky-blue blouse. We have variety—A-lines, pleats—but office standards. Rosalie will wedge her toes into Nicole's mules and hope for the best. Nicole approaches me with pencils and liners for a touch-up. I unfold my script.

Then we hear the piano and the children's thin voices. "Climb Every Mountain." "Sound of Music." "I Believe."

"Nicole," I whisper, "those blind children, we weren't told about an opening act."

"Reggie, don't you worry. With those old tunes, there won't be a dry eye. Those ladies are gonna open their checkbooks and clear out their closets for StyleSmart. When I come back next week to collect the donations, our inventory will be through the roof."

Twenty minutes later, the test. The choir's back in the bus, and the spotlight is on us. Nicole is spellbinding, a natural-born motivational speaker. "Scripture says, 'In the day of prosperity, be joyful,' and our joy at StyleSmart is helping wonderful women prosper and find their joy in the world of gainful work—with the support of the Newton Home and Garden Alliance!"

Here we go. Renee leads off, and I read, "To soar with flying colors in a simple silhouette." She's down the aisle. The ladies smile with trembling chins, still teary from the blind children. I continue. "Midcalf skirt looks like a million dollars and spells out one word: *professional*."

Renee pauses at the far end, as planned, to state her new job. "A receptionist in a dental clinic." All applaud as she pivots and starts back up while our own version of Naomi Campbell, a suited Rosalie, totters forward in the mules.

"Payroll clerk!" she booms. More applause.

And so it goes to the finale, when all six stand in the aisle and Nicole poses the scripted question. "For joyful prosperity, for style-smart success, what does it take?" In turn, each speaks her line.

"It takes job skills."

"It takes focus."

"Takes a budget."

"Patience."

"Enterprise."

"Commitment."

Applause thunders from a group of women who never had to face the life and times of these six. Including me.

Then it's over. The models retreat to the greenroom while Nicole and I work the room. "Inspiring" is the word that echoes from table to table as impressive donations are pledged. We smile serenely, and I recall that Nicole will pay each "model" her hourly lost wages.

The end-of-luncheon signal is lipsticks twisted and applied, and yet I haven't had the chance to ask about Sylvia Dempsey. Where is Caroline French? Alongside Nicole, saying she wants to join the models for a few moments to give each a "small token of our appreciation." She has a tote with little ribboned boxes. They walk arm in arm down the hall.

Plan B: find Sissie Hehrborg, who stands with a departing group and looks a bit unsteady on her feet. I approach to hear her say, "Perfectly fine to drive. Know my way blindfolded . . . oops, better not say that today. Tactless. Weren't they darling?"

The group is thinning. I hear auto ignitions outside. Sissie's friends say good-bye, the last one a woman in a robin's-egg-blue fluted skirt. "So uplifting," she says to me. "A refreshing change from our horticulture."

Sissie and I are alone. "Trellises and arbors," she says, "perennials and pruning tips. But not today."

I step closer as caterers clear the tables around us. "Sissie, thanks for your help. I was wondering . . . the luncheon has been so festive, but it must be difficult knowing that someone in your community died so recently, so horribly."

She hiccups and struggles to focus. "You're Regina."

"I am."

"You knew our Sylvia?"

"I feel as though I knew her."

Sissie points at my shoes. "She stood right where you're standing."

"She was an Alliance member?"

"It was last March . . . no, Valentine month, February. We had a speaker, friend of hers, talked about the environment. She introduced him. So you knew her too?"

"Sylvia was killed near my home."

"Right where you're standing. Now they hush it up."

"What?"

"Big insurance policy her husband took out. Millions."

"I understand her husband is a skin doctor."

"Skin off anybody's nose. Skin-deep. Dr. Bernard Dempsey." Sissie's gaze wanders as she sways, widens her stance, pinches the skin of my wrist. "Bernie's got a skin factory. Fake skin, plastic."

"Synthetic skin?"

"Skin's fake, but the money trouble was real. Going broke, but the insurance on Sylvia got him out. Paid up, cup runneth over. Dumb Newton cops, dumb Boston cops. Nobody adds two and two, 'less it's a cover-up."

"You think her husband—"

"Swear on a stack of Bibles. Hey, time to go. Be careful if somebody's got a big policy. Too dangerous, life and limb." Sissie begins to move away, fumbles at the clasp of her handbag, looks back at me. "Right where you're standing, last time I saw her alive."

"February."

"Her pink Chanel, fabulous, never out of style. 'Ladies, I present the next lieutenant governor of the Commonwealth.' Classic. Last words we heard her speak. Sylvia was classic. 'Ladies, today I present my good friend, friend of the environment . . . Senator Jordan Wald.'"

Chapter Seventeen

W hat about cast iron? Or nonstick?"

"Frank, please—"

"Skillets, Reggie. Skillets are on my mind. It's the *Iron Chef* idea. Is a twenty-two-inch more versatile?"

"You refuse to talk about the Faiser case, is that what you're telling me?" Devaney pops two Tums and loosens his necktie, rows of red roosters crowing at dawn.

Anger rises in my chest. We're in my front room facing one another on the sofa and rocker. It's after seven. I'm exhausted from the StyleSmart extravaganza but bursting with these tips about the Dempseys. I'm the star informant, but as before, Devaney is dismissive.

"Sylvia Dempsey was possibly killed for insurance money, Frank. That's a lead. Can't you put others to work on this and get back to Faiser? I think you're blowing me off."

"I listened. I didn't interrupt."

"You promised me the latest on the Faiser-Wald case. And you wished for more time to spend on Faiser. I got you new information on Sylvia Dempsey. Ten minutes ago you said—"

"I said exchanging information is always a good possibility."

"You promised."

"Reggie, you heard what you want to hear."

A brick wall, this man. I ought to stop, but silence is somehow beyond me at this instant. "What about my thumb? I felt excruciating pain today at the Newton Home and Garden Alliance. It's the same exact feeling as when I held the stopwatch from the weedy vacant lot on Eldridge."

"Maybe it's like a phantom limb."

"Tell me, Frank, did you treat Jo this way?"

He crunches two more Tums, and his Adam's apple bobs. "Reggie, it's been a long day. One thing Jo knew: the police and her sixth sense had different timetables. They zigged and zagged. She had patience."

Unlike her niece? "A multimillion-dollar insurance policy at the very moment when the husband's new business is nearing bankruptcy—doesn't that tell you something? Don't I get credit for tips? Don't I deserve to hear about Faiser? Don't you want to work harder on his case?"

He gives me a basset hound look and sighs. "How about this, Reggie? The Dempseys had huge policies on one another. They got them before a trip to Hong Kong because they feared a SARS-type outbreak. They joked with friends about it."

"But his artificial skin business—"

"Advent Tissue Science. It got a big infusion from a venture capitalist three months before Mrs. Dempsey was killed."

The man has a knack for deflation. The air fills with tension and disappointment. He says, "Is there anything else?"

I'm about to say I learned that Sylvia Dempsey introduced Senator Jordan Wald at the garden club and called him a good friend. But I save my breath. Frank Devaney's likely reply is utterly predictable: that a garden club naturally invites a campaigning environmentalist to make a speech. As for political friendship, any primate classifiable as *Homo sapiens* will do. Given their social circles, Sylvia Dempsey's acquaintance with the state senator would be no surprise, merely two or three degrees of separation.

"Anything else, Reggie?"

"Did Jo ever report psychic phantom limbs?"

"Not to me. Never." He leans my way. "I know you want to help. You are helping. But homicide doesn't follow Newton's law. Everybody wants security, day or night. A brutal crime out of nowhere scares everybody. The public wants an immediate arrest."

"Peter Wald's murder and the arrest of Henry Faiser?"

"I meant Mrs. Dempsey."

"Frank." I lower my voice and try to speak slowly. "Frank, have you changed your mind about the Faiser case?" He blinks and looks sheepish. "Have you had a change of heart?"

He rubs a palm across his face as if to wash it. "These days, Reggie, Homicide is focused hard on the Dempsey case."

"Including you."

"There's only so many hours in a day."

"So Faiser rots in jail—"

"Prison."

"Prison. He rots in Norfolk Prison while the Homicide Division caters to Boston's wealthy whites, isn't that it?"

"You're a white woman yourself, Reggie, and Barlow Square is close enough to the Charles. Look—" He leans forward, a hand on each knee. "Consider this: any given day, I'm working cases that the public forgets all about once they're off TV and out of the papers. Out of nowhere we get a Dempsey. All hell breaks loose. Do I need it? No. Is it political? You tell me. But it comes with the territory. We have to deal with it."

He grips his knees as though they're softballs. "You're a civilian. When it comes to a crime, you can think full-time about Faiser. Dempsey isn't on your plate. You want to believe the husband plotted her death. Sure you do— because in a weird way, it frees your mind. The husband did it, so the police should grab the evidence and make the arrest. The fact is, we have no evidence that Sylvia Dempsey knew her killer. Her purse was retrieved from the Charles. The wallet was gone."

"Why was she walking by the river alone at night?"

"That's a big one. We don't know."

"Was she wearing high heels?"

"A pink suit. She shopped at Copley Place the afternoon of her death. According to credit card transactions, she returned purchases at Saks Fifth Avenue. A clerk remembers her being worried about rush-hour traffic on the turnpike."

"She drove out of the city?"

He shakes his head no. "Her car remained in the Copley garage. Nobody saw her after five p.m. The Lexus key was found in her purse, and the ME says she died between midnight and two a.m. That's all I know. I gotta get going. *Iron Chef*'s on tonight."

"You think Henry Faiser watches *Iron Chef*?"

"I think we're out of gas, you and me, the tank's empty."

Devaney leaves, and I sit for a moment eating a limp

salad, then take Biscuit out as darkness falls. It's a sober moment. I've assumed that Devaney simply withheld information about Faiser. Doubtless he has. But right now it's clear the young black man's case is on hold. Simply put: Devaney's workdays are committed elsewhere; for now, Sylvia's death trumps Henry Faiser's life.

Where does that leave me? Stalled? In free fall? I pause while Biscuit sniffs a spindly maple and barks at a bird that sounds like a trip-hammer. Along the block, neighbors nod in passing, including Trudy Pfaeltz in her nurse's uniform and carrying cartons of Milky Ways. She'll stock her vending machines and head to night shift at the hospital. She has focus, purpose.

Turning onto Tremont, I remember a book, *The Death and Life of Great American Cities*. The "life" force is city people watching the scene on the streets and from their windows. The "death" is isolation, nobody on the walkways, nobody to deter an attacker or summon help. Windswept plazas and dark alleys and a desolate path by the river—they're death.

A suburban matron knows this in her bones, which is why women like Sylvia Dempsey—or Regina Baynes—live in leafy Newton, or on the Main Line, or Winnetka or Westchester or Shaker Heights. Yes, Sylvia might take calculated risks, perhaps a fling with the club's tennis pro or a snorted few lines of cocaine. But a stroll by the Charles River at midnight? It makes no sense. Sylvia would come into the city at night solely to dine and attend the theater or a concert, then perhaps have a nightcap before returning directly to her home turf, Newton.

Now she's obstructing a mission to find out what happened on Eldridge Street thirteen years ago. Dead, Sylvia sucks up Devaney's time and energy. Am I therefore sidelined, a lady in waiting until her case is solved? Not at all. The shortest distance to Henry Faiser is not patience, but action. If I can help the Dempsey case, Devaney can get back to work on Faiser. If I help out, it'll speed things up, get the Faiser case back on track.

For instance: why did Sylvia introduce Jordan Wald at the Garden Alliance meeting? Devaney thinks it's not important. Maybe not. But I ask, why Sylvia in particular? Surely, a number of the garden club members know Senator Wald through social or business connections. Any of them could introduce him. Why Sylvia? As a Garden Alliance officer or program chair, the task would fall to her. But Sissie Hehrborg said nothing on this. My instinct says check it out. Push.

Sissie Hehrborg is waiting the following Wednesday at 2:00 p.m. at the back entrance of the Newton Home and Garden Alliance. She looks confused as I get out. "You're not Nicole. I expected Nicole."

"I'm Regina. We met last week." I flash my brightest smile. We're both wearing camel slacks. "Nicole couldn't come, so I'm subbing." It's a lie. I had to beg Nicole to let me pick up the donated clothes.

"Of course, now I remember." But her puffy eyes are blank, as if she does not.

"We also talked about the sad loss of your good friend Sylvia."

"Terrible." She looks away. "Mickey, give a hand with these boxes, please. The van is here."

"Oh, could I just sit for a moment?" I say. "I've never driven a big van before. It's terrifying." Which is true and which is why Nicole was reluctant to let me do this pickup. Two near misses on Storrow Drive nearly proved her right.

Sissie motions me to a back door garden bench as Mickey hoists carton after carton into the van. "The donations have poured in all this week. Your fashion show was a big hit." She fumbles in her purse for a cigarette, offers me one, and lights up, her hands slightly trembling as she inhales and blows out a thin blue column.

I start my pitch. "Sissie, you said that Sylvia wore Chanel. Do you suppose Dr. Dempsey would consider making a donation from his late wife's wardrobe?"

Startled, she squints at me. "Ask Bernie for Sylvia's clothes?"

"I know it's a sensitive topic, but StyleSmart holds an annual auction of classic ensembles and couture items that come our way—a Gaultier gown, Givenchy coat, Dior accessories. Some of these donations come from the deceased. Could we approach Dr. Dempsey?"

Her mouth tightens, and she frowns. "I'm not sure."

"Maybe I will take that cigarette." It's a bonding strategy, though I never fared well as a smoker, never mastered the hand positions. Pretend you're Susan Sarandon, Reggie. Take the Newport, accept the light, but do not inhale lest you choke. Puff in, puff out. "Thanks. Now and then a cigarette—"

"Nothing like it."

A quiet moment passes. Mickey loads the last carton. I'm on borrowed time. "Sissie, did you tell me Sylvia served as program chair of the Garden Alliance?" She squints, puzzled. "Or was she an Alliance officer?"

She exhales. "Neither one. Just a member in good standing."

"But she introduced Senator Wald."

"She got him for the program. It's what we're about, landing the big fish from time to time."

"Politicians?"

"Sure. And sports celebrities, TV personalities. We run the gamut. Don't think for a minute we're just ladies on the sidelines."

"So Sylvia got Wald all by herself?"

"She showed her clout. The members took notice. Sylvia's stock shot up. A garden can be a battleground. Sylvia had her goals. Mickey, would you flatten the left-over cardboard? Thanks." To me: "Now, what's this about her clothes?"

I focus my pitch. "Sometimes in grief a family disposes of a loved one's possessions too hastily and then regrets doing so. Dr. Dempsey would serve a good cause and qual-ify for the appropriate deduction. Needless to say, a Chanel suit would enhance our auction."

Sissie flicks her ash. "Ah yes, Dr. Dempsey, the griev-ing widower." Her sarcasm sounds an alarm.

"We find that requests are best made early."

"Believe me, Bernie is the king of early."

"I beg your pardon?"

"They take their comfort where they find it, don't they? On the prowl already, the younger the better. You know Bernie?"

"Let's say I know the type." I flick my ash and make a move. "I was married to one. Call it themes and variations."

"Sylvia's barely in the grave. And the insurance pol-icy . . . rumors are flying like B-52s."

"About Sylvia's murder?"

"And Bernie's money pit."

"You mean his skin business? Advent Tissue Science?"

"It's his ATM."

We puff. Eager to pepper her with questions, I control myself and stay neutral. "I understand Advent got venture capital investment."

"For his lab and his plane, so he can ski the Tetons." Sissie crushes her cigarette underfoot. "Bernie's looking beyond pimply teens and skin cream. The clinic was just the start. He's always had his eye on money and the social circuit. Some thought Sylvia was his stepping-stone. His charm paid off."

"Doesn't it always?"

She nods. "But his temper, that's Bernie's Achilles' heel."

"I've heard rumors."

"All true. Provoke him and he'll stare you down with those fire-and-brimstone eyes. You've met him?"

"Maybe once."

"Never rub him the wrong way. You don't want to meet those eyes." Sissie looks at me with a watery gaze. "Sylvia's Chanel at auction . . . ghoulish, don't you think?"

"Didn't Jackie Kennedy's suit and pillbox hat go to the Smithsonian?"

"I don't remember."

Actually, neither do I. "Could you call him for us?"

She hesitates. "Where is this auction held?"

"The Four Seasons." Which is a lie. "Next year, possibly the Ritz."

This is how I gain entrance to Sylvia Dempsey's dressing room.

It's the next Tuesday, a hellishly hot afternoon, when I climb the stairs behind the Dempsey housekeeper, the

broad-faced, bushy-browed Mrs. Manosa, whose black
polyester swishes as she leads me across the carpeted balcony of the Chestnut Hill Tudor. The house is furnished
in heavy Queen Anne mahogany with virgin-white porcelain *objets,* mostly figurines of children. Sissie Hehrborg,
bless her, played the middlewoman. I'm led to understand
that as the StyleSmart representative, I can select
wardrobe items under Mrs. Manosa's watchful eye, with
the stipulation that I provide proof that StyleSmart is a
registered 501(c)(3) not-for-profit agency. I must also
provide wardrobe appraisal of each donated item. Dr.
Bernard Dempsey, it seems, is not too devastated to think
about tax deductions.

The Dempseys, it's clear, had separate bedrooms.
Sylvia's is decorated in toile wall covering and furnished
with a sleigh bed and Empire dresser decked with the
couple's wedding photos. The eight-by-tens show a slender, ivory-complexioned Sylvia in her twenties, blond
hair swept into a French twist, eyes gazing heavenward
in the classic expression of faith and staged bliss. She's
in a gown of organza with seed pearls, a popular design
of twenty years ago. Facing opposite is the tuxedoed,
olive-complexioned Bernard, slight of build with a narrow face and receding hairline. Sloe-eyed, I'd say, but
not hellish. At the time of his wedding, he looked about
thirty-five.

Oddly, there are no other photos in the room, no record
of life's progression. The polished picture frames, I notice, rest on surfaces that are coated with dust, as if the
room has been neglected and the wedding photos placed
here within the last day or two. The night tables and mirror, too, are dusty, and a cobweb loops from a lamp finial
to the shade. What housekeeper would fail to notice and

act? Unless perhaps superstition keeps Mrs. Manosa out of this room. Or orders from Dr. Dempsey.

In the doorway to Sylvia's walk-in, the housekeeper stares straight ahead, mute and still. Finally, she says, "The doctor, he says you can take from here."

I begin to sort and select from among the newest goddess gowns in pastel chiffons, then the club suits with midthigh skirts, finally the jackets and shoes, most with five-inch spike heels. Sylvia definitely liked her heels high and in browns and blacks, tan, pinks, pale pistachio, open-toed and closed. Apart from two pairs of flats, none of these shoes were meant for walking any distance, certainly not from Copley Place to the Charles. Perhaps Sylvia took a taxi. Or someone gave her a ride. Her killer?

I shudder, then spot a dusky pink Chanel suit, whose proximate value I list before slipping it into a garment bag. Mrs. Manosa nods, and I wipe my perspiring face and proceed to a cocoa Valentino gown and two Jil Sander pantsuits. Several outfits hang with the store tags still on. A sign of planning ahead or compulsive shopping? Or an incentive to lose five pounds?

"May I use a restroom?"

Mrs. Manosa points to Sylvia's bath, and I'm suddenly surrounded by the marble Jacuzzi, three sinks, lavender, linens, Khiel's lotions. Running the cold tap at a high splash with the door closed, I open the medicine cabinet and scan shelves of eyedrops, a razor, floss, a tube of sunscreen. Each shelf shows gaps, as if containers were removed. There's not one expired antibiotic or prescription medicine of any kind. What did she take? Paxil? Zoloft? Xanax? I count six empty slots and close the cabinet.

The clock is running, and Mrs. Manosa waits outside the door, from which a lemon terry robe hangs on an inside hook. I reach to the bulging pocket, find tissues and a lip balm, then lift up the hamper lid to see a mesh bag of soiled hosiery. I flush, wash my hands in the cool water, and emerge with a question about purses or handbags. The housekeeper shows me a drawerful of beaded evening bags.

"Mrs. Manosa, do you have a box for these?"

She slips downstairs to search for one, and I open Sylvia Dempsey's lingerie drawer to find a surprise: a neat stack of pale cotton panties, chaste bras, neutral camisoles and slips. It's as if the era of Victoria's Secret passed Sylvia by. Under the Chanel and Valentino, she wore the lingerie of a nun. A nun in spike heels?

In the next moments, like a dry cleaner, I go through pockets, retrieving hairpins, handkerchiefs, and a few coins, all of which I set aside on the dusty dresser. In the purses are papers, a CVS receipt, a cosmetologist's card, a theater ticket stub, a to-do list, and a note, which I scan in haste: "Just to say I appreciate what you do for me—J." At the sudden sound of Mrs. Manosa's footsteps, I cram these papers into my pocket. I box the purses, complete the appraisal paperwork, and make my way to the front door under Mrs. Manosa's escort.

It's hot and windy as I begin to load my Beetle and hear an engine roar. A huge black Mercedes zooms up fast behind me. The tires spit gravel. Clutching the garment bag, I jump back as the car stops about a foot from my bumper. I catch my breath and watch a slender, bald, dark-suited man get out. He yanks off dark glasses, plants his legs apart, and stares. In his mid-fifties, he's olive-skinned with sloe eyes.

"Dr. Dempsey?" He neither speaks nor nods. His gaze hardens to a stare. "Dr. Bernard Dempsey?"

He slams the Mercedes door and glares in silence. Two fat robins hop nearby, but the glaring gaze does not shift. It intensifies. Awkwardly, I load the car. My mouth is dry, my scalp prickling in the heat. Those eyes lock on my every movement. "I left paperwork with Mrs. Manosa . . ."

My words die in the face of the silent stare. I feel it on my back as I get into my own car and shut the door. I feel it through the back window as I turn the key and nudge the gas. I try to look straight ahead, but the rearview mirror is a summons. In the glass is a statue of a man, taut as a palace guard, his fixed glare beamed at me like twin black lasers. Those eyes follow me all the way back to the city.

Chapter Eighteen

J ust to say I appreciate what you do for me—J."
The card pocketed from Sylvia Dempsey's purse is vellum, the message in blue ballpoint in a crabbed handwriting.

Is J Jordan Wald?

The chill of Dempsey's cold stare lingers, so I'm wearing a sweater as I sit at the kitchen table where I've spread the miscellaneous bits from Sylvia's purses. Technically, this is all the widower Bernard's property. Would he have a ready guess about J's identity?

J for Jordan? The signature letter swings wide with a bold flourish. Perhaps Sylvia worked on his campaign and contributed money and got this thank-you. Perhaps the doctor is also a supporter of Carney-Wald. If so, the card is more protocol than personal.

Then again, it could signal deeper acquaintance.

Suppose, however, the Dempseys were as politically split as their bedrooms. If Wald was a big fish to land for the Garden Alliance program, Sylvia would conceal the effort here at home. The purse might have been a hiding place. Maybe other notes lie in various cracks and crevices of her bedroom. Did the police find them?

Biscuit squeals and yaps at the rap of the door knocker. Stark is due to pick her up, and he appears on the dot of 7:00 p.m. in jeans, a sleeveless navy T-shirt, and sandals with soles that probably started life as snow tires. "Why the sweater, Cutter? You sick?"

"Fighting a chill. Where's the bike?"

"Fatso's in the shop for maintenance. I drove a buddy's pickup." He scoops up Biscuit and roughs her ears. She loves it. "Are you serving coffee, or is your work stoppage still on?"

"Stark, you're getting far too much mileage out of one moody mini-moment. Come on, the galley's open." The three of us troop to the kitchen, and I count the scoops and set out mugs. Biscuit thinks it's a party.

"The Motorcycle Safety Foundation folks tell me they're reviewing your application."

This from my own Mr. Hell's Angel. "Tell them to take their sweet time."

"Gotta get in training, just like the pup." Biscuit obligingly wiggles from head to tail. Stark says, "Sit," and she sits. "Roll over." She rolls. "By the way, I'm extending her program."

"Oh?"

"Gonna take her to Spy Pond, let her swim. I know a guy with a dock. I want to see how she dives."

"Biscuit a diving beagle? I don't like this."

He looks coy. "You know, like dog triathlons. There's extreme sports for dogs. She's a sporting dog."

"Stark, are you mad? She could be injured. Biscuit is a household pet."

"She's an athlete in training. I get her up off your couch."

"She's not allowed on the couch to begin with."

He scratches her white belly and rocks her by her front paws. "I'm building aquatics into her program. She'll learn new skills."

"A tub bath is plenty of aquatics. And SeaWorld doesn't feature diving dogs."

"Don't worry, I treat her right." I can't disagree. The coffeemaker gurgles and sighs. Agitated, I pour two mugs and hand him the big one with the Bruins logo. "You need a program too, Cutter. We'll borrow a bike for you, maybe a V-Star rice burner, but what the hell."

"A rice burner?"

"Made in Japan."

"Stark, that's crude racism."

"It's one biker's patriotism."

"Blind devotion to a motorcycle factory in Milwaukee?"

"Made in USA, that's Harley. Where are these mugs from? China? Pakistan?" He lifts one. "Yeah, China. Used to be America that made stuff. Now they're gutting us like fish."

"Here." I slide the sugar bowl. "Domino. Pure cane sugar made in America."

"With sugar subsidies to fatten the fat cats."

"Hey, what's going on with you?"

"The working stiffs are getting stiffed, that's what. It's taxation without representation. Today the rich bloodsuckers get it all. For everybody else, table scraps." He dumps in his five sugars, stirs, and chugs, then eyes my table. "What's all this stuff?"

"Call it lint from a woman's pocket. I'm learning new life skills—pickpocketing and purse snatching."

"Uh-huh. Who's this J character?"

"I don't know. Really, I don't." Coffee at this time of evening means surefire insomnia. I'll lie awake worrying about the dog, my kids, whether I heard a man murdered in the fog on Dartmouth Street. And of course, the constant: Henry Faiser. "What do you know about handwriting analysis?"

"Camp Lejeune does not teach graphology, Cutter. Marines' handwriting is lead and brass shell casings." Stark leans to read the vellum card. "Very fancy, this J. 'Appreciate what you do for me.' Woowee, you got a secret admirer, Cutter?"

A flush rises from my neck at the thought of a card signed by a certain man traveling in the Middle East. I continue to watch the mail. "This wasn't sent to me," I say. "All the stuff you see here came from donated clothing."

"So it's trash, right?" I nod. "Then how come it's all spread out in order like exhibit A?"

"It's my neatness compulsion."

"Try again, Cutter."

I face him. "Okay, how's this. It's from the pockets and purses of a woman who was bludgeoned to death by the Charles last April."

He blinks. Biscuit whimpers. "The Newton woman?" I am silent. "The one that's all over TV? Is this one of your psychic cop gigs?"

"Yes and no."

"What about the senator's son? What about the black guy in Norfolk?"

"Henry Faiser, he's the main case. This one is . . . related."

He bites his lip. "The Newton woman is connected to the black guy in prison for murder?"

"Not the way you think. In fact, they're actually separate." His eyes narrow, and dark clouds gather across his brow. He'll stay right here until he gets an explanation, knowing Stark. "I'm trying to help a certain detective. He's swamped right now. I'm saving him some time."

"With evidence on your kitchen table? This saves time?"

"In a way, yes, it does."

"The cop knows what you're up to?"

"We have an understanding."

"That's not what I asked, Cutter."

"Maybe it's not your business, Stark. Anyway, I don't need a chaperone. But for what it's worth, I'm on my own on this."

"Seriously?"

"Seriously."

His mug slams down on the countertop. It startles Biscuit, but Stark ignores her. His knuckles are white as foam. "You're dancing with the devil, Cutter. You're scaring me."

I don't answer. Stark reaches for the dog, who bays like a primal hound. I try to laugh, but it catches in my throat.

It's Wednesday morning and still hot. In a twill skirt and checked yellow shirt, I set out on foot for the Eldridge neighborhood, following a wretched sleepless night and the dawn's dead-end effort at "Ticked Off." The items from Sylvia Dempsey's purses are put away in a shoe box. My rib's hot pulsing started up again at sunrise, a prod to action. You might say my rib is my conscience. This morning I'll pound on strangers' doors. Devaney would call it legwork, but he knows nothing about my morning's whereabouts.

Forster Street, which Suitcase Mary named as her former home, is the first side street off Eldridge, the street where sparks and cinders flew through the night sky when the Eldridge houses and the chop shop burned. One block over is Remmer Street, then Sorrington and Werfair, mostly all dilapidated triple-deckers. I want to find out about the properties bought and sold to make way for Eldridge II. I want to know whether conditions are ripe for an arson repeat.

First house is a grimy white clapboard on Forster with a riotous blooming lilac bush in the front yard. Nobody answers the bell. A half dozen yellowed rolled newspapers lie on the porch in sodden lumps, and the house has an empty feeling. Next I knock at a pale gray house with bashed-in aluminum siding. A woman with heavy eyes and teeth like pegs answers and lets out a verbal barrage, which may be Estonian or Kazakh. She gestures with wide sweeps of her arms, but I can't pick up a word.

Across the street, a man in ruby pants and hair like dust tells me that whatever I'm selling, he won't buy it. "Magazines, right? Forget it."

"No, not magazines."

"Whatever. You're in the wrong neighborhood. People are moving out."

"That's what I'd like to talk about."

"Evacuation. We're all refugees. It's an outrage." The door slams shut. I peck on the window glass, but it's futile. If only Biscuit were here with me, my goodwill ambassador. As a social lubricant, she rivals a cooing baby in a carriage.

Three more houses on Forster, and nobody answers.

It's a workday, so it might be smarter to make these rounds in the evening hours. I'm on the next block on Remmer Street when a young woman in a calico skirt with a backpack descends an outside stair and heads toward a Corolla with an Illinois plate. "Miss, may I ask you a question?"

Her expression of midwestern openness reminds me of my years in Chicago. "Sure thing."

"I'm interested in an apartment around here. But I hear people are moving."

"Yeah, it's a shame. They call us tenants at will. Nobody has a lease anymore."

"Why is that?"

"Somebody's been buying the houses. My own landlord sure sold out fast."

"Maybe he got a price he couldn't refuse?"

"Gee, I don't know. He didn't seem happy. I think it's more like take-the-money-and-run. He moved to the South Shore. They say a big development is coming."

"Is the development company buying the houses? Is it the Bevington Partners Group?"

"I don't know. I'm a grad student. I'm moving myself next month. You might talk to this guy who lives on Sorrington—no, on Werfair. Yeah, on Werfair Street, two blocks over. His name's Danny something. He tried to organize a neighborhood association."

"Friends of Eldridge?"

"That's it. He's kind of an activist. I think he's a grad student too." She leans to unlock her car door. "One good thing about everybody leaving: it's easy to get a parking place. Well, good luck."

The third house on the left on Werfair is supposedly Danny Conaway's apartment, according to a woman outside in a flowered robe and slippers whistling for her cat, Peaches. "Peaches! Peaches, come here, kitty kitty! Here, boy!"

There's no sign of tomcat Peaches when the door is opened by a straw-haired, freckled young man in khakis and a plaid shirt desperate for the pass of an iron. He's in his late twenties, barefoot, and looks as though the doorbell woke him up. It's now almost noon. "Danny Conaway?" He nods, rubs his eyes. "I'm Reggie Cutter. I understand you're the head of the Friends of Eldridge."

He yawns. "Friends, yeah. You're too late. It's disbanded."

"Were you the president?"

"No. I hate hierarchy. I'm no hegemon."

"But you were the group leader? Organizer?"

His laugh is dry. "I got up the petitions and called meetings. I went door-to-door and facilitated. Yeah, I put in some time." He scratches a stubbly cheek. "You looking for somebody in particular?"

"I'm scouting an apartment for my daughter. I hear you're the man to see."

He scowls. "Lady, tell your daughter to look someplace else. The wrecking ball's due any day in this neighborhood. It's our own local Big Dig."

"I don't understand."

"This neighborhood is sold out from under. Kiss it good-bye. Tell your daughter."

"These houses are scheduled for demolition?"

"You got it."

"By whom? The city? The state? Is it eminent domain?"

A bitter laugh breaks as he shakes his head. "It's eminent domain, all right. Eminent big money, another crib for rich people. Forget civic action. Forget workers, students, Russian immigrants. We're history. We learned something: the grass roots die when vultures want to eat your liver. Why do you ask? You a civics teacher?"

"I'm a voting citizen. What's going on?"

"They bought off the zoning board and sent undercover errand boys to steal the properties."

"Who's 'they'?"

"Big money. Kleptos. Oligarchs."

"But who?" He shrugs. "And everyone simply sold?"

"They're slick. They sent flacks to front for them. Flacks with checkbooks."

"Agents? Surrogates?"

"Totally. I lived here three years before I caught on. First was this guy from Southie, Irish like me, claimed he was a roofer and doing real well. He bought half a dozen houses. Good cash offers, every one. Then comes a Portuguese fella from Rhode Island, says he's got a big extended family from the Azores and they all want to live in the same neighborhood. Before you know it, he's bought nearly every house on Sorrington. Cash up front. But the Azores people never showed up. We were neutron-bombed but didn't know it. The media wasn't interested. They're in their pod."

"It's hard to believe that every owner was so willing to sell. How many houses on these three streets, about forty?"

"Yeah. There were incentives."

"High offers?"

His laugh is high, bitter. "There's a homeless woman around here who raves about live coals and cinders."

"Suitcase Mary."

"That's her. Some of the old-timers remember a fire before the first Eldridge Place went up. Word got around it could happen here—*would* happen. Big guys showed up with Dobermans and walked up and down at odd hours. A neighborhood guy got mauled. Then a woman on Remmer Street refused to sell. She got killed in a weird accident."

"A car wreck?"

"No, a live power line. She was electrocuted. There was no storm, just the live wire down in front of her house. Nobody knows how or why she touched it. Her daughter sold the house right away. All the holdouts knuckled under fast and took the cash."

"The whole neighborhood was terrorized?"

He looks left and right down the block and lowers his voice. "Nobody said sabotage or death threats, not in so many words. We couldn't pin it down. And hey, I can't get into hearsay. Cross a line, it's a legal mess. We tried to get owners to come forward, go on the record, see a lawyer. Nobody would talk, not even the guy attacked by the Dobermans. Maybe because we're students. Grad students, but students."

"Let me ask about the new buyers. Was one of them named Perk?"

"Perk?" He shakes his head. "No."

"How about Carlo?"

"Carlo? I don't think so."

"The one who claimed to be Portuguese? Did he quote lines from Dante's *Inferno*?"

"No. I'd remember."

"Was there also an Asian man making offers and buying the houses?"

"The Chinese guy, yeah. He showed up right after the Irish and Portuguese. He smiled a lot and tried to sell us cars."

"Steve, Steve Yung."

"That's him. How'd you know? How come you're so interested?" He cocks an eyebrow. "That stuff about your daughter, it's fake, right?"

"Let's say I'm looking into a situation."

He pulls a shirt button. "Look, it's none of my business, but whatever you're thinking, this fight's lost. The neighborhood is finished. But mainly, these guys don't fool around. They have money and tactics. That downed live wire was enough for us. Go up against them, it's not worth it. Try to buck them, one morning they have a live wire ready for you."

I ache to call Devaney but refrain. We haven't spoken since the *Iron Chef* dustup. If I tell him about the door-to-door search, he'll reproach me for amateur adventuring, then promise to "pass along" my information. He'll shove a scribbled note into a pile of papers while the Homicide Division works round the clock on the Dempsey case. No, I won't call, not yet. Instead, I wash up a few dishes, straighten the kitchen, and do my morning free-weight workout and sets for the thighs and calves.

If I'm correct, Steve Yung is Jeffrey Arnot's man, and so were the Irish roofer and the Portuguese too. This makes Arnot's role in the Bevington Partners Group clear: it's land procurement. Whatever the cost of "persuasion," Arnot gets title to properties even if it takes ethnic front men, Dobermans, and a lethal high-voltage wire—or an arsonist's torch thirteen years ago. The houses that Yung and the others bought were doubtless sold immediately to dummy shell companies. No wonder Danny Conaway's Friends of Eldridge couldn't track them down. Ownership lines blur through leasing arrangements, as I well know from Marty's business mantra on outsourcing and externalizing costs and special partnerships. The Bevington Partners Group wouldn't necessarily hold title to the land. No blood on its books.

Did such deals turn Jeffrey Arnot into a high-profile Boston businessman? Did they vault him from women's wrestling and nightclubs to Bevington Partners Group? At what point did death become one cost of doing business. Was it the arson and the accidental death of squatters on Eldridge Street?

If Arnot had ordered B&B Auto and the Eldridge houses torched, was it Carlo who did the dirty work? Why else would the B&B worker turn up as the Eldridge Place night manager? He was probably rewarded for the firestorm of his own making. Big Doc's rant about Carlo and "flames of hell" makes sense in a new way. The incineration of Eldridge Street is the *real* inferno.

But how does this tie in with Peter Wald's murder? The fatal shooting and the fire occurred the same day. Big Doc remembers young Wald; he called him a "pale wanderer" and "child of death." And he acknowledged that Faiser lived in the cult house. What's more, the Tsakis brothers remember Henry hawking jewelry and shoes at B&B Auto, so the young man had access there. The chop shop workers knew him on sight. Does Carlo know anything about the murder? Or Perk?

It's a struggle to calm down long enough for household tasks, making a bed, tossing in a load of laundry. Every minute is a mental strategy session. My thoughts stampede—Henry Faiser, Jeffrey Arnot, Carlo Feggiotti.

I need Detective Frank Devaney. I do. But he's off-limits until the Dempsey furor dies down. On that front, I have a plan. In ten minutes, I'm expecting my neighbor, Trudy Pfaeltz, whose day off from the hospital is crammed with sales pitches for Cutco knives, her newest side business. She wants an hour with me, and I've agreed, mostly to ask this veteran nurse about artificial skin. I'll buy a kitchen knife if I must.

Trudy will make sure I do. She enters the front door like a weather front in cross trainers. I barely have a minute's breezy chat about her parakeet's vocabulary with the new talking-bird seed diet. "The jury's out, Reggie. Kingpin still says 'pretty bird,' but it's weird, his feathers are turning orange. He's healthy but looks like a feathered carrot. Imagine the marketing potential of orange parakeets shipped online. I'm testing ten young birds now, but my kitchen's small. I don't suppose you'd—"

"Raise test parakeets? I'm afraid not, Trudy."

"Then let's get to Cutco. This is a wonderful product." We sit across the table, and Trudy sets down her bundle of cutlery wrapped in red felt and begins to unroll it. "Home sales cuts the middlemen, so the cost benefit is to you, the customer. This is a 440A chrome-molybdenum steel blade, least likely to rust or corrode. It holds a chef-standard edge."

"How much?"

"We'll get to that. As a nurse, I know what 'surgical steel' means. These knives are surgical steel for the home." She shows how a serrated knife cuts a piece of leather. "Imagine that this is the toughest steak." In moments, she snips a penny in half with the demo scissors. I marvel.

"Trudy, sales are your calling in life."

She gives me a frank stare. "Believe me, it's refreshing

to talk to healthy people after what I see every night in the ICU, the oncology floor, the burn unit—"

"That's actually what I want to ask you about."

"Burns?"

"Skin. Artificial skin."

"It's a modern miracle, Reggie. When you've seen what I have . . . the can of spray paint that explodes when the nine-year-old lights a match. I tell you, tissue engineering is amazing stuff."

"But what is it?"

"The 'skin'? Usually, it's a combination of living cells held together with a scaffold of biodegradable plastic or protein, plus chemicals to stimulate growth. It'll be fabulous when they work out the kinks and the business problems. Right now it's business problems holding them back."

"What kind of problems?"

She smooths the red felt and straightens the knives. "I hear about struggles with financing. A couple companies went into Chapter 11. Their sales aren't high enough, plus there's the nightmare of jumping the regulatory hoops. Right now they're just not profitable enough."

"Is Advent Tissue Science one of them?"

"Advent?"

"Here in town, in Cambridge. It's headed by a dermatologist, Bernard Dempsey."

"Dempsey? Oh God, not that guy again."

"Married to Sylvia Dempsey. You've heard about the Sylvia Dempsey case? It's all over the media."

Trudy blushes. "Reggie, with my schedule, days pass without a newspaper or glance at TV. Sitcom reruns, maybe a *Globe* that's left in a lounge. I go for the latest on the Sox or Patriots. But, God, I haven't thought about Bernard Dempsey in years."

"How many?"

She shrugs. "He was a researcher at a hospital where I worked right out of nursing school, St. Clement's. I remember his creepy dark eyes, but he was a hotshot. He patented an acne cream and supposedly had the cure for eczema. He published a ton of papers, but the data were cooked. He pressured a lab technician to alter the notes. He resigned, and the technician got fired. She got prosecuted. He got off, mostly because the docs protect their own. I heard he went to another lab, charmed everybody, and got in more trouble. He's a major sleaze. No, a crook."

Trudy picks up a knife and tests the edge. "I wouldn't ordinarily say this much, but the lab technician was a friend of mine at the time. He groped her, threatened to get her visa canceled, made her life miserable. She took the rap for him. She'll be paying off her fine until her last day on earth. It doesn't surprise me that Dempsey's in the thick of the artificial skin business. The man smells money. Whichever companies make it big, I hope his goes down the toilet."

She stands. "Hey, I'm due at another sales call. How about the Homemaker Plus Eight Set."

"Trudy, my homemaker days are over. I'll take the scissors and spend lonely Saturday nights slicing pennies."

"Better pennies than anything connected with Dempsey. Stay away from him. Whatever the deal is with his wife, he'll get off free. She'll pay the price."

Chapter Nineteen

Devaney phones on Tuesday afternoon, his voice brusque and blunt. "Reggie, can you come downtown to the federal courthouse? There's somebody you want to meet."

"Who?" Bernard Dempsey is on my mind. Could it be?

"Get here by four. Come around the back. Look for me."

I drop everything, grab my purse and keys. The traffic snarls on Milk Street, and I feel like Devaney's gofer. There's no place to park on the courthouse block, so I stow the Beetle in a pricey garage and hoof it.

Platoons of briefcases swarm the gray granite courthouse, and bicycle messengers weave in and out. At the rear, a FedEx truck idles and five motorcycle police sit with radios crackling. Where is Devaney? Why am I here?

Then I see him by the curb. In a blue suit and loud green tie, he signals to me with a quick hand gesture. He's by himself near a state police car with dark windows. Who is it he wants me to meet? "Frank, what's up?"

"Tune in to your psychic channel, Reggie. This is not by the book. The troopers are doing me a favor."

"What is it?"

He steps close, his voice low. "They're transporting a prisoner who testified in a trial today. You're gonna meet the prisoner."

"Who is it?"

"You'll check your sixth-sense message, okay? Any visual pictures, be alert. They're gonna open the front door and let you inside for a minute. The prisoner's in back. He's cuffed. You'll have just a minute or two. Make the most of it. They're taking him back to Norfolk."

"MCI Norfolk. It's Henry Faiser."

"It is."

There's no time for questions. At Devaney's signal, the front passenger door is opened from within. I see a trooper's flat hat brim and hefty hand with a signet ring with the Massachusetts state seal, the Indian and symbolic stars. Then I'm inside next to the trooper, who smells like Polo aftershave. I twist around to look through a steel mesh grille. In the backseat between two more uniformed troopers sits—

"Henry Faiser?"

"Yeah."

The liquid-eyed youth in the snapshot that Kia showed me is long gone. The slender, smiling boy with short hair has given way to a saturnine man who's dwarfed by his prison blue denims. His thin frame is hunched yet angular, a stick figure wedged between two uniforms. His face looks sallow, his dark hands and wrists spotted with red welts, which he rubs as if the handcuffs are a Chinese nail puzzle to be uncoupled. What do I say?

"My name is Reggie Cutter. Detective Devaney told me about you."

"Uh-huh."

"I met your sisters. I met both of them. And your niece and nephew too."

"Uh-huh."

"And I heard Big Doc preach." He says nothing, looks at his wrists. I feel no psychic currents, hear no message, visualize no image. "I know you lived in his house on Eldridge Street. I spend some time on Eldridge myself. Does Big Doc ever visit you?"

He rubs the steel cuffs at his wrists as if it's occupational therapy. "Big Doc, no, he don't come out."

"Or others from the house?" Maybe he'll name someone. He shakes his head no.

The trooper who's driving taps the car key, which is my signal to get going. Mere seconds remain. There's no way to touch Henry Faiser, and I feel no vibe. My rib is quiet, and my thumb too.

All I'm getting from Henry Faiser is a blank stare.

"A lead doesn't have to be psychic, Frank." I press the point. The police car is gone. Devaney and I linger at Courthouse Square by a curbside vendor in a quilted truck as homebound office workers swirl to the T stop. "The Carlo connection—Frank, this is hot as fire."

"You want a soda, Reggie? Let me buy you a cold soda. Make it two Sprites." He doesn't hear me because he's sulking. His huge gamble did not pay off, and now he's embarrassed and owes the troopers. *Men.* "Frank, the paranormal is not a teleconference, for godsake. You know that."

"Straw?"

"Will you listen to me? Carlo Feggiotti worked in the chop shop that burned to the ground the day Peter Wald was shot. He's now a night manager at Eldridge Place. The Greek grocers in my neighborhood remember him because he sold them a stolen car. I suspect Carlo torched the shop on someone's orders. I think it's a good bet that he witnessed the shooting of Peter Wald or knows someone who did. He could testify."

Devaney pops the Sprite, takes a long pull, stifles a burp. "Reggie, do you believe in rehabilitation?" This is classic Devaney, out of left field. Wherever he's going with this, I want to scream. "You believe in paying your debt to society?"

I could strangle the man. Instead, I open the soda can, insert the straw, fiercely sip. "Of course."

"Then you need to know that Feggiotti was convicted as an accomplice in vehicle theft. He'd served thirteen months when his conviction was overturned on appeal. He was released. The Eldridge contractors hired him when the high-rise went up, and he did so good the company put him on the management payroll. He's a model employee."

"I suppose he coaches Little League."

"Soccer."

I could bite the man. "Don't fool yourself, Reggie. Faiser's a sick man but also a hustler. Feggiotti has no other criminal record, but Faiser had a long rap sheet. He could be in for any number of offenses besides murder."

"And free by now."

"Or back in for something else."

"Tough talk, Frank. I thought Faiser was on your conscience. I thought justice and morality were the point of all this."

"Handling the case right, that's the point. Do it right, you sleep at night. The system takes it from there. I'm just saying, don't get sentimental. Where're you parked?"

"In a platinum garage that's costing me a fortune to argue with you."

"Here." He holds out two limp fives. I refuse them, turn on my heel, and walk off in a huff.

It's after six when Meg phones, her voice sounding chipper and tense. I've just finished a hard-boiled egg and a glass of merlot just this side of salad vinegar. Meg and I haven't spoken since our tiff, and I'm glad to hear from her, glad for distraction from Devaney. "How's the Red Hat sister?"

"On that score, terrific. I just found the prettiest cherry-red straw for the season, in Filene's Basement no less, a fabulous bargain. I'm shopping for a hatbox for the overhead compartment because this chapeau is going to the Red Hat convention. Reggie, no hard feelings, okay?"

"Meg, let's schedule lunch. My treat."

"Good deal. But are you free this evening? It's not an innocent question. Tania wants you."

Wants me—like a bossy recruiting poster that pokes its finger at my eye. "Sorry, Meg. I'm settled in."

"Reggie, don't make me beg. Tania's out of her mind. I swear the woman's bipolar. Workmen doing duct work in the Marlborough attic found a piece of old cloth stuck in the rafters."

"So what?"

"So it's like she's found the Shroud of Turin. Tania thinks the cloth is so old you can do your psychic thing. She says it dates from the 1800s. She had a textile expert examine it."

"Forget it, Meg. I turned in my book report on Marlborough. And I already made a try at a psychic reading today. You can tell Tania it was a total flop. Besides, I'm persona non grata to her husband. He banned me from the property."

"I know. But Jeffrey's out of town."

"That's no comfort."

"Tell me about it, Reggie." Meg pauses. Her shallow breath is audible. "I try to keep my problems to myself. Everybody's got their burdens to bear. But Jeffrey Arnot's a one-off. He threatened to kill a deal of mine if I couldn't rein in his wife." Her voice is grave. "Really threatened, Reggie. I can't laugh it off."

"Meg, please don't put me in this position."

"Reggie, I'm a workingwoman. I have to pay my bills. Arnot holds me accountable for the Marlborough house. He thinks Tania's hysteria is my fault. If you'd just stop by and hold the cloth in your hand and say . . . say the trail is cold or you feel a ghost or it's going to rain cats and dogs. It doesn't matter what. I can't rile Jeffrey Arnot with this deal of mine pending. This is the last favor I'll ask on this, promise, cross my heart."

"Meg—" I start to refuse. If I set foot in the Marlborough house, Tania is certain to tell her husband. In pique or passion, she'll tell because she's incapable of *not* telling. And there will be consequences. Suppose I'm summoned to the limo, that lair, and subjected to Jeffrey's harangue, my slice of the Boston cream pie slammed in my face?

Would he stop there? What could he do if he knew I'd been to the Brighton Auto Mart and the Eldridge II streets? "Meg, I—" From my window, the charming gas lights of Barlow Square glow a greenish yellow.

Electrical power lines aren't visible, but suppose my house were the site of a gas explosion? Regina Cutter could be the sole casualty of a freak "accident." A downed wire, a burst gas pipe—if only Meg hadn't asked this favor.

Yet I voluntarily walked the walk in the Eldridge neighborhood and felt my rib burn at the bone-white birches where I'm sure Peter Wald died. I snooped and talked to Carlo and went to the Brighton Auto Mart. No one made me do these things. Sometimes a woman must step out.

Is this my moment? I find myself yielding, seeing new possibilities in the chance to speak with Tania alone. If I can cut through the glitz, she might—just might—talk about Jeffrey, his deals, his partners, especially his past. A private one-on-one with her might forge that link to Carlo. I could learn more about Carlo's link to Faiser, then confront Devaney and press the issue of a possible witness to the shooting of Peter Wald. Maybe it's a long shot to the Henry Faiser innocence project, but I'm in no position to pass it by. The image of Henry chafing his cuffed wrists is too vivid in my mind. The red welts on his hands are a symptom of his hepatitis. The man is a wraith. He needs care. If innocent, he needs to get out of there to stay alive.

My watch says 6:23 p.m., June 11. It's worth recording because it marks the risk involved. There's that certain moment when the light changes, a chill wind blows, and the season suddenly shifts. Or the makeup mirror shows a new facial line, and you're up a notch on life's cycle. This is one such instant. It's not just for fun but for keeps. It's not a hobby I can exit and leave to the pros. I'm too far in it for that. This is a moment when a woman realizes she's got to go deeper than she thought.

It's a humid, drab evening, and the fading daylight gives the Marlborough house an ocher cast. If Tania is indeed alone, she hasn't turned on the lights. I'm thinking one hour in and out. I'll be back home before dark. From the sidewalk, the white limo is nowhere in sight, not that Arnot could park it out front. His absence is crucial, my act of faith.

Here's my plan—first, to hold the rafter fabric and close my eyes as if communing with the cosmos, then to deliver the message in a radio-play voice echoing the history of the house. "Through time's generations," I'll say, "the cloth conveys to me a certain feeling of sadness, or in French, *tristesse.*"

I'll emphasize Edmund Wight's yearning through worlds of spirit and matter. To add heft and a woman's twist, I'll bring in the architect Dehmer: "Both of the gentlemen's spirits are upset that the rightful mistress, Clara Eddington, did not take her place in residence." Here's my message: that Tania must be patient with the spirits and trust they will recognize her as the rightful lady of the house.

She'll buy it. At that point, I'll segue to Jeffrey, then Carlo. I'll pace it, frame it in psychic terms.

I climb the stairs, but before I ring, the door opens just wide enough, and Tania peers from the door frame. She's watched me approach from a window. "Mrs. Arnot . . . Tania, good evening."

She stands sideways, as though the door is her shield. I manage to step inside. No lamps glow, and the recessed system is not switched on. "I understand Mr. Arnot is out this evening."

She doesn't respond. The furniture casts dark shadows, and Tania herself is shadowy, all in black from the neck down, with little makeup and no jewelry. Her hair is piled up and pinned, but loose strands have fallen across her temples like cobwebs. Her cheeks look hollow, her eyes restless. Along the jawline—is that a bruise?

"Is there anything you'll need for the psychic experience? My household staff have been sent out for the evening. It's true, Jeffrey is away." Minus the breathy Zsa Zsa glamour, Tania's voice is as flat as her appearance. Her feet are bare. The house feels muggy, and Tania's face glistens with a patina of sweat. The blades of the chandelier glimmer, the suspension wires like filaments of a spiderweb. "I could close all the shutters if you think there's too much light. How about music? Do you need music?"

"Oh no. I mean, music isn't necessary and the light will do."

"Come this way. Follow me." She gives the chandelier a wide berth. "Jeffrey says it's cowardly if you don't walk under this thing."

"The chandelier?"

"I want to have it tested. I'm afraid it could fall and kill somebody. He just laughs it off. In here. The casket is in the reception room."

My God, a casket, as if it's a funeral. Tania's black silk trousers hiss as I circle around the chandelier and follow her past a staircase with a newel-post carved into a dragon's head. Avoiding the wall-mounted breastplate, I nearly trip on a jamb. It's too much like that terrible night here with Meg, even the sandalwood vapors. Why isn't

the central air cranked to cool? The room needs oxygen.
We enter a small side room with an ornate mantel and
plaster rosettes. On a side table is a small carved box.

"Here it is, the casket. Why do you smile?"

"I'm sorry. I misunderstood casket."

"It's eighteenth-century French chestnut. The fabric is
inside, Regina, for your clairvoyant touch."

"First, would you tell me about this cloth?"

"Workmen found it. They brought it to me. I summoned an expert from the Merrimack Valley Textile Museum. It is vigogne, a neutral-colored wool in a twill
weave and authentic to the period of our home. The textile expert thinks it most probably a remnant of a winter
outergarment. Don't expect a sumptuous fabric. It has
succumbed to the ravages of time and, yes, insects. Whatever its secrets, you must unlock them. I've lost so much,
my beautiful things, my peace of mind." She puts a hand
to her forehead and wipes the perspiration just as another
strand of hair falls. She seems oblivious. That jawline
darkness—definitely a bruise. Why no shoes? She asks,
"Are you ready?"

"Yes, I am."

"You will touch the fabric and . . . report to me."

"I'll describe whatever paranormal experience I might
have, especially in connection with the origins of your
home. Did you read my research report on the first owner,
Edmund Wight? And the architect, Charles Dehmer?"

"I think I remember . . . so many names these days.
There's too much to think about. My mind gets crowded."
She stands close, and I see her dilated pupils. Is it the lack
of light, or is Tania drugged?

"You're ready?" I ask her.

"I am."

The little chestnut box hinges creak, and I reach in and pull out a piece of woven cloth. It's dull, stiff, and filthy. I hold it away from my kelly-green light jacket and promise myself a bar of Dial when this is done. The cloth is about the size of a handkerchief and full of holes chewed by generations of ancestral moths.

It's pitiful, worse than a rag. But yet here's a button. Tania said nothing about the button, which looks like ivory. I want to ask what the textile expert said about it. Yet my script has no room for a button.

Tania stands with arms at her sides, waiting for the secrets. "Through time's generations," I say, "the cloth conveys to me a certain feeling of sadness, or in French, *tristesse*. Through spirit and matter—"

Listening, Tania is still as a post. I'm about to bring in Edmund Wight, but just as I say his name, a crystal shiver starts across my sight line, like breaking glass. No, ice. It's frost on a windowpane. It's a sky filled with ice crystals. The whole sky—

"Regina, are you all right?"

"Mr. Edmund Wight," I begin. The air is turning cool, then cold. I grip the cloth with both hands as drafts chill my ankles, my neck.

"Regina, are you shivering?"

It's not air-conditioning. This cold is different. It comes from the cloth; it's blasting from it and swirling into something white.

"What is it, Regina?"

"White. It's something white."

She clutches her throat. "The limo. Jeffrey's limousine."

"Where? Coming back? Is he here?"

"He talks about you. Yesterday he said you're too

close. You're on his mind. He made me promise." Her voice comes from the bottom of a well.

"Promise what?"

"Not to do this."

My heart thuds. The whiteout swirls—a cold premonition of Jeffrey Arnot? Is he about to burst through the door? Yes or no, I can't move. I'm surrounded by a thick whiteness that blows and blinds me.

"I promised Jeffrey. But the plates ... and my Lalique mirror in pieces."

It's like a blizzard. I see no shape, no form. Every cell in my body is chilled. I'm cold to the very core. Tania raises her arm to wipe sweat from her face. She's next to me but miles from me. She's in summer heat, yet a foot from where she stands, I stand naked in a winter blast of arctic cold.

Chapter Twenty

So, Mom, you're okay, right?"

I grip the phone and try to sound jaunty. "Molly, I assure you I am free of frostbite." I know this tone. Upset as I am, I recognize my daughter's genuine concern, which is undershot with angst about the possible chore of nursing an ailing mother. "Nothing bad happened, Mol. I left quickly. I didn't see the husband. I came right back home here."

"Maybe you have myxedema?"

"Never heard of it."

"People who are perpetually cold. They wear coats all year round. It's an endocrine disorder."

"I am not perpetually cold. It was just this once." Bringing up last evening's episode with my daughter is a mistake, though Jo talked with her about so many things, and Molly has her own psychic side too. "Mol, I only wondered whether you'd ever had a similar kind of vision. Or maybe Jo reported something like it?"

"No, Aunt Jo never said anything about psychic cold spells. Maybe it was a summer virus you were fighting off."

"Maybe so." Let it go. Change the subject. Try not to blame yourself for mission failure, Reggie. Regain your balance and recoup. Maybe Meg could set up something with just Tania and me, a café or a walk in the Public Garden where we could talk and I could probe about Jeffrey. "How's the exhibit coming? How's Barbie?"

"Great. She's talking dirty to G.I. Joe about anthrax spores."

"Oh, Molly." And to think of my mink, the sacrificial fur.

"The opening will be totally fab, Mom. You'll love it. We'll serve pink champagne, twenty bucks a case, and it's even drinkable. What's on your agenda today? I think you should stay home and rest."

"Sounds sensible."

"Promise you'll rest. I'll e-mail Jack to tell him you're taking it easy." We say bye. My daughter thinks she's tucked me in. Think again, dear.

Half an hour later, I'm Googling "psychic" and "ice" when Devaney calls. He sounds a bit sheepish. "How's life, Reggie?"

"One of the best, Frank, one of the best."

"I want to apologize for that courthouse business. I sprung it on you."

"Let's call it bygones. Tell me this: did Henry Faiser get back to Norfolk okay?" He says yes. "It was shocking to see him, wasn't it, Frank? He looks terrible, so thin and sick, wasting away. And weakened, of course, by the hepatitis. He must weigh heavily on your conscience. Do you sleep at night?"

"Don't bait me, Reggie."

"Whatever do you mean?"

"And don't play dumb. I get the message. I'm doing what I can. Anyway, I got tied up right after you left."

"With the Dempsey case? With round-the-clock Sylvia?"

"Okay, rub it in, Reggie. Bull's-eye to the gut." I remain silent. He clears his throat. "Actually, this is about the night you heard the scuffle in the fog. We're questioning a guy that went to high school with the caterer, and that's why I'm calling. It looks like Alan Tegier was nowhere near the Back Bay the night he died. He was seen at a pool hall in Southie around nine o'clock. If this checks out, you can set your mind at rest on that score. Whatever you heard on the street was probably just a scuffle. You take it easy now."

Dismissed again and consigned to a rocking chair.

I'm due at StyleSmart because an expert is coming to consult about seasonal storage for the designer clothing, including Sylvia's. Nicole is worried about theft, fading, and vermin. Next autumn's auction is slated to be a major fund-raiser, and StyleSmart needs to protect its capital.

So I spend the morning with Nicole and a bleached-blond young man who represents a climate-controlled vault that will give StyleSmart a deep discount for summer storage. We survey the "boutique" inventory as he tsk-tsks about our hangers and cramped quarters. You might call this my second day of Operation Fabric, but wrenching because I find myself the docent for Sylvia Dempsey's wardrobe.

"Here's the authentic Jil Sander," I manage to say evenly to the young man as we examine the designer racks.

"Before her hiatus with Prada. Excellent."

"And here, of course, the classic."

"Coco." He fingers the sleeve of Sylvia's deep pink Chanel jacket and says, "Priceless."

"Not exactly."

"I beg your pardon?"

"She paid the ultimate price. I mean, the suit will do well at our auction."

"But only with proper, professional preservation."

"Indeed."

He finally exits. We promise to call.

Nicole says, " 'Thou clothest thyself with crimson' in vain."

"What a snot, acting as though we're Dumpster divers."

"But it's a good price for storage, Reggie. This is business. We better sign up." I agree. I gather my purse and keys. Nicole walks me to the door. "Reggie, it's none of my business, but is something going on?"

"Why?" I face her furrowing brows, the expression of concern in her eyes. "Nicole, you look as though a test came back positive."

"Reggie, I spent years in social work. You know my heart was with the folks in the neighborhoods. I have contacts. I hear stuff."

"What stuff?"

"Your name came up. Somebody says you're asking questions."

"What kind of questions?"

"Around town, in different places. Some feel like you need to mind your own business. Some feel you're out of your zone. There's folks that play real rough. Watch yourself, Reggie. You hear me? Watch yourself."

Of course, I'm watching myself. I'm also watching the calendar. June is ticking away, and Meg has not yet scored a private meeting with Tania for me. But I have another idea. The Arnots host numerous events, and caterers start work in the Marlborough house hours before a scheduled event begins. Caterers have ears. They have memories. Maybe Carlo has been inside the house, or a conversation about him has been overheard.

Can I open a memory bank? For Henry Faiser, I've got to try. Devaney dismissed the Faiser-Carlo link, but I want to know more. That catering company at the Wald-Carney fund-raiser . . . the servers' pocket stitching said "Ambrosia." The nameplate of the woman who offered me an aspirin and swept up the shattered Limoges—was it Linda? No, it was Brenda.

Ambrosia's company policy, as it turns out, prohibits the disclosure of employee names. "Oh, of course, how silly of me." Breathless and effusive, I make my pitch to the stonewalling receptionist. "You see, I'm calling on behalf of my aunt, a dear soul up in years. She's convinced that your employee Brenda is the granddaughter of a close but deceased friend. My aunt, you see, attended a political fund-raiser at the Arnot home on Marlborough Street on the twenty-seventh of last month. Ambrosia catered it, and Aunt Jo has become, well, almost obsessed. She's in frail health. Could you give it a try?"

The moment teeters, but the woman finally reports three Brendas. "I'm not positive, and I'm not supposed to do this. We use contract workers. No one is full-time." She then gives me phone numbers. "These aren't necessarily current. Good luck with your aunt."

The first Brenda hasn't worked for Ambrosia since last fall. Number two runs a movie concession stand and is surprised to hear her name's still on the company roster. Brenda number three, Brenda Holstetter, isn't home. A thin male voice thinks she may have today's lunch shift.

"At an Ambrosia event?"

"At the Renaissance. Downtown."

The Renaissance restaurant is off Stuart Street in the theater district, its interior dark with yellowish sconces, possibly cozy in winter but drab in June. I request a lunch table at Brenda's station, hoping this hairsbreadth connection isn't a dead end.

At Brenda's name, thank heaven, the hostess leads me to a table against a side wall.

"Good afternoon." In knee breeches, a brocade vest, and velvet tam stands the woman who offered me an aspirin at the Marlborough house fund-raiser. She recites the specials, and I order the Elizabethan salad, a mix of greens and "hand-carved" croutons, then force myself to eat slowly, shoving aside the jaw-breaker croutons. I sip a cup of coffee until the 2:00 p.m. lunch closing, then leave a hefty tip.

"Thank you so much."

"Brenda, you don't remember me, but we met briefly last month. I'm Reggie Cutter. Could we talk for a few minutes when your shift ends? I'd like to ask a couple of questions about someone you might know."

"Who is it?"

"Let's wait till you're off, okay?" With a shrug, she agrees, and at 2:15 we slip across the street to a deli, which smells of pickles. "At least it's not meat. I'm a vegetarian. The meat smell gets in my hair, as bad as cigarettes." She orders herbal tea. I have coffee. She's in jeans and a T-shirt and sets down a tote bag. "Your uniform?"

"We have to buy them. Management thinks they're good for business."

"And are they?"

She brushes back her auburn hair. "Theme park costumes are a sure sign a restaurant is going downhill. I give the Renaissance another eight months. I'm looking, but jobs are tight. They could replace me in five minutes. I have to hang on for now." Brenda, I see, is not so young. Lines etch her mouth and eyes. "A job's a job," she says. "So what's going on?"

"Brenda, you and I met at a Back Bay political fund-raiser last month. It was on Marlborough Street. Ambrosia catered it."

"Oh yeah, that big dark stone house, right? With the chandelier made out of swords?"

"That's it."

She laughs. "We dare each other to walk under it. Nobody will. It sort of clicks sometimes, like it's going to fall. Those wires are so thin. And the drafts too . . . those cold-air blasts. There must be some problem with their heat or AC. I always wear extra layers."

"How about the noises?"

"What noises?"

"Slamming? Banging? No? Never mind. I understand the owners host many parties."

"Campaign years are great. I've worked five or six receptions in that one house. No offense, but I don't remember you in particular."

"You offered me an aspirin. And you swept up some broken china."

"Those plates that fell off the mantel, the rare plates? Talk about Humpty-Dumpty. And the house got freezing cold that night." She sips her tea. "Good thing none of our crew crashed the plates. Look, I've got about fifteen minutes. I got another job to get to. What's on your mind?"

"Someone you might have seen or known about while working in the house. It's about an insurance claim."

"I hate insurance companies. They screw you right and left."

"It's for an individual I'm trying to help. I can pay you for your time."

She pokes at the teabag. "We sign a client confidentiality sheet. Ambrosia bonds us."

I slip a ten from my purse and lay it on the table. Talk may be cheap, but Henry Faiser is costing me. "I'll say a name, and you could nod if it rings a bell. The name is Carlo. Carlo Feggiotti." She shakes her head. "He has a flattop, dark-complexioned."

"Nobody I can think of."

"He quotes poetry and chews bubble gum. The poet is Dante. No? You're sure? Then how about this name— Perk?"

"Perk's a man? What's he look like?"

"I don't know. I've only heard the name."

"Nope. Sorry, I can't help you."

"Take the ten dollars anyhow. Maybe if you could give me a name or two of coworkers who've worked at the Marlborough house, and phone numbers?"

"Can't do it."

"Just one?"

"I don't even know last names. The crews are always different, and there's a lot of turnover. The pocket name tags, we need them for each other." She blows to cool the hot tea. "I've worked Ambrosia events for four years, and I can count on one hand the crew I know. Some of us saw each other a couple weeks ago at a memorial service. It was like a reunion for a few of us." She pauses. "Poor Al . . ."

"Al? Al who?"

"He always worked the bar."

"At Marlborough?"

"Beacon Hill and Back Bay events. Wherever. Sure, Marlborough too."

"His last name . . . what's the last name?"

"He had one crazy fifties haircut, but he was a pro."

"Al? With a pompadour?"

"Yeah."

Could it be Alan Tegier? "You say he worked with you at the Marlborough house?"

"Sometimes." She looks past my shoulder. "His family had his photograph at the service. They played doo-wop records. He loved that." She looks back at me. "How'd you know about his hair? Just a good guess?"

"Maybe I'm psychic. Al's last name . . . what is it?"

"No last names. Why do you want to know all this?"

"Did everyone call him Al?"

"Al or Alan. Why?" Her sideways glance is pure suspicion. She swirls her tea and drinks. "He worked different jobs, like most of us. Knock yourself out, you still don't get ahead. He was saving for a car. He had his eye on a red Mustang."

"When was the last time you saw him?"

"Late April, early May. What's this about?"

"His last name, won't you tell me?"

"What do you want to know for?"

"How did he die?"

She reaches for the tote. "I gotta go."

"Is it Tegier? Is it Alan Tegier?"

But Brenda Holstetter grabs the tote and dashes for the door. I try to follow, but she's too fast. Outside, she disappears. I look up and down the block, but she's gone. Back inside the deli, my ten-dollar bill lies in a pool of spilled tea.

Chapter Twenty-one

Woburn, pronounced *woo-burn*, is best known for the John Travolta movie *Civil Action*. He played a lawyer who sues a chemical company that has polluted Woburn's drinking water and has given its children cancer. It's *Erin Brockovich* without Erin.

Woburn is also the hometown of the late Alan Tegier, and thus my immediate destination. It's a long shot, but if Pompadour Al is Alan Tegier, he might have told his family something about Marlborough and Carlo. Something I can use with Devaney to steer him to Henry Faiser.

Stark insists that we take the Harley. "We'll take Biscuit. I've improved the harness. We'll stop at Fresh Pond on the way back so you can see her new flying-leap dive."

"Stark, don't tease me. I have things on my mind."

"So do I, Cutter. What time do you want to go?"

"Immediately."

"We're gonna hit rush hour."

"So be it."

"Get out your brain bucket."

This is bikerese for helmet. I have not told him that my

purpose is a drop-in visit to the Tegier family, whose address I got off the Net.

The Fat Boy roars to my curb at 4:11 p.m., and the harnessed Biscuit warms my heart with her furry full-body ecstasy of wiggles and yelps, clearly happiest with both of her custodial "parents." On the touchy subject of the motorcycle harness, I cave in like a reluctant mother—"just this once." Stark wears jeans and lightweight leather. I am in a linen-silk-blend pantsuit, which Stark warns isn't warm enough.

He's right. I'm shivering as we pull onto Fordyce Street, a block of modest brick bungalows in Woburn. I have gambled that showing up unannounced is my best bet. Stark says he'll exercise Biscuit and pick me up in an hour. He lingers at the end of the block, watching as I knock at 653 Fordyce. A woman opens the door with the chain lock on, and one blue eye surveys me from a lined face framed by strawberry-blond hair held in a banana clip.

"Yes?"

"Mrs. Tegier? I'm Regina Cutter. I'm helping the Boston police. If you're Alan's mother, I'd like to talk with you." The eye blinks and squints. "I'm not selling anything," I say. "I'm helping a Boston police detective trace your son's whereabouts the night he died." It's cheap of me to add this, but "I have a son in his twenties. Believe me, I wouldn't come to your door otherwise."

The chain bolt slides. I'm in. The room smells of pine cleaner. I stifle a sneeze. "Sit anywhere. I'm Alma." It's a small living room dwarfed by the overstuffed blue sofa and matching chairs. I sit across from a sofa wall covered with decorative crosses, Maltese, Latin, Celtic. Somewhere a sound system plays marching band music. "I was just mopping the kitchen." Alma Tegier gestures toward her rolled jeans and shirt knotted at the navel, then turns on a lamp and calls out, "It's okay, Franzie. I'll deal with this."

Franzie, a slim-hipped twenty-something with brunet ponytail, nods from the dining room, her bare arms reaching and grabbing to box up items on the dining table, which is set up like a home factory. She moves in rhythm to John Philip Sousa's "Stars and Stripes Forever."

"We buried Alan. He's at rest. I'm his stepmother, but I raised him and Franzie like my own. Their mother passed away when they were babies. My husband was a widower." I force myself to meet the gaze of this woman whose eyes are like stones, her voice metallic. "The police were here three—no, four times. If they'd paid attention when first he went missing . . ."

"On May third."

"They brush you off. They don't take you serious until it's too late." She meets my gaze. "You got the date right, the third of May. He did not have one enemy in the world, our Alan. He was a hardworking, good boy. Maybe if he went in the navy like his dad. It's all hindsight."

"I understand he worked for a caterer."

"And cleaned carpets. He had two, three jobs the way people do nowadays. I begged him to take a vacation. He worked with Franzie assembling the kits too."

"Sewing kits?"

"First aid, needlework, headphones, whatever they bring her. She makes a dime a kit. On a good day, she boxes six hundred. The march music keeps her speed up. They come pick up the kits twice a week. It's a job, if they don't move it to China."

The piccolo trills, the cornets speak. "Mrs. Tegier, I

know you've answered many questions about Alan. I'm hoping to learn something the police might have missed so far."

"I told them over and over, he got a ride to the Arlington T stop and went from there to his five o'clock job, a cocktail party somewhere in the Back Bay. He wore his bartender outfit, the white shirt, black pants, and cummerbund. He said he'd get a ride back or else take the T to Arlington and call for a ride. He never called, and he never made it back."

"What time did you expect him?"

"We never knew for sure. Sometimes he worked a night shift cleaning carpets. Or he'd go on to another caterer job if they were shorthanded."

"At Ambrosia?"

"Or Fife's or Holiday's. But Ambrosia, they're big. Alan liked the work. He called his corkscrew his six-shooter. 'Got my trusty six-shooter,' he'd say."

With eyes filming, she reclips her hair. "When he started out, I knew every address where he worked, State Street, Washington Street, Alewife Brook Parkway . . . I got out the atlas. I always knew."

"Mrs. Tegier, did Alan ever work at a house on Marlborough Street?"

"Like the cigarettes?"

"Same name. Did he ever mention working there?"

She lowers her head, shakes it, and mumbles. "I always knew at first. But he was a man, he wanted to come and go on his own. So he did." I wait while she dabs her eyes.

"Did he ever talk about a Back Bay house with a custom chandelier made of old swords?"

"No."

"The owners, he's black and she's white. Maybe you remember anything he said about their house? Any conversations?" She pauses, shakes her head again. "Did he ever mention a Carlo or Perk? No? When a job was done, did he usually leave alone? Did he walk by himself?" She says she doesn't know. "Did he have a friend or acquaintance in the Back Bay, anyone he might visit after work near Dartmouth Street?"

"Nobody we know. The police asked us all that."

"Did he ever mention working in a house that got cold or drafty? Sudden drafts?" Once again she shakes her head no. "I understand a high school friend has come forward to tell the police that he saw Alan at a pool hall in South Boston on the night he disappeared."

She scoffs. "That's Rudy Cavitch. What's the word when they show off to get attention?"

"An exhibitionist?"

"That's it. Rudy's a sweet kid but completely nuts. He tells whoppers. He'll say anything to get attention. In high school, nobody believed a word he said. The Woburn police know all about him. The Bostons, they'll learn." The sofa wall of crosses catches my eye. "That's my collection," she says. "Only crosses, no crucifixes. I like how they look. They're from all over the world, Malaysia, Korea, Ireland. It wasn't for religion. I mean, at first it was just a hobby, until Alan—"

I nod. "So you have no reason to think anyone would want to harm your son?"

"No, nothing. You raise them. You do what you can. My husband served on navy frigates, and I had the kids and their problems, Franzie's boyfriends, Alan with his skin when it was so bad. I can show you 'before' and 'after.'"

At least I owe Alma Tegier this moment of reverie. She goes to the far side of the room and pulls down framed photos. "Here's Alan at high school graduation." I look at a sharp-faced boy, eyes lowered, his chest in the commencement robe and his mortarboard at a rakish angle to show his pompadour. His face is covered with blemishes.

"It was deep acne. It was on his neck and chest. They had him on tetracycline, but it didn't really help. They tried to cover it with makeup. He was shy, it made him miserable. Now look."

She swaps picture frames to show the new Alan, flirting with the camera lens and sporting a thin mustache. In the background, a Christmas tree twinkles. His complexion is entirely clear. "My husband took this last December. It was a good Christmas. That's what I tell myself, we had good times, and Alan had a good, worthwhile life. He had friends, a loving family. He was saving for a car. He had a thing for Mustangs. Mustangs and doo-wop music. We put a model Mustang in his Christmas stocking. This last year he found a doctor to help him. I mean, if it wasn't for Dr. Dempsey—"

"Dempsey? Bernard Dempsey?"

"You know him? Of course you do, he's famous. Oh, the tragedy that's happened to him with his wife . . . we sent a card."

With both hands planted in my lap, I force my voice low and steady. "Dr. Dempsey treated Alan?"

She nods. "Alan wasn't an ordinary patient. Dr. Dempsey accepted him in an experimental plan. It was very select."

"Really?"

"And very secret. It involved injections, but that's all

we knew about it. Alan got the shots at his skin laboratory near Kendall Square."

"Advent Tissue Science."

She nods. "Alan signed a consent form and a secrecy agreement too. He wouldn't tell me or Franzie anything about it. He wouldn't tell his dad either. If anything got out about it, he'd be expelled from the program. That was Dr. Dempsey's rule." She fingers the knot of her blouse. "I mean, his skin cleared right up. We couldn't complain."

"About the secrecy?"

"About his moods. He got down in the dumps, he couldn't sleep. We wondered if maybe the shots . . . then again, it was like a miracle, and Alan followed the rules. He said that if he told, he wouldn't get a second chance. He said if he told, he'd be finished."

"For acne, Reggie, there's topical ointments. For deep acne, antibiotics."

"What else?" Impatient, just back home from Woburn, I've called Trudy Pfaeltz, who's about to leave for the hospital. Biscuit is at my ankles, Stark gone. I'm fighting a cold. "What about shots?"

"If antibiotics don't work, the last-resort treatment is isotretinoin. Jeez, it's almost six—"

"Iso . . . spell it." Parakeets chirp in the background. Trudy spells. "That drug, is it experimental?"

"No, but the side effects are serious. The trade name is Accutane. It's been in the news. Can we talk about this tomorrow morning?"

"What side effects?"

"Dry eyes and chapping are common. Blood and liver

disorders too. Cholesterol levels get screwed up, and triglycerides too. It causes serious fetal damage and psychiatric problems. A few people have died. Patients sign consent forms and get regular blood tests. Hell, where's my keys?"

"And this iso . . . isotretinoin, it's injected?"

"Oh no, the dosage is oral. Capsules. Damn keys."

"The particular treatment that I heard about was definitely injected."

"I don't know what it could be. Ye gods, this purse is hopeless. You sure the doc's a dermatologist?"

"That's what I was told." I do not reveal the name, sparing Trudy and myself a scorching rerun on Dempsey.

"Great, they're right here in my pocket. Listen, I have no idea what's in the syringe, Reggie. Probably it's a clinical trial. Trade secrets and all that. I'm out the door. Tell me, do you like the scissors? Then how about the summer barbecue set with extra-long Wedge-Lock handles, the fork, turner, and tongs. I can show you over this weekend."

"Maybe next season, Trudy. Bye."

I feed Biscuit, then phone the Renaissance restaurant to learn that Brenda Holstetter is not working tonight's dinner shift and is off tomorrow. "I have something of hers," I say, "something I want to return personally."

The good news: Brenda will most probably stop by the Renaissance tomorrow afternoon for her weekly paycheck. I'll be there too. Strategy is crucial. Do I confront her at the restaurant door? Or follow her down the street when she departs with her check? No, she'll outrun me again, bolt and disappear. Call Stark? Again, no. I need to come up with a way to get to Brenda. Because one good lead for Frank Devaney can feed the fires of the Dempsey case and lure Frank back to Henry Faiser.

At noon the next day, I'm standing in front of a novelty shop across from the Renaissance, wearing slacks and my spongiest Nikes because this could be a very long afternoon. It's overcast and in the low eighties, and my knit top is hot. The novelty shop window features itching powder, rubber fried eggs, and varieties of plastic animal droppings. I'm on edge, eyeing the restaurant traffic, which looks steady if not bustling. The minutes drag, each quarter hour a week long. Twice I dash into the street, mistaking a restaurant patron for Brenda. If she uses a back entrance through an alley, I'd miss her entirely.

Finally, I see her. It's after 2:30 when she comes down the block in black pants and a white shirt. She goes inside. I quickly follow, which is my plan. Brenda stands at the hostess desk talking to a sandy-haired manager who shuffles pay envelopes. Her back is turned, but the manager sees me. "I'm sorry, we're closed until dinner."

"I understand, but here's my favorite server—Brenda. How are you, hon?"

She turns, recognition souring to hostility. "Mitch, this woman came in yesterday—"

"Indeed I did. For my money, Brenda is Ms. Renaissance. That darling tam and breeches, the sweet brocade vest—why, I'd come for the decor and the authentic toggery. I tell all my friends to ask for Brenda's table." I step toward the manager. "So I was surprised to hear Brenda tell me she's not so crazy about the Shakespearean costumes."

He frowns. "Our servers all work in the spirit of the restaurant."

Brenda protests. "I didn't say . . . I never—"

"You were just having an off day, right, Brenda dear? You didn't mean to reflect badly on the Renaissance, not a bit."

She reaches for her pay envelope. He holds it back. A few lunch customers linger in the dining room. He says, "Whatever the misunderstanding, we want to make it right."

"Well, I wouldn't want to be a tattletale," I say. "A bad day, am I right, Brenda? I know deep down you appreciate working at a distinctive Boston landmark restaurant. You wouldn't for a minute intend to criticize. How about this: let me treat you to a dessert, if your good manager here will permit. I see a few patrons lingering. We can both sit down for just a bit."

"I don't have time. I came for my check."

"Oh? My goodness, and to think, I'd planned to urge our book club to hold the *Midsummer Night's Dream* banquet dinner here."

"Brenda, could you give our customer twenty minutes? I'll bring you both a slice of strawberry cheesecake. And here's this week's check."

We sit at a far table with the cheesecake. Her eyes are pure fury, her jaw clenched. "What the hell is this?"

"It's a pressure point moment, Brenda. I need information on Alan Tegier. He was in treatment for his skin. Did he talk about it?" She pockets the check and presses fork tracks in the cheesecake. "Don't waste my time, Brenda. What about the acne?"

"He said something once, in a general way."

"Did he ever mention Dr. Bernard Dempsey?"

"Dempsey?" She shrugs. "I don't remember."

"Think hard. Did he talk about injections? Experimental treatment?"

"No. Are you some kind of cop?"

Ignore the question, Reggie. Press ahead. "I understand Alan's personality changed shortly before his death. Did you notice any dark moods? It's a simple question: any moods?"

"I didn't see much of him the couple months before he died. He didn't work much for Ambrosia." She rakes at the strawberries on the cheesecake and avoids my gaze. "You know how they found him?"

"I do."

"It's horrible. Hard to believe something like that could happen to a friend." She puts down the fork. "But yeah, he got moody. He had plenty to be moody about."

"Like what?"

"He was stressed-out."

"From work?"

"Different things. You know about his jobs, the rug cleaning?" I nod. "One thing led to another. It really got to him."

"What do you mean?"

She swipes a gooey strawberry with her finger and licks it. "How about that ten from yesterday? From on the table?"

"Sorry, Brenda, it expired when you left the deli. What about Alan's moods?" She bites her lip. "Or do I show up at your station every shift you work here, lunch and dinner, day in and day out? Believe me, I'll do it."

"That's a threat?"

"It's a promise."

She sighs, frowns, bites a cuticle. "Alan was a great

bartender. He got first call. The months before he died, he cleaned rugs at night. He'd leave a cocktail buffet gig and work straight through till morning."

"Offices?"

"Mainly, he cleaned at a fancy high-rise. He was making good money, but he got to be a gofer for a certain guy. He was on the guy's payroll. It was do this, do that, not one minute to himself. The last time I saw Alan, he was real tense. He said the red Mustang wasn't worth it."

"What's the name of the high-rise?"

She pauses. "It was L-something."

"Not Eldridge."

"Hey, yeah, Eldridge. That's it."

I'm on the edge of the seat. "Brenda, the man Alan worked for, who was it?"

"I don't know. He said the guy was all about hell and damnation. Fancy words for hell, old-fashioned."

"Dante. The *Inferno*." She looks blank. "Did you tell any of this to the police?"

"I went to the memorial service, not the police."

"The police didn't question you?"

"Nobody did."

"The man who talks about hell, he's the night manager at Eldridge."

"Managers," she says with a huff. "They get you one way or another."

Chapter Twenty-two

I'm working on "Ticked Off," waiting for a call-back from Devaney to urge the police to question Brenda Holstetter. The phone rings. I say, "Frank," and hear a familiar, unmistakable voice cry, "Regina!"

"Tania?"

"He's furious. Didn't I tell you this would happen? He's never been so angry. He won't let me out of his sight. I'm watched every minute."

"By your husband?"

"The blazer men. Watch them, they wear body armor."

"From Eldridge? The staff?"

"They could be watching you too. I had to call. Don't worry, this won't be traced. I bought a phone card."

"Tania, where are you?"

But the line is dead. "Biscuit, here, girl." I want the dog with me as I walk to the front window and peer outside. It's early afternoon, and Barlow Square is quiet. It's less than twenty-four hours since the cheesecake talk with Brenda, and I'm impatient for a callback from Devaney, who's gone silent on me. The only person visible is the pipe-smoking man in the argyle sweater who lives across the square. I watch him walk up the block and cut between two cars recognizable as my neighbors'. Trudy's van is directly across the median. My Beetle is two blocks away, not a bad distance in the street parking game we all play here in the South End.

Biscuit whines, and I take her in my arms. My head is jammed from the dander allergy on top of this cold. The dog and I both look out. The sun is high, the afternoon shadows just beginning to stretch out. Glare blocks the visibility through several windshields, but it seems hardly likely that Jeffrey Arnot's enforcers would stake out my home in a parked car on my block.

Was Tania simply hysterical?

"Biscuit, let's go outside." I grab her leash and put on a jacket, and we walk around the square. I stride boldly. The sun feels good. Everything looks normal, not a blue blazer in sight. At the corner, a hefty man with thick brown hair rolls up the sleeves of his tan flannel shirt and reaches under the hood of his curbside station wagon. His tools lie on a pad on the walk. I tug the leash and step around. We circle back in about twenty minutes, all okay. The flannel shirt man is buried in his car's engine compartment, practically mooning the sidewalk.

How does a person know she's being watched? By hunch? Intuition? By echoing footfalls? I fill Biscuit's water bowl and finish "Ticked Off," this week's topic the public nuisance of humming, whistling, and singing aloud. I tap the e-mail "send."

Devaney still hasn't phoned back. I decide to go to the Boston Public Library. "No, Biscuit," I say at the door, "you can't go this time. Doggies aren't allowed in the library." No one follows me as I walk down public streets that are filled with plenty of pedestrians.

At this hour of the day, the BPL main reading room feels like a church. Call this my Mission Unfinished. This dreary head cold, you see, goads me. It's a pale echo of the icy arctic episode with Tania, that whiteout blizzard days ago in the muggy, hot June twilight. The polar-white paint of Jeffrey's limo can explain the incident only to a point. It does not account for the bone-chilling cold that clutched me in its icy grip. It does not account for the chill that Meg and I felt that first night, nor Igloo Sue, nor Brenda's remark on the sudden cold drafts. The Marlborough house harbors secrets, and another bout of research might pry them loose.

But it's not to be. For genealogy, I'm directed to the Social Science department, where I find a catalog system worthy of CIA codes. "I'm looking for the full date of death of Edmund Wight, who died in 1888. The funeral was held on March 20." A pleasant young librarian with a whippet waist pulls a microcard and helps me load a machine that throws a gloomy image roughly comparable to the first TV broadcast in 1939.

"Can you read it?" he asks.

The eye chart from hell. "Barely."

He shows me how to focus, and I have a momentary flashback to high school biology when the amoeba was nowhere to be seen under the microscope. But in minutes, I find the death date—March 17, 1888.

"Wight died of the grippe and bronchitis," I say to the librarian. "I'm looking for specifics. I want to know what happened in Boston on March 17."

In the high-ceiling Newspaper Room, I'm offered microfilm reels of historic dailies, the *Boston Evening Traveller,* the *Boston Daily Advertiser,* the *Boston Evening Transcript,* the *Boston Daily Globe.* It's as if March 17,

1888, never happened, because every one of these papers was consumed with the aftermath of a days-old monster snowstorm. "Crippled" and "paralyzed" are the words for the entire East Coast from Washington, D.C., to Maine on March 11 to 13. "Everywhere horse cars were lying on their sides, entrenched in deep snow, jammed together in every conceivable position . . . The city's surface was like a wintry battlefield."

It was the nineteenth century's version of a multivehicle interstate pileup. The storm, it seems, began on Saturday night, March 10, and the next morning Bostonians awakened to a meter of drifting snow. Some managed to reach their places of work and commerce on Monday but were trapped by the day's driving snowfall. In the *Boston Evening Transcript* is a post-storm feature on "Heroic People and Hat Chasers" who braved the blizzard with impromptu outerwear. "A few men pulled a pair of woolen socks over their shoes and then covered their legs with leggins." But the snow and cold were relentless. On Tuesday it continued to snow, temperatures dropped well below freezing, and wind speed reached seventy miles per hour. Fallen telegraph wires marooned each seaboard city. Up and down the coast, four hundred people died.

This stops me. This is not mere historical curiosity but circumstantial evidence. The newspaper accounts make it clear that Edmund Wight was probably one of the storm victims, a casualty of this blizzard of 1888. The weekly Monday Club dinner was his responsibility. He probably set out in good faith on Monday from Marlborough Street, and then hours later struggled back toward the Back Bay in driving, drifting snow. Exhausted, Wight most likely took sick from his exertion in the storm. Grippe and bronchitis are diseases brought on by chills.

Let's say he made it back to Marlborough, took to his bed, failed to respond to the beef tea and toddies and plasters doubtless administered. His strength ebbed, and he died on the seventeenth of March, buried on the twentieth. He wouldn't actually have died *in* the storm, but from it, of it.

My own arms and neck suddenly prickle, my teeth chatter as I shiver. Not from picturing myself in the blizzard, but from a thought. If I am right, the piece of cloth in Tania's chestnut casket connects with Edmund Wight. If I'm right, the cloth remnant pulled from the rafters is an actual relic of the storm. It's the remains of Wight's improvised outerwear. It marks his desperate effort to protect himself from the blizzard that brought on his death.

If I'm right, the stiff, filthy rag signals the spirit of Edmund Wight continuing in the Marlborough house. It has spoken to me, telling me that Wight is both ice-cold and deeply disturbed. The disturbance, of course, could come from the guilt of a man who engineered Charles Dehmer's death in the coach "accident."

Guilt alone, however, would not express itself in smashing the Arnots' valuables. The breakage means anger and hostility. The house is haunted. Edmund Wight's ghost is there. The Bostonian is furious, and a ghost has no deadline. Outside of time, it can rage into perpetuity. No wonder the Marlborough house goes on the market so often.

The summer hour with the Blizzard of '88 has been a historic distraction, an interlude while I await Devaney's call. It might prove useful for Meg, but my task now is to exit the library and walk to Barlow Square on high alert to detect surveillance.

Exiting the library on Boylston, I duck panhandlers and cross the granite library plaza. At the Copley T stop entrance, a man with thick brown hair pauses and disappears down the steps. My heart stutters. He's the guy working on his car on my block this afternoon.

Isn't he? Isn't the tan shirt the same? Commuters jostle and swirl down the T station stairs. He's gone. I should have scrutinized more carefully the facial features of the sidewalk mechanic.

Or maybe I'm just imagining things, chilled from the library episode. As for the walk back, forget it. My plans are suddenly changed. I'm heading for the precinct house on Harrison Avenue. I'll walk there and sit myself down and wait for Devaney and refuse to budge until he comes out.

At Columbus, I wait for the walk sign, and nobody halts behind me. On to Kneeland, where I mix in the pedestrian flow, an odd lot of walkers and dogs and vehicles. A horn sounds, a German shepherd barks. Everyone is minding their own business. Young women with gym bags alight from a van and enter a social center. Their laughter is lovely, like flowers. I make a left and find myself the sole pedestrian on the sidewalk as I climb the steps of the fortress of a precinct house on Harrison.

"Detective Devaney is not available? Then I'll be happy to wait."

The desk sergeant's nod is indifference itself. Her nameplate says "V. Ramirez," and her hair glows with henna highlights set off by the blue of the uniform. She turns back to her computer screen, and I sit against a far wall in one of the plastic chairs that bump the lower back. The clock says 5:38. Uniformed cops come and go without a glance in my direction. I spend twenty minutes with a well-thumbed *USA Today,* then go to the water fountain, mostly to remind Sergeant Ramirez of my existence. She doesn't look up. From the plastic chair, I call Devaney on my cell phone and leave the message that, unlike Elvis, I haven't left the building. It's 6:17 p.m. My stomach grinds and growls.

"Well, Reggie."

"Well, Frank. I should've brought a sleeping bag." By now, it's 7:02. With his jacket over his shoulder, his catsup red tie loosened, his shirtsleeves rolled, Frank Devaney looks like a man stuck at a roadblock. When I say, "I wanted to catch you in person for a few minutes," he grunts. "I walked here," I add. As if foot power means anything. "It's important, Frank. I have a message."

"A psychic message?" I shake my head. "Then how about tomorrow?"

"This won't wait. How about right now?"

We go into a stuffy side room with a Formica table scarred with cigarette burns. I sit. He straddles a chair. "Okay, what's up?"

"Two things. A woman who worked catering jobs with Alan Tegier has important information for the police. Brenda Holstetter. She's a server at the Renaissance restaurant off Stuart Street. Frank, why aren't you writing this down?"

Reluctantly, he makes a note. "What else?"

"The witness who says he was with Alan Tegier at the poolroom the night he disappeared is a notorious liar. His name is Rudy Cavitch. He's a local legend in Woburn."

"So you've been to Woburn."

"And to Chestnut Hill to the Dempsey house. I think Bernard Dempsey is involved in Tegier's murder. Possibly his wife's death too."

Devaney gnaws a knuckle and studies my face. "So correct me—you did actually feel psychic vibes at Dempsey's house?" I shake my head no. "How about Woburn? Not at Tegier's house?"

"Don't insult me, Frank. I talked with Alan Tegier's stepmother. Alan was enrolled in Dempsey's secret medical trial for severe skin problems. Dempsey injected him and swore him to secrecy. The injections affected his state of mind. He became withdrawn and moody."

"Which doesn't make it criminal."

"Advent Tissue Science must be investigated. Dempsey has a corrupt past. He was involved in a laboratory scandal. Data was falsified. And there's more: the restaurant server, Brenda Holstetter, says Alan Tegier cleaned carpeting at night at Eldridge Place. Frank, he worked for Carlo Feggiotti."

"Feggiotti . . . the guy who'll spring Faiser?"

"You don't seem interested."

Devaney crunches two Tums and says "appetite suppressant" as if I don't know it's dinnertime. "Not to insult you, Reggie, but there's too much *CSI* and *New Detectives* and God knows what. It's nuts. Everybody's a detective."

Against better judgment, against judgment itself, I hear myself blurt out, "Okay, listen to this. Sylvia Dempsey knew Jordan Wald. She introduced him at the Newton Home and Garden Alliance."

I could lip-synch Devaney's comeback. "A garden club that invites the politician responsible for environmental laws in the Commonwealth of Massachusetts—am I supposed to investigate that too?" He tugs his open collar and starts to rise. "Reggie, let me drive you home."

I am silent all the way from the precinct house to Barlow Square. "Frank, that station wagon . . . I may have been followed by a brown-haired man who worked on that car."

"The Olds?" Its hood is half raised. Devaney double-parks, and we get out. A hammer lies on the pad on the walk. The brown-haired man is nowhere around. Frank leans to see the VIN number. "I'll run it through the DMV and NCIC." In minutes, he makes calls and says, "It's clean. Nothing to worry about."

"Who's the owner?"

"Oh no. No, you don't. No more going to knock on strangers' doors. Reggie, you're going way too far. You gotta pull back." He puts a hand on my shoulder and faces me with a kindly gaze. "Take my advice, get some rest. Walk in the Public Garden. Go to the museum and look at the impressionists."

"Monet's water lilies won't solve murders."

"That's the point. Look, we're grateful for the tip about the lying Woburn witness. We'll definitely look into it. But I'm going home now. My new slow cooker is turning shoulder chuck into *boeuf bourguignon*. You take care. I mean it. Take care."

It's nearly 8:00 p.m. when I walk Biscuit down the block and see that the Olds front passenger door is open. Two thin legs with pointy black oxfords stick out toward the sidewalk. Then he sits up, this evening's Olds mechanic. He's a wiry, short, sallow man in a gray T-shirt and black pants. He picks up a wrench and nods as I pass, then pats Biscuit with a hand whose nails are spotless. A mechanic without one drop of grease under his nails?

My skin prickles as Biscuit and I circle back around. Wrench in hand, the man fiddles with the radio buttons as if tuning in a station. Biscuit dawdles to sniff the tires, but I tug her leash and double-lock my door. Nightlong, I keep an eye on the station wagon, a hulk in the darkness on my block. The Oldsmobile is intrusive, as if it's giving off bad energy, a feng shui violation. I look out my front window at midnight, then again at two, and finally in the predawn hour. It looks like a docked gunboat, and I sense someone inside it. The small dark man? The brown-haired one?

Could both men camp in the car to watch me? No, that's nuts. A man who works on his car, he's in the American tradition. He pulls up at a curb and uses his know-how with his own tools, even in Boston's gentrified South End. His buddy lends a hand and tunes in to a Sox game. I saw the hammer, the wrench, the pad on the side-walk.

That's it, I realize, the source of my unease. From yesterday to today, no actual work seems in progress. The wrench and hammer look more like props.

If Tania's right, Jeffrey Arnot is enraged enough to have me watched. Do the men track my whereabouts for Arnot? Is Carlo in on it?

Or do they work for Bernard Dempsey? Had he somehow found out that I went to Alan Tegier's house? He could try to drive me frantic with crude intimidation. If Dempsey killed his wife and caused Alan Tegier's death, who would stop him from coming after me?

The Olds station wagon is still there this morning at eight, and I decide to call Stark, who promises to come check it out. At nine, he's still not here. I think about the two handguns in Jo's file drawer. Should I get bullets?

I step into the study, pull down the blinds, and look at the guns. The Colt looks too John Wayne, a western period piece. The .38 revolver, though, looks usable. It seems ice-cold, the barrel a steel gray-blue. Biscuit whines as I pick it up. I'm just aiming it at the microwave when the door knocker sounds. I shove the gun in the drawer.

It's Stark at the door. The dog is overjoyed. "Thanks for coming." He roughs her belly. "It's that Oldsmobile station wagon down the block. I think I'm being watched." He scratches her ears. "Down there . . . down the block." But it's gone. There's not a trace of it. We stand at the open door. "This morning I walked Biscuit past it. Maybe it dripped oil. We could go see."

"Whatever you want." Stark's is the tone of voice people use with the mentally ill.

"No, really, Stark. Yesterday a brown-haired man seemed to work on it, and then a short dark man. Detective Devaney checked the car out. It's not stolen or linked to a crime. I think the two men were here to watch me."

"Who?"

"I . . . I'm not sure."

"Guys work on cars."

"Of course. Of course they do."

"Guys like to install a fuel pump, put on a muffler. I do a lot of my own work on Fatso."

"Yes."

He jams his hands in his jeans. "You want me to hang around? You want a ride someplace?"

"Yes . . . I mean no."

"How about if I take Biscuit for the day? You get some rest. I'll bring her back anytime you say. You take it easy. Call me." I watch him get the dog harness from the motorcycle saddlebag, strap the dog in, pull on his gloves and helmet, drop the visor, start the engine, wave, and ride off, with Biscuit's eager little nose to the air.

On Barlow Square, a roofer is at work across the grassy median. A dry cleaner makes a pickup. Nobody else is outside. If I screamed, who would hear? Who would run to the rescue? Who safeguards me as I race against a killer's clock?

Chapter Twenty-three

A rainy summer evening ought to feel nice. Open the windows, smell the wet earth, hear the muffled hum of the city. Instead, I watch the black VW Beetle that now circles Barlow Square every six to eight minutes, its driver a man or woman with a pony-tail. I first noticed it while walking Biscuit after Stark brought her back and left. That was an hour ago. The slot occupied by the Olds is now filled by a sedan with a Boston College sticker, and the "mechanics" are nowhere in sight. But the VW is identical to my own car, eye-catching in the way one's own possessions command attention. The driver seems to be circling for a parking spot.

In fact, Trudy Pfaeltz pulled out twenty minutes ago. I watch from my front window as the Beetle twice by-passes her huge van-size space. At 8:14 p.m., the Beetle circles for the third time this hour. Though it's darkish gray outside, I haven't switched on any lamps, instead watching the street in the vanishing light and counting reappearances from the window frame.

Could this Beetle actually be my very own car? I'd

parked two blocks over and, of course, locked up. I haven't driven it since the night of Tania and the rafter cloth.

Would Dempsey try to terrorize me this way? Would Jeffrey Arnot? Or Carlo? And why? To lure me out into the street? Rattle me? Do me harm?

I want to walk the two blocks to find out whether a thief taunts me with my own automobile. But I linger in the safety of my own home. Well founded or absurd, fear is fear. The sounds of struggle that I heard May 3 could have been Alan Tegier's death throes. So much for aiding Henry Faiser if I, too, end up in a barrel of beef fat.

Biscuit paces the floorboards, sensing my mood, puzzled by the darkening of the rooms. I scratch her neck, try to pick her up. She's having none of it and takes shelter under the love seat.

I try to settle down by thinking of the lessons of my sixth sense. There's my burning rib, my painful thumb, even the ice-cold message of the century-old rafter cloth. Signs and signals, every one, but coded. They may be linked or not. Their logic is veiled. There's a Buddhist saying: the mind knows what the body feels.

What does my mind know? I stand here at the window on this rainy evening and sort the pieces. Start with Faiser, now serving a twenty-to-life sentence for a murder someone else might have committed. Henry, whose guilt or innocence is as much of a mystery today as on the morning Devaney showed up here with the leather notebook.

Then there's Carlo. Do all roads lead to Carlo? The night manager of a condo high-rise is not the food chain's biggest fish. Would that be Jeffrey Arnot? I'm betting the truck pulling out of Eldridge at midnight carried something illegal, that the condo high-rise is a shipping point. And who is Perk? Short for Perkins? If only I'd asked Big Doc. He linked Carlo to the *Inferno,* and his pothead ravings on sewers and parts-per-billion poison might have yielded a clue on Perk.

Biscuit whimpers, and the VW goes round again. I refuse to spend the night here at the window frame, so I creep along the wall back toward the kitchen, startled by the fridge light as I grab yogurt and an orange, then shut the door fast and wolf down the food. It feels like house arrest. I'm being held hostage.

No, I'm a woman exercising caution for self-preservation, a woman ready to fight another day. Tonight's low profile guarantees my tomorrow.

At 6:00 a.m., I'm out inspecting my car. There's no sign of the circling Beetle. The silk rose blooms in the bud vase. The Beetle is locked snug at the curb, yet several spaces up from where I'd parked it. Five or six spaces.

Inside the unlocked car, I turn the key and check the odometer but can't recall my mileage. It's the Goldilocks feeling that someone's been inside. The seat seems to be moved back a notch or two. Biscuit jumps and sniffs a carnival of new odors.

I'm sliding out when I see daylight glint on a strand of hair, which is blond and very long, too long to be mine, and the wrong color too. I hold it up. It's over a foot long. From the ponytail of the joyrider? Devaney would now ask, "Who's been your passenger in the car these past weeks, Reggie?" Okay, Frank, the answer is the StyleSmart "models." I pick up the hair between thumb and forefinger, wrap it in tissue, and drive to StyleSmart.

"So do you think it could be Monique's?" I'm at the door when Nicole opens up. Her keys jangle on a big brass ring. "Monique's hair was the longest of all the models who drove with me."

"Reggie, let me get the lights turned on and the coffee going. What's this all about?"

"I want to know whether you think it could be Monique's. She rode in my VW to the Newton show."

Nicole holds the single strand to the window's light. "Monique's is russet blond, Reggie. This one here is more cornsilk. You ready to toss out this old hair?"

"Oh no. I need it."

Nicole's look is sly. "You find the hair close-up on a man's collar?"

I force a chuckle, rewrap the hair, and tuck it in my purse. "Let's just say that this single hair has me going round in circles. First thing, I want to check on the couture. The storage people are coming?"

"For pickup tomorrow. Everything's ready."

"Let me check anyway. Give me a moment." Actually, I have a plan. In the back room, all by myself, I want to touch Sylvia Dempsey's Chanel suit. I'm thankful to hear a customer come in. Nicole will be distracted. Good.

The back room is fragrant with a mixture of scents from the designer clothes in the garment bags— Boucheron, L'Or, Escada. Moving down the rack, I unzipper each bag and peek until I find the Sylvia collection.

I prepare myself. First, relax the shoulders. Take note of Nicole's voice in the distance, her lilting words entwined with the customer's own. Let their voices fall away. Let the moment be clear and open. Let the mind be receptive. Now reach for the clothing, which Sylvia once wore. Take hold of the sleeve of the pink suit. Feel the connection. Open both mind and body and let the moment speak.

My palms dampen against the fabric. In the distance, I hear Nicole say, "Let's try you in a fourteen." The fluorescent light buzzes. The moment empties. Then something stirs. It's a faint hum, a light flutter on the surface of my skin. Will it crescendo? Will I next feel turmoil and the violence of her death, the bludgeoning? My legs tense, toes grip. I prepare for this as a certain sensation rises in my chest . . . in my breast. My nipples prickle. A great warmth surges, a liquid thickness, then a driving wink between my thighs. This throbbing . . . it's sex. It's lust. Not fear or murder, but lust. This is Sylvia Dempsey's message—hot pink, hot sex. Her lingerie drawer so chaste, but the Chanel suit a pulsating cry of sex. *For* sex.

I let go of the sleeve. I struggle to contain the pulse and pounding throb. The room whirls. I'm panting. My God . . . I am flushed with arousal, weak, my vision blurry. Ground yourself, Reggie. Pull out of this. Breathe deep. Center yourself.

"Reggie, you okay in there?"

"Fine, Nicole. I'm fine. Be right out."

Lie. My shirt is wet, knees buckling. I stand here for what seems eternity. Sylvia's partly unzipped garment bag gapes, but I won't touch it. Every fiber of the pink suit throbs. I turn away, run a hand through my hair, straighten my collar, freshen my lipstick. Shoulders back, I exit this back room as though my life depends on it.

*   *   *

Breathless from brisk walking in the darkness, I linger in the shadows at the Eldridge Place entrance until a car clears the security gate and disappears into the garage. I parked two blocks away and wasn't followed—not noticeably—but I still feel exposed. It's two hours before Carlo begins his shift, a two-hour window of opportunity. High in the night sky, a bird cries. A crow? A jackal? I press the front door buzzer and hope against hope the night staff is the navy retiree with the thatchy gray hair and thick glasses.

When he comes, I'll say, "Good evening. I'm Regina Cutter. I believe we met a few weeks ago." Through the glass doors, he'll face a woman in a black linen pantsuit with pearls. How can he possibly not let me in? I'll ask certain pointed questions. I have an agenda.

Here comes someone, squinting, peering. It's him, but he reaches for his pager to summon help. I flash my brightest smile, and he pockets the pager and taps a remote. The electronic lock releases, and I open the door. "Hello again. It's Walt, isn't it?"

"Walt Kane."

"I'm Regina Cutter." My fib is on the tip of my tongue. "I'm expecting Mr. Albritten from the realty company. He's showing me a two-bedroom unit."

"Nobody told me."

"It's a late-night appointment, just like the last time. Mr. Albritten is so nice about my impossible schedule. Surely you remember me, the night owl? I helped you with your puzzle." Bat your eyelashes, Reggie, and hold that smile. "I'll just wait here in the lobby, okay?"

"Our guests park in the garage." He stares at me through the yellowish lenses.

"I took a taxi. Mr. Albritten will be here any moment."

"They're supposed to notify me."

"No doubt a tiny slipup." I saunter toward the desk to appear casual, then lean to see a book of crossword puzzles lying open on the desktop, and supermarket tabloids too. The eight surveillance monitors glow gray. "Well, I see you're doing crosswords once again." My smile muscles strain. On one monitor, a car is shown parking in a lower-level garage slot on level D, and a couple gets out and walks to the elevator. A second monitor shows them inside the elevator. Walt Kane sits down at his console. "Tell me, Mr. Kane, did you work crosswords in the navy?"

"You remember I'm a navy man?"

"Navy chief, right?"

"Right as rain. I started as a bosun's mate at seventeen and worked up. If my country ever needs me again, I'm ready. Say, would you happen to know who in ancient history first used the horse in battle? The third and fourth letters are t's."

"Try the Hittites." The couple now exits the elevator. Another screen shows them in a hallway. "I've been thinking, Walt, about how much services matter in a high-rise residence. For instance, window cleaning."

"Twice a year, spring and fall, like clockwork. They're pros. Hittites it is!"

"And carpets? How about rugs and carpets? Who cleans them?"

"Well, an outside team does the Orientals here in the lobby. The hallway carpets, though, we take care of that ourselves."

"And residents can make a request for their own rugs to be cleaned too? If I move in, I can arrange carpet cleaning?"

He puts down the crossword. "If you want to. The night manager sees to it."

"Carlo Feggiotti. I met him. Actually, a Realtor told me the man to call for carpets is . . . let's see, I jotted it down. It's Alan Tegier."

The watery eyes remain opaque, unblinking. "Al, that's Pompadour Al. Hardworking young guy, a jack-of-all-trades."

Is it possible Walt Kane does not know that Alan is dead? "So you know him?"

He nods. "Carlo took him under his wing. He was with us for the better part of a year."

"But he doesn't work here now?"

"Not now." Walt shakes his head as if Alan Tegier has simply left the payroll. He's missed the local news story—by cocooning himself in national tabloids? "Young Al had some kind of falling-out with Carlo. Believe me, you never want to cross Carlo. It's too bad because the kid liked the night shift. He worked the check times too."

"Check times?"

"Part of our security." He falls silent and reaches for the puzzle.

"You seem to have a marvelous security system."

"The best. The perimeter, the premises, it's state-of-the-art. You move in here, you can set your mind at ease."

"Twenty-four/seven?"

"Yep. Except for check times."

"And what are those check times?"

"Nothing to worry about. Carlo and the boys cover everything."

"I don't believe Mr. Feggiotti or Mr. Albritten told me about them."

"A Realtor wouldn't know. A good many of the residents don't know."

I lean toward him. "Believe me, Walt, if I'm going to move into Eldridge Place, I want to know everything."

"How about a talking machine, eleven letters?"

"Try Graphophone. See, if I move in, you can count on me. Carlo's check time, please explain that."

"A safety feature. He shuts down the whole system to check it out."

"The surveillance system?"

"Surveillance and alarms, twice a week between two and three a.m. It takes about an hour. Say, Graphophone works. You're a big help."

"So your monitors go blank?"

"The alarm system too, every Tuesday and Thursday night. But don't worry, Carlo's in charge. The security crew on duty, they're cream of the crop."

"Perk too?"

He looks up and squints. "Who's Perk?"

"Maybe it's Perkins?"

"Never heard of him."

"Anyway, it sounds like twice a week you can count on a long break in the wee hours."

He squares his shoulders as if to salute. "No, ma'am, I man my station here at the door. It's a drill. If the power ever goes out, we have a procedure. Carlo's my commander. I'm under orders to man the front door every minute."

"Well, that's impressive. I've heard so many good things from Mr. Arnot too. Perhaps you've met Mr. Jeffrey Arnot?"

"The African-American gentleman? Yes, he's here

sometimes. He's like the rear admiral. Say, where's that real estate man of yours?"

I look at my watch and pretend surprise. "Golly, it's twenty after. Perhaps I should call." Cell phone out, I fake the call and a message. "He must be on his way. I see you read the *National Enquirer* and the *Star.* I do too."

"I like to follow Lisa Marie and the Kennedys."

"Anything on Elvis or Princess Di, I can't resist."

He licks his lips. "You know, the fact is, we have *Enquirer* material right here at Eldridge Place."

"Really?"

"If you move in, you'll find out."

"Ooh, interesting." Bat those lashes, Reggie. "I imagine nothing slips by you, Walt. A navy chief knows the score."

He sucks in his stomach and puffs out his chest. "Some think I'm the old guy at the night desk. They'd be surprised what I see. The goings-on, I'm not fooled."

"I bet you're not."

"High-ups, you'd be surprised."

"Celebrities?"

"TV stars too. From Channel 5."

"Really?"

"And politicians. Like a certain statehouse official."

"I see."

"A certain senator. Up for election this year."

"You mean reelection."

"Nope. *E*-lection." His eyes twinkle behind the lenses. "Who's up for lieutenant governor?"

My heart thuds. "You mean Jordan Wald?"

"They think with thick glasses, you can't see two feet in front of you."

"Jordan Wald has a condo here?"

"Every guy with gray hair is past it, that's what they think. But I knew who it was."

"Wald? Jordan Wald lives here at Eldridge?"

"There's a crow's nest and a love nest. A navy man knows the difference."

"Senator Wald has a love nest?"

"The unit that's still up for sale. That woman in pink. Pink lady, pink condo."

"The unit with the Valentine theme? The sixth floor, 603, I saw that unit."

"You talk about young Al. He cleaned those carpets."

"The carpets in the Valentine condo?"

"Used the steam machine. He said things were plenty steamy up there with the two of them. Then, too, folks try to sneak by me. They get in the elevator and forget about the camera and monitor. The pink lady carried on in the elevator. She and him put on a show."

"With Jordan Wald? Are you sure?"

He nods. "I understand she's the one that got herself killed. Careless lady."

"Sylvia Dempsey."

"Out by herself by the Charles River at all hours. You say you took a cab?"

"I did."

"I'll call one tonight when you're ready. I called the pink lady a cab lots of times. Middle of the night, whatever. She slipped me a heck of a holiday bonus last February. Put it in a Valentine card with Cupid shooting arrows. A month later, though, it was all over. The love nest, it was a tiger cage."

"They fought?"

"Tiger by the tail, both of them. A man came here one night and waited till the lady came down the elevator. The look on her face when she saw him . . . like the ad says, priceless. He danced her out so fast her toes didn't touch the floor."

"What did he look like?"

"Just a middle-age man in a suit. He got her in an arm-lock like he had a black belt in jujitsu. She called him Bernie. He had the darkest, blackest eyes I ever saw."

Chapter Twenty-four

A mmo? Sure thing. What'll it be?"

"I'd like some bullets for a .38 handgun."

"FP? HP?" I stare like a dumb fool. I'm at Buck & Buck Sports in Burlington. The news about Jordan Wald and Sylvia Dempsey kept me up till all hours, and I read and reread the note. "I appreciate what you do for me— J." So now I know for sure.

"Flat point? Hollow point?" The chunky salesclerk has round shoulders and a round face. "You going to practice at a range?"

"Yes. This is for target shooting, my first time."

"Revolver or semiautomatic?"

"Uh, revolver." Behind the counter, a wall-mounted boar thrusts its tusks and glares. Hunting rifles surround me. The clerk wears camo pants.

"Try the half jacket. See what you think." He shows me a two-toned bullet with a brass casing and gray head. I buy a box and a holster too. "You want a high-ride holster with a muzzle rear rake. They call it the FBI tilt. Make sure your belt fits the slits or it'll ride up. And hold your gun two-handed and lock your thumbs left over right, clear of the trigger. Unless you want to lose your right thumb."

I get on I-95 and go home to call Stark and brew a pot of his favorite coffee robusta.

"What do you mean, how do you load a hypothetical revolver? What crap is that?" Stark scratches Biscuit's back. By this time, it's late afternoon.

"I mean, if I actually bought a gun. And bullets. Maybe a holster too."

He scowls and runs a hand through his ginger hair. "You talkin' single- or double-action revolver?"

"What's the difference?"

"Cutter, if you're interested in guns, take a course. I'm not your gun buddy. You're almost out of sugar. Did you call me for a gun quiz or what?"

I fill the sugar bowl. We sit at my kitchen table, and Biscuit settles at Stark's feet. "Okay, here's why I called. I want to go to Eldridge Place on Tuesday night between two and three a.m. I want you to go with me. We have to sneak in."

"We?"

"You and me."

He stirs his coffee to a whirlpool. "Is this about your cop pal and the wrongful conviction?"

I nod. "A man named Carlo Feggiotti is the night manager at Eldridge. He's the link to the old chop shop days and the arson fire. And Henry Faiser knew him."

"Faiser. The guy in Norfolk."

I nod again. "These days Carlo's up to something else. Twice a week he shuts down the Eldridge surveillance and alarm systems in the name of security checks. The night I met him, he seemed upset when a worker tried to tell him about a shipment that came in. There was a truck." I stop. Stark will get angry if I talk about parking by the service road. "I think Carlo could help Faiser. I want to know what he's up to."

"Why not call your homicide detective pal?"

"I thought about it. I gave it careful consideration."

"You decided he'd blow you off, right? Or he'd cut you out. And that's what bothers you, doesn't it? I see the glint in your eye. You want to be in the middle of the action. You don't want to be sidelined."

"I just thought if we went together—"

"The condo rent-a-cops could shoot at both of us?"

"We could find out what's going on. Then I can go to the police if it's worth investigating. So what do you say? How about it?"

He chugs coffee as though it's a shot of espresso. "What makes you think that Feggiotti's up to anything?"

"Why else would he shut down the security system?"

"To check it out."

"Twice a week? No. I think he's running an illegal operation. A truck is involved, and some of the Eldridge workers too. The young guy from Woburn—Alan Tegier—he worked the night shift at Eldridge. He was involved in the check times. That's what they're called, check times. There's someone by the name of Perk or Perkins too. I think he's also in on it, but I haven't found him."

"But Tegier was offed."

"Yes."

"And maybe this Perk too?" I shrug. Who knows? Stark puts his cup down and plays with the dog. "So if anything screws up, you and I get buried in beef fat? Cutter, these people are nasty. I recommend the cops. They get paid for high risk. Sometimes it's best not to dance. What do they call that?"

"Wallflower?"

"Sounds good to me."

"Then I'll go by myself."

He gives me a hard stare. "You wouldn't."

"Try me. Just try me." Somewhere a clock strikes the hour. Biscuit whimpers and licks my hand. "I'll go alone." It's a weak hand, but still I play it, maybe for the sake of pride. "Tuesday night at two, Stark, you know where to find me."

Four days lie between now and Tuesday. The countdown turns each daily event surreal, and my broken sleep brings on borderline hallucinations. At StyleSmart, the racks of clothes look psychedelic. The fruit and canned soup at Tsakis Brothers look like infrared Warhols. I grab the first available parking space here on Barlow Square and stare until the grass and trees seem radioactive. The Olds wagon with its fake mechanics does not reappear. There's no sign of the brown-haired or the pointy-shoed man. No person of driving age sports a ponytail either.

Yet it feels like calm before the storm, as if a category 5 hurricane is incubating offshore while I stay inside, my doors locked as I work on "Ticked Off," answer mail, and read. My tenant, Dr. Forest Buxbaum, reports a stuck window screen. I spray it with silicone. And pretend that all's well on the phone with my kids. Molly's exhibit is nearing installation. Jack tells me he's now data mining on the computer. I make a crack about mother lodes of data, and my son pretends amusement. If my children pressed, what would I tell them?

Stark makes no effort to contact me.

Late Sunday afternoon, I close the blinds, get out the .38, and lay it on the kitchen table. Did my Aunt Jo sit at this table and load the gun? Did she keep it in her night table drawer, just in case? Did she ever fire it? Its barrel is four inches long and gleams blue.

My fingers tremble. But I pick up the gun, take a couple deep breaths, and wrap my fingers around the grip. I put it into the holster and pull it out, pointing the barrel away from me, keeping my thumb clear of the hammer.

A flick of the thumb against a little switch by the hammer, and presto, the cylinder releases sideways. Left-handed, I reach for the bullet box, take out six cartridges, and line them in a row on the tabletop. I insert one in each chamber, then push the cylinder shut. I put the gun down and stare at my tabletop arrangement: salt shaker and peppermill with loaded revolver.

A loaded gun belongs in a locked drawer. There's a small walnut cabinet with a skeleton key, an antique of Jo's. I put the .38 inside, lock it, put the key on my ring. All day Monday, I avoid the cabinet. The skeleton key looks primitive. I try not to think about it.

Then finally it's Tuesday. I drink a Diet Dr Pepper at dawn and make a run to StyleSmart for a long-sleeved black jersey and dark sneakers.

Nicole is suspicious. "First it's a blond hair, Reggie, then you're in the back room communing with the couture. Now high-tops? What do you want with black canvas high-tops?" Yet she digs for an old pair of Converse while I rummage for a long-sleeved jersey. "Most Junes in Boston, Reggie, we go in for short sleeves. And what about our Operation Peacock?"

"I'm your Technicolor project, Nicole. I just need a

black sweater at the moment. This one ought to fit. It's bulky and too pilly for the racks. I'll just take it off your hands."

And so I do.

Night falls at last. I've paid some bills, downed two servings of spinach soufflé, flipped through the channels, tried on the noir outfit twice. I take Biscuit out as usual. At eleven, I watch the news and weather and switch back and forth between the two late-show monologues, Leno's one-liners on breast implants on WHDH and Letterman's hypochondria jokes on WBZ. I'm not a bit sleepy but put on the X-large T-shirt I've been wearing as a nightgown and get into bed.

At 1:00 a.m., I'm wide awake. The TV's off. Maybe I should call Devaney. I have his home number. No, he'd stop me cold. No question about that. Then I remember: he's in Orlando at the prison convention. I couldn't summon him if I tried. Which makes me uneasy, as if half my body is exposed.

Suddenly, I think about my hair. A night foray requires a cap. It's 1:15 as I root through Jo's scarves, then finally settle on a dark brown cashmere cloche from the coat closet. By 1:35, I'm inspecting myself in the whole outfit in the full-length mirror. The sneakers are a half size too big, but a second pair of socks helps. I unlock the cabinet drawer and buckle on the holster to a stout leather belt. The sweater pulls down and covers the gun.

All this wool is hot. Biscuit wakes and whimpers, but two treats settle her down. I decide to step outside to test the air—and am startled to see Stark at my doorway.

"Stark. My God, you scared me."

"Get your helmet. It's time to go."

The motorcycle gleams in the quarter-moon. "I didn't hear your engine."

"I walked the bike up from Tremont. Come on, get the helmet. It's pushing two o'clock." Mouth dry, I try to give him the directions, but he waves me off. "I scouted Eldridge in case you were nuts enough to keep your word. There's a back way with pylons where the bike can get through. Here's the plan. We're gonna park a little way off and go through a fence and climb a wall by a Dumpster. We'll look over their loading dock. No talking. Follow my lead. How's your shoes?" He feels my sneakers and grunts. He's in all black too, with a watch cap.

I start to admit to second thoughts, but the Harley growls to life. There's no time to tell him about the gun. I climb aboard, grab his hips, and we roar into the night.

In minutes, we pass the Eldridge complex and double back to an alley that dead-ends at the concrete pylons. Stark guides the bike between two of them, and we proceed slowly on rutted, broken pavement to a weed-choked chain-link fence. Stark cuts the engine. Truck traffic roars on the Mass Pike. We dismount and take off our helmets. I look for razor wire coils atop the fence but see none. From the saddlebag, Stark gets out bolt cutters and clips the chain link up from the bottom to let each of us through. Eldridge Place looms before us. A few condo lights glow, but the grounds are dark. This means it's just past 2:00 a.m., check time. I hear my own breath as Stark motions me to the wall.

Fifteen feet high at least, it's a ridged stone boundary barrier at the rear of the building. Stark motions me behind him, flattens his palms against the base of the wall, and crouches down. I understand I'm to climb onto his back and then stand on his shoulders to reach the top.

Stepping onto his muscle and bone boulder of a back, one foot on each shoulder, I touch the wall for balance as he slowly stands up. At last, I'm high enough to grasp the top of the wall, which is flat, maybe a foot thick. Biting my lip to stay silent, shoulders and arms straining, I work to pull myself up. The holster bulks awkwardly, and I shift my weight. Eyes closed, I finally lie flat on my stomach on the top of the wall, my right cheek against rock and mortar. My workouts pay off. I'm just a bit out of breath.

It's a barrier, not a climbing wall, and Stark is clawing his way up to join me. His stifled grunts mix with night-bird sounds—and with a stench. Something's sour, rotten, like fermenting milk and meat. Didn't Stark say a Dumpster was near? Yes, the dark hulking big steel box is just below, maybe six feet down. I could gag.

Then I hear talking. It's two men's voices.

"Where the hell is he?"

"Relax. We're on schedule."

Stark flattens himself on the top of the wall. We're head-to-head, each staring sideways over the Dumpster. The holster digs into my hip. The voices drift up. Coals of cigarettes glow in the dark below.

"He's late. I coulda stayed at Fenway. They were in the tenth."

"Shut up."

Through his cap, Stark's hair smells of the clean odor of leaf tobacco. I start to whisper but stay silent when an engine sounds. It's a truck. It's approaching, lights dim, then off. It makes a tight turn and backs up. I see the shape. It's a tank truck. The door opens, the driver's footfalls thud. "Shit, Denny, where you been?"

"Parking my ass on the expressway. A semi jackknifed by the gas tanks, it was down to one lane. You wanna complain? You make the run and watch out for the state cops. I'll stand here at the pipe and have a smoke."

" 'Ah, our sandy place of squalor—' "

"Cap off? You ready with the hose?"

" '—and charred features scorched of hair.' "

That's got to be an *Inferno* quote. It's Carlo.

"Okay, nozzle's in. Hold it." A low grinding hum begins. "Shit, hold it. I said hold it. Now look, a fuckin' spill. It's a mess. Get a rag. Wipe it up. Do it the way Al used to. Al never let it spill. Goddamn." More curses and grunts. Then, "Okay, good to go. Now start it up. Keep it steady."

The grinding hum resumes. Facing sideways, my cheek pressed against the wall, I see the tank truck emptying its contents into a pipe protruding to the left of the loading dock. Is it oil? Heating oil for the building? Do Stark and I risk life and limb to watch a heating oil delivery? In summer?

"Friggin' hot."

" 'Because the soles of both feet were aflame, so violently, it seemed their joints could burst.' "

"Shit, Carlo, that stuff gets on my nerves. I'm gettin' earplugs."

"Dante's good for the soul. In the first circle, the only curse is hopelessness. So hang on. Two more loads of Perk, then it's over."

"No more Perk? I thought Perk was forever."

"Not from the Cape. We drained that swamp—excuse

me, wetlands. Next comes chrome. They got to get rid of some chrome. Tests came out bad."

"Shit, I'm drinkin' only bottled. Period."

"When check times pay out, Arnie, you can drink mother's milk."

"Like you order custom suits? And what are those shoes anyway? Crocodile?"

" 'I get my payment, date for fig.' Canto 33. You wait. Come chrome, the sky's the limit."

Muffled words, then laughter. What am I hearing? Is it chrome from old car bumpers? Or liquid chrome, as in the water in *Erin Brockovich*? Toxic chrome, a deadly pollutant, soon to be hosed from this truck into a drain? A drain leading where?

And Perk? Perk pours down the drain at this minute. It's not a person, but a liquid in a tank truck. Suddenly, Big Doc's rant comes to mind—on poisons, parts per billion, and sewers. Sewers of death in the City on a Hill, which is Boston. Is this the deadly sewer? Am I watching poison being pumped into a sewer pipe?

Has Carlo Feggiotti dumped toxins on this site for years and years? With Big Doc's knowledge? And Henry Faiser's? Was he framed for Peter Wald's murder so he wouldn't get a chance to rat?

My right arm is asleep. I flex the muscles. It's hot and clammy and rock-hard on this wall. The holster hurts. My scalp itches, and I want to pull off the hat. Garbage thickens the air. Every breath stinks. Stark is perfectly still. We wait, and wait longer. I hear "Fenway" and "Martinez," as if these are regular night shift guys talking baseball. I listen closely, but the back-and-forth dies as the pump grinds on, then finally stops.

"Okay, hose clamped, all set. Toss that wet rag in the

Dumpster. Shit no. Denny, take it. Get rid of it on the way back. Go on, it won't bite."

Denny objects, yields, slams the truck door, and pulls away. Carlo and the other man, Arnie, stand in place till the rig disappears. A metal door shuts as they go inside. Somewhere a cat howls. The sole noise now is the Mass Pike traffic. Stark stirs. He pulls sideways, knees bent. It's a signal. He'll hang over the back side of the wall and jump down, then stand against the wall as I hang over and guide my feet to his shoulders. We'll reverse the climb.

But the pipe and Perk beckon me. We could drop to the Dumpster and then to the ground. Whatever Perk is, I can get a sample. I can swipe the hem of my sweater on the spill. It'll take almost no time. It'll be easy.

I signal Stark, but he's already halfway down the back side of the wall. If I follow him, my chance is gone. I won't get it back. It must be now. The instant is more reflex than decision, but I push off as from a pool edge.

My feet hit the Dumpster like thunder. I crouch down atop it, wait for Carlo to burst through the door.

He doesn't come. A minute passes. Then two. The night holds still. The pitch-blackness continues. No Eldridge lights come on. How long before Carlo reactivates the surveillance system? Five minutes? Three?

Stark waits on the back side of the wall. He heard me land here. Will he follow? I can't wait to find out.

I hang over the Dumpster edge and drop down. But my hand slips, and I land crooked. My left ankle twists, and pain zings to the knee. I yelp and kneel and curse the too-big sneakers. I get up and stagger forward, the pipe and spill just feet away. When I'm there, I grab the sweater hem and swipe the pipe and mop at the ground. I have not touched the liquid directly. The sample is secured.

I start to hobble back, but the steel door snaps open, and a flashlight catches my face. I'm frozen in the blazing white beam.

"Ah, 'you have fared to this unhappy world, and yet arrive unpunished.'"

A black-gloved hand reaches out and grabs for me. Air swirls as I duck. I try to run, but my ankle won't let me. I sink down.

"Yes. 'Move on all fours along the dismal track.'"

I scuttle sideways on my knees, feeling faint, sick. Carlo laughs. "'Distance can deceive the senses—so spur yourself a little more.'"

His light plays over my body, then back to my face. He's toying with me. I want to vomit.

"'Climb up toward me with cautious step . . . grapple the hair, as someone climbing would.' Canto 34."

I move my arms, and my elbow bumps something at my right side. It's the holster. Under the sweater is a gun. I have to get it out. Turning just enough to keep my right side hidden in shadow, I use my left hand as a decoy. I move those left fingers like puppets. Meanwhile, my right thumb unsnaps the holster safety strap. I work the gun loose. The .38 is now in my hand, heavy, weighty. There's only one chance. I rise and step back, weight on the right foot, and point at the light. Thumb steady, I pull back the hammer.

At the click, the flashlight shifts to my gun hand, then zigzags as Carlo reaches to his belt line for his own gun. He's drawing. If he fires, he's defending Eldridge. If I fire, it's self-defense. Or is it murder?

The instant goes into slow motion. A cat howls in the darkness, and the howl becomes a crackle and roar. It's an engine. I turn as a Cyclops of white light roars and blazes at me and at Carlo. He, too, stands frozen as the Harley

bears down, slices between us, and brakes to a quick stop.
I mount and grab Stark's hips, gun in hand, as he throttles
fast away from Eldridge, Fatso's engine mixing with a
pop-pop of the bullets that miss as Stark guides us off into
the night.

Chapter Twenty-five

The phone rings at the fourth lap of the Ace bandage around my swollen ankle. "This is Tania. You need to come see me."

"I can't."

"Regina, you can. You must. I'll send a car."

"I'm not feeling well." This is the understatement of a day spent icing my ankle, mentally reliving the *Inferno* escape and Stark's 4:00 a.m. blistering lecture on reckless handgun use. The black sweater is sealed in a Ziploc, ready for dispatch to a police lab. The gun is back in the cabinet. Stark spent the early morning hours making compresses for my ankle and keeping a lookout. He took Biscuit with him when he left at noon. On four hours' sleep, I'm mobilized by coffee and Dr Pepper and an old malacca cane Jo once used to scatter pigeons from the rear fire escape. It's now after 5:00 p.m. of a day on which this woman is thankful to be alive.

Tania's laugh is acid. "Come anyway."

"Sorry, I have plans."

"Cancel them. There's somebody here who wants to talk to you. It's important."

Jeffrey. Of course, she's calling for Jeffrey. Carlo told him everything. It's a trap. Tania is baiting me, and the timing is terrible because Devaney's at the prison convention in Orlando. Till he returns, I won't budge. My doors are locked, blinds closed. Go back again to the Marlborough house? How stupid do they think I am?

"Regina, let me assure you the coast is clear. Jeffrey is out of town. I'm by myself."

"What about the Eldridge guards who don't let you out of their sight?"

"There's only one. He's at the corner. You can come through the back alleyway. There's a parking space right beside my SUV. He won't see you. I'll close the draperies. Believe me, Regina, it's just me here by myself . . . and a special person who has new information." I say nothing. "Don't you want to know who it is?"

"Tania, this won't work."

"Aren't you curious?"

"Maybe another time."

"It's Brenda Holstetter."

"Brenda—"

"From Ambrosia Catering. She talked to you at a restaurant days ago. She's ready to talk to you again."

"We spoke twice."

"That was different. She's ready to say much more. Her troubled conscience brought her here. I counseled her. She has secrets to tell. One secret especially . . . you'll never guess."

"Probably not."

"About a prisoner you're interested in?"

My heart leaps. "What prisoner?"

"Serving a murder sentence in Norfolk."

"How do you kn—I mean, what does Brenda say? Put her on the phone. Please put Brenda on the phone."

"Regina, that's the very last thing we'd want to do. She's finally calmed down. She arrived in a silly uniform with a brocade vest and pantaloons. I gave her a spa robe and chamomile tea in my majolica pot. She's resting on a chaise in the sunporch. She'll be receptive if you simply arrive. Otherwise, I can't predict her mental state. I can't promise she'll tell her secrets tomorrow or next week. She's ready today, right now. You needn't worry about Jeffrey. He's in New York for a two-day meeting. He's a partner of a developer named Bevington. Frankly, it's peaceful here."

"I sprained my ankle."

"I'm on tiptoe myself. The quiet is comforting. It centers oneself. I may have a Zen meditation room installed. Why don't you let me call my driver? I'll send the Town Car."

I draw the line at Tania's car. "Let me think it over. If I'm not there by six, don't expect me." We hang up.

"Quandary" puts it mildly. What could Brenda know about Henry Faiser? *How* could she know? From Alan? But how? What if Brenda appeared at the Marlborough house, and Tania seized the chance to dramatize, to whip the waitress into flights of dark fantasy? I could be sandwiched between two hysterics, Brenda and Tania. And Tania would hover, sucking up every word. Resolved to keep silent, she'd sooner or later spew everything to Jeffrey, fact or fiction. But I'm the one he'd target.

Yet something brought Brenda to the Arnots' doorstep. What is it?

How much risk to find out? Last night I could have died, my body disposed of before dawn, vanished forever.

I swore to Stark that I'd hunker down here in the house until Devaney gets back.

I peek outside, where today's weather is bright and sunny, one of the longest days of the year, a mockery of my seclusion. If I go to Marlborough, I can be back long before dusk. Plus, Barlow Square looks clear, and my car is at the curb. I can manage with this cane. Hobbling around the condo all day, I've learned some maneuvers. If Brenda Holstetter has important information, perhaps she'll come back with me. Maybe we'll go directly to the police this very evening. Daylight is an ally.

I call Stark to let him know where I'm going, but his cell phone is off. I leave him a message and toy briefly with the idea of buckling on the .38. No, not after his Marine Corps ultimatum on guns and amateurs. In slacks and a blue shirt, car key in hand, gripping the cane, I head out.

On Marlborough, I turn my black Beetle into the rear alleyway, which is rutted and full of "Private, No Parking, Tow Away Zone" signs. Behind the Arnot house sits a Cadillac SUV—Tania's—and an empty space. Nobody's in sight. I pull in and press a bell marked "Deliveries."

The first impression as I enter the kitchen is that Tania's lipstick is crooked, like an elderly woman who misses the lip line. "Regina," she says, "here you are, with a walking cane." She's in a tangerine shirt, black wrap skirt, and espadrilles. Her hair is pulled back and held with a clip. Her voice is strangely flat, a strained monotone. "I doubted you'd come. I'd bet you wouldn't. I counted on it."

"Where's Brenda?"

"Now it's too late."

"She's gone?"

"Late, late, late."

"But it's not six. I said by six. Since she's not here, I'll leave right now."

A man suddenly emerges from the butler's pantry holding a meat cleaver. He looks familiar. That thick brown hair . . . it's the man who worked on the Olds, who followed me to the library. Silently, he stands in front of the kitchen back door, blocking it.

"I'm leaving, Tania. Excuse me." He doesn't move a muscle.

"Come into the front room, Regina. You must."

Plan B: I'll go straight to the front door and out into the street and flag down a vehicle. It'll take a cool head and two minutes' time. Carefully, I clear the cane tip in the thick hallway carpeting. My ankle hurts. Tania doesn't look well herself. The woman who pranced in platforms at the fund-raiser now trudges as if dejected, her shoulders hunched.

At the archway to the front room, there's a clear view of the front door. I lengthen my stride to make a beeline. I've fifteen feet to go when a figure suddenly stirs from a sofa and rises—a short, wiry man in a double-breasted suit, no tie, his shirt open. It's Jeffrey Arnot.

"Ms. Cutter, welcome. Sit down. You too, Tania. Both of you, sit."

"Jeffrey, you promised—"

"Shut up, Tania. Behave yourself."

So Tania followed her husband's orders to lure me here.

"I collect single-malt scotches, Ms. Cutter," Jeffrey says. "Let me offer you a drink."

"No thank you." I perch on a Sheridan chair about twelve feet from the front door. The draperies are drawn, and the mounted armor plates are silhouetted in the gloom. The blades of the chandelier glint as if greased.

"Tania, pour our guest a drink." Tania reaches for the cut crystal and pours me a glass nearly brimming with scotch. Jeffrey leans against the archway, still standing. If I splash scotch at his face, can I make it to the door?

"To your health, Ms. Cutter. I see you're hurt. How did that happen?"

"I fell near my home."

"In daytime?"

"Early this morning."

"Too bad. Drink up, Ms. Cutter. I insist." It's an order. I comply, and fiery whisky streaks from throat to navel. "You must be tired. The dead of night is no time for a scavenger hunt. A person can wind up where it's none of their business. A person can injure himself—or herself. That's why a property has walls, for protection. Do drink up."

I sip again and endure the burn. Tania sits slumped on an Empire sofa, eyes on her husband, who rocks back on his heels. The wall-mounted armor casts a sickly sheen. "My lawyers, Ms. Cutter, tell me that criminal trespass is a punishable offense. And then there's property theft."

"Theft?"

"Anything stolen from private property."

The sample I swiped on the sweater, what else could he mean? And what does he want from this prolonged cat-and-mouse game? Me pleading for my life? "A dab of Perk," I say with a staged shrug. "It's hardly grand theft."

He laughs. "Ah, our good friend perchlorate. Perch."

"Perchlorate?"

"A business opportunity, waste disposal of perchlorate. And it's patriotic. Did you know that, Ms. Cutter? Did you know it's red, white, and blue?"

"No."

"Indeed. The disposal project assists our nation's defense industry. NASA, the air force, all the military branches—perch is the crap in their diaper. Every rocket they fired for the last fifty years, the leftover shit is perchlorate. Science says it's contaminated the lettuce fields all over America, gives us cancer salads. The problem is hushed up in Washington, of course, so we're really doing the government a favor. Perch is all over Cape Cod, in case you didn't know. It drives the eco freaks crazy. The trial lawyers would love it, but perch won't pad their wallets. Not when it's disposed of. Customers count on us for disposal."

"In the Eldridge drainpipe."

"Wherever. As a businessman, Ms. Cutter, I jump at new ventures but take care of the old ones too. If it's making money and not broke, we don't fix it. We stay in for the long haul."

What long haul? The days of B&B Auto up to now? The days of Big Doc's cult house and his ravings on sewers, toxins, and parts per billion? Living on-site before the fire, Doc knew about the toxic waste disposal. Did Henry Faiser know too, because he was in and out of B&B Auto hawking his stolen watches and shoes?

That's the Carlo connection. It has to be Carlo who made certain the chop shop drain stayed in place when the deluxe high-rise was built. He worked construction then. What did Devaney call him? A model employee.

I have to get out of here.

"My wife told you there's someone special here to see you."

"Jeffrey, I'm going upstairs—"

"Hell you are. You sit still and keep your mouth shut. Next time you'll follow orders and do what you're told." Jeffrey snaps his fingers toward the shadows of the dining room. A gangly man steps forward. He has long blond hair in a ponytail. He stands with his back to the front door, and I'm suddenly face-to-face with the very man who circled Barlow Square days ago in my car. Now he barricades the Arnots' front door.

"This is the man I'm going to meet?"

"Oh no, I can do much better than that. Much better."

Then it's Carlo. The *Inferno* fanatic lurks somewhere in this house, waiting for Jeffrey's signal. My ankle throbs, my left hand is sweaty on the cane.

Jeffrey calls out, "We're ready. Come down, please." He sounds oddly deferential. Then I understand why. The man who's coming down the stairway is recognizable from the jutting jaw, the blazing white teeth of the smile. It's the face I've seen on TV, the face I saw up close in this very house.

It's Senator Jordan Wald.

Chapter Twenty-six

Regina Cutter, I believe we've met before." In a navy blazer, khakis, and running shoes, Wald bounds forward boyishly. Then, my God, we are shaking hands. For the second time, I feel the strangeness of his handshake.

"Drink, Jordan?"

"Mineral water sounds good. A runner has to stay in training." Tania jumps to the bar, grabbing ice cubes with silver claw tongs. The water fizzes. "Tania, my dear, thank you." Tania sits back down, still grasping the tongs. Wald flashes his smile and faces me. "Jeff and Tania are the motor of the Carney-Wald campaign. They've been on board from the beginning. They're charter members of the Green Circle, our most valued supporters. Did you know that, Ms. Cutter?"

"Not until now."

"Opening one's home repeatedly takes very special people. The best." Wald lifts his glass to toast the Arnots. Jeffrey nods. A pale Tania clutches the tongs. Wald seems perfectly cheerful, as if the room were now buzzing with political supporters, wine, and the riffs of the jazz trio. He looks like a man ready to collect campaign checks.

He conspicuously ignores the ponytailed man who stares out into the middle distance, unmoving as a figure from a wax museum.

"So, Ms. Cutter—or may I call you Regina? Reggie? Which do you prefer? Or is it Gina Baynes?"

My heart stops. "I don't answer to 'Gina' anymore. Or 'Baynes.'"

"Not since moving to Boston? That was last winter, wasn't it?"

"February." The word sounds choked.

"And before that, Chicago, wasn't it?"

"Yes." My smallest voice.

He laughs. "We politicians need to know our constituents' backgrounds. How else can we serve the Commonwealth? Am I right, Jeff?" Arnot grins. "Don't worry, Regina, your private life is safe with me. But you'll see our Boston families enjoy nothing more than family history. For us, genealogy is, well, it's either our tic or our trademark. Your choice."

He winks at me, actually winks. I feel rigid as wood. Could a front window provide escape? Could I smash a big pane and get out?

"Here's a little surprise I've been saving for Jeff and Tania. There's a Wald family connection to the Arnots' house, a true fact I've learned lately. And, Tania, you'll be interested to hear this, with all your fine antiques."

Tania looks up. Jeffrey frowns and looks wary. All eyes are on Wald. "Here it is. My great-great-great-grandfather was an architect. He designed a number of Boston houses, particularly here in the Back Bay. Yours, I understand, is one of them."

My God, that's Dehmer. Dehmer, who married Clara Eddington. I sit stock-still. Is this a trick? Jeffrey grunts. Tania murmurs something unintelligible.

"Yes, indeed, I'm descended from Charles Dehmer, who lived on Beacon Hill, though unfortunately, my great-great-great-grandfather died in a carriage accident. But on my mother's side, I am a Dehmer. That makes me kin to this house. Here's to all of us." He drains his glass and gives it to Tania, whose hand is shaking. Wald seems oblivious. It seems that he knows nothing about the breakage and nighttime mayhem. Or Edmund Wight. Or his calamitous courtship of Clara Eddington.

Tania bites her lip and pinches the tongs. Her face is stone gray, her eyes two coal-dark pits. Jeffrey looks at his watch. "Jordan, if you don't mind, the schedule—"

"Of course. Let's move on." He faces me. "Regina, political life is complex. A candidate must always know the score. It seems you've been tampering with the scoreboard."

"I—"

"Maybe not purposely. You had good intentions, right? But you got out of your depth. You plunged into the Boston of the past, into an incident very painful to me personally." His voice drops low. "My own son was gunned down by a drug-crazed man on Eldridge Street. You know that?"

Silent, I nod.

"Thirteen years ago Eldridge Street was full of addicts and drug dealers. My son, tragically, sought drugs there. As a father, I live daily with that knowledge."

I nod again, my ankle throbbing as a new pain sensation rises in my right thumb. It feels suddenly hot and raw.

"As a parent, I'm haunted by what I could have done to prevent my son, Peter, from turning to drugs. A good student, he was college age."

My thumb is searing. It looks normal, but burns as it once did in the donut shop with Devaney when I held the stopwatch. And in Newton at the Home and Garden Alliance. I close my eyes and see blood ooze at the knuckle.

"A tragic, senseless killing that robbed my son of his future."

My thumb is on fire, my vision a scene of spurting blood. I can hardly bear it. Wald stands over me, towers over me.

"But fortunately, the killer was brought to justice and is in prison. Norfolk Prison."

Does he expect me to say Henry Faiser's name? Wald's own thumb is inches from my eyes. It's malformed. And shiny, likely from scar tissue. That's why his handshake feels odd. Because of his right thumb. His right thumb . . . Didn't the gun dealer warn me about holding a gun, locking down the right thumb? Hold it two-handed, he said, clear of the trigger. *"Unless you want to lose your right thumb."*

"The jury convicted the assailant. No one else will die as his victim. Justice was served."

I see Wald's own thumb bloodied, ripped, and mangled. My gaze drops to his shoes, running shoes. What did he call himself at the microphone here at the fundraiser? A runner to go the distance for Massachusetts? The love nest condo in Eldridge Place had a track suit. And the stopwatch that made my thumb burn raw was a runner's stopwatch, the watch found in the weeds near the weapon.

"My son, you see, was an environmentalist. Greenpeace, Sierra, the Wilderness Society—he was their captive." His gaze locks on mine. "Peter was an idealist, as young people often are."

I nod, thumb blazing.

"But idealists won't compromise. Reasoning with my own son was out of the question. The environment was nonnegotiable. You can understand the problem. Anyone in public life understands the basics of compromise."

"Compromise," I echo in a whisper out of fiercest pain.

Wald goes on. "In life, in business, to serve the greater good. Our heating oil business, for instance, where Peter learned of certain . . . activities. He worked part-time in my trucking business, you see. He drove certain routes."

Sick with pain and revulsion, I stare.

"A father-son standoff was the last thing in the world I wanted. He brought it on. He went to Eldridge Street. He had no business there. That route was for other drivers, other deliveries, not his—"

Jeffrey interrupts. "He went for drugs, Jordan. He had a habit."

"He had no business. No business on Eldridge Street."

"Buying drugs," Jeffrey says. "Drugs."

"No business there at all."

"Cocaine and hash. He met his dealer."

"A father in public life had no choice," Wald says. "Measures had to be taken. Everything was at stake. He wouldn't listen, wouldn't keep his mouth shut. His conscience, really. He became . . . dangerous."

Through the fog of pain, I make sense of what Wald is telling me. Peter Wald learned his father's trucks dumped toxic waste. Peter went to Eldridge and found out. Peter was adamant. No compromise was possible. Vowing to tell authorities, he posed a threat.

"Yes, it was drugs." Wald begins to parrot Jeffrey. "It was. And self-defense on my part. I came immediately, but he provoked me in the street. A father tries to help, but things happen . . . it was self-defense." Wald recites the words as if they're anchors that will hold me steady to his version of the past. I meet his gaze. Piety and righteousness gleam in his eyes, but I know I'm looking at the face of Peter Wald's killer.

"Life goes on, Regina, as it must. My memorial to Peter is environmental law. I continue my son's passion for green causes. My fatherly duty endures in the Massachusetts Senate. As lieutenant governor, I can make certain those efforts will not stop."

He leans close. His breath smells of clove and rot. "Providing we're not smeared by rumors and allegations. Providing a certain Boston police detective stops his personal mission and comes to his senses. We don't blame you, Regina. We're prepared to wipe the slate clean, but we need to know a few things. We need to know the so-called new evidence." He crosses his arms like a TV prosecutor. "We need to know who else the detective has talked to. Who you've talked to."

So this is why Wald's here. It's damage control by diplomacy. And if that doesn't work, then what?

"I . . . I have nothing to say."

"Take your time, Regina. No harm is meant. Consider your own future. When the Carney-Wald administration takes office, my door will be open. We'll have positions to fill. The Commonwealth needs good people such as yourself. Right now I simply want information so we can correct any falsehoods. As a citizen, you can help prevent campaign mudslinging. You don't want to be implicated in slander."

"No."

He flashes his white teeth. "So we agree. The rest is simple."

Simple indeed. And crystal clear. The clean slate begins with the elimination of Reggie Cutter.

I walked into this snare with eyes wide open, yet I must not give in. The cane—can I use it? The mounted armor, the breastplate? Can I get to a phone and hit 911?

"I'd like to stand up, please. Powder room . . ."

"But of course." Wald steps aside as if he's gallantry itself. With the cane in my left hand, the whisky in the right, I exaggerate my halting steps across the shag carpet. I'm in the middle of the room, suddenly drawn to the chandelier I've so shunned. It gives me an idea. Jeffrey, Wald, and ponytail there at the door—they're a triangle. I'm in the middle, and Tania is nearly in a heap off to the side.

Cold sweat runs down my back. I stand directly under the chandelier, the steel blades too high to reach. "Regina, we need to hear from you." Wald is prodding. "Visit the powder room, collect your thoughts, and let's proceed."

My hands are icy. In this instant, a new current wafts here in the room. It's chilly. The AC? No, it's sharp, more like winter. And it comes with a jangling of what sounds to be metal on metal.

I shiver and look up. Is the draft swinging the chandelier back and forth? And did the lamplight shift? Because the blades have turned dull gray, as if coated with dust. No, with frost. Before my eyes, snowflakes begin to swirl. Wald and Jeffrey Arnot stand in place. Don't they hear this? See or feel the cold? Tania is unmoving. It's freezing in here. I look up again.

Wald's voice comes from afar. "Regina, let's not abuse the Arnots' hospitality. Gazing at the ceiling won't help us. I'm ready to listen. Speak up."

Ice is coating the halberds and swords and knives of the chandelier. The glaze thickens before my eyes. It coats the slender wires suspending the entire light fixture. The whole mass glitters, with a snow squall whirling like a storm. Cold flashes against the back of my throat. My eyes water. I think of airplanes forced down from ice on the wings. Ice storms split winter's stoutest trees from end to end.

I know what I must do. The cane goes first, my one and only weapon sacrificed for the moment. I drop it as the wires of the chandelier ping and tick like a ship's rigging strained to the hilt. "Oops, Senator, would you please?" Trust Old Boston manners. He springs.

Now the whisky. I let the glass go. "Oh, Scotch on your rug. Jeffrey, I'm so sorry." The wires groan. Jeffrey glances up, then back down at the whisky-wet rug. The onetime Boston street tough who wears a suit—will he retrieve the glass and stand with Wald by my side? How many seconds? Five?

Here comes Jeffrey to pick up the glass, but Tania steps up too, as the wires click and twing. Wald hands me the cane, and Jeffrey holds the glass. Both men are right beside me, the three of us directly under the frosted blades. I have one chance, one chance only in this instant.

I clasp the cane in my hand, prepare to raise it up above my head as Tania steps forward. I can't warn her. There's no time. Braced on one leg, I raise my head, look up, thrust the cane, and jump. The cane's crook catches on the blades and wires, grabs fast. Tania takes another step. I yank the cane hard. Once, twice, then one last time.

For a split second, I hang suspended from the cane as the ceiling crunches. Cracks open, whole crevasses. The plaster rains, tumbles, and the room shudders and quakes. Dropping down, I lunge and shove Tania, the two of us thudding to the floor, away from the chandelier, while Wald and Jeffrey Arnot scream out, both buried in a cascade of plaster and an avalanche of steel.

Chapter Twenty-seven

S o you crawled out?"

"Not exactly. Tania and I were both winded, but she got herself up and helped me. We wheezed and choked, but she helped to steady me."

"Helped *you* but not her husband? Interesting." Devaney shifts in the love seat and uses a handkerchief very delicately on his sunburned, peeling nose, his memento of Orlando. I face him in the rocker, my ankle at rest on a footstool.

"The house felt bombed, Frank. Plaster and blood were everywhere. It was like Armageddon."

"Reggie, you could have been killed." His voice is more plaintive than reproachful. "You came way too close."

"I took a chance, all on my own. It was for Henry Faiser, Frank, my 'innocence project' paid off. But who'd imagine a sprained ankle as good luck? Because that cane was crucial." I pause for a couple of deep breaths to help calm the days' long aftershocks from Marlborough.

"Tell me again, Reggie, how you pulled the chandelier down."

"I jumped, hooked the wires and blades, and gave it

three hard yanks. It let go. That contraption looked ready to crash from the first night I saw it."

"What about the frost and ice on the swords?"

I've told him twice. But Frank's face shows his concern about my state of mind. He's trying to talk me into a soft landing, as if by repeating the story, I'll be free of it. It's probably a cop version of therapy.

"You think maybe a psychic presence was involved?"

"A resident ghost, Frank. Paranormal power came into play, I know that for sure. The Marlborough house has a troubled history. No wonder it gets sold frequently. I think it's haunted. Someday I'll tell you the story of the house and Senator Wald's connection to an angry ghost spirit. But believe me, timing was everything at that instant. When the chandelier crashed, we choked and coughed and made our way out the front."

"What about the blond-haired guy with the ponytail?"

"He ran to help Jeffrey, who was pinned down and howling like a beast. Wald was facedown in the rubble. He wasn't moving. The blades were so treacherous, Tania and I groped our way along the wall to the door. The guy with the cleaver came running too. Tania and I . . . well, it was like we were in a three-legged race to the door. Once in the street, we flagged down a woman. We were trying to talk her into taking us to the precinct, but my friend came. I'd called him earlier to let him know where I was going."

"He drove you?"

"He's a biker. We worked it out." I don't describe Stark roaring up Marlborough, hailing us a cab, then riding ahead, like a motorcade escort, to the precinct house. It was three days ago but feels like five minutes. I ask, "Is Jeffrey Arnot conscious?"

"He's still too doped up to talk. He was stuck like a pig. The EMTs took him to Boston City with blades still in his gut. He has deep lacerations. They're watching for internal bleeding."

"What about Wald?"

"The senator is in intensive care at Mass General. That chandelier did a job on him too. He's got a collapsed lung and a bucket of blood in the chest cavity from severed blood vessels. The trauma surgeon got a workout. Of course, Wald's lawyers are massing like an armed camp. It's gonna be hardball all the way. The prosecution has its work cut out."

"Frank, I know how you hate to tell a civilian about a case—"

"There's no exact case yet, Reggie. We got a search warrant for Eldridge Place. We got Carlo Feggiotti in for questioning, and we'll look into medical records for treatment of the injury of Wald's right thumb. If it matches the death date of his son, we're in business."

"And Henry Faiser can count down the days till his release and medical treatment." I pause. "So Peter Wald's death was never about drugs, was it?"

"Sure it was—to a point, because Peter flirted with the Rastafarians. He smoked weed and used a lot of other junk too. But the drug connection fooled us. His murder seemed like a street killing."

"And it was. He threatened to expose the waste disposal racket, and his father shot him in the street. We both know hypocrisy drives young people crazy. It had to be a bombshell for him—his dad, the state's green politician, being a major polluter." Silence falls. "Does it all surprise you, Frank?"

He hesitates, shakes his head. "Yes and no. A guy like

Wald is probably arrogant to start with. Then his greed mixes with privilege."

"The aristocrat teamed up with Jeffrey Arnot?"

"Why not? Let's say Arnot first okayed dumping grease and solvents in the B&B Auto days. Carlo ran it. Then Wald bought in. Why? Because he's got a fleet of tank trucks sitting parked in warm weather and mild winters. The dumping brought in nice money, probably everything from petroleum waste to banned pesticides. And Carlo's still their guy."

"Though they needed helpers, like Alan Tegier. When his acne treatment made him moody and tense, Carlo wanted him out, but doubtless suspected he might talk about it. He had to be eliminated."

Devaney nods. "We'll look hard to find out if Arnot or Wald signed off on the Tegier murder, or if Carlo ordered it on his own. Maybe the operation expanded in the perchlorate phase."

"The hard evidence, Frank, is my sweater, which ought to provide plenty of perchlorate. I looked it up online. It's awful. It plays havoc with the endocrine system, wrecks the thyroid, and damages the neural system. Perchlorate is found in underground plumes and has spread into water systems. And it's nationwide. Massachusetts is just one of many states."

"Equal opportunity poison."

"So to speak. It's even linked to auto air bags and fireworks and imported fertilizer but mainly to spent rocket fuels. It's our souvenir of the Cold War. We've fouled our own nest in so many ways. Jeffrey Arnot and Jordan Wald knew from the first exactly what they were doing."

Devaney nods. "And young Peter Wald knew too, at least about his father."

I shift my leg on the stool. "But how did they get away with dumping for so long? Surely, Boston tests its sewer water. What about the EPA?"

Devaney rolls his shoulders, loosens his tie. "Bureaucracies and budgets, Reggie. Agencies are understaffed, and people do what they can with skeleton crews and thin resources. Here in town, there's two agencies, the Water and Sewer Commission and the state Water Resources Authority. They're obliged to test drainage discharges in representative areas."

"But not everywhere?" He shakes his head no. "How about reported sickness? Or deaths?"

"We'll try to get the Environmental Strike Team of the Public Health Commission on this. But, Reggie, you know how these cases play out. A cancer cluster isn't proof. Hot spots aren't definite. And don't think I'm blowing you off. I'm mad as hell we missed our cue years ago." He reaches for his Tums.

"Will the Eldridge arson and murder be investigated now?"

"Believe it." Devaney chews the tablets and pats his tender nose. "I don't want to get ahead of things, but if Carlo Feggiotti cuts a deal with the prosecutor, we can go after Arnot hard and heavy."

"And Wald?"

"Wald for sure."

"Do I dare bring up Sylvia Dempsey?"

He cringes. "You got a theory about the skin doctor?"

"Yes, but I now suspect Wald. A high-profile love triangle would be too messy for an ambitious politician. A man who'd kill his son for jeopardizing his career wouldn't hesitate to bludgeon a lover if she pressured him into making her Mrs. Lieutenant Governor. And Sylvia was ambitious."

"Spoken like a true rocking-chair deputy."

"Spoken like a woman thrilled to think Henry Faiser will be free." In fact, the mental image of Faiser's hands unshackled soothes and excites me at once. "How long before Faiser is released, Frank? What's the time frame?"

"A while, Reggie. The system grinds at its own pace."

"Promise you'll stay with it. Promise me Faiser will be your top priority even if another tabloid-size crime erupts." I give him my hardest stare.

He meets my gaze. "It's a deal. You can remind me."

"Nag?"

"Nag. But I don't want you in harm's way. I don't like the look of that ankle."

"It's healing nicely. I'll be fine. I have my daughter's gallery show to attend, and lunch with a Red Hat friend."

"Red Hat? A communist organization?"

"Try spunky women who speak their mind. Also, Frank, a social life to move from a back burner to the front. Who knows, maybe a new flame . . ." Though the Hong Kong/Cairo postcard man still hasn't called.

"I'm thinking flames too, Reggie, back and front burners, restaurant kitchens. The big heat."

"That's where I want to be, Frank, in the heat."

He blinks. I blink back. Then we laugh.

References

The author wishes to acknowledge the use of the following sources:

Bunting, Bainbridge. *Houses of Boston's Back Bay: An Architectural History, 1840–1917.* 1967.

Gross, Kim Johnson, and Jeff Stone. *Dress Smart Women: Wardrobes That Win in the Workplace.* 2002.

Howe, Helen. *The Gentle Americans, 1864–1960.* 1965.

Howell, William Dean. *The Rise of Silas Lapham.* 1885.

Mergen, Bernard. *Snow in America.* 1997.

O'Connor, Thomas H. *The Hub: Boston Past and Present.* 2001.

Pinsky, Robert, editor and translator. *The "Inferno" of Dante.* 1994.

About the Author

Cecelia Tishy, a Pittsburgh native who has also lived in West Palm Beach, Florida, and Fairmont, West Virginia, made her home in Boston, Massachusetts, for twenty years. She left in 1987 to relocate to Nashville, Tennessee, with her husband, Bill, and two daughters. When she isn't writing crowd-pleasing mysteries, she is professor of American Literature at Vanderbilt University. She has also written, under the name Cecelia Tichi, several nonfiction works on such diverse subjects as country music and muckraking in America.

More
supernatural thrills from
Cecelia Tishy!

~o

Please turn this page
for a preview of

All in One Piece

Available in hardcover.

Chapter One

I've never been a careless person. Crossing the street, I look both ways. Of course I do. My reflexes are razor sharp, and I'm a brisk walker. At the end of this city block, a small blue car is moving slowly up Barlow Square as I tug my dog's lead and step off the curb at a good clip.

The car speeds up, its squealing tires a signal that it's gaining on me. The dog trots ahead, but my gut radar says to step it up. A power walker in slacks and a sweater, I clutch my purse and, stupidly, a hot latte in my right hand.

The car is racing. My left arm signals *slow down*. Instead, it speeds up. The dog tugs, and I grip the latte and break into a run. There's too much glare to see the driver. The sidewalk is just a few feet ahead. The dog springs to the curb. The car aims like a missile. I sprint.

Bang!—it clips me. I pitch forward. Knee and elbow strike the asphalt, and the latte arcs and splashes as I sprawl flat, my handbag flying as pain rockets to my shoulder. My cheek smacks into a pool of steaming coffee and the car speeds off, the car that hit me. Spangles of light flash behind my eyes as the dog whines and everything goes black.

Do minutes pass? Seconds? I'm still here in the street, sipping air, too winded to move. I breathe a mix of coffee, tailpipe exhaust, and burning rubber. The pavement is cold, and my knee is on fire.

Footsteps. I hear footsteps.

"Are you all right?" A tenor voice at my ear says. "I saw you fall. Can you speak?"

My lips are gritty, my mouth full of sand and stones. My eyes water from the pain. Quietly I spit.

"Let's get you off the street. Don't worry, your dog is right here." Strong arms tug at my good arm. I see ruddy cheeks, chestnut hair, and soft gray eyes. He wears a bomber jacket like the one I sent my son, Jack, last winter. Confused, I murmur, "Jack—"

"No. Steven."

Steven, of course. It's Steven Damelin, my new upstairs tenant. He holds the dog's lead, and Biscuit stays close at my side as I limp a step or two. "My calf—" Pain scissors the back of my right leg where the bumper hit. There's no sign of the hit-and-run car. "Did you see the license plate?" My voice quavers.

"Here," he says, "sit down on the curb." The latte cup scuds away in a chill gust of October wind. Biscuit whines. No one else is on the sidewalk.

"It was blue." I shiver. "A small car, maybe Japanese."

"Maybe a BMW."

Nausea rolls in waves. My slacks are ripped at the knee. Blood seeps through. I wipe a sleeve across my wet cheek. "It's as though it aimed for me. It came right at me."

"You crossed at midblock." He gets my handbag from the street and holds it awkwardly. "Can you move your arms and legs? Try to move."

I do. Everything hurts. My best wool slacks are ruined. "Nothing seems broken." It takes great energy to say this. I'm winded, bruised, maybe sprained. Fracture? I look up at his kind face, a man in his early thirties. "That car came right at me."

"I saw you fall. I saw you from my window on the second floor. Let's get you inside."

Clutching his arm, I rise and smell his aftershave— tropical lime in humid midautumn Boston. The granite stoop is torture. These Victorian brick town houses all have high steps, a stretch even for a beagle. I take my bag and fumble for keys to the outside door, then to my vestibule entrance.

"Let me help you into your place, Ms. Cutter."

Cutter? Yes, it is my name, although I'm still getting used to it after twenty-five years as Mrs. Martin Baynes and as Gina, which was my ex's, Marty's, choice. But now it's back to Reggie, which was my childhood nickname here in this South End town house condo which I inherited from my late Aunt Jo.

"Step in, Ms. Cutter."

"Reggie," I say, then push my voice above the pain in my elbow and knee. "Call me Reggie."

He guides me to the love seat, settles me against the cushions, and unclips Biscuit's lead. She sits. I unzip my bag and grope for the phone. "I'm calling the police."

"Let me get you some ice. Try to relax."

But my cell phone is dead. I take out a Kleenex and daub my bloody knee, a city Purple Heart after years in the sanctuary of the suburbs, where the biggest kick was a double espresso at Starbucks.

Was the latte my undoing? Free of that cup, would I have beaten the bumper, or would the driver have chased me onto the sidewalk? What if the dog hadn't jumped in time?

Stop the mental replay, Reggie. Take comfort in your new home of these last months, surrounded by Aunt Jo's familiar old furniture, the bentwood rocker, kilim rugs, chenille throw, books crammed everywhere. A few of my own pieces are in place as well. As Marty's long-term corporate wife, I got my share of nicer things and brought a few of them when the divorce was finalized and I moved to Boston last winter. None of it comforts me now.

"Let's put these on your knee and elbow."

Steven offers two neat packets of cracked ice in Ziplocs wrapped in kitchen towels. I thank him. Would my own grown kids be this attentive? Jack would skip the towels. Molly would turn the ice pack into a funky art object. Or am I just feeling sorry for myself? "Look outside at the street," I say. "About ten feet up from my VW Beetle, see the coffee spill?"

"Yes."

"That's where the car hit me."

"You crossed at midblock."

"Do you think the driver was joyriding?"

"I doubt it."

"Maybe it was some kind of initiation rite?"

"No way."

"Or somebody who's seen too many action movie car chases? Or plays video games? Because it aimed at me."

"I'm sure the driver didn't see you. It was an accident."

"Sped at me. Another second crossing that street, I'd be in . . ." The word I want to use is "morgue," but I say, "ICU."

"Perhaps you're not quite used to the city."

"You think I was jaywalking?"

He points at my scuffed, dirty handbag. "A little saddle soap, it should clean up nicely."

"It was hit-and-run."

But his eyes do not meet mine.

"Hit-and-run," I repeat.

He gives me the same pitiful caregiver look that the hospital aides gave my aunt in her final days last winter.

"I'm calling the police right now."

"Why not give the ice a chance to work first?" He faces me in Jo's rocker, obviously at ease in my late aunt's home. Well, that's why I agreed to the six-month sublet—

because Steven Damelin knew my late aunt. Otherwise I'd require the long-term tenant, a dentist, to meet his lease obligations while he tests experimental novocaine in developing countries, meaning the parts of the world that Marty called Emerging Markets, as if those places don't have actual names.

"Steven, please hand me the phone on that table. I want to call the police, actually a certain detective."

"Your Aunt Jo's favorite detective? Is he yours now?"

My favorite? I'd never call Homicide Detective Francis Devaney anybody's personal detective, not Jo's and certainly not my own. Is Steven Damelin being ironic? "The detective is an acquaintance," I say. "It's on a professional basis."

"So you work for cops, too. Are you a psychic, like your aunt?"

What to say to this? Being psychic is a touchy topic. Skeptics sneer in disbelief, while true believers think you're an extraterrestrial. Both sides expect a *Twilight Zone* trick instantly.

"Your aunt told me psychic powers run in families."

"That's true. But abilities vary, Steven. It's not like the TV shows, instantly *on* and flowing like tap water. Jo was very advanced, probably because she embraced her sixth sense throughout her lifetime. The paranormal faculty needs, well, a certain cultivation. It's like, use it or lose it. For me, it's a relatively recent thing. Let's say that I'm playing catch-up with my psychic ability. I have a learner's permit."

"But you're the next generation of Cutter psychics. So let me tell you, that detective kept your Aunt Jo busy. Between Boston crime and the terrorism threats, you'll be in high demand."

Steven Damelin seems to think the first aid entitles him

to full familiarity, but I'm finding this Boy Scout a bit too brash. "Jo took her psychic ability very seriously," I say. "She considered it a great responsibility. It was as serious as her teaching career."

"Oh yes, I know. You see that glass bottle there on the top bookshelf?"

I turn. "The pale green glass?"

"It's an old whiskey bottle handed down from my family. I gave it to Jo. That's when I found out she was psychic. She said when she held it, the bottle gave her a picture of people yelling and a cracked skull too."

"Oh . . ."

"But she accepted the gift because she also felt strong currents of hope. She said teaching high school was an act of hope, too." He shrugs. "I mean, whatever. I'm from an old mill town north of Boston, and it was just a bottle around the house when I was a kid. I thought your aunt would like it. She liked old stuff. The psychic reaction, it was like an allergy."

He sounds too flip.

"Jo Cutter never trifled with her psychic power," I say. "Until her final days, she used her sixth sense for the cause of criminal justice and was equally committed to social justice. To her, the two were entwined, and her community activism was legendary. That's how you met her, right, Steven?" This is a prompt. I want to hear him recite what I already know from my Realtor friend's background check on this man, who is a financial analyst needing a place for a few months while his own condo is renovated.

Steven pushes back his thick chestnut hair. His face is open and eager. "That's right. I met Jo through the Big Buddies mentoring program. She's the reason I got linked up with Luis. We go to movies, shoot pool, sit together in the bleachers at Sox games. His mother works two jobs, no dad in the picture. How's that elbow?"

"The cold feels good."

"Okay. Anyway, I try to keep Luis in school, help him with homework projects. He's already taller than me. Fifteen years old, and he's pushing six feet. I'm starting to talk to him about college. But yeah, your Aunt Jo got the program organized. What a dynamo. It seems like she was in every good cause in the South End, maybe the whole city. Retirement didn't slow her down one bit. She had a gang of us here for chowder once. I remember this cute dog." He reaches down to scratch Biscuit's rump and admires her markings. "This was Jo's dog, wasn't it? I guess she's yours now."

"Yes, you could say Biscuit's mine." In fact, she's half mine. Jo willed her equally to two owners. Don't ask me why.

"This dog's a chowder hound . . . Jo made the best chowder in New England."

"Steven, I ate it as a child in this very house."

"You must have your aunt's recipe."

But I don't. To Marty, shellfish are the filth of the sea. He likes Omaha steaks. I could run the grill at Morton's or Palm or Ruth's Chris. "The chowder," I say, "Jo made it by . . . by heart." The moment sags. Biscuit lies down. I shift the ice packs.

Steven says, "Reggie, you're perfectly free to call the police, but do you really want the aggravation?"

"Someone hit me. I'm a citizen. I have a duty."

"First duty to yourself. You're upset. You need to rest for a while."

"Resting isn't my style. The police need to know about the hit-and- . . ." But I realize Steven won't corroborate my story. He'll call it an accident and say I was jaywalking, in effect discrediting me. "Steven, you've been wonderful, but I must let you get back upstairs to work. I have some things to do." Reggie, I tell myself, assert your authority as landlady. "Is everything okay upstairs? Are you getting enough heat?"

"It's toasty, everything's great. Let me see your eyes . . . checking for dilation."

"I'm fine."

But he plants himself in the rocker. "So here's something to think about, Reggie. You could use some good cheer today. Here's an opportunity." Suddenly the medic sounds like a telemarketer. One way or another, I want him out. Every joint and muscle cries its protest as I swing my legs down and sit straight, inching forward to signal *enough*.

"Your Aunt Jo and I got close over the last year before she got sick, Reggie. There was a deal we were working on together. We kept it confidential. Something good for both of us. I'd like to tell you about it as soon as you feel better. Maybe you'd be interested."

"Maybe some other time." "Deal" was Marty's mantra, a word I can't stand.

"A very favorable investment. As conservative as your aunt was about money, she saw the wisdom of this deal."

"Steven, from now on, I'm a woman of modest means."

His smile broadens. "No problem. There are ways."

"Maybe we can talk about it in a week or so."

And that ends it for now. The light is fading, but Steven's smile is a halogen lamp. The youngish man silhouetted in my door frame—that's the parting image. Sometimes I think back and wish it was just that innocent, a moment when time hung still—just before events again shoved me from behind, shoved me with a force of flesh and bone smashed against cold rock. Shoved me so hard that today's hit-and-run was just a teaser.

Chapter Two

Let me summarize the next hours, a countdown to disaster. I bandage my knee, pop pain pills, eat a light meal on Jo's old Fiestaware—and decide with huge reluctance not to call Detective Frank Devaney. It's about my credibility. Under questioning, I'd say hit-and-run, while Steven would insist that I jaywalked. My Boston police "street cred" would go down the drain in a he-said, she-said waste of Devaney's time. Worst of all, I could seem like a drama queen, the psychic who cries wolf. Devaney could decide to handle his cases without the help of psychic Reggie Cutter, the cornerstone of my Boston life would crumble to dust. The Homicide Division work, my life's fizz and sizzle, finis. I work as a volunteer on an unofficial basis. I can't risk it.

By 10:00 P.M., I reluctantly sink down into bed, vowing to rethink the whole thing in the morning. I've always been a fairly sound sleeper, but something does go bump in the night even with the heating pipes banging now and then. I hear thudding, rumbling. Biscuit gets restless, growls, and barks, and I let her onto the bed to calm her down. Fitful sleep, no rest.

At last, dawn. Slipping a raincoat over my robe, I take Biscuit out and then feed her. Downing pain pills and coffee, I simply sit in the front room, too sore and sleepy to turn on a radio. The swelling in my knee and elbow is down. My gaze is drawn to the top shelf's green whiskey bottle that Jo held in her hands, surprising Steven when his gift became a psychic prompt. I, too, must touch a thing to "read" it. The bottle is a curiosity, but my main thought at the moment is that the whole shelf needs dusting.

So I sit, rethinking a call to Devaney. And the dripping at first sounds clocklike. Drip ... drip ... drip ... drip. The intervals are irregular even to my so-so musical ear. All right, get up and check the faucets. From the kitchen to the bath, no leaks, no droplets.

A second coffee poured, I sit back down. Still the insistent drops. Is it a leaking radiator? The roof? Boston's having a wet autumn, but it's doubtful that the roof ... anyway, my ceiling is Steven Damelin's floor, so it's unlikely that a leak would escape his notice. Maybe one of his sinks is stoppered, or his bathtub is overflowing.

Wide-awake, I go room to room scanning the ceiling. Plaster, moldings, everything's okay starting from the two bedrooms in back, mine and the smaller second one, which is the study. Then to the bathroom off the hall, forward to the kitchen, once again to the hall and back to the front room right to the corner behind the sofa—

Where I see the spatter on the floor by the radiator.

Droplets dashed on the hardwood have formed a small puddle. A phase of my Molly's art flashes, her Pollock period. I lean down and touch and smell it. That iron odor. The darkening red.

"Biscuit, no, get away from there." I pull her back and scoop her into my arms. Then a drop falls into my hair, the sticky wet on my scalp.

I look up. Drops are falling where the steam pipe runs from my radiator upstairs to Steven's.

From Steven's down onto my floor.

Let it be paint.

Let it be enamel, finger paint, rustproofing, any kind of paint. Pray for paint. Because in that frozen moment, denial is the lifeline. Please, God, paint—because the minute you let go, the world will rupture forever.

Dashing upstairs, I try Steven's door—locked from inside—and bang the brass knocker. And slam my palm on the door panel. And I scream his name.

Tripping on my robe going back downstairs, I ask, *where's that key?* Where did I put the key to the upstairs flat? In the hall table drawer. The dog squirms and yelps, but I hold her tight against me and root among coupons, stamps, rubber bands. No key.

The phone book—nutty, but I call Steven's number—tethered by the cord of one of Jo's old landline phones. Fourth ring, and here's his upbeat voice. "Leave me a message . . ."

Back to that spot by the heat pipe. The slow drip. The pool of blood. Then I remember—the key is on a hook by the kitchen window. I grab the key, dash upstairs, open the door—and find fifties-sixties furniture, fake zebra pillows, boomerang tables all tumbled and knocked over. A sideways Lava lamp forms a slow blue belch.

Biscuit leaps, dives, and hits the floor. "Here, Biscuit!" But she barks frantically and runs to the next room. "Come here! Here!" She's back a moment later, her white muzzle stained, her paw marks rusty red against my robe.

Back and forth she runs as if to show the way, barking and whining me to Steven's radiator.

First, a sneakered foot, then a jacked-up knee. Then his body lying on its back, a twisted mannequin, arms out stiff, something dangling from the wrists, dark strips, like shoelaces. Mouth open, a ridge of teeth, wax museum eyes that stare at nothing.

And so much blood, his shirtfront mapped in blood,

continents of blood. Small blood circles up and down his arms are a polka-dot pox of wounds that weep.

The floor slants. I retch, grab at a wall, stumbling on something hard that slides when my foot kicks at it—a yellow drill that's slick with blood . . . the murder weapon, could it be?

It touched the hem of my robe.

Then something else. I lean close to see . . . nailheads. They pin down the skin of Steven's calf and ankle, and his wrists and neck too. A few inches apart, they stretch the skin tight. It looks upholstered, like a button-back sofa. Human flesh treated like upholstery—I lean closer and fight for balance. It takes everything not to throw up.

Chapter Three

Sudden as lightning, the thought occurs to me that a killer could still be inside. In his kitchen, or a back bedroom?

I grab the dog, run back downstairs, slam my door, and call 911. Unreality sets in, like a jerky handheld camera. Whose voice do I hear reporting a dead body at 27 Barlow Square? Whose words say the unspeakable? Me and not me. Steven and not Steven.

The patrol car comes fast, the cop like on TV. I give him Steven's key.

"Lady, you stay inside here."

Still in my robe, I slip into moccasins. Stupid quandary: can I dress? Is a witness required to stay as is? For that matter, am I a witness?

"Settle down, Biscuit," I say as much to myself as to the dog. The sight of Steven Damelin. My gorge rises.

More sirens, then heavy footfalls upstairs.

Steven's leg, his splayed fingers and purpled throat. Those strips. The nails.

The lights of patrol cars flash up and down Barlow Square. Blue uniforms are everywhere on the sidewalk out front. Clutching my robe, I step outside on the stoop. Yellow crime tape already bands the front of my building like crazy gift wrap. *Police Line Do Not Cross Police Line Do Not . . .*

"Lady, get back inside."

"Yes, Officer." In the vestibule, however, I'm stopped by the sight of big rust-red smears on the outside of my own door. Did I somehow get blood on my door when I ran downstairs minutes ago? No, there's not enough blood on me to leave those marks. They don't look random. They're not smears. They're too definite. Patterned, they're patterned. They're like . . . brushstrokes.

How did they get there? Who marked my door in blood? I go inside, grab my phone, call Frank Devaney in the Homicide Division, and fight hysteria as I leave him a voice mail.

Seated near the phone, I wait out an eternity. Finally there's a knock on my door and a voice calling, "Ms. Cutter?"

"Come in, Frank," I yell, then move toward my door as it opens.

But it isn't Frank Devaney.

"I'm Detective Edward Maglia. You called 911?" Before me in the door frame stands a compact man in his late thirties, with short dark brown hair, narrow face and features. He wears a blue suit with a certain sheen, and his nails look manicured. "I'd like to ask you some questions."

"But I called Detective Devaney. I left a message for

him." As if he were a custom-ordered dial-a-detective. Reggie, get a grip. "Please come in."

At the flash of the badge, he's in like a weather front. I gather my robe around me as he stares at a disheveled woman whose robe is stained with blood. A woman who hasn't washed after kicking that drill. The hem of my robe is streaked the color of iodine.

"I didn't know whether to get dressed. Still in my robe."

Maglia nods. He's in the rocker where Steven Damelin sat less than twenty-four hours ago. I excuse myself a moment to put Biscuit in the study and close the door. Refusing coffee, Maglia opens a notebook and starts into my background. Who am I? How long have I resided here? What relation to the owner of record, Josephine Cutter?

"I am her niece and heir. My aunt died last February, of cancer, and I moved in the same month. Steven Damelin was my upstairs tenant." I spell "Damelin." "He moved in about a month ago. He was subletting."

"When last did you see the deceased alive?"

"Yesterday, about two in the afternoon, I was crossing the street out front here on Barlow Square with my dog, and a small blue car hit me. Hit-and-run, actually." His eyes narrow. I part my robe just enough to show the deep bruise on my calf and gauze pad on my kneecap. "The car clipped me. I barely made it across. I fell forward—"

He stares at the gauze pad. *Face it, Reggie, Steven's murder dwarfs your near miss. Natter on about the blue car and you'll sound worse than callous.* "I fell forward on the pavement," I say, "and Steven ran out to help and came inside with me until I felt better, about an hour altogether. That's the last I saw him."

He makes a note. "So he left here at approximately

three P.M." Maglia's voice is soft but probing. "As land-lady, you had a key to his apartment?"

"To his door, which is off the second-floor landing."

"And you used it to enter the apartment this morning when you discovered his body? Any sign of anybody in the stairwell or hallway?" I shake my head. "The first-floor door to the street, Ms. Cutter, was it also locked?"

"The door to the street?" It's the main door at the top of the granite stoop. I'd opened it to let the uniformed cops in. It has a spring bolt. In my frantic state, had I twisted it open? Is there blood on it, too? "I think it was locked."

"You're not sure?"

"I think . . . surely it was." But "surely" isn't good enough. If the killer came in the front, he or she—or they?—first had to enter through the street door, pass my door, then take the inside vestibule stairs up to Steven's apartment.

It hits me—Steven's killer then came back down and marked my door. The marks are Steven's own blood. Life blood, death blood. Nausea rolls from the pit of my stom-ach, and it's all I can do to focus on the door, the outside door that I'd paid no attention to. "I was very upset," I said. "I didn't really think about the outer front door. It wasn't on my mind." My arm and leg throb. Maglia's eyes narrow as if the lapse is a mark against me.

Like a good hostess of twenty-five years, I try to com-pensate, mentioning Luis and the Big Buddies charity. I tell the detective that Gibralter Reality did a background check on Steven and might provide additional informa-tion. Breathless, I also tell about the night bumping noises and the dripping, how I came to find the body. My state-ment lasts at most ten minutes, a monologue from hell.

"Let's go back to yesterday, Ms. Cutter. When Steven paid a visit."

"It wasn't a visit. It was first aid."

He looks at me as though I'm an NPR word quiz lady. Ed Maglia shows no real empathy for a civilian reeling from carnage in her own home, blood on her door. "Like I was saying, after Steven left you, he went back upstairs?"

"I assumed he was up there. He's a financial analyst. He worked part of the time in his apartment."

"But you have no actual knowledge."

"Well, no, I didn't see or hear him. I was resting from the hit-and- . . . the fall. My kitchen and bedroom are to the rear of the house, away from the square. Whoever came or went last night, I didn't see him. Or her. Them."

Maglia taps a nail against his wedding band. I assume that his gun is holstered inside his suit jacket. "A few minutes ago, Ms. Cutter, you referred to a nighttime bumping noise. Yet you say the building seems soundproof."

"The walls are very thick. These Victorian town houses are built like fortresses."

"When you woke up in the night and heard the bumping, the noises you called violent—"

"I didn't say violent." Or did I?

"What about voices?"

"No voices. None." Should I try to make the actual bumping sounds, like when you take your car in? "It was like a storm, like thunder. It felt both close and distant. Maybe it was somebody's fireworks left over from the Fourth. Or it might have been a nightmare. A dream not related to Steven—"

"Isn't that unlikely? I mean, the noises woke you, isn't that right?"

"My dog was agitated. Maybe a sleep cycle was interrupted. I didn't get up and look at a clock, if that's what you're asking."

"So you heard the violent bumping noises, Ms. Cutter, and stayed in bed? Can you make a best guess about the time?"

"I'd rather not." A minute ago, he was all for *supposing*. Now he wants guesswork. I'm a hit-and-run victim, lucky to be alive, but he acts as though I deliberately lounged in bed listening to a homicide in progress. Maglia reminds me of Marty, even though the homicide detective looks nothing like my ex-husband. One thing I know for sure: Detective Frank Devaney wouldn't treat me like this.

"How about you show me where you saw the blood drip?" We troop to the radiator, but Maglia bars me from getting too close, as if I have no judgment on my own. He says something about getting a photographer and a tech to take a sample. "Could I see your bedroom, please?"

He follows me back, sees the unmade bed and all, and he taps the walls, stares at the ceiling like a building inspector, opens the window, and leans out to look up and down at the narrow back alley. Cold October air blows in.

I, too, try leaning out to see, but Maglia shuts the window, and we go back to the front room and sit back down. He faces me. "One reason all this is important for you, Ms. Cutter . . . there's a stain on your own front door. We think tests will prove it's blood."